G.A. HENTY
December 8, 1832 — November 16, 1902

Under Wellington's Command
A Tale of the Peninsular War

by

G. A. Henty

ILLUSTRATED BY WAL PAGET

PrestonSpeed Publications
Pennsylvania

A note about the name PrestonSpeed Publications:
The name PrestonSpeed Publications was chosen in loving memory of our fathers, Preston Louis Schmitt and Lester Herbert Maynard (nicknamed "Speed" for his prowess in baseball).

Originally published by Blackie & Son, Limited,
June 2, 1898
Blackie & Son Title Page Date: 1899

Under Wellington's Command: A Tale of the Peninsular War
by G. A. Henty
© 2001 by PrestonSpeed Publications
Published by PrestonSpeed Publications, 51 Ridge Road, Mill Hall, Pennsylvania 17751.

All rights reserved. No part of this publication may be reproduced, stored in a retrieval system, or transmitted by any means, electronic, mechanical, photocopy, recording, or otherwise, without the prior permission of the publisher, except as provided by USA copyright law.

This book is printed on acid-free paper, and its binding materials have been chosen for strength and durability.

Heirloom Hardcover Edition ISBN 1-887159-94-0
Popular Softcover Edition ISBN 1-887159-95-9

Printed in the United States of America

PRESTONSPEED PUBLICATIONS
51 RIDGE ROAD
MILL HALL, PENNSYLVANIA 17751
(570) 726-7844
www.prestonspeed.com
May, 2001

INTRODUCTION

G. A. Henty's life was filled with exciting adventure. After completing his work at Westminster School, he attended Cambridge University, where he undertook a rigorous course of study and also enjoyed boxing, wrestling, and rowing. The strenuous study and healthy, competitive participation in sports prepared Henty for his adventures. To name just a few, he fought with the British army in the Crimea, served as a war correspondent during Garibaldi's fight for independence in Italy, visited Abyssinia, witnessed the Franco-Prussian war while in Paris, observed the Carlists in Spain, attended the opening of the Suez Canal, toured India with the Prince of Wales (later Edward II), and visited the California gold fields.

G. A. Henty lived during the reign of Queen Victoria (1837-1901) and began his story-telling career with his own children. After dinner it was his custom to spend an hour or two telling them a story that often continued for days. In fact, some stories lasted for weeks! One evening a friend happened to be present during Henty's "story hour." Watching the children as they sat spell-bound, he urged Henty to write down his stories so others could enjoy them. Happily for us, Henty did so. One of his secretaries reported that he often would pace rapidly back and forth in his study dictating stories as fast as the secretary could record them. He became known to his readers as "The Prince of Story-Tellers" and "The Boys Own Historian."

Henty's stories revolve around a fictional boy hero during fascinating periods of history. His heroes are diligent, courageous, intelligent, and dedicated to their country and cause in the face of, at times, great peril. Respected historians have acknowledged his histories, particularly the accounts of battles, for their accuracy. His ability to bring his readers action-packed adventure in an accurate historical setting makes the study of history exciting, and removes the drudgery often associated with such study.

Henty's heroes fight wars, sail the seas, discover new lands, conquer evil empires, prospect for gold, and embark upon a host of other exciting adventures. They meet such famous personages as Josephus, Titus, Hannibal, Robert the Bruce, Sir William Wallace, General Marlborough, General Gordon, General Kichner, Robert E. Lee, Frederick the Great, the Duke of Wellington, Huguenot leader Coligny, the explorer Cortez, King Alfred, Napoleon, and Sir Francis Drake, to name just a few. The heroes experience the fall of Jerusalem, the Roman invasion of Britain, the Crusades, the Viking invasion of Europe, the Reign of Terror in France, and the exciting events of the Reformation in various countries, etc. In short, Henty's heroes live during tumultuous times in history and meet many of the most prominent leaders of those times.

PrestonSpeed is delighted to offer the long-out-of-print works of G. A. Henty to a whole new generation of adults and young people. Our Henty titles contain the complete text and all maps and/or illustrations included in the original editions. Although the books have been newly typeset, the original grammar and spelling remain the same as in the original versions.

"We surrender, sir, as prisoners of war."

PREFACE

MY DEAR LADS,

As many boys into whose hands the present volume may fall will not have read my last year's book, "*With Moore in Corunna*," of which this is a continuation, it is necessary that a few words should be said to enable them to take up the thread of the story. It was impossible, in the limits of one book, to give even an outline of the story of the Peninsular War without devoting the whole space to the military operations. It would, in fact, have been a history rather than a tale, and it accordingly closed with the passage of the Douro, and the expulsion of the French from Portugal.

The hero, Terence O'Connor, was the son of the senior captain of the Mayo Fusileers, and when the regiment was ordered to join Sir Arthur Wellesley's expedition to Portugal, the colonel of the regiment obtained for him a commission, although so notorious was the boy for his mischievous pranks, that the colonel hesitated whether he would not get into some serious scrapes, especially as Dick Ryan, one of the ensigns, was always his companion in mischief, and both were aided and abetted by Captain O'Grady.

However, on the way out, the slow old transport, in which a wing of the regiment was carried, was attacked by two French privateers, who would have either taken or sunk her had it not been for a happy suggestion of the quick-witted lad. For this he gained great credit, and was selected by General Fane as one of his aides-de-camp. In this capacity he went through the arduous campaign, under General Moore, that ended at Corunna. His father had been so seriously wounded at Vimiera that he was invalided home and placed on half-pay; and in the same battle Captain O'Grady lost his left arm, but, on its being cured, returned to his place in the regiment. At Corunna, Terence, while carrying a despatch, was thrown from his horse and stunned, and on recovering found that the British had already embarked on board the ships of the fleet.

He made his way to the frontier of Portugal, and thence to Lisbon; he was then appointed to the staff of Sir John Cradock, who was now in command, and sent in charge of some treasure for the use of the Spanish general, Romana, who was collecting a force on the northern border of Portugal. Terence had orders to aid him in any way in his power to check the invasion of Portugal from the north. Of this order he took advantage when, on the way, the agents of the junta of Oporto endeavoured to rob him, attacking the house where he and his escort had taken up their quarters, with a newly-raised levy of two thousand five hundred unarmed peasants.

By a ruse he got their leaders into his hands, and these showed such abject cowardice that the peasants refused further to follow them, and asked Terence to take the command of the force. He assented, formed them into two battalions, appointed two British orderlies as majors, the Portuguese officer of his escort lieutenant-colonel, and his troopers captains of companies, put them in the way of obtaining arms, and by dint of hard drill and kindness converted them into an efficient body of soldiers. Finding that little was to be expected from Romana's force, he acted as a partisan leader, and in this capacity performed such valuable service that he was confirmed in the command of his force, which received the name of the Minjo regiment, and he and his officers received commissions for the rank they held in the Portuguese army.

At Oporto he rescued from a convent a cousin, who, at the death of her father, a British merchant there, had been shut up by her Portuguese mother until she would consent to sign away the property to which she was entitled, and to become a nun. She went to England to live with Terence's father, and came into possession of the fortune which her father, foreseeing that difficulties might arise at his death, had forwarded to a bank at home, having appointed Captain O'Connor her guardian.

The present volume takes the story of the Peninsular War up to the battle of Salamanca, and concludes the history of Terence

O'Connor. My readers will understand that in all actions in which the British army took part, the details are accurately given, but that the doings of the Minho regiment, and of Terence O'Connor as a partisan leader, are not to be considered as strictly historical, although similar feats of daring and adventure were accomplished by Trant, Pack, and other leaders of irregular forces.

> Yours sincerely,
>
> G.A. HENTY.

CONTENTS

I.	A DETACHED FORCE,	1
II.	TALAVERA,	16
III.	PRISONERS,	32
IV.	GUERILLAS,	47
V.	AN ESCAPE,	61
VI.	AFLOAT,	76
VII.	A FRENCH PRIVATEER,	91
VIII.	A SMART ENGAGEMENT,	106
IX.	REJOINING,	122
X.	ALMEIDA,	138
XI.	THE FRENCH ADVANCE,	155
XII.	FUENTES D'ONORO,	171
XIII.	FROM SALAMANCA TO CADIZ,	188
XIV.	EFFECTING A DIVERSION,	203
XV.	DICK RYAN'S CAPTURE,	219
XVI.	BACK WITH THE ARMY,	235
XVII.	CIUDAD RODRIGO,	251
XVIII.	THE SACK OF A CITY,	264
XIX.	GRATITUDE,	280
XX.	SALAMANCA,	295
XXI.	HOME AGAIN,	313

ILLUSTRATIONS

"WE SURRENDER, SIR, AS PRISONERS OF WAR"
                              FRONTISPIECE

"YOU MAY AS WELL MAKE YOUR
REPORT TO ME, O'CONNOR," 24

STOOPING SO THAT THEIR FIGURES SHOULD
NOT SHOW AGAINST THE SKY, ... 73

"SHE IS WALKING ALONG NOW," 88

A DESPERATE FIGHT WAS
GOING ON FORWARD, ... 112

"THIS IS COLONEL O'CONNOR, SIR," 124

"GOOD NEWS. WE ARE
GOING TO TAKE COIMBRA," 168

"I WANT TO GET AWAY FROM HERE, NITA," .. 185

THE MEN LEAPT TO THEIR
FEET, CHEERING VOCIFEROUSLY, ... 205

"SEARCH HIM AT ONCE," 221

THE MAN FELL, WITH A SHARP CRY, ... 272

A SHELL HAD STRUCK TERENCE'S HORSE, .. 309

MAPS

PLAN OF THE BATTLE OF TALAVERA, ... 30
PLAN OF THE BATTLE OF BUSACO, ... 152
PLAN OF LINES OF TORRES VEDRAS, ... 165
PLAN OF THE BATTLE OF
FUENTES D'ONORO, ... 175
PLANS OF THE FORTS AND
OPERATIONS ROUND SALAMANCA, ... 303

Under Wellington's Command

Chapter I

A Detached Force

"Be jabers, Terence, we shall all die of weariness with doing nothing if we don't move soon," said Captain O'Grady, who, with Dick Ryan, had ridden over to spend the afternoon with Terence O'Connor, whose regiment of Portuguese was encamped some six miles out of Abrantes, where the division to which the Mayo Fusileers belonged was stationed. "Here we are in June, and the sun getting hotter and hotter, and the whisky just come to an end, though we have been mighty sparing over it, and nothing to eat but ration beef. Begorrah, if it wasn't for the bastely drill, I should forget that I was a soldier at all. I should take meself for a convict, condemned to stop all me life in one place. At first there was something to do, for one could forage for food dacent to eat; but now I don't believe there is as much as an old hen left within fifteen miles; and as for ducks and geese, I have almost forgotten the taste of them."

"It is not lively work, O'Grady, but it is worse for me here. You have got Dicky Ryan to stir you up and keep you alive, and O'Flaherty to look after your health and see that you don't exceed your allowance, while practically I have no one but Herrara to speak to, for though Bull and Macwitty are excellent fellows in their way, they are not much as companions. However, I think we must be nearly at the end of it. We have got pretty well all the troops up here, except those who are to remain at Lisbon."

"I see the men," O'Grady said, "but I don't see the victuals. We can't march until we get transport and food, and where they are to come from no one seems to know."

"I am afraid we shall do badly for a time in that respect, O'Grady. Sir Arthur has not had time yet to find out what humbugs the Spaniards are, and what wholesale lies they tell. Of course he had some slight experience of it when we first landed, at the Mondego, but it takes longer than that to get at the bottom of their want of faith. Craddock learnt it after a bitter experience, and so did Moore. I have no doubt that the Spaniards have represented to Sir Arthur that they have large disciplined armies, that the French have been reduced to a mere handful, and that they are only waiting for his advance to drive them across the frontier. Also, no doubt, they have promised to find any amount of transport and provisions as soon as he enters Spain. As to relying upon Cuesta, you might as well rely upon the assistance of an army of hares, commanded by a pig-headed owl."

"I can't make out meself," O'Grady said, "what we want to have anything to do with the Spaniards for at all. If I were in Sir Arthur's place, I would just march straight against the French and thrash them."

"That sounds well, O'Grady, but we know very little about where the French are, what they are doing, or what is their strength; and I think that you will allow that, though we have beaten them each time we have met them, they fought well. At Rolica we were three to one against them, and at Vimiera we had the advantage of a strong position. At Corunna things were pretty well even, but we had our backs to the wall. I am afraid, O'Grady, that just at present you are scarcely qualified to take command of the army, except only on the one point, that you thoroughly distrust the Spaniards. Well, Dick, have you been having any fun lately?"

"It is not to be done, Terence. Everyone is too disgusted and out of temper to make it safe; even the chief is dangerous. I would as soon think of playing a joke on a wandering tiger as on him. The major is not a man to trifle with at the best of times, and, except O'Flaherty, there is not a man among them who has a good word to throw at a dog. Faith, when one thinks of the good time one used to have at Athlone, it is heartbreaking."

A DETACHED FORCE

"Well, come in and refresh yourselves; I have a bottle or two still left."

"That is good news!" O'Grady said fervently. "It has been on the tip of me tongue to ask you, for me mouth is like an oven, but I was so afraid you would say it was gone that I daren't open me lips about it."

"To tell you the truth, O'Grady, except when some of you fellows come over, there is not any whiskey touched in this camp. I have kept it strictly for your sergeants, who have been helping to teach my men drill, and coaching the non-commissioned officers. It has been hard work for them, but they have stuck to it well, and the thought of an allowance at the end of the day's work has done wonders with them. We made a very fair show when we came in, but now I think the two battalions could work with the best here, without doing themselves discredit. The non-commissioned officers have always been our weak point, but now my fellows know their work very fairly, and they go at it with a will. You see, they are all very proud of the corps, and have spared no pains to make themselves worthy of it.

"Of course, what you may call purely parade movements are not done as they are by our infantry; but in all useful work I would back them against any here. They are very fair shots, too. I have paid for a lot of extra ammunition, which, I confess, we bought from some of the native levies. No doubt I should get into a row over it if it were known, but as these fellows are not likely ever to fire a shot against the French—and it is of importance that mine should be able to shoot well—I didn't hesitate to do it. Fortunately the regimental chest is not empty; and all the officers have given a third of their pay to help. But it has certainly done a lot of good, and the shooting has greatly improved since we came here."

"I have been working steadily at Portuguese, Terence, ever since you spoke to me about it. One has no end of time on one's hands, and really I am getting on very fairly."

"That is right, Dicky. If we win this campaign I will certainly ask for you as adjutant. I shall be awfully glad to have you with me, and I really do want an adjutant for each battalion; and you, O'Grady?"

"Well, I can't report favourably of meself, at all, at all. I tried hard for a week, and it is the fault of me tongue, and not of meself. I can't get it to twist itself to the outlandish words. I am willing enough, but me tongue isn't; and I am afraid that, were it a necessity that every officer in your corps should speak the bastely language, I should have to stay at home."

"I am afraid that it is quite necessary, O'Grady," Terence laughed. "An adjutant who could not make himself understood would be of no shadow of use. You know how I should like to have you with me, but, upon the other hand, there would be inconveniences. You are, as you have said many a time, my superior officer in our army, and I really should not like to have to give you orders. Then again, Bull and Macwitty are still more your juniors, having only received their commissions a few months back, and they would feel just as uncomfortable as I should at having you under them. I don't think that it would do at all. Besides, you know, you are not fond of work by any means, and there would be more to do in a regiment like this than in one of our own."

"I suppose that it must be so, Terence," O'Grady said resignedly, as he emptied his tumbler; "and, besides, there is a sort of superstition in the service that an adjutant should be always able to walk straight to his tent, even after a warm night at mess. Now, although it seems to me that I have every other qualification, in that respect I should be a failure, and I imagine that in a Portuguese regiment the thing would be looked at more seriously than it is in an Irish one, where such a matter occurs occasionally among men as well as officers."

"That is quite true, O'Grady; the Portuguese are a sober people, and would not, as you say, be able to make the same allowance for our weaknesses that Irish soldiers do, seeing that it is too common for our men to be either one way or the other. However, Ryan, I do hope I shall be able to get you. I never had much hopes of O'Grady, and this failure of his tongue to aid him in his vigorous efforts to learn the language seems to quite settle the matter as far as he is concerned."

At this moment an orderly rode up to the tent. Terence went out.

"A despatch from headquarters, sir," the trooper said, saluting.

A DETACHED FORCE

"All right, my man! You had better wait for five minutes and see if any answer is required."

Going into the tent he opened the despatch. "Hooray!" he said, as he glanced at the contents. "Here is a movement at last."

The letter was as follows: *Colonel O'Connor will at once march with his force to Plasencia, and will reconnoitre the country between that town and the Tagus to the south, and Bejar to the north. He will ascertain, as far as possible, the position and movements of the French army under Victor. He will send a daily report of his observations to headquarters. Twenty Portuguese cavalry, under a subaltern, will be attached to his command, and will furnish orderlies to carry his reports.*

It is desirable that Colonel O'Connor's troops should not come in contact with the enemy, except to check any reconnoitring parties moving towards Castello Branco and Villa Velha. It is most necessary to prevent the news of an advance of the army in that direction reaching the enemy, and to give the earliest possible information of any hostile gathering that might menace the flank of the army while on its march.

The passes of Banos and Periles will be held by the troops of Marshal Beresford and General Del Parque, and it is to the country between the mountains and Marshal Cuesta's force at Almaraz that Colonel O'Connor is directed to concentrate his attention. In case of being attacked by superior forces, Colonel O'Connor will, if possible, retreat into the mountains on his left flank, maintain himself there, and open communications with Lord Beresford's forces at Banos or Bejar.

Colonel O'Connor is authorised to requisition six carts from the quartermaster's department, and to hand over his tents to them, to draw 50,000 rounds of ball cartridge, and such rations as he may be able to carry with him. The paymaster has received authority to hand over to him £500, for the payment of supplies for his men. When this sum is exhausted Colonel O'Connor is authorised to issue orders for supplies payable by the paymaster to the forces, exercising the strictest economy, and sending notification to the Paymaster-general of the issue of such orders. This despatch is confidential, and the direction of the route is on no account to be divulged.

"You hear that, O'Grady; and you too, Dicky. I ought not to have read the despatch out loud. However, I know you will keep the matter secret."

"You may trust us for that, Terence, for it is a secret worth knowing. It is evident that Sir Arthur is going to join Cuesta and make a dash on Madrid. Well, he has been long enough in making up his mind, but it is a satisfaction that we are likely to have hot work at last, though I wish we could have done it without those Spaniards. We have seen enough of them to know that nothing beyond kind words are to be expected of them, and when the time for fighting comes I would rather that we depended upon ourselves than have to act with fellows on whom there is no reliance whatever to be placed."

"I agree with you there heartily, O'Grady. However, thank goodness we are going to set out at last, and I am very glad that it falls to us to act as the vanguard of the army, instead of being attached to Beresford's command and kept stationary in the passes. Now I must be at work. I dare say we shall meet again before long."

Terence wrote an acknowledgement of the receipt of the general's order, and handed it to the orderly who had brought it. A bugler at once sounded the field-officers' call.

"We are to march at once," he said, when Herrara, Bull, and Macwitty arrived. "Let the tents be struck and handed over to the quartermaster's department. See that the men have four days' biscuit in their haversacks. Each battalion is to take three carts with it. I will go to the quartermaster's department to draw them; tell off six men from each battalion to accompany me, and take charge of the carts. Each battalion will carry 25,000 rounds of spare ammunition and a chest of £250. I will requisition from the commissariat as much biscuit as we can carry, and twenty bullocks for each battalion, to be driven with the carts. As soon as the carts are obtained, the men will drive them to the ordnance stores for the ammunition, and to the commissariat stores to load up the food. You had better send an officer in charge of the men of each battalion. I will myself draw the money from the paymaster. I will go there at once. Send a couple of men with me, for of course it will be paid in silver. Then I will go to the quartermaster's stores and get the carts ready by the time that the men arrive. I want to march in an hour's time at latest."

A DETACHED FORCE

In a few minutes the camp was a scene of bustle and activity; the tents were struck and packed away in their bags and piled in order to be handed over to the quartermaster, and in a few minutes over an hour from the receipt of the order the two battalions were in motion. After a twenty-mile march, they halted for the night near the frontier. An hour later they were joined by twenty troopers of a Portuguese regiment under the command of a subaltern. The next day they marched through Plasencia, and halted for the night on the slopes of the Sierra. An orderly was despatched next morning to the officer in command of any force that there might be at Banos, informing him of the position that they had taken up. Terence ordered two companies to remain at this spot, which was at the head of a little stream running down into an affluent of the Tagus, their position being now nearly due north of Almaraz, from which they were distant some twenty miles. The rest of the force descended into the plain, and took post at various villages between the Sierra and Oropesa, the most advanced party halting four miles from that town. The French forces under Victor had, in accordance with orders from Madrid, fallen back from Plasencia a week before, and taken up quarters at Talavera.

At the time when the regiment received its uniforms, Terence had ordered that twenty suits of the men's peasant clothes should be retained in store, and specially intelligent men being chosen, twenty of these were sent forward towards the river Alberche to discover Victor's position. They brought in news that he had placed his troops behind the river, and that Cuesta, who had at one time an advanced guard at Oropesa, had recalled it to Almaraz. Parties of Victor's cavalry were patrolling the country between Talavera and Oropesa.

Terence had sent Bull with five hundred men to occupy all the passes across the Sierras, with orders to capture any soldier who might come along; and a day later four men brought in a French officer who had been captured on the road leading south. He was the bearer of a letter from Soult to the king, and was at once sent under the escort of four troopers to headquarters. The men who had brought in the officer reported that they had learned that Wilson, with his command of four thousand men, was in the mountains north of Escurial, and that spies from that officer had ascertained that there was great alarm in Madrid, where the news of the British advance towards Plasencia was already known, and that it was feared that this force, with Cuesta's army at Almaraz and Venegas' army in La Mancha, were about to combine in an attack upon the capital.

This, indeed, was Sir Arthur's plan, and had been arranged with the Supreme Junta. The Junta, however, being jealous of Cuesta, had given secret instructions to Venegas to keep aloof. On his arrival at Plasencia the English general had learned at once the hollowness of the Spanish promises. He had been assured of an ample supply of food, mules, and carts for transport, and had, on the strength of these statements, advanced with but small supplies, for little food and but few animals could be obtained in Portugal. He found on arriving that no preparations whatever had been made, and the army, thus early in the campaign, was put on half rations. Day after day passed without any of the promised supplies arriving, and Sir Arthur wrote to the Supreme Junta, saying that although in accordance with his agreement he would march to the Alberche, he would not cross that river unless the promises that had been made were kept to the letter.

He had by this time learned that the French forces north of the mountains were much more formidable than the Spanish reports had led him to believe, but he still greatly underrated Soult's army, and was altogether ignorant that Ney had evacuated Galicia, and was marching south with all speed with his command. Del Parque had failed in his promise to garrison Bejar and Banos, and these passes were now only held by a few hundreds of Cuesta's Spaniards. A week after taking up his position north of Oropesa, Terence received orders to move with his two battalions, and to take post to guard these passes, with his left resting on Bejar and his right in communication with Wilson's force. The detachments were at once recalled. A thousand men were posted near Bejar, and the rest divided among the other passes by which a French army from the north could cross the Sierra. As soon as this arrangement was made, Terence rode to Wilson's headquarters. He was received very cordially by that officer.

"I am heartily glad to see you, Colonel O'Connor," the latter said. "Of course I have heard of the doings of your battalions, and am glad indeed to have your support. I sent a messenger off only this morning to Sir Arthur telling him that, from the information brought in by my spies, I am convinced that Soult is much stronger than has

A DETACHED FORCE

been supposed, and that if he moves south I shall scarce be able to hold the passes of Arenas and San Pedro Barnardo, and that I can certainly spare no men for the defence of the more westerly ones by which Soult is likely to march from Salamanca. However, now you are there, I shall feel safe."

"No doubt I could hinder an advance, Sir Robert," Terence said, "but I certainly could not hope to bar the passes to a French army. I have no artillery, and though my men are steady enough against infantry, I doubt whether they would be able to withstand an attack heralded by a heavy cannonade. With a couple of batteries of artillery to sweep the passes one might make a fair stand for a time against a greatly superior force, but with only infantry one could not hope to maintain one's position."

"Quite so, and Sir Arthur could not expect it. My own opinion is that we shall have fifty thousand men coming down from the north. I have told the chief as much, but naturally he will believe the assurances of the Spanish juntas rather than reports gathered by our spies, and, no doubt, hopes to crush Victor altogether before Soult makes any movement, and he trusts to Venegas' advance from the south towards the upper Tagus, to cause Don Joseph to evacuate Madrid as soon as he hears of Victor's defeat; but I have certainly no faith whatever in either Venegas or Cuesta.

"Cuesta is loyal enough, but he is obstinate and pig-headed, and at present he is furious because the Supreme Junta has been sending all the best troops to Venegas instead of to him, and he knows well enough that that perpetual intriguer Frere is working underhand to get Albuquerque appointed to the supreme command. As to Venegas, he is a mere tool of the Supreme Junta, and as likely as not they will order him to do nothing but keep his army intact. Then, again, the delay at Plasencia has upset all Sir Arthur's arrangements. Had he pressed straight forward on the 28th of last month, when he crossed the frontier, disregarding Cuesta altogether, he could have been at Madrid long before this, for I know that at that time Victor's force had been so weakened that he had but between fourteen and fifteen thousand men, and must have fallen back without fighting. Now he has again got the troops that had been taken from him, and will be further reinforced before Sir Arthur arrives on the Alberche, and of course Soult has had plenty of time to get everything in readiness to cross the mountains and fall upon the British rear as soon as he hears that they are fairly on their way towards Madrid.

"Here we are at the 20th, and our forces will only reach Oropesa to-day. Victor is evidently afraid that Sir Arthur will move from Oropesa towards the hills, pass the upper Alberche, and so place himself between him and Madrid, for a strong force of cavalry reconnoitred in this direction this morning."

"Would it not be as well, sir," said Terence, "if we were to arrange some signals by which we could aid each other? That hill-top can be seen from the hill beyond which is the little village where I have established myself. I noticed it this morning before I started. If you would keep a look-out on your hill, I would have one on mine. We might each get three bonfires a hundred yards apart, ready for lighting. If I hear of any great force approaching the defiles I am watching, I could summon your aid either by day or night by these fires, and, in the same way, if Soult should advance by the line that you are guarding, you could summon me. My men are really well trained in this sort of work, and you could trust them to make an obstinate defence."

"I think that your idea is a very good one, and will certainly carry it out. You see, we are really both of us protecting the left flank of our army, and can certainly do so more effectually if we work together. We might, too, arrange another signal. One fire might mean that, for some reason or other, we are marching away. I may have orders to move some distance towards Madrid, so as to compel Victor to weaken himself by detaching a force to check me; you may be ordered, as the army advances, to leave your defiles in charge of the Spaniards, and to accompany the army. Two fires might mean: spies have reported a general advance of the French coming by several routes. Thus, you see, we should be in readiness for any emergency. I should be extremely glad of your help if Soult comes this way. My own corps of 1200 men are fairly good soldiers, and I can rely upon them to do their best; but the other 3000 have been recently raised, and I don't think that any dependence can be placed upon them in case of hard fighting; but with your two battalions we ought to be able to hold any of these defiles for a considerable time."

A DETACHED FORCE

Two days later Terence received orders to march instantly with his force down into the valley, to follow the foot of the hills until he received orders, and check the advance of any French force endeavouring to move round the left flank of the British. The evening before, one signal-fire had announced that Wilson was on the move, and thinking that he too might be summoned, Terence had called in all his outposts and was able to march a quarter of an hour after he received the order. He had learned on the evening he returned from his visit to Sir Robert, from men sent down into the plain for the purpose, that Cuesta's army and that of Sir Arthur had advanced together from Oropesa. He was glad at the order to join the army, as he had felt that, should Soult advance, his force, unprovided as it was with guns, would be able to offer but a very temporary resistance, especially if the French marshal was at the head of a force anything like as strong as was reported by the peasantry.

As to this, however, he had very strong doubts, having come to distrust thoroughly every report given by the Spaniards. He knew that they were as ready, under the influence of fear, to exaggerate the force of an enemy as they were at other times to magnify their own numbers. Sir Arthur must, he thought, be far better informed than he himself could be, for his men, being Portuguese, were viewed with doubt and suspicion by the Spanish peasantry, who would probably take a pleasure in misleading them altogether. The short stay in the mountains had braced up the men, and with only a short halt, they made a forty-mile march to the Alberche by midnight. Scarcely had they lit their fires when a Hussar officer and some troopers rode up. They halted a hundred yards away, and the officer shouted in English:

"What corps is this?"

Terence at once left the fire and advanced towards them.

"Two Portuguese battalions," he answered, "under myself, Colonel O'Connor."

The officer at once rode forward. "I was not quite sure," he said, as he came close, "that my question would not be answered by a volley. By the direction from which I saw you coming, I thought that you must be friends. Still, you might have been an advanced party of a force that had come down through the defiles. However, as soon as I saw you light your fires, I made sure it was all right; for the Frenchmen would not likely have ventured to do so, unless, indeed, they were altogether ignorant of our advance."

"At ten o'clock this morning I received orders from headquarters to move to this point at once, and as we have marched from Banos, you see we have lost very little time on the way."

"Indeed, you have not. I suppose it is about forty miles, and that distance in fourteen hours is certainly first-rate marching. I will send off one of my men to report who you are. Two squadrons of my regiment are a quarter of a mile away awaiting my return."

"Have you any reason to believe that the enemy are near?"

"No particular reason that I know of, but their cavalry have been in great force along the upper part of the river for the last two days. Victor has retired from Talavera, for I fancy that he was afraid we might move round this way, and cut him off from Madrid. The Spaniards might have harassed him as he fell back, but they dared not even make a charge on his rearguard, though they had 3000 cavalry. We are not quite sure where the French are, and, of course, we could get no information from other people here; either their stupidity is something astounding, or their sympathies are entirely with the French."

"My experience is," Terence said, "that the best way is to get as much information as you can from them, and then to act with the certainty that the real facts are just the reverse of the statements made to you."

As soon as the forces halted, a picket had been sent out, and Terence, when the men finished their supper, established a cordon of advanced pickets with strong supports at a distance of a mile from his front and flanks, so as to ensure himself against surprise, and to detect any movement upon the part of the enemy's cavalry who might be pressing round to obtain information of the British position. At daybreak he mounted and rode to Talavera, and reported the arrival of his command and the position where he had halted for the night.

"You have wasted no time over it, Colonel O'Connor. You can only have received the order yesterday morning, and I scarcely expected that you could be here till this evening."

A DETACHED FORCE

"My men are excellent marchers, sir; they did the forty miles in fourteen hours, and might have done it in an hour quicker had they been pressed. Not a man fell out."

"Your duty will now be to cover our left flank. I don't know whether you are aware that Wilson has moved forward, and will take post on the slopes near the Escurial. He has been directed to spread his force as much as possible, so as to give an appearance of greater strength than he has."

"I knew that he had left his former position," Terence said. "We had arranged a code of smoke signals by which we could ask each other for assistance should the defiles be attacked, and I learned yesterday morning in this way that he was marching away."

"Have you any news of what is taking place on the other side of the hills since you sent off word two days ago?"

"No, sir; at least all we hear is of the same character as before. We don't hear that Soult is moving, but his force is certainly put down as being considerably larger than was supposed. I have deemed it my duty to state this in my reports, but the Spaniards are so inclined to exaggerate everything that I always receive statements of this kind with great doubt."

"All our news—from the juntas, from Mr. Frere, and from other quarters—is quite the other way," the officer said. "We are assured that Soult has not fifteen thousand men in condition to take the field, and that he could not venture to move these, as he knows that the whole country would rise did he do so. I have no specific orders to give to you. You will keep in touch with General Hill's brigade, which forms our left, and as we move forward you will advance along the lower slopes of the Sierra and prevent any attempt on the part of the French to turn our flank.

"I dare say you do not know exactly what is going on, Colonel O'Connor. It may be of assistance to you in taking up your position to know that the fighting is likely to take place on the line between Talavera and the mountains. Cuesta has fallen back in great haste to Talavera. We shall advance to-day and take up our line with him. The Spaniards will hold the low marshy ground near the town. Our right will rest on an eminence on his left flank, and will extend to a group of hills separated by a valley from the Sierra. Our cavalry will probably check any attempt by the French to turn our flank there, and you and the Spaniards will do your best to hold the slope of the Sierra should the French move a force along there. I may say that Victor has been largely reinforced by Sebastiani, and is likely to take the offensive. Indeed, we hear that he is already moving in this direction. We are not aware of his exact strength, but we believe that it must approach, if not equal, that of ourselves and Cuesta united.

"Cuesta has indeed been already roughly handled by the French. Disregarding Sir Arthur's entreaties, and believing Victor to be in full retreat, he marched on alone, impelled by the desire to be the first to enter Madrid, but at two o'clock on the morning of the 26th of July the French suddenly fell upon him, drove the Spanish cavalry back from their advanced position, and chased them hotly. They fled in great disorder, and the panic would have spread to the whole army had not Albuquerque brought up 3000 fresh cavalry and held the French in check while Cuesta retreated in great disorder, and, had the French pressed forward, would have fled in utter rout. Sherbrooke's division, which was in advance of the British army, moved forward and took up its position in front of the panic-stricken Spaniards, and then the French drew off. Cuesta then yielded to Sir Arthur's entreaties, recrossed the Alberche, and took up his position near Talavera.

"Here even the worst troops should be able to make a stand against the best. The ground is marshy and traversed by a rivulet. On its left is a strong redoubt, which is armed with Spanish artillery; on the right is another very strong battery on a rise close to Talavera, while other batteries sweep the road to Madrid. Sir Arthur has strengthened the front by felling trees and forming abattis, so that he has good reason to hope that, poor as the Spanish troops may be, they should be able to hold their part of the line. Campbell's division forms the British right, Sherbrooke comes next, the German legion are in the centre, Donkin is to take his place on the hill that rises two-thirds of the way across the valley, while General Hill's division is to hold the face looking north, and separated from the Sierra only by the comparatively narrow valley in which you have bivouacked. At present, however, his troops and those of Donkin have not taken up their position."

A DETACHED FORCE

The country between the positions on which the allied armies had now fallen back was covered with olive and cork trees. The whole line from Talavera to the hill, which was to be held by Hill's division, was two miles in length, and the valley between that and the Sierra was half a mile in width, but extremely broken and rugged, and was intersected by a ravine, through which ran the rivulet that fell into the Tagus at Talavera.

Chapter II
Talavera

On leaving the Adjutant-general, Terence, knowing that Mackenzie's brigade was some two miles in advance on the Alberche river, and that the enemy was not in sight, sent off one of the orderlies who accompanied him, with a message to Herrara to fall back, and take up his station on the lower slopes of the Sierra facing the rounded hill, and then went to a restaurant and had breakfast. It was crowded with Spanish officers, with a few British scattered among them. As he ate his food he was greatly amused at the boasting of the Spaniards as to what they would accomplish if the French ventured to attack them, knowing as he did how shamefully they had behaved two days before, when the whole of Cuesta's army had been thrown into utter disorder by two or three thousand French cavalry, and had only been saved from utter rout by the interposition of a British brigade. When he had finished breakfast he mounted his horse and rode to the camp of his old regiment.

"Hooroo, Terence!" Captain O'Grady shouted as he rode up, "I thought you would be turning up when there was going to be something to do; it's yourself that has the knack of always getting into the thick of it. Orderly, take Colonel O'Connor's horse and lead him up and down. Come on, Terence, most of the boys are in that tent over there; we have just been dismissed from parade."

A shout of welcome rose as they entered the tent, where a dozen officers were sitting on the ground or on empty boxes.

"Sit down if you can find room, Terence," Colonel Corcoran said; "wouldn't you like to be back with us again for the shindy that we are likely to have to-morrow?"

"That I should, but I hope to have my share in it in my own way."

"Where are your men, O'Connor?"

"They will be in another hour at the foot of the mountains over there to the left; our business will be to prevent any of the French moving along there and coming down on your rear."

"I am pleased to hear it. I believe that there is a Spanish division there, but I am glad to know that the business is not to be left entirely to them. Now, what have you been doing since you left us a month ago?"

"I have been doing nothing, Colonel, but watching the defiles, and as no one has come up them we have not fired a shot."

"No doubt they got news that you were there, Terence," O'Grady said, "and not likely would they be to come up to be destroyed by you."

"Perhaps that was it," Terence said, when the laughter had subsided; "at any rate they didn't show up, and I was very pleased when orders came at ten o'clock yesterday for us to leave Banos and march to join the army. We did the forty miles in fourteen hours."

"Good marching," Colonel Corcoran said. "Then where did you halt?"

"About three miles farther off at the foot of the hills. We saw a lot of camp-fires to our right, and thought that we were in a line with the army, but of course they were only those of Mackenzie's division; but I sent off an orderly an hour ago to tell them to fall back to the slopes facing those hills where our left is to be posted."

"You are a lucky fellow to have been away from us, Terence, for it is downright starving we have been. The soldiers have only had a mouthful of meat served out to them as rations most days, and they have got so thin that their clothes are hanging loose about them. If it hadn't been for my man Doolan and two or three others who always manage, by hook or by crook, to get hold of anything there is within two or three miles round, we should have been as badly off as they are. Be jabers, I have had to take in my sword-belt a good two inches, and to think that while our fellows are well-nigh starving, these Spaniards we came to help, and who will do no fighting themselves, had more food than they could eat, is enough to enrage a saint. I wonder Sir Arthur puts up with it. I would have seized that stuck-up old fool Cuesta, and popped him into the guard-tent and kept him there until provisions were handed over for us."

"His whole army might come to rescue him, O'Grady."

"What if they had! I would have turned out a corporal's-guard and sent the whole of them trotting off in no time. Did you hear what took place two days ago?"

"Yes, I heard that they behaved shamefully, O'Grady; still I think a corporal's-guard would hardly be sufficient to turn them, but I do believe that a regiment might answer the purpose."

"I can tell you that there is nothing would please the troops more than to attack the Spaniards. If this goes on many more days our men will be too weak to march; but I believe that before they lie down and give it up altogether, they will pitch into the Spaniards in spite of what we may try to do to prevent them," the Colonel said. "Here we are in a country abounding with food, and we are starving, while the Spaniards are feasting in plenty, and by St. Patrick's beard, Terence, it is mighty little we should do to prevent our men from pitching into them. There is one thing, you may be sure we shall never co-operate with them in the future, and as to relying upon their promises, faith, they are not worth the breath it takes to make them."

As everything was profoundly quiet, Terence had no hesitation in stopping to lunch with his old friends, and as there was no difficulty in buying whatever was required in Talavera, the table was well supplied, and the officers made up for their enforced privation during the past three weeks. At three o'clock Terence left them and rode across to his command, which he found posted exactly where he had directed it.

"It is lucky that we filled up with flour at Banos before starting, Colonel," Bull said, "for, from what we hear, the soldiers are getting next to nothing to eat, and those cattle you bought at the village half-way yesterday will come in very handy. At any rate, with them and the flour we can hold out for a week, if need be."

"Still, you had better begin at once to be economical, Bull. There is no saying what may happen after this battle has been fought."

While they were talking, a sudden burst of firing at a distance was heard.

"Mackenzie's brigade is engaged!" Terence exclaimed. "You had better get the men under arms at once. If the whole of Victor's command is upon them, they will have to fall back. When the men are ready, you may as well come a few hundred feet higher up the hill

TALAVERA

with me, then you will see all over the country and be in readiness to do anything that is wanted. But it is not likely the French will attempt anything serious to-day; they will probably content themselves with driving Mackenzie in."

Terence went at once up the hill to a point whence he could look well over the round hills on the other side of the valley, and make out the British and Spanish lines stretching to Talavera. The troops were already formed up in readiness for action. Away to his left came the roll of heavy firing from the cork woods near the Alberche, and just as his three officers joined him the British troops issued pell-mell from the woods. They had, in fact, been taken entirely by surprise, and had been attacked so suddenly and vigorously that for a time the young soldiers of some of the regiments fell into confusion, and Sir Arthur himself, who was at a large house named the Casa, narrowly escaped capture. The 45th, however, a regiment that had seen much service, and some companies of the 60th Rifles, presented a stout front to the enemy. Sir Arthur speedily restored order among the rest of the troops, and the enemy's advance was checked. The division then fell back in good order, each of its flanks being covered by a brigade of cavalry. From the height at which Terence and his officers stood they could plainly make out the retiring division, and could see heavy masses of French troops descending from the high ground beyond the Alberche.

"The whole French army is on us!" Macwitty said. "If their advance guard had not been in such a hurry to attack, and had waited until the others came up, not many of Mackenzie's division would have got back to our lines."

It was not long before the French debouched from the woods, and as soon as they did so a division rapidly crossed the plain towards the allies' left, seized an isolated hill facing the spur on to which Donkin had just hurried up his brigade, and at once opened a heavy cannonade. At the same time another division moved towards the right, and some squadrons of light cavalry could be seen riding along the road from Madrid towards the Spanish division.

"They won't do much good there," Terence said, "for the country is so swampy that they cannot leave the road. Still, I suppose they want to reconnoitre our position and draw the fire of the

Spaniards to ascertain their whereabouts. They are getting very close to them, and when the Spaniards begin they ought to wipe them out completely."

At this moment a heavy rattle of distant musketry was heard, and a light wreath of smoke rose from the Spanish lines. The French cavalry had, in fact, ridden up so close to the Spaniards that they discharged their pistols in bravado at them. To this the Spaniards had replied by a general wild discharge of their muskets. A moment later the party on the hill saw the right of the Spanish line break up as if by magic, and to their astonishment and rage they made out that the whole plain behind them was thickly dotted by fugitives.

"Why, the whole lot have bolted, sir!" Bull exclaimed. "Horse and foot are making off. Did anyone ever hear of such a thing!"

That portion of the Spanish line nearest to Talavera had indeed broken and fled in the wildest panic, 10,000 infantry having taken to their heels the instant they discharged their muskets, while the artillery cut their traces, and, leaving their guns behind them, followed their example. The French cavalry charged along the road, but Sir Arthur opposed them with some British squadrons. The Spanish who still held their ground, opened fire, and the French drew back. The fugitives continued their flight to Oropesa, spreading panic and alarm everywhere with the news that the allies were totally defeated, Sir Arthur Wellesley killed, and all lost.

Cuesta himself had for some time accompanied them, but he soon recovered from his panic and sent several cavalry regiments to bring back the fugitives. Part of the artillery and some thousands of the infantry were collected before morning, but 6000 men were still absent at the battle, and the great redoubt on their left was silent from want of guns. In point of numbers there had been but little difference between the two armies. Prior to the loss of these 6000 men, Cuesta's army had been 34,000 strong, with seventy guns; the British, with the German Legion, numbered 19,000, with thirty guns; the French were 50,000 strong, with eighty guns. These were all veteran troops, while on the side of the allies there were but 19,000 who could be called fighting men.

TALAVERA

"That is what comes of putting faith in the Spaniards!" Bull said savagely. "If I had been Sir Arthur I would have turned my guns on them and given them something to run for. We should do a thousand times better by ourselves; then we should know what we had to expect."

"It is evident that there won't be any fighting until to-morrow, Macwitty. You will place half your battalion on the hill-side, from this point to the bottom of the slope. I don't think that they will come so high up the hill as this, but you will, of course, throw some pickets out above. The other wing of your battalion you will hold in reserve a couple of hundred yards behind the centre of the line, but choose a sheltered spot for them, for those guns Victor is placing on his heights will sweep the face of this hill.

"This little watercourse will give capital cover to your advanced line, and they cannot do better than occupy it. Lying down they would be completely sheltered from the French artillery, and if attacked they could line the bank and fire without showing more than their heads. Of course you will throw out pickets along the face of the slope in front of you. Do you, Bull, march your battalion down to the foot of the hill and take up your post there. The ground is very uneven and broken, and you should be able to find some spot where the men would be in shelter; move a couple of hundred yards back, then Macwitty would flank any force advancing against you. The sun will set in a few minutes, so you had better lose no time in taking up your ground. As soon as you have chosen a place, go on with the captains of your companies across the valley. Make yourselves thoroughly acquainted with the ground, and mark the best spots at which to post the men to resist any force that may come along the valley. It is quite possible that Victor may make an attempt to turn the General's flank to-night. I will reconnoitre all the ground in front of you, and will then, with the colonel, join you."

The position Terence had chosen was a quarter of a mile west of the spur held by Donkin's brigade. He had selected it in order that, if attacked in force, he might have the assistance of the guns there, which would thus be able to play on the advancing French without risk of his own men being injured by their fire.

Bull marched his battalion down the hill, and as Terence and Herrara were about to mount, a sudden burst of musketry from the crest of the opposite hill showed that the French were attempting to carry that position. Victor, indeed, seeing the force stationed there to be a small one, and that from the confusion among the Spaniards on the British right the moment was very favourable, had ordered one division to attack, another to move to its support, while a third was to engage the German division posted on the plain to the right of the hill, and thus prevent succour being sent to Donkin. From the position where Terence was standing, the front of the steep slope that the French were climbing could not be seen, but almost at the same moment a dense mass of men began to swarm up the hill on Donkin's flank, having, unperceived, made their way in at the mouth of the valley.

"Form up your battalion, Macwitty," he shouted, "and double down the hill!" Then he rode after Bull, whose battalion had now reached the valley and halted there. "We must go to the assistance of the brigade on the hill, Bull, or they will be overpowered before reinforcements can reach them. Herrara, bring on Macwitty after us as soon as he gets down. Take the battalion forward at the double, Bull."

The order was given, and with a cheer the battalion set out across the valley, and on reaching the other side began to climb the steep ascent, bearing towards their left, so as to reach the summit near the spot where the French were ascending. Twilight was already closing in, and the approach of the Portuguese was unobserved by the French, whose leading battalions had reached the top of the hill, and were pressing heavily on Donkin's weak brigade, which had, however, checked the advance of the French on their front. Macwitty's battalion was but a short distance behind, when, marching straight along on the face of the hill, Bull arrived within a hundred yards of the French. Here Terence halted them for a minute, while they hastily formed up in line, and Macwitty came up. The din on the top of the hill just above Bull's right company was prodigious, the rattle of musketry incessant, the exulting shouts of the French could be plainly heard, and their comrades behind were pressing hotly up the hill to join in the strife.

TALAVERA

There was plainly not a moment to be lost, and, advancing to within fifty yards of the French battalions struggling up the hill in confused masses, a tremendous volley was poured in. The French, astonished at this sudden attack upon their flank, paused and endeavoured to form up and wheel round to oppose a front to it, but the heavy fire of the Portuguese, and the broken nature of the ground, prevented their doing this, and, ignorant of the strength of the force that had thus suddenly attacked them, they recoiled, keeping up an irregular fire, while the Portuguese, pouring in steady volleys, pressed upon them. In five minutes they gave way, and retired rapidly down the hill. The leading battalions had gained the crest, where, joining those who had ascended by the other face of the hill, they fell upon the already outnumbered defenders.

Donkin's men, though fighting fiercely, were pressed back, and would have been driven from their position had not General Hill brought up the 29th and 48th, with a battalion of detachments composed of Sir John Moore's stragglers. These charged the French so furiously that they were unable to withstand the assault, although aided by fresh battalions ascending the front of the hill. In their retreat, the French, instead of going straight down the hill, bore away to their right, and although some fell to the fire of the Portuguese, the greater portion passed unseen in the darkness.

The firing now ceased, and Terence ordered Bull and Macwitty to take their troops back to the ground originally selected, while he himself ascended to the crest. With some difficulty he discovered the whereabouts of General Hill, to whom he was well known. He found him in the act of having a wound temporarily dressed, by the light of a fire which had just been replenished—he having ridden in the dark into the midst of a French battalion, believing it to be one of his own regiments. Colonel Donkin was in conversation with him.

"It has been a very close affair, sir," he said, "and I certainly thought that we should be rolled down the hill. I believe that we owe our safety in no small degree to a couple of battalions of Spaniards, I fancy, who took up their post on the opposite hill this morning. Just before you brought up your reinforcement, and while things were at their worst, I heard heavy volley firing somewhere just over the crest. I don't know who it could have been if it was not they, for there were certainly no other troops on my left."

"You may as well make your report to me, O'Connor."

TALAVERA

"They were Portuguese battalions, sir," Terence said quietly.

"Oh, is it you, O'Connor!" General Hill exclaimed. "If they were those two battalions of yours I can quite understand it. This is Colonel O'Connor, Donkin, who checked Soult's passage at the mouth of the Minho, and has performed other admirable services. You may as well make your report to me, O'Connor, and I will include it in my own to Sir Arthur."

Terence related how, just as he was taking up his position for the night along the slopes of the Sierra, he heard the out-break of firing on the front of the hill, and seeing a large force mounting its northern slope, and knowing that only one brigade was posted there, he thought it his duty to move to its assistance. Crossing the valley at the double, he had taken them in flank, and, being unperceived in the gathering darkness, had checked their advance and compelled them to retire down the hill.

"At what strength do you estimate the force which so retired, Colonel?"

"I fancy there were eight battalions of them, but three had gained the crest before we arrived. The others were necessarily broken up, and followed so close upon each other that it was difficult to separate them, but I fancy there were eight of them. Being in such confusion, and, of course, unaware of my strength, they were unable to form or to offer any effectual resistance; and our volleys from a distance of fifty yards must have done heavy execution upon them."

"Then there is no doubt, Donkin, Colonel O'Connor's force did save you, for if those five battalions had gained the crest, you would have been driven off it before the brigade I brought up arrived, and, indeed, even with that aid we should have been so outnumbered that we could scarcely have held our ground. It was hot work as it was, but certainly five more battalions would have turned the scales against us. Of course, O'Connor, you will send in a report of your reasons for quitting your position, to headquarters, and I shall myself do full justice to the service that you have rendered so promptly and efficaciously. Where is your command now?"

"They will by this time have taken up their former position on the opposite slope. One battalion is extended there; the other is at the foot of the hill, prepared to check any force that may attempt to make its way up the valley. Our line is about a quarter of a mile in rear of this spur. I selected the position in order that, should the French make an attempt in any force, the guns here might take them in flank, while I held them in check in front."

The general nodded. "Well thought of," he said; "and now, Donkin, you had better muster your brigade and ascertain what are your losses. I am afraid they are very heavy."

Terence now returned across the valley, and on joining his command told Herrara and the two majors how warmly General Hill had commended their action.

"What has been our loss?" he asked.

"Fifteen killed and five-and-forty wounded, but of these a great proportion are not serious."

Brushwood was now collected, and in a short time a number of fires were blazing. The men were in high spirits. They were proud of having overthrown a far superior force of the enemy, and were gratified at the expression of great satisfaction, conveyed to them by their captains by Terence's order, at the steadiness with which they had fought. At daybreak next morning the enemy was seen to be again in motion, Victor having obtained the king's consent to again try to carry the hills occupied by the British. This time Terence did not leave his position, being able to see that the whole of Hill's division now occupied the heights, and, moreover, being himself threatened by two regiments of light troops, which crossed the mouth of the valley, ascended the slopes on his side, and proceeded to work their way along them. The whole of Macwitty's battalion was now placed in line, while Bull's was held in reserve behind its centre.

It was not long before Macwitty was hotly engaged, and the French, who were coming along in skirmishing order among the rocks and broken ground, were soon brought to a stand-still. For some time a heavy fire was exchanged. Three times the French gathered for a rush, but each time the steady volleys from their almost invisible foes drove them back again with loss, to the shelter they had left. In the intervals Terence could see how the fight was going on across the valley. The whole hillside was dotted with firs, as the French worked their way up, and the British troops on the crest fired down upon them. Several times parties of the French gained the brow, but only to be hurled back again by the troops held in reserve in readiness to move to any point where the enemy might gain a footing.

TALAVERA

For forty minutes the battle continued, and then, having lost 1500 men, the French retreated down the hill again, covered by the fire of their batteries, which opened with fury on the crest as soon as they were seen to be descending the slope.

At the same time the light troops opposed to Terence also drew off. Seeing the pertinacity with which the French had tried to turn his left, Sir Arthur Wellesley moved his cavalry round to the head of the valley, and obtaining Bassecour's division of Spanish from Cuesta, sent them to take post on the hillside a short distance in rear of Terence's Portuguese. The previous evening's fighting had cost Victor 1000 men, while 800 British had been killed or wounded, and the want of success then, and the attack on the following morning, tended to depress the spirits of the French and to raise those of the British.

It was thought that after these two repulses Victor would not again give battle, and, indeed, the French generals Jourdan and Sebastiani were opposed to a renewal of hostilities, but Victor was in favour of a general attack. So his opinion was finally adopted by the king, in spite of the fact that he knew that Soult was in full march towards the British rear, and had implored him not to fight a battle till he had cut the British line of retreat, when, in any case, they would be forced to retire at once. The king was influenced more by his fear for the safety of Madrid than by Victor's arguments. Wilson's force had been greatly exaggerated by rumour. Venegas was known to be at last approaching Toledo, and the king feared that one or both of these forces might fall upon Madrid in his absence, and that all his military stores would fall into their hands. He therefore earnestly desired to force the British to retreat, in order that he might hurry back to protect Madrid.

Doubtless the gross cowardice exhibited by the Spaniards on the previous day had shown Victor that he had really only the 19,000 British troops to contend against, and as his force exceeded theirs by two to one, he might well regard victory as certain, and believe he could not fail to beat them.

Up to midday a perfect quiet reigned along both lines. The British and French soldiers went down alike to the rivulet that separated the two armies, and exchanged jokes as they drank and filled their canteens. Albuquerque, being altogether dissatisfied with Cuesta's arrangements, moved across the plain with his own cavalry, and took his post behind the British and German horse, so that no less than 6000 cavalry were now ready to pour down upon any French force attempting to turn the British position by the valley. The day was intensely hot, and the soldiers, after eating their scanty rations, for the most part stretched themselves down to sleep, for the night had been a broken one, owing to the fact that the Spaniards, whenever they heard, or thought they heard, anyone moving in their front, poured in a tremendous fire that roused the whole camp, and was so wild and ill-directed that several British officers and men on their left were killed by it.

Soon after midday the drums were heard to beat along the whole length of the French line, and the troops were seen to be falling in; then the British were also called to arms, and the soldiers cheerfully took their places in the ranks, glad that the matter was to be brought to an issue at once, as they thought that a victory would at least put an end to the state of starvation in which they had for some time been kept. The French had by this time learned how impossible it was to surmount the obstacles in front of that portion of the allies' line occupied by the Spaniards. They therefore neglected these altogether, and Sebastiani advanced against the British division in the plains, while Victor, as before, prepared to assail the British left, supported this time by a great mass of cavalry.

The French were soon in readiness for the attack. Ruffin's division were to cross the valley, move along the foot of the mountain, and turn the British left. Villatte was to guard the mouth of the valley with one brigade, to threaten Hill with the other, and to make another attempt to carry it. He was to be aided by half the division of Lapisse, while the other half assisted Sebastiani in his attack on the British centre. Milhaud's dragoons were placed on the main road to Talavera, so as to keep the Spaniards from moving to the assistance of the British. The battle began with a furious attack on the British right, but the French were withstood by Campbell's division and Mackenzie's brigade, aided by two Spanish columns, and were finally pushed back with great loss, and ten of their guns captured; but as Campbell wisely refused to break his line and pursue, the French rallied on their reserve, and prepared to renew the attack.

TALAVERA

In the meantime Lapisse crossed the rivulet, and attacked Sherbrooke's division, composed of the Germans and Guards. This brigade was, however, driven back in disorder. The Guards followed hotly in pursuit, but the French reserves came up, and their batteries opened with fury and drove the Guards back, while the Germans were so hotly pressed by Lapisse that they fell into confusion. The 48th, however, fell upon the flank of the advancing French, the Guards and the Germans rallied, the British artillery swept the French columns, and they again fell back. Thus the British centre and right had succeeded in finally repelling the attacks made upon them. On the left, as the French advanced, the 23rd Light Dragoons and the 1st German Hussars charged the head of Ruffin's column. Before they reached them, however, they encountered the ravine through which the rivulet here ran. The Germans checked their horses when they came upon this almost impassible obstacle. The 23rd, however, kept on; men and horses rolled over each other, but many crossed the chasm, and, forming again, dashed in between the squares into which the French infantry had thrown themselves, and charged a brigade of light infantry in their rear. Victor hurled two regiments of cavalry upon them, and the 23rd, hopelessly over-matched, were driven back with a loss of 207 men and officers, being fully half the number that had ridden forward. The rest galloped back to the shelter of Bassecour's division. Yet their effort had not been in vain. The French, astonished at their furious charge, and seeing four distinct lines of cavalry still drawn up facing them, made no further movement. Hill easily repulsed the attack upon his position, and the battle ceased as suddenly as it had begun, the French having failed at every point they had attacked.

Terence had, on seeing Ruffin's division marching towards him, advanced along the slope until they reached the entrance to the valley, and then, scattering on the hillside, had opened a heavy and continuous fire upon the French, doing much execution among their columns, and still more when they threw themselves into square to resist the cavalry. He had given orders that should Ruffin send some of his battalions up the hill against them, they were to retire up the slopes, taking advantage of every shelter, and not to attempt to meet the enemy in close contact. No such attack was, however, made. The French battalion most exposed threw out a large number of

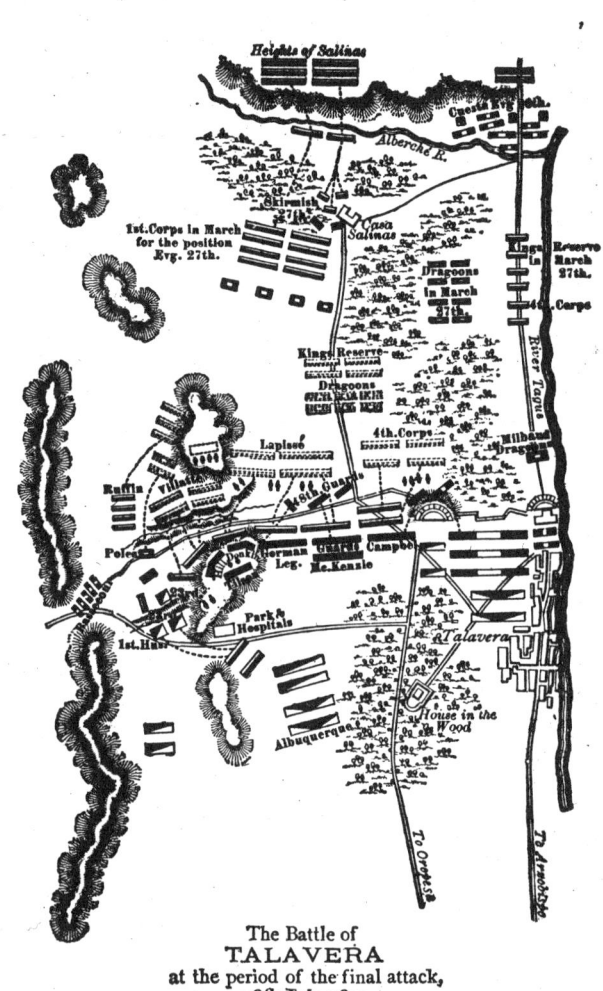

The Battle of
TALAVERA
at the period of the final attack,
28th July, 1809.

skirmishers, and endeavoured to keep down the galling fire maintained from the hillside; but as the Portuguese took advantage of every stone and bush, and scarcely a man was visible to the French, there were but few casualties among them.

The loss of the British was in all during the two days' fighting 6200, including 600 taken prisoners; that of the French was 7400. Ten guns were captured by Campbell's division, and seven left in the woods by the French, as they drew off the next morning at daybreak to take up their position behind the Alberche.

During the day Crauford's brigade came up after a tremendous march. The three regiments had, after a tramp of twenty miles, encamped near Plasencia, when the alarm spread by the Spanish fugitives reached that place. Crauford allowed his men two hours' rest and then started to join the army, and did not halt until he reached the camp, having in twenty-six hours, during the hottest season of the year, marched sixty-two miles, carrying kit, arms, and ammunition—a weight of from fifty to sixty pounds. Only twenty-five men out of the three regiments fell out, and immediately the brigade arrived it took up the outpost duty in front of the army.

Terence was much gratified by the appearance in general orders that day of the following notice:

The general commander-in-chief expresses his warm approbation of the conduct of the two battalions of the Minho regiment of Portuguese, commanded by Colonel O'Connor. This officer, on his own discretion, moved from the position assigned to him, on seeing the serious attack made on Colonel Donkin's brigade on the evening of the 27th, and, scaling the hill, opened so heavy a fire on the French ascending it that five battalions fell back without taking part in the attack. This took place at the crisis of the engagement, and had a decisive effect on its result.

At eight o'clock a staff-officer rode up with orders for the Minho regiment to return at once to the pass of Banos, as the news had come in that the enemy beyond the hills were in movement. Terence was to act in concert with the Spanish force there, and hold the pass as long as possible. If the enemy were in too great strength to be withstood, he was given discretion as to his movements, being guided only by the fact that the British army would probably march down the valley of the Tagus. If Soult crossed, "his force," the order added, "was estimated as not exceeding 15,000 men."

Chapter III
Prisoners

On the 31st of July Terence reached the neighbourhood of Banos, and learned from the peasantry that a French army had passed through the town early on the preceding day. No resistance whatever had been offered to its passage through the pass of Bejar, and the Spanish at Banos had retreated hastily after exchanging a few shots with the French advanced guard. The peasantry had all deserted their villages, but had had some skirmishes with small foraging parties of cavalry. Several French stragglers had been killed in the pass. Hoping to find some of these still alive, and to obtain information from them, Terence continued his march for Banos, sending on two of the best mounted of the Portuguese horse men to ascertain if there was any considerable French force left there. He was within half a mile of the town when he saw them returning at full speed, chased by a party of French dragoons, who, however, fell back when they saw the advancing infantry.

"What is your news?' Terence asked, as the troopers rode up.

"Banos is full of French troops," one of them replied, "and columns are marching down the pass. From what I can see I should think that there must be 16,000 or 20,000 of them."

In fact, this was Soult's second army corps—the first, which had preceded it, having that morning reached Plasencia, where they captured 400 sick in the hospitals, and a large quantity of stores that had been left there from want of carriage when the British army advanced. Terence lost no time in retreating from so dangerous a neighbourhood, and at once made for the mountains he had just left. Two regiments of French cavalry set out in pursuit as soon as the party that had chased the Portuguese troopers entered Banos with the news that a body of infantry, some 2000 strong, was close at hand. They came up before the Portuguese had marched more than a mile. The two battalions were halted, and thrown into square. The French rode fearlessly down upon them, but were received with so hot and steady a fire that they speedily drew off with considerable loss. Then the regiment ascended the hills, and half an hour later halted.

"The question is, what is to be done?" Terence said to Herrara and his two majors. "It is evident that for once the information we obtained from the Spaniards is correct, and that Soult must have at least 30,000 men with him. Possibly his full strength is not up yet. By this time the force that passed yesterday must be at Plasencia, and by to-morrow may be on the Tagus, and Sir Arthur's position must be one of great danger. Putting Cuesta and the Spaniards altogether aside as worthless, he has, even with that brigade we saw marching in soon after we started, only 22,000 or 23,000 men; and on one side of him is Victor, with some 40,000; on the other is Soult, with perhaps as many more. With starving and exhausted troops his chances are small indeed, unless he can cross the Tagus. He might beat one marshal or the other, but be can hardly beat the two of them.

"The first thing to do is to send two troopers off with duplicate despatches, telling Sir Arthur of Soult's passage. He might not otherwise hear of it for some time, and then it might be too late. The peasantry and the village authorities will be too busy carrying off their effects and driving their animals to the hills to think for a moment of sending information. That is evidently the first thing to be done. Until we see what is going to happen, I don't think we can do better than cross the Sierra and encamp at some spot where we can make out the movements of the French on the plain. At the same time we can keep an eye on the road to Plasencia, and be able to send information to Sir Arthur if any further bodies of French troops come down into the valley. Our position is evidently a dangerous one. If the news has reached Sir Arthur, he will have fallen back from Talavera at once. Victor will no doubt follow on his heels, and his cavalry and those of Soult will speedily meet each other. Therefore it will be in all ways best to see how matters develop themselves before moving down into the plain."

UNDER WELLINGTON'S COMMAND

Accordingly two of the troopers were sent off with information that 15,000 French were already in the valley, and that as many more would be there on the following day. Then the regiment marched across the Sierra and took post high up on the slope, with Plasencia ten miles away on the right, and the spires of Oropesa visible across the valley. On the following day another army corps was seen descending from Banos to Plasencia, while a large body of troops marched from that town to Navalmoral, thus cutting off the retreat of the British by the bridge of boats at Almaraz. Clouds of dust on the distant plain showed that a portion at least of the Allied Army had arrived at Oropesa, and bodies of French cavalry were made out traversing the plain and scattering among the villages. Two more troopers were sent off with reports, and warned, like the others, to take different routes and make a wide circuit so as to avoid the French, and then to come down upon Oropesa. If the troops there were British they were to deliver their reports to the general in command. If it was occupied by Spaniards they were to proceed to Talavera and hand them in at headquarters.

On the following day still another army corps marched down to Plasencia, raising Soult's force to 54,000. On that day Cuesta, who had undertaken to hold Talavera, retreated suddenly, alarmed by Victor's army making an advance, and leaving to their fate the 1500 British wounded in the hospital. These, however, were benefited by the change. They had been dying of hunger, for, although there was an abundance of provisions in Talavera, the inhabitants refused to sell any to the British, and jealously concealed their stores in their houses. Nor would Cuesta do anything to aid them; and thus the men who had fought and suffered for the Spanish cause were left to perish while there was abundance around them.

The conduct of the Spaniards, from the moment the British crossed the frontier to the time of their leaving Spain, was never forgotten or forgiven by the British troops, who had henceforth an absolute hatred for the Spanish, which contributed in no small degree to the excesses perpetrated by them upon the inhabitants of Badajos and other places, taken subsequently by storm. The French, on entering Talavera, treated the British wounded with the greatest kindness, and henceforth they were well fed and cared for.

PRISONERS

The first report sent by Terence reached Sir Arthur safely ten hours after it was sent out, and apprised him for the first time of the serious storm that was gathering in his rear, and he had without an hour's delay given orders for the army to march to Oropesa, intending to give battle to Soult before Victor could come up to join his fellow-marshal. The second report informed him of the real strength of the army towards which he was marching, and showed him the real extent of his danger. So he at once seized the only plan of escape offered to him, marching with all speed to Arzobispo, and crossing the Tagus by the bridge there, Cuesta's army following him.

As soon as the Tagus was passed, Crauford's brigade was hurried on to seize the bridge of boats at Almaraz, and prevent the French from crossing there.

Fortunately, Soult was as ignorant of the position of the Allies as Sir Arthur was of his, and believing that the British were following Victor and pressing forward towards Madrid, he had conducted his operations in a comparatively leisurely manner. Therefore, it was not until the British were safely across the Tagus that he ascertained the real state of affairs, and put himself in communication with Victor. On the morning following the crossing, Terence was apprised by a note sent back by one of the troopers of the movement that had taken place. It was written upon a small piece of paper, so that it could be destroyed at once by the bearer if he should be threatened with capture, and contained only the following words:

Your report invaluable. The Allied Army moves to Arzobispo and will cross the Tagus there. You must act according to your judgment. I can give no advice.

"Thank God the British army has escaped!" Terence said, after reading the despatch to his officers. "Now we have only to think of ourselves. As to rejoining Sir Arthur, it is out of the question; the valley is full of French troops. Ney has joined Soult, and there are 100,000 Frenchmen between us and our army. If I had any idea where Wilson is, we might endeavour to join him, for he must be in the same plight as ourselves. Our only chance, so far as I can see, is to cross their line of communications and to endeavour to join Beresford, who is reported as marching down the frontier from Almeida."

"Would you propose to pass through Banos, Colonel?" Herrara asked. "The mountains there are almost, if not quite, impassable, but we might get a peasant to guide us."

"I don't like going near Banos, Herrara; the French are almost sure to have left a strong body there, and the chances are against our finding a peasant, for the inhabitants of all the villages for ten miles round have almost certainly fled and taken to the hills. I think it would be safer to follow along this side of the Sierra, cross the road a few miles above Plasencia, then make for the mountains, and come down on the head of the river Coa. Beresford is probably in the valley of that river. We are more likely to find a guide that way than we are by going through Banos. We shall have tough work of it whichever way we go, even if we are lucky enough to get past without running against a single Frenchman."

"Would it not be better to wait till nightfall, Colonel?" Bull asked.

Terence shook his head. "There is no moon," he said; "and as to climbing about among these mountains in the dark it would be worse than running the risk of a fight with the French. Besides, we should have no chance whatever of coming across a peasant. No, I think we must try it as soon as it gets light to-morrow morning. We had better dress up a score of men in peasant clothes, and send them off in couples, to search among the hills. Whoever comes across a man must bring him in, whether he likes it or not. The Spaniards are so desperately afraid of the French that they will give us no information whatever unless forced to do so, and we shall have even more difficulty than the British. There must have been thousands of peasants and others who knew that Soult had come down upon Plasencia, and yet Sir Arthur obtained no news. There is one comfort, there can be little doubt that Soult is just as much in the dark as to the position of the British army."

By nightfall three peasants had been brought in. All shook their heads stolidly when questioned in Portuguese, but upon Terence having them placed against a rock, and twelve men brought up and ordered to load their muskets, one of them said in Spanish: "I know where a path across the mountains leaves the road, but I have never been over the hills, and know nothing of how it runs."

PRISONERS

"Ah! I thought you could make out my question," Terence said. "Well, you have saved the lives of yourself and your comrades. Take us to the path to-morrow and set us fairly on it, and you shall be allowed to go free and be paid five dollars for your trouble." Then he turned to Bull.

"Put four men to guard them," he said, "and let the guard be changed once every two hours; their orders will be to shoot the fellows down if they endeavour to make their escape. They are quite capable of going down into Plasencia and bringing the French upon us."

At daybreak they were on the march, and two hours later came down into the valley through which the road from Banos ran down to Plasencia. They had just crossed it when the head of a column of cavalry appeared coming down the valley. It at once broke into a gallop.

"How far is it to where the path begins to ascend the mountains?" Terence asked, holding a pistol to the peasant's head.

"Four miles," the man replied sullenly, looking with apprehension at the French.

Terence shouted orders to Bull and Macwitty to throw their men into square, and as they had been marching, since they reached level ground, in column of companies, the movement was carried out before the enemy arrived.

The French cavalry, believing that the battalions were Spanish and would break at once, charged furiously down upon them. They were, however, received with so heavy a fire that they drew off discomfited, leaving many men and horses on the ground.

"They are a strong body," Terence said quietly to Bull, in the centre of whose square he had taken up his position. "I should say there are 3000 of them, and I am afraid they are the head of another division."

"Yes, there are the infantry coming down the valley. We must press on, or we shall be caught before we get into the hills."

The battalions were soon in motion, but immediately they started the cavalry prepared to charge again.

"This will never do, Bull. If we form square every time we shall be delayed so much that the infantry will soon be up. You must do it now and quickly, but we will start next time in column eight abreast, and face the men round in lines four deep either way if they charge again."

The French this time drew off without pressing their charge home, and then, trotting on, took their place between the Portuguese and the mountains.

"Form your leading company in line, four deep, Bull; the column shall follow you."

The formation was quickly altered, and, preceded by the line to cover them from the charge in front, the column advanced at a rapid pace. The cavalry moved forward to meet them, but as the two parties approached each other the line opened so heavy a fire that the French drew off from their front both to the right and left. Bull at once threw back a wing of each company to prevent an attack in flank, and so in the form of a capital T the column kept on its way. Several times the French cavalry charged down, compelling them to halt, but each time, after repulsing the attack, the column went on.

"It would be all right if we had only these fellows to deal with," Terence said to Bull, "but their infantry are coming on fast."

The plain behind was indeed covered with a swarm of skirmishers coming along at the double.

"We must go at the double too, Bull," Terence said, "or they will be up long before we get to the hills; we are not half-way yet. Keep the men well in band, and don't let them fall into confusion. If they do, the cavalry will be down upon us in a minute."

The cavalry, however, were equally conscious of the importance of checking the Portuguese, and again and again dashed down upon them with reckless bravery, suffering heavily whenever they did so, but causing some delay each time they charged.

"I shall go back to the rear, Bull. Mind my orders are precise, that whatever happens behind to us, you are to push forward until you begin to climb the hills." Then without waiting for an answer he galloped back.

Although the column pressed on steadily at the double, the delay caused by the cavalry, and the fact that the French infantry were broken up, and able, therefore, to run more quickly, was bringing the enemy up fast. Herrara was riding at the head of the second battalion, and to him Terence repeated the instructions he had given Bull.

"What are you going to do, Colonel?" the latter asked.

"There is some very broken ground a quarter of a mile ahead," be replied. "I intend to hold that spot with the rear company. It will be some little time before the French infantry will be able to form and attack us, and the ground looks to me too broken for their cavalry to act. As soon as I can see that you are far enough ahead to gain the hill before they can overtake you again, I shall follow you with the company; but mind, should I not do so, you must take the command of the two battalions, cross the mountains, and join Beresford."

He galloped on to Macwitty, who was riding in the rear, and repeated the order to him.

"Well, Colonel, let me stop behind with the company instead of yourself."

"No, no, Macwitty. It is the post of danger, and as commanding officer I must take it. It is a question of saving the two battalions at the cost of the company, and there is no doubt as to the course to be taken. Do you ride on at once and take your post at the rear of the company ahead of this, and keep them steady. Here come their cavalry down again on the flank."

There was another charge, three or four heavy volleys, and then the French drew off again. The bullets of their infantry were now whistling overhead.

"A hundred yards farther," Terence shouted, "and then we will face them."

In front lay an upheaval of rock, stretching almost like a wall across the line they were following. It was a sort of natural outwork pushed out by nature in front of the hill, and rose some fifty feet above the level of the plain. There were many places at which it could be climbed, and up one of these the track ran obliquely. Hitherto it had been but an ill-defined path, but here some efforts had been made to render it practicable by cutting away the ground on the upper side to enable laden mules to pass up.

Terence reined up at the bottom of the ascent and directed the men to take up their post on the crest, the leading half of the company to the right and the other half to the left of the path. Before all were up the French light troops were clustering round, but a rush was prevented by the heavy fire that opened from the brow above, and the company were soon scattered along the crest a yard apart. In five minutes some two thousand French infantry were assembled. A mounted officer rode some distance to the right and left, to examine the ground. It was evident that he considered that the position, held by 200 determined men, was a formidable one. Lying down, as they were, only the heads of the Portuguese could be seen, while a force attacking them would have to march across level ground, affording no shelter whatever from the defenders' fire, and then to climb a very steep ascent. Moreover, the whole force they had been pursuing might be gathered just behind.

After another five minutes' delay half a battalion broke up into skirmishers, while the rest divided into two parties, and marched parallel to the rocks left and right. Terence saw that these movements must be successful, for with 200 men he could not defend a line of indefinite length. However, his object had now been achieved. The descent behind was even and regular, and he could see the column winding up the hill somewhat over half a mile away. Of the French cavalry he could see nothing. They had, after their last charge, ridden off, as if leaving the matter in the hands of their infantry. He ordered the bugler to sound the retreat in open order, and the Portuguese, rising to their feet, went down the gentle slope at a trot. They were half-way to the hills when the long lines of the French cavalry were seen sweeping down upon them from the right, having evidently ridden along the foot of the steep declivity until they came to a spot where they were able to ascend it.

At the sound of the bugle the rear company instantly ran together and formed a square, and, as the French cavalry came up, opened a continuous fire upon them. Unable to break the line of bayonets, the horsemen rode round and round the square, discharging their pistols into it, and occasionally making desperate efforts to break in. Suddenly the cavalry drew apart, and a battalion of infantry marched forward and poured their fire into the Portuguese. Terence felt that no more could be done. His main body was safe from pursuit, and it would be but throwing away the lives of his brave fellows did he continue the hopeless fight. He, therefore, waved a white handkerchief in token of surrender, shouted to his men to cease fire, and riding through them with sheathed sword made his way to the officer who appeared to be in command of the cavalry.

"We surrender, sir," he said, "as prisoners of war; we have done all that we could do." He could speak but a few words of French, but the officer understood him.

"You have done more than enough, sir," he said. "Order your men to lay down their arms and I will guarantee their safety."

He ordered his cavalry to draw back, and, riding up to the infantry, halted them. Terence at once ordered his men to lay down their arms. "You have done all that men could do," he said. "You have saved your comrades, and it is no dishonour to yield to twenty times your own force. Form up in column ready to march."

The commander of the cavalry again rode up, this time accompanied by another officer.

"The general wishes to know, sir," the latter said in English, "who you are and what force this is?"

"I am Colonel O'Connor, holding that rank in Lord Beresford's army, and have the honour to be on the staff of Sir Arthur Wellesley, though at present detached on special service. The two battalions that have marched up the hill are the Minho regiment of Portuguese under my command. We were posted on the Sierra, and being cut off from rejoining the British by the advance of Marshal Soult's army, were endeavouring to retire across the mountains into Portugal when you cut us off."

The officer translated the words to the general.

"Tell him," the latter said, "that if all the Portuguese fought as well as those troops, there would have been no occasion for the British to come here to aid them. I have never seen troops better handled or more steady. This cannot be the first time they have been under fire."

Terence bowed when the compliment was translated to him.

"They fought, General, in the campaign last year," he said, "and the regiment takes its name from the fact that they prevented Marshal Soult from crossing at the mouth of the Minho, but their first encounter with your cavalry was near Orense."

UNDER WELLINGTON'S COMMAND

"I remember it well," the general said, "for I was in command of the cavalry that attacked you. Your men were not in uniform then or I should have known them again. How did you come to be there, for at that time the British had not advanced beyond Cintra?"

"I had been sent with a message to Romana, and happening to come across this newly-raised levy without officers or commander, I took the command, and, aided by two British troopers and a Portuguese lieutenant, succeeded in getting them into shape, and did my best to hold the pass to Braga."

"Peste!" the general exclaimed. "That was you again, was it? It was the one piece of dash and determination shown by the Portuguese during our advance to Oporto, and cost us as many men as all the rest of the fighting put together. And now, Colonel, we must be marching. Major Portalis here will take charge of you."

In a few minutes the French cavalry and infantry were on their march towards Plasencia, the Portuguese prisoners guarded on both sides by cavalry marching with them, their captain being, like Terence, placed in charge of an officer. The Portuguese marched with head erect. They were prisoners, but they felt that they had done well, and had sacrificed themselves to cover the retreat of their comrades, and that had it not been for the French infantry coming up, they might have beaten off the attacks of their great body of cavalry. On their arrival at Plasencia the troops were placed in a large building that had been converted into a prison. Here were some hundreds of other prisoners, for the most part Spaniards, who had been captured when Soult had suddenly arrived. Terence was taken to the quarters of General Foy, who was in command there. Here he was again questioned through the officer who spoke English. After he translated his answers to the general, the latter told him to ask Terence if he knew where Wilson was.

"I do not, sir," he replied; "we were together on the Sierra a fortnight ago, but he marched suddenly away without communicating with me, and I remained at Banos until ordered to march to the Alberche. We took part in the battle there, and were then ordered back again to support the Spaniards at Banos, but Marshal Soult had marched through the pass, and the Spaniards had disappeared before we got there. We remained among the mountains until yesterday, when, hearing that the British had crossed the Tagus, and seeing no way to rejoin them, I started to cross the mountains to join Lord Beresford's force wherever I might find it."

"General Heron reports that the two battalions under your command fought with extraordinary steadiness and repulsed all the attempts of his cavalry to break them, and finally succeeded in drawing off to the mountains with the exception of the two companies that formed the rear-guard. How is it that there is only one officer?"

"They were, in fact, one company," Terence said; "my companies are each about 200 strong, and the officer captured with me was its captain."

"General Heron also reports to me that your retreat was admirably carried out," General Foy said, "and that no body of French veterans could have done better. Well, sir, if you are ready to give your parole not to escape, you will be at liberty to move about the town freely until there is an opportunity of sending a batch of prisoners to France."

"Thank you, general; I am ready to give my parole not to make any attempt to escape, and am obliged to you for your courtesy." Terence had already thought over what course he had best take should he be offered freedom on parole, and had resolved to accept it. The probabilities of making his escape were extremely small; there would be no chance whatever of rejoining the army, and a passage alone across the all-but-impassable mountains was not to be thought of. Therefore he decided that, at any rate for the present, he would give his promise not to attempt to escape. Quarters were assigned to him in the town in a house where several French officers were staying. These all showed him great courtesy and kindness. Between the English and French the war was throughout conducted on honourable terms, prisoners were well treated, and there was no national animosity between either officers or men.

When he went out into the town one of the French officers generally accompanied him, and he was introduced to a number of others. He set to work in earnest to improve the small knowledge of French that he possessed, and, borrowing some French newspapers, and buying a dictionary in the town, he spent a considerable portion of his time in studying them. He remained three weeks at Plasencia. During that time he heard that the army of Venegas had been completely routed by Victor, that Cuesta had been badly beaten soon after crossing the Tagus, and Albuquerque's cavalry very roughly treated. Five guns and 400 prisoners had been taken. Ney had marched through Plasencia on his way back to Valladolid to repress an insurrection that had broken out in that district, and on his way met Wilson, who was trying to retreat by Banos, and who was decisively beaten and his command scattered.

Terence was now told to prepare to leave with a convoy of prisoners for Talavera. He was the only British officer, and, being on parole, the officer commanding the detachment marching with the prisoners invited him to ride with him, and the two days' journey was made very pleasantly. At Talavera he remained for a week. The Portuguese prisoners remained there, but the British who had been captured in Plasencia, and the convalescents from the hospital at Talavera, in all 200 strong, among whom were six British officers, were to march to the frontier, there to be interned in one of the French fortresses.

The officer who had commanded the escort on the march from Plasencia spoke in high terms of Terence to the officer in charge of the 200 men who were to go on with them. The party had been directed not to pass through Madrid, as the sight of over 200 British prisoners might give rise to a popular demonstration by the excitable Spaniards, which would possibly lead to disorder. He was therefore directed to march by the road to the Escurial, and then over the Sierra to Segovia, then up through Valladolid and Burgos. The escort was entirely composed of infantry, and as Terence could not therefore take his horse with him, he joined the other officers on foot. To his great surprise and joy he found that one of these was his chum, Dick Ryan.

"This is an unexpected pleasure, Dicky!" he exclaimed.

"Well, yes, I am as pleased as you are at our meeting, Terence, but I must own that the conditions might have been more pleasant."

"Oh, never mind the conditions!" Terence said. "It is quite enough for the present that we both are here, and that we have got before us a journey that is likely to be a jolly one. I suppose that you have given your parole, as I have, but when we are once in prison there will be an end of that, and it is hard if, when we put our heads together, we don't hit on some plan of escape. Do you know the other officers? If so, please introduce me to them."

As soon as the introductions were completed, Terence asked Ryan where he had been wounded.

"I was hit by a piece of a French shell," the latter replied. "Fortunately it did not come straight at me, but scraped along my ribs, laying them pretty well bare. As it was a month ago, it is quite healed up, but I am very stiff still, and am obliged to be very careful in my movements. If I forget all about it and give a turn suddenly I regularly yell, for it feels as if a red-hot iron had been stuck against me. However, I have learned to be careful, and as long as I simply walk straight on I am pretty well all right. It was a near case at first, and I believe I should have died of starvation if the French had not come in. Those brutes of Spaniards would do nothing whatever for me, and I give you my word of honour that nothing passed my lips but water for three days."

"Perhaps it was a good thing for you, Dicky, and kept down fever."

"I would have run the chance of a dozen fevers to have got a good meal," Ryan said indignantly. "I don't know but that I would have chanced it, even for a crust of bread. I tell you, if the French had not come in when they did there would not have been a man alive in hospital at the end of another forty-eight hours. The men were so furious that if they could have got at arms I believe everyone who could have managed to crawl out would have joined in a sally and have shot down every Spaniard they met in the streets till they were overpowered and killed. Now let us hear your adventures. Of course I saw in orders what good work you did, that day when you were in our camp, against the French when they attacked Donkin. Some of our fellows went across to see you the morning after the big battle, but they could not find you, and heard afterwards from some men of Hill's division that you had been seen marching away in a body along the hills."

Terence then gave an account of the attack by the French upon his regiment, and how he had fallen into their hands.

"That was well done, Terence. There is some pleasure in being taken prisoner in that sort of way. What will become of your regiment, do you suppose?"

"I have no idea. Herrara may be appointed to the command; I should think that most likely he would be, but of course Sir Arthur may put another English officer at its head. However, I should say that there is no likelihood of any more fighting this year. Ney's corps has gone north, which is a sign that there will be no invasion of Portugal at present, and certainly Sir Arthur is not likely to take the offensive again, now that his eyes have been thoroughly opened to the rascality and cowardice of the Spaniards, and by next spring we two may be back again. We have got into so many scrapes together, and have always pulled through them, that I don't think the French will keep us long. Have you stuck to your Portuguese, Dicky?"

"I have, and am beginning to get on very fairly with it."

"That is right. When we get back I will apply for you as my adjutant, if I get the command of the regiment again."

Chapter IV
Guerillas

The marches were short, as many of the prisoners were still weak, and, indeed, among their guard were many convalescents who had recently been discharged from the hospital at Toledo, and who were going back to France. The little column was accompanied by four waggons, two of which were intended for the conveyance of any who should prove unable to march, and the others were filled with provisions for consumption by the way, together with a few tents, as many of the villages that would be their halting places were too small to afford accommodation for the 400 men, even if every house was taken up for the purpose. Although the first day's march was only twelve miles, the two empty waggons were quite full before they reached their halting-place, and many of the guard had placed their guns and cartridge-boxes on the other carts.

It was now the middle of August, and the heat in the valley of the Tagus was overpowering. The convoy, however, had marched at six in the morning and halted at eight, in the shade of a large olive wood, and did not continue its march until five in the afternoon. The night was so warm that the English prisoners, and many of their guards, preferred lying down in the open, and throwing the blanket, with which each had been furnished, over him to keep off the dew, to going into the stuffy cottages, where the fleas would give them little chance of rest. On the third they arrived at the village of Escurial; the next morning they began to mount the pass over the Sierra, and slept that night in an empty barracks at Segovia. Here they left the main road leading through Valladolid and took one more to the east, stopping at small villages until they arrived at Aranda on the Douro.

Thence they marched due north to Gamonal. They were now on the main road to the frontier, passed through Miranda and Zadorra, and began to ascend the slopes of the Pyrenees. The marches had for some days been considerably longer than when they first started. The invalids had gained strength, and having no muskets to carry, were for the most part able to march eighteen or twenty miles without difficulty. Four had been left behind in hospital at Segovia, but with these exceptions all had greatly benefited by steady exercise and an ample supply of food.

"I could do a good deal of travelling in this way," one of the officers said, as they marched out from Miranda. "Just enough exercise to be pleasant; no trouble about baggage or route, or where one is to stop for the night; nothing to pay, and everything managed for you. What could one want for more!"

"We could do with a little less dust," Dick Ryan said with a laugh; "but we cannot expect everything."

"Unfortunately, there will be an end to our marching, and not a very pleasant one," Terence said. "At present one scarcely recognises that one is a prisoner. The French officers certainly do all in their power to make us forget it, and their soldiers and ours try their best to hold some sort of conversation together. I feel that I am making great progress in French, and it is especially jolly when we halt for the night and get the bivouac fires burning, and chat and laugh with the French officers as though we were the best friends in the world."

The march was, indeed, conducted in a comfortable and easy fashion. At starting, the prisoners marched four abreast, and the French two abreast at each side, but before a mile had been passed the order was no longer strictly observed, and the men trudged along, smoking their pipes, laughing and talking, the French and English alternately breaking into a marching song. There was no fear of the prisoners trying to escape. They could at night have got away from their guards easily enough, but there was nowhere for them to go if they had done so. The English, smarting from the cruelty and ill-faith of the inhabitants of Talavera and the Spanish authorities, felt a burning hatred of the Spanish, while the Spaniards, on their side, deceived by the lying representations of their Juntas, had no love whatever for the English, though ready enough to receive money and arms from them.

On leaving Zadorra, the French officer in command said to Terence: "Now, Colonel, we shall have to be more careful during our marches, keeping a sharp look-out at night. The country here is infested by guerillas, whom all our efforts cannot eradicate. The mountains of Navarre and Biscay are full of them. Sometimes they are in bands of fifteen or twenty strong, sometimes they are in hundreds. Some of them are at ordinary times goatherds, shepherds, muleteers, and peasants, but a number of them are disbanded soldiers—the remains of armies we have defeated and broken up, and who prefer this wild life in the mountains to returning to their homes. Our convoys are constantly attacked, and have always to be accompanied by a strong guard."

"As we have no waggons with us, I should think that they would hardly care to molest us," Terence said.

"That renders it less likely certainly, Colonel, but they fight from hatred as much as for booty, and no French soldier who falls into their hands is ever spared; generally they are put to death with atrocious tortures. At first there was no such feeling here, and when my regiment was quartered at Vittoria some three years ago, things were quiet enough. You see, the feeling gradually grew. No doubt some of our men plundered. Many of the regiments were composed of young conscripts with very slight notions of discipline. Those from the country districts were, as a rule, quiet lads enough, but among those from the towns, especially such places as Toulouse, Lyons, and Marseilles, were young scoundrels ready for any wickedness, and it is to these that the troubles we now have are largely due. Of course the peasants, when they were able to do so, retaliated upon these marauders. The feeling of hatred grew on both sides; straggling parties of our men were surrounded, captured, and then hung, shot, or burnt alive.

"Then, on our side, villages were destroyed and the peasants shot down. Lately, that is, after the defeats of their armies, numbers of fugitives took to the hills, threw away their uniforms, obtained peasants' dresses, and set up as what they called guerillas, which is only another term for bandits; for although their efforts are chiefly directed against us, they do not hesitate to plunder their own people when they need provisions, and are a perfect scourge to all the villages among the hills between the Bay of Biscay and the Mediterranean. Of course, they are strongest along the line of communication with

France, but it may be said that, roughly, where there are mountains there are guerillas, though there are but few of them along the hills we crossed between the valley of the Tagus and that of the Douro.

"This is for two reasons: in the first place, there are very few villages, and they would have difficulty in maintaining themselves; and in the second place, because hitherto Leon and Old Castile on the north of the Sierra have always been under different commands to that in the Tagus Valley, and therefore there has been but small communication between them, except by messengers with despatches from Madrid. The passes have scarcely been used, and indeed in winter they are practically altogether impassable, except that along the valley of the Ebro. We found that to our cost when we marched with Napoleon to cut off your British General Moore. We lost nearly two days getting through them, and the delay saved your army."

"Yes, it was a very close thing," Terence said. "As I have told you, I was with Moore, and if the troops from the south had come up but six hours earlier, it would have gone very hard with us."

"It was an awful time," the officer said, "and I think our army must have suffered quite as much as yours did. Soult's force was reduced fully to half its strength when he first arrived on that hill near Corunna. Of course the stragglers came in rapidly, but a great number never returned to their colours again—some died of cold and hardship, others were cut off and murdered by the peasantry. Altogether we had an awful time of it. Your men were in one respect better off than ours, for your stragglers were not regarded with hostility by the peasants, whereas no mercy was shown to ours."

"Yes, major, one of the battalions that fought at Talavera was entirely composed of men who had straggled in the retreat, and who afterwards succeeded in gaining the Portuguese frontier."

That evening they halted for the night at a small village high up in the passes. The French officer took every precaution against surprise; twenty sentries were placed at various points round the village, and as many more were posted in pairs three or four hundred yards farther out. At three in the morning several shots were fired, the troops all got under arms, and parties were sent out to the outposts. At two of these posts both the sentries were found stabbed to the heart, at others men had been seen crawling up towards them, and

GUERILLAS

the shots that had aroused the troops had been fired. The outposts were recalled to the village, and the soldiers remained under arms until morning.

As soon as it was daybreak a scattered fire opened from the hills on either side of the valley, and it was evident that these were occupied by strong parties. The villagers, on being questioned, denied all knowledge of these bands; but under threats said that they heard that Minas, with a very strong force, was in the neighbourhood, and that the Impecinado had been reported to be among the hills between the pass and that of Roncesvalles.

"What strength do you put them down at, Colonel?" the major asked Terence.

"I should say, from what we can see of them, that there must be four or five hundred on each hill."

"They must have had information from their spies at Zadorra, Colonel, and half a dozen bands must have united to crush us. *Diable,* that was a good shot!" he exclaimed as his shako was struck from his head by a bullet. "That is the worst of these fellows, they are uncommonly good shots. You see, almost all these mountain men are accustomed to carry guns, and the charcoal-burners and shepherds eke out a living by shooting game and sending it down to the towns."

"What are you thinking of doing, major?"

"I shall hold the village," the latter replied; "we might get through the pass, but I doubt whether we should do so, and if we did, my men and yours would suffer terribly. Can I rely upon your fellows keeping quiet?"

"I think so. At any rate we will all go round and order them to do so."

There was, however, no necessity to impress this on the men; two of them had already been wounded by the guerilas' fire.

"Why, sir," one of them said, "if we had but muskets here, we would turn out and help the French to drive those fellows off. The French have behaved very well to us, while the Spaniards did their best to starve us to death, and there ain't one of us who wouldn't jump at the chance of paying them out."

"All right, men!" said Terence. "I agree with you as to the treatment you have received; however, we are not here to fight. We are prisoners, and have nothing to do with the fray one way or the other, though I don't mean to say that I should not myself be glad to see the French beat the guerillas off."

The other officers found the same spirit among the soldiers they questioned.

"I quite agree with them," one of the officers said, "and if there were muskets handy I would not mind leading them myself if it were not for the uniform. Sir Arthur would scarcely be pleased if, among all his other worries, he got a despatch from the central Junta, complaining that a large number of innocent peasants had been killed by English troops fighting by the side of the French."

Gradually the guerillas drew in towards the village, taking advantage of every stone and bush, and rarely giving a chance to the French infantry. Their aim was exceedingly accurate, and whenever a French soldier showed himself from behind a hut to fire, he was fortunate if he got back again without receiving a bullet.

"This is getting serious," the French major said, coming into the cottage where the English officers were gathered. "I have lost thirty-eight killed and wounded already. I have had the wounded carried into the church, and some of your men are unloading the provision waggons and taking the contents inside. They have requisitioned every utensil that will hold water in the village. No doubt we shall be able to hold out there till some other detachment comes along the road."

"I think that it is a very good plan, major," Terence said. "They would hardly be able to carry it by assault unless they burnt down the door, and you ought to be able to prevent them from doing that."

Half an hour later the whole French force was collected in the church. As soon as the Spaniards found what had happened, they speedily entered the village and opened fire from every window giving a view of the church, and from loopholes that they quickly made in the walls. Terence noticed that when the British soldiers entered the church, most of them carried heavy staves. A sergeant came up and saluted.

GUERILLAS

"We have had four men killed and eight wounded, sir. The men declare that they are not going to stand still and see the French murdered by these fellows, and I doubt if any orders will keep them back."

"Very well, sergeant. I will speak to them presently. Now, gentlemen," he said to the other officers, "three of you are senior to me in our own army, and though I own that I don't know how matters should stand, holding as I do Lord Beresford's commission as colonel, I am perfectly willing to place myself under the orders of whoever may be senior of you."

"I believe I am the senior," one of the captains said; "but I should imagine that Lord Beresford's commission would, for the time, rank as if it had been signed by our own authorities. Moreover, you are on Wellesley's staff. You have seen more service out here than any of us, and I think that you are certainly entitled to the command, though really I don't see what we can do in our uniforms."

"I quite agree with you, Captain Travers, and therefore my proposal is, that we shall all take them off and fight in our shirt-sleeves. The guerillas will then not be able to affirm that there were any men in English uniforms assisting the French."

"I think the idea is an excellent one," Captain Travers said.

"Then in that case I will act upon it;" and Terence went up to the English soldiers, who were standing in a group in the middle of the church.

"I am sure you quite understand, my men," he said, "that it would never do for you to be fighting in British uniforms against the Spaniards; otherwise I leave the matter in your hands. But I may mention that it is the intention of myself and the officers to defend this church without our coats and caps. If any of you like to do the same, of course you can join us. I give no orders whatever on the subject, but you see that it would get rid of the inconvenience of soldiers in British uniforms fighting against the Spaniards."

The men answered with a shout of satisfaction mingled with laughter, and in less than a minute the scarlet uniforms had disappeared. The muskets of the French killed and wounded were appropriated, and the rest of the English prisoners seized their clubs. For some hours the fight continued, and from the roof of the church belfry and windows a hot fire answered the incessant fusillade of the

Spaniards. The French and English officers were obliged constantly to impress upon the men that they must husband their ammunition, as there was no saying how long they might be besieged before a detachment, strong enough to turn the scale, arrived.

"Maintain a fire heavy enough to make them keep at it. Their ammunition is likely to run short as soon as ours, and there is not much chance of their being able to replenish it. But don't fire at random; let every bullet tell. Take a steady aim at the windows through which they are firing."

Late in the afternoon the fire of the guerillas slackened a good deal, and it was evident that their leaders were enjoining them not to waste their ammunition. As it became dark the officers gathered again in the body of the church. The total loss had risen to thirty-two killed and fifty wounded, the English casualties being about a third of the whole.

"It is a heavy loss," the major said, "and I have noticed that as the fire slackened the proportion of men hit has been larger. I suppose that they are only keeping their best shots at work."

"I should fancy," Terence said, "that if we were to make a sortie we could scatter them altogether. As soon as it is dark we might get out by that sacristy door at the rear. They gave up the attack on that side some time ago, as they could not get any shelter, and when they found that was so, they betook themselves to houses where they were better covered. If we were to go out noiselessly and sweep round the village so as to fall upon it in two bodies, one at each end, they will take us for a body of troops just arrived. Even if they do hear us as we go out we can go straight at them, and should, I have no doubt, be able to clear the place with a rush. The only thing is, major, I should be glad if your soldiers would take off their coatees too, so that there would be nothing to distinguish our men from yours. What do you think?"

"I think that it will be much the best plan," Captain Travers said. "In the first place, it is probable that they will try to burn us out to-night, and we could not hope to prevent their piling faggots against the doors in the dark; for that reason alone I think that it will be much better to attack them than wait for them to attack us. We need only leave some twenty of the less seriously wounded men to guard the place. When we sally out, the guerillas will have plenty to do without making an attack on the church. I certainly think that we are not likely to lose so many lives in a sortie as we should do in the defence here against a night attack."

"I certainly am of your opinion, Colonel," the French major said; "and if you and your men will join us, I have no doubt that we shall be able to clear the village."

As soon as it became quite dark the men on the roof were all called down, with the exception of one or two, who were ordered to continue to fire from various spots there and in the belfry, so that the Spaniards should not discover that the garrison had been withdrawn. Then the French were drawn up and divided into two parties. The English who had muskets were told off in equal numbers to each of these parties, as were those who had nothing but their clubs. The major then ordered his soldiers to take off their coats, and to leave their shakos behind them. The French major took the command of one party, and asked Terence to take command of the other.

This he declined.

"No, sir, it is better that one of your own officers should be in command; we will divide ourselves between the two parties."

The major now impressed upon his men the necessity for absolute quiet, and for marching as lightly and silently as possible. The English officers gave similar instructions to their men. It was arranged that when the door was opened the two parties should issue out simultaneously two abreast, so that if the alarm was given before all were out, they would be able to turn right and left, and attack in both directions at once. A French lieutenant was appointed to remain in the church and command the little garrison of wounded men. Those who sallied out were to stoop low as they went, and were to keep a few paces apart. Some hangings in the church were pulled down and torn up into strips, with which the men were directed to muffle their boots.

There was no mistaking the ardour with which the soldiers prepared for the sortie. Both English and French were indignant at being pent up by a foe they thoroughly despised, and were eager to be at the enemy. The casualties added to their wrath; one of the French officers had been killed and another hurt seriously, while three of the English had also been wounded, though in each case but slightly. The bolts of the door were noiselessly drawn and that of the lock forced back; then the two little parties stole out in the order in which they had been directed. The guerillas had just begun to fire heavily, as a prelude, Terence had no doubt, to a serious attack upon the church. Fortunately there were no houses at the back of the church, and no shout indicated that the party were seen; they, therefore, kept together until fifty or sixty yards from the door; then they separated and continued their way to the ends of the village to which they had been respectively assigned.

Then at one end of the village a French trumpeter sounded the charge, and two drummers at the other beat the same order vigorously, and with loud cheers they rushed down the street, the French and English alike shouting. It had been arranged that while the French held their way straight on, shooting down the Spaniards as they poured out into the street, the British should break up into small detachments, burst their way into the houses, and overpower the enemy there. They found the first houses they entered deserted, and the soldiers uttered exclamations of impatience as they heard the heavy roll of firing in the main street. As they approached the centre of the village, however, they came upon a number of the Spaniards rushing from their houses.

The men who had arms opened fire at once upon them, while those with clubs dashed forward, levelling the panic-stricken guerillas to the ground with their heavy blows, and arming themselves with their muskets and bandoleers. Thus the firing soon became general, and the Spaniards, struck with utter dismay, and believing that they had been attacked by a heavy column that had just arrived, speedily took to head-long flight, most of them throwing away their arms as they fled. In some of the houses there were short but desperate conflicts, but in a quarter of an hour after the first shot was fired there was not a guerilla remaining alive in the village, upwards of a hundred and fifty having been killed, while on the side of their assailants only some fifteen had been killed and twenty-eight wounded. They soon formed up in the street, and were told off in parties of twelve to the houses in the outskirts of the village. Three in each party were to keep watch by turns while the rest slept. An English officer was to remain in charge on one side of the street, and a French officer on the other; the rest went back to the church, whose doors were now thrown open.

GUERILLAS

"I thank you most heartily, gentlemen," the French officer said to Terence and to the other British officers, "for the immense service that you have rendered us. Had it not been for your aid our position would have been a very precarious one before morning. As it is, I think we need fear no further interruption. We are now all armed, and as, with the wounded fit for work, we are still three hundred strong, we should beat off any force likely to attack us, though, indeed, I have no belief that they will rally again. At any rate their losses have been extremely heavy, and the streets were completely strewn with guns, so that I doubt whether half of those who got away have carried their weapons with them."

The next morning, indeed, it was found that in all about 400 muskets had been left behind: all that remained over after arming the British soldiers were broken up and thrown down the wells. Enough provisions were collected among the houses to furnish the whole with three or four days' rations. The dead were buried in a field near the village, those wounded too severely to march were placed in the waggons, and the rest, who had now resumed their uniforms, set out in high spirits. They were in the same order as before, but the prisoners were told to carry their muskets at the trail, while the French shouldered theirs, so that, viewed from a distance, the British should appear unarmed.

"That has been a grand bit of excitement, Terence," Dick Ryan said gleefully to his friend as they marched along together. "Those fellows certainly fight a good deal more pluckily than the regular troops do. It was a capital idea to make all the men take off their uniforms, for I don't suppose the Spaniards even for a moment dreamt that we were among their assailants; at any rate they have no proof that we were. You really must get me as your adjutant, Terence. I see there is very much more fun to be got out of your sort of fighting than there is with the regiment. I am very pleased now that I stuck to Portuguese as you advised me, though it was a great bore at first."

"I hope, Dicky, we sha'n't find, when we get back in the spring, that the corps has been turned over to Beresford as part of his regular command, for I must say that I quite appreciate the advantage of independence. Well, this business ought to do us some good. No doubt, the major will report in warm terms the assistance we have rendered him, and we shall get good treatment. Of course, some of their prisons must be better than others, and if they will confine us in some place near the frontier, instead of marching us half through France, it will make it all the easier for us to get away. It is not the getting out of prison that is the difficulty, but the travelling through the country. I am getting on well with my French, but there is no hope of being able to speak well enough to pass as a native. As for you, you will have to keep your mouth shut altogether, which will be mightily difficult."

"You will manage it somehow, Terence. I have no fear of you getting me through the country; it is getting out of the country that seems to me the difficulty."

"There is one thing, Dicky, we need be in no hurry about it. There is little chance of fighting beginning for another six or seven months, and directly we come to the end of our march, wherever it may be, we must begin to pick up as much French as we can from our guards. In three or four months I ought at least to be able to answer questions, not perhaps in good French, but in French as good as, say, a Savoyard workman or musician might be able to muster."

"Oh, Lor'!" Dick Ryan said with a deep sigh. "You don't mean to say that I must begin to work on another language, just after I have been slaving for the last six months at Portuguese?"

"Not unless you like, Dicky. I can either start alone, or with someone else who has some knowledge of French, but I am not going to run the risk of being recaptured by taking anyone with me who cares so little for liberty that he grudges three or four hours' work a day to get up the means of making his escape."

"Oh, of course I shall learn," Ryan said pettishly. "You always get your own way, Terence. It was so at Athlone: you first of all began by asking my opinion, and then carried out things exactly as you proposed yourself. Learning the language is a horrid nuisance, but I see that it has to be done."

"I expect, Dicky, you will have to make-up as a woman; you see, you are not much taller than a tallish woman."

"Well, that would be rather a lark," Ryan said; "only don't you think I should be almost too good-looking for a French-woman?"

"You might be that, Dicky; it is certainly a drawback. If I could get hold of a good-sized monkey's skin, I might sew you up in it."

GUERILLAS

"A bear-skin would be better, I should say," Dicky laughed; "but I don't think anyone would think that it was a real bear. I saw a chap with one once at Athlone: no man could open his mouth as wide as that beast did; and as to its tongue, it would be four times as long as mine. No, I think the woman idea would be best; but I should have to shave very close."

"Shave!" Terence repeated scornfully. "Why, I could not see any hair on your face with a magnifying glass. If that were the only drawback, the matter could be arranged without difficulty."

Without farther adventure they crossed the mountains and came down to Bayonne. At each halting-place where the French troops were stationed, the British prisoners were received with warm hospitality by them, when they learned from their comrades that the British had fought side by side with the French against the guerillas, and had saved them from what might have been a very serious disaster. The French shook hands with them warmly, patted them on the shoulders, with many exclamations of "*Braves garçons!*" and they were led away to cafes, and treated as the heroes of the day, while the officers were entertained by those of the garrison. At Bayonne they and their escort parted on the most cordial terms, the French exclaiming that it was a shame such brave fellows should be held as prisoners, and they ought to be released at once and sent back in a ship with a flag of truce to Portugal.

The major, after handing over the soldiers to the prison authorities, took Terence and the other British officers to the headquarters of the governor of the town, and introduced them to him, giving him a lively account of the fight with the guerillas, and the manner in which the prisoners, armed only with clubs and the muskets of the soldiers no longer able to use them, had made common cause with the French, and, joining them in the sortie, defeated the Spanish with heavy loss. The governor expressed courteously his thanks to the officers for the part they had taken.

"I shall forward Major Marcy's report to headquarters, gentlemen, and shall be happy to give you the liberty of the town on parole. I have no doubt that, if no other good comes of your adventure, you will be placed among an early list of officers to be exchanged."

"I am very much obliged to you, General," Terence said, "but I and Lieutenant Ryan would prefer not to give our parole. I don't say we are likely to make our escape, but at any rate we should like to be able to take any opportunity if we saw one."

The general smiled. "Of course it must be as you like, sir, but I think that you are wrong. However, at any time, if you like to change your minds, I will give instructions to the officer in command of the prison to release you immediately you give your parole not to leave the town."

The matter had been talked over on the march and the others now expressed their willingness to give their parole. They had told Terence they thought he was wrong, and that it would be impossible to make an escape, as it would be necessary to traverse either the whole of Spain or the whole of France before he could find any means of rejoining the army, and that before long they might be exchanged.

"I don't think there is a prospect of an early exchange," Terence said. "There cannot have been many prisoners taken during this short campaign, and I don't suppose there will be any talk of exchanges for some time to come. I am particularly anxious to get back again if I possibly can, as I am afraid that my regiment will be broken up, and that, unless I get back before the campaign begins in spring, I shall not get the command again. So I mean to get away if I can; anyhow, I would just as soon be in prison as walking about the streets of Bayonne. So I have quite made up my mind not to give my parole."

The officers all returned to the prison quarters assigned to them, the difference being that those on parole could go in and out as they chose, and could, at will, take their meals in the town; while Terence and Ryan were placed together in a room, with a sentry at each door, whose instructions were to accompany them whenever they wished to go beyond the door and to walk in the prison-yard, or on the walls surrounding it.

Chapter V
An Escape

"Well, here we are, Terence," Ryan said cheerfully, as the door of their cell closed behind them; "and now what next?"

"The next thing is to look around, Dick; other matters can wait. One cannot form the remotest idea as to the possibilities of an escape until one has found out everything about the place. I should say that it will be quite soon enough to discuss it in another couple of months. Now as to the room; there is nothing to grumble at here. Two truckle-beds, not altogether luxurious in appearance, but at any rate a good deal softer than the ground on which we have been sleeping for months past; a couple of chairs designed for use rather than comfort, but which will do to sit on while we take our meals, and at other times we can use the beds as sofas; a good-sized piece of carpet, a table, and what looks like a pudding-dish to wash in.

"Things might have been better, and they might have been a great deal worse. As to our food, we must reserve comment until they bring us some. Now, as to funds, I had only twenty-five crowns on me when I was captured. You were rather better off, as you had ten pounds in gold and eight crowns in silver. You see, had we given our parole like the others and gone in for luxurious feeding outside, our stock would soon have given out; and money is an essential for carrying out an escape, when that escape involves perhaps weeks of travelling, and certainly disguises of different kinds. We have not a penny too much for that, and must resolve to eschew all luxuries except tobacco, and perhaps a bottle of wine on Sundays.

"Our windows, as you observe, are very strongly barred. They look westward, but that range of buildings opposite prevents our getting a view of the sea. One thing is evident at once, that it is no manner of use for us to think of cutting through those bars or dislodging them, for we should only, on lowering ourselves, be in the court-yard, and no nearer escape than we were before we began the job. It is a good thing to get at least one point off our mind. Now, Dick, before we go further, let us make an agreement that we will always talk in French. I know enough of it to be able to assist you, and it will be an amusement as well as a help to accustom ourselves to talk in it."

"All right," Ryan said resignedly, "but I bargain that for an hour a day we drop it altogether. It will be an awful nuisance, and one must give one's tongue a rest occasionally by letting it straighten itself out a bit."

The door now opened, and one of the wardens entered with two large bowls of broth, a fair-sized piece of the meat from which it was made, a dish of vegetables, a large piece of bread, and a bottle of wine.

"This is your supper, messieurs. In the morning you have coffee and a piece of bread; at twelve 'clock a meal like this, with a bottle of wine between you."

"Thank you," Terence said cheerfully; "that will do extremely well. Are there any other British officers here?"

"None except your comrades. There were some naval officers here last week, but they have been sent into the interior. We do not have many prisoners here. Those captured at sea by warships or privateers are generally taken to Brest, and, so far, we have not had many of your nation sent from Spain. There are Spaniards sometimes, but they do not count. Those that are taken are generally drafted into the Spanish corps of our army."

"Can we buy tobacco?" Terence asked.

"Certainly, monsieur. There is a canteen in the courtyard. It is open from eight till nine o'clock in the morning, and from five to six in the evening. But you are not allowed to get things in from the town; but nevertheless"—and he smiled—"as your comrades are on parole, doubtless, should you need anything beyond what is sold in the canteen, it may chance that they may bring you just the things you want."

"Thank you. You had better get something from the canteen for yourself," Terence said, handing him a crown.

AN ESCAPE

"Thank you, monsieur. I have heard from the soldiers who came in with you that you fought bravely with them against the Spanish brigands, and they think that it is very hard that you and your companion should be shut up here after having proved such good comrades. I have a cousin among them. He, like myself, is a native of Bayonne, and should it be in his power, I am sure that he and his comrades would do anything they could for monsieur—as far, of course, as their duty as French soldiers will allow them."

"Thanks! By the way, what is your name?"

"Jean Monier, monsieur."

"Well, Jean, will you please tell your cousin that I am obliged to him for his good-will? It was a pleasure to fight side by side with such brave soldiers, and, should an occasion offer, I will gladly avail myself of his services. The detachment is not going farther, is it?"

"No, monsieur. They will remain here for perhaps two or three months, till the good French air has invigorated them; then they will join some column marching south again. There is nothing more that you will want to-night, monsieur?"

"No, thank you, Jean. Good evening!"

"Good evening; good sleep!" and the warden retired.

"What is all that jabber about, Terence?"

"Very satisfactory jabber, and jabber that is likely to lead to a very good result. A cousin of his is one of the guard that came down with us. He has told this warden about our fight, and asked him to say that he and his comrades were very angry at our being shut up here, and as much as said that they would aid us to escape if it was in their power, so we may consider that our first difficulty is as good as arranged. No doubt in a short time they will be put on regular garrison duty, and will take their turn in furnishing prison guards. This warder is evidently ready to do anything he can, so that we may look upon our escape from prison as a matter of certainty. I don't suppose that, in any case, the guard is a very vigilant one, for they would not expect that prisoners of war here would try to escape. At Verdun and other prisons within a few days' journey of the frontier it would be different."

"Well, that is good news, Terence, though I see myself that our difficulties will really begin only when we get out. There is no doubt that the fight with the guerillas was a lucky thing for us. I would not have missed it for anything, for I must say there was much more excitement in it than in a battle, at least as far as my experience of a battle goes. At Talavera we had nothing to do but stick up on the top of a hill, watch the French columns climbing up, and then give them a volley or two and roll them down the hill again, and between times to stand to be shelled by Victor's batteries on the opposite hill. I cannot see that there is any fun about that. This fight, too, has turned out a very good thing for us. I expect we should not have been so well treated if it had not been for it, and the fact that some of these French soldiers are ready to give us a helping hand is first-rate. You see, it is all your luck, Terence. There never was such a fellow for luck as you are."

"There is no doubt about that," Terence agreed. "Now, Dick, you must really break into French."

"To-morrow morning will be time enough for that," Ryan said, in a tone of determination. "I want to talk now, really talk, and I can't do that in French, especially after what you have just told me. By the way, I don't see myself why we should make this journey through France. Why not try to get a boat and land somewhere on the coast of Spain?"

"I have been thinking of that, Dick, but it seemed to me before altogether too difficult; still, if we can get help from outside, I don't know why we should not be able to manage it. We should have to go some distance along the Spanish coast, for there are sure to be French garrisons at Bilboa and Santander, but beyond that I should think we might land at any little village. Galicia must certainly have been evacuated by the French, for we know that Ney's corps were down in the Tagus valley, and I should think that they cannot have any great force in the Asturias. The worst of it is, we have not got enough money to buy a boat, and if we had, the soldiers could hardly bargain with a fisherman for one. Of course, if we were free we might arrange with a man to go with us in his boat, and pay him so much for its hire for three or four days."

"We might make our way down the river and steal one, Terence."

"Yes, we might do that, but it would be a heavy loss to some poor fellow. Well, I shall look forward to the morning, when we go out and see all about the prison arrangements."

"Then you have given up the idea of waiting for two months before you do anything, Terence?" Ryan remarked.

AN ESCAPE

"Certainly. You see, these French convalescents may be marched back again in another month's time, and at present our plans must be formed upon the supposition that they are ready to help us. It would never do to throw away such an opportunity as that. It would be little short of madness to try and get out unless we had disguises of some sort. My staff-officer's uniform, or your scarlet, would lead to our arrest at the first village we came to. Besides, before this news, one was willing to wait contentedly for a time till some good opportunity presented itself. Now that we have such an unexpected offer of assistance, the sooner we get out of the place the better."

The next morning they went out into the court-yard of the prison. The soldiers who had been captured with them were walking about in groups, but the sentry who accompanied the two British officers led them through these and took them up to the top of the wall surrounding the prison.

"Messieurs," he said, "when the others are shut up you can go where you please, but my orders are that you are not to communicate with your soldiers."

He fell back some distance, and left them free to wander about on the wall. From this point they had a view over the city. Bayonne was a strongly fortified place, standing on the junction of the Nive and Adour, and on the south side of the latter river two miles from its mouth. The Nive ran through the town, and its waters supplied the ditches of the encircling wall and bastions. The prison was situated on the Nive at some three or four hundred yards from the spot where it entered the Adour.

"I should say this quite decides it," Terence said, when they had made the circuit of the walls, upon which sentries were placed at short intervals. "Once out of the town the river would be open to us, but it would be next to impossible to pass those semicircles of fortifications on both sides of the town. You can see the masts of the craft lying at the quays, and though I should not like to rob a fisherman of his boat, I should not feel the smallest scruple in taking a ship's boat, which would be comparatively a small loss to the owner. The worst of it would be, that directly we were found to be missing, and the owner of the boat reported its loss, they might send out some of their gunboats in search of us, and we should very soon be overtaken."

Discipline was not very strict in the French army, except when in an enemy's country, and the sentries, knowing well that there was really no occasion for watchfulness, answered willingly the questions that Terence asked them, as to the names of places within sight.

"It must be rather tedious work for you on the wall here," Terence said to one whose post was shielded by a building close by from observation from below.

"Very dull," the soldier said, "and we shall be glad enough when we are relieved and marched into Spain. Here we are doing no good. There is no chance whatever of the prisoners attempting an escape, for if they did get out of here they could get no further; but they say that we shall not stop here long, and we shall be heartily glad when the order comes. They say the convalescents who came in yesterday will take over the prison duties next week."

Terence's motive for speaking to the men was to discover whether they were forbidden to talk, and it was satisfactory to find that, if there was such a rule, it was by no means strictly observed. Leaning on the parapet, he and Ryan stood for some time looking at the sea. There were many fishing-boats dotting its surface, and the tapering masts of two schooners could be seen near the mouth of the river.

"I have no doubt that they are privateers," Terence said. "They have just the appearance of that fellow we captured on the way out. One would not have much chance of getting far in a boat with those fellows after us. It seems to me that, if it could possibly be managed, our safest plan would be to lie quiet in the town for a week or so after we got out; then it would be comparatively safe to get hold of a boat and make off in it."

"Yes, if that could be managed it certainly would be the safest plan. If we changed our minds about making off by sea, we might then be able to pass out through the fortifications without question. Of course, they would be vigilant for a short time after we were missing, but I suppose that at ordinary times the country people would go in and out unquestioned just as in any other town, for with no enemy nearer than Portugal, there could be no occasion whatever for watchfulness."

Terence and his companion had seen nothing of their friends on parole, as these, they found, although lodged in prison for their own convenience, were not permitted to have any communication

AN ESCAPE

with the other prisoners. Ten days after they arrived at Bayonne, the warder, who had, since he first spoke to them, said nothing beyond the usual salutations, remarked carelessly:

"The soldiers who came down with you took up the prison duties last night. My cousin told me to say that you will know him and four or five of his comrades of the 72nd of the line, all of whom are thoroughly in agreement with him, by their saying as you pass them, *'The morning is fair, Colonel.'* To any of them you can speak when you find an opportunity of doing so unobserved."

"Thank you; but would it not be safer for them were you to carry my messages?"

"No; I cannot do that," the warder said. "I think that it is quite right that my cousin and his comrades should do anything in their power to aid those who stood by them when attacked, but I wish to know nothing about it. It must be between you and them, for I must be able to swear that I had no hand in the matter, and that I locked you up safely at night."

"You are quite right, Jean; it is much the best plan that it should be so. I certainly should not myself like to know that in making my escape I might endanger the life of one who had acted simply from kindness of heart, and trust that no suspicion whatever will fall upon you. I thank you most heartily for having brought me the message from your cousin, and for the good-will that you have shown us."

When Terence and Ryan went out as usual after their breakfast, all the sentries they passed saluted, as if to one of their own officers. They of course returned the salute and made a cheery remark to each, such as, "Rather a change this from our work up in the hills, lad," to which each gave some short and respectful answer, three of them prefacing it with the words: "The morning is fair, mon Colonel." Two of these had the number of their regiment on their shako; the other, who had a deep and scarcely-healed scar over the ear, only wore a forage cap, having evidently lost his shako when wounded.

"What do you mean by saluting a prisoner?" a French staff-officer, when he was passing, angrily asked an old soldier. "You have been long enough in the service surely to know that prisoners are not saluted."

The soldier stood at attention. "Monsieur le Capitaine," he said, "I am not saluting a prisoner. I am saluting a brave officer, whose orders I have obeyed in a hard fight, and to whom I and my comrades probably owed our lives. A mark of respect is due to a brave man whether a prisoner of war or not."

The officer passed on without answering, and arriving at headquarters reported the circumstances to the general.

"I am not surprised, Captain Espel," the latter replied with a slight smile. "A French soldier knows how to respect bravery, and in this case there is little doubt that, but for the assistance of their prisoners, it would have gone very hard with that detachment. That young officer, who, strangely enough, is a colonel, was a prisoner when he fought side by side with these men, and it is but natural that they scarcely regard him as one now. He has refused to give his parole, and I am afraid he means to try to make his escape. I am sorry, for should he do so he is sure to be captured again."

The third one of the 72nd men, the one with a forage cap, chanced to be posted at the point of the wall that was not overlooked, and after he had repeated the formula agreed upon, Terence said to him: "You are one of those lads who sent me a message that you would assist me if you could?"

"That is so, mon Colonel; you assisted us when we were somewhat hotly pressed, and 'tis but good comradeship to repay such a service if one can. We have been thinking it over, and although it would not be difficult for you to escape from here, we do not see how you are to be got out of the town."

"That is the difficulty I see myself," Terence replied; "we could not hope to pass through the circle of fortifications, and were we to take a boat and make off, we should be pursued and recaptured to a certainty, for, of course, as soon as our escape was known there would be a hot search made for us. There are two things needed, the first is disguises, the second is a shelter until the search for us slackens, after which it would be comparatively easy for us to make off."

"What sort of disguises would you want, monsieur?"

"If we go by land, peasant dresses; if by water, those of fishermen. We have money which I can give you to purchase these."

"That we could do for you, monsieur, but the hiding-place is more difficult. However, that we will see about. I am a native here, and have of course many friends and acquaintances in the town. When we have made our plans I will let you know. I will manage that when it is my turn for duty. I will always be posted here, and then I can tell you what is arranged, and give you whatever is necessary to aid you to make your escape. My cousin, Jean Monier, will shut his eyes, but he will not do anything himself, and I think that he is right, for of course he will be the first to be suspected. As for us, it will be no matter. Everyone knows how you stood by us, and they will guess that some of us have had a hand in it, but they will never find out which of us was chiefly concerned. I expect that soon we shall all be taken off this prison duty, for which we shall not be sorry, and sent back to Spain with the first detachment that comes along; but, after all, one is not so badly off in Spain, and certainly Madrid is a good deal more lively than Bayonne."

"I suppose," Terence said, nodding towards their guard, who was standing a few paces away gazing over the country, "he knows nothing about this."

"No, monsieur, we have kept it to just the men of our own regiment, but all feel the same about your being kept a prisoner, and there is no fear of his telling anyone that you spoke to one man more than another, when it is found out that you have escaped. Still, it might be as well that you should not speak to me again until I tell you that it is a fine morning, for, although all our own men can be trusted, if any of the regular prison-warders was to notice anything, he would not be slow in mentioning it, in hope of getting promotion."

Accordingly Terence made a point of only passing along that part of the wall once a day and merely saying a word to the soldier, as he did to others, on the occasions when he was on duty. Ten days later the man replied to his salutation by remarking that it was a "fair day." It happened that the man told off to guard them on this occasion was another of the 72nd; there was therefore nothing to be feared from him.

"I have arranged the matter, monsieur," the soldier said; "my sister's husband, Jules Varlin, will shelter you; he is a fisherman, and you can be safely hidden in the loft where he keeps his nets and gear. He is an honest fellow, and my sister has talked him over into lending his aid so far, and although he has not promised it yet, I think we shall get him to go down the river with you so as to reply if you are challenged. You can put him ashore a mile or two along the coast. Now as to the escape, monsieur. Here is a sharp saw; with it you can cut round the lock of your door. There are two outside bolts whose position I dare say you have noticed; by cutting a hole close to each of them you can get your hand through and draw them. Here is a short-handled auger to make a hole for the saw to go through. There are four sentries at night in the court-yard. We shall manage to get all our men on duty to-morrow evening. Our sergeant is a good fellow, and, if he guesses anything, will hold his tongue, for I have heard him say more than once that it is monstrous that you should be kept a prisoner.

"Therefore you need not be afraid of them, they will take care to keep their eyes shut. I shall be on sentry duty here, and will get the disguises up, and a rope. When you have got down I shall let the rope drop, and you will carry it off and take it away with you; thus there will be no evidence where you descended. Here are two sharp files with which you can cut through the bars of your window and remove some of them; then it will not be known whether you escaped that way or down the stairs, and the men on sentry in the court-yard at the bottom cannot be blamed, because, for aught the governor will know, you may have gone out through the window into the other court-yard, and got over the wall on that side; so they would have no proof as to which set of men were negligent.

"No doubt we shall all be talked to, and perhaps kept in the guard-room a few days, but that won't hurt us, and soldiers are scarce enough, so they will hardly keep ten or twelve men long from duty: there are not enough in the town now to furnish all the guards properly, so you need not worry about us. I will give you instructions how to find my sister's house to-morrow night. You must not escape until you hear the bell strike midnight. Our party will relieve guard at that hour. You see we have four hours on duty, and as you may have gone either on the first watch, the second, or the third, they will not be able to pitch on us more than the others, so that, in fact, the blame will be divided between forty of us. You will, of course, put on your disguises over your uniforms and destroy your clothes when you get to Jules's house."

AN ESCAPE

"I thank you very warmly, my good fellow, for running all this risk for me. Here are two hundred francs to pay for the disguises."

"That will be more than enough," the soldier said; "Jules put it down at a hundred and fifty."

"Things may cost more than he expects. At any rate, please hand these to him; I can arrange matters with him when I see him. Then at about a quarter past twelve we will sally out. We will walk on now lest any of the warders should happen to notice that we have been a long time on this part of the wall."

Ryan had understood but little of what was happening, and when Terence told him what had been arranged, he exclaimed:

"Well, after this, Terence, I will never say a word against a Frenchman. Here are these soldiers going to run a lot of risk, and a certainty of getting into a row, for us, merely because we did the best we could against those wretched Spaniards, and without getting any reward whatever, for they must know that prisoners are not likely to have any money to spare about them."

"Quite so, Ryan; and what is more, if I had a hundred pounds in my pocket, I would not offer them a penny, for certainly they would take it as an insult if I did so. They would feel that it would be a sort of bribe, and though they are ready to help us as comrades, I am sure they would not do it for money. I sincerely hope they won't get into any serious row. As he said, authorities won't be able to tell which party was on guard at the time we went, and they could hardly put the whole of them under arrest—at least not keep them under arrest. No doubt there will be a close search in the town for us, but there is little fear of our being discovered: our dangers won't begin until we are fairly afloat. I know nothing about sailing. I have rowed a boat many a time at Athlone, but as for sailing, I have never once tried it."

"Nor have I," Ryan said. "But I suppose there is no difficulty about it. You put up the sail, and you take hold of the rope at the corner, and off you go."

"It sounds all right, Dicky, and I dare say we shall manage to get along somehow, but these things are not half as easy as they look. Now we had better have four or five hours' sleep this afternoon, for I expect it will take us the best part of the night to file through the bars. You must not cut quite through them, but just leave them so that we can finish them off in a short time to-morrow night."

"But the warder might notice them?"

"He is not likely to look very sharply, Dicky, but, at the same time, it is just as well not to put too great a strain on his loyalty. We will keep a piece of bread left over from our supper, work it up into a sort of paste, fill up any cuts we make, and rub it over with dirt till it well matches the bars. Certainly they have planned the affair capitally, so as to throw doubt as to which way we descended, and so divide the blame between as many of the sentries as possible."

It took four hours' work that night to get through the bars. They were most careful not to let any of the filings fall outside, for had any of them dropped into the court-yard below they might well catch the eye of a warder, and in that case an examination of all the windows of the rooms above would certainly be made at once. Before the warder's visit the next morning the holes had been filled up with bread worked into a putty and smeared over with dust, which so nearly matched the bars that it could not be observed except by a careful examination. The next day they abstained from saying more than a passing word to any of the French soldiers. They waited after being locked up for the night for two or three hours, and then began their work at the door.

The saw was a very narrow one, and when they had made a hole with the auger they found no difficulty in cutting the wood; therefore they thought it was well to leave that for the last thing, and so betook themselves to their files, and soon removed enough of the bars to enable a man to crawl through. Then they returned to the door, and had cut round the lock and made holes through which they could pass their hands to draw back the bolts, a short time before the clock struck twelve. Then they went to the window and listened. They heard the bells strike midnight, and then a stir below as the sentries were relieved. Waiting for a few minutes until all had become quiet again, they drew back the bolts, took off their shoes, and went noiselessly down the stairs.

The night was very dark, and although they could hear the tread of the sentries in the court-yard, they could not make out their figures. They crossed the yard, keeping as far as possible from the

AN ESCAPE

Stooping so that their figures should not show against the sky.

sentries. They had no doubt that all would happen as arranged, but there was, of course, the possibility that at the last moment some change might have been made, and it was in any case as well that the men there should be able to declare honestly that they had seen no one. They were glad when they reached the archway leading to the stairs that led to the top of the wall. Mounting, they kept along by the parapet, stooping so that their figures should not show against the sky, for, dark as it was below, they might have been noticed had they not done so. Presently they saw the sentry.

"*Diable,* messieurs!" he said in a low tone as they came up to him. "You gave me a start; I was expecting you, but I did not hear your footsteps nor see you, and had you been enemies you might very well have seized and disarmed me before I could give the alarm. Well, here are your clothes."

They soon pulled the blue canvas leggings over their breeches, and over these, high boots, in which their feet felt lost. A rough blouse and a fisherman's oilskin cap completed the disguise. They put their boots into the capacious pockets in the blouses, and were then ready to descend. They had left their shakos in their cell when they started. While they had been putting on their clothes, the sentry had fastened the rope and lowered it down.

"We are ready now, Jacques," Terence said. "Good-bye, my good friend; we shall remember with gratitude all our lives how a party of French soldiers were ready to show their sides, even though the two nations were at war with each other. We shall always feel a kindness towards the French uniform in future, and if you or any of your comrades of the 72nd should chance to fall into British hands, and you can send word to me or to Mr. Ryan, I can promise you that we will do all we can to have you released at once and sent back, or to aid you in any other way."

"We have done but our duty to brave comrades," the soldier said. "Now, as to where to find my cousin. You will go down that street below, and take the third turning on the right—that will lead you down to the wharves. Keep along by the houses facing them, until you come to the fourth turning. It is a narrow lane, and there is a cabaret at each corner of it. My cousin's house is the twelfth on the left-hand side. He will be standing at the door. You will say to him as you pass, '*It is a dark night,*' and he will then let you in. Don't walk

AN ESCAPE

as if you were in a hurry: fishermen never do that. It is not likely that you will meet anyone, but if you do, and he sees two fishermen hurrying, it will strike him as singular, and when there came news of two prisoners having escaped, he might mention the matter, which might lead to a search in the right quarter."

"Will you go first, Ryan, or shall I?" Terence said.

"Just as you like."

"Well, then, you may as well go, as then I can talk with this good fellow till it is my turn."

Ryan shook the soldier's hand heartily, took hold of the rope, slung himself over the parapet, and began the descent. Terence and the soldier leaned over, and watched him until they could no longer make out the figure with certainty. As soon as the tension on the rope slackened, Terence grasped Jacques's hand, said a few more words of thanks, and then followed his companion. As soon as he reached the ground he shook the rope, and a minute later it fell on the ground beside him. He coiled it up, and then started down the street. Following the instructions that they had received, in ten minutes they reached the end of the lane.

"We were to throw away the rope, were we not?" Ryan said.

"Yes, but now we are here, there can be no use in our doing so. If a length of rope were found lying in the road, people would wonder who had thrown it away; besides, it is a good stout piece of new rope, and may be of use to the fisherman."

Counting the doors carefully as they went along, they came to the twelfth, where, before they reached it, the red glow from a pipe showed that a man was standing outside.

"It is a dark night, mate," Terence said in a low tone, as he came up to him.

"That is right," the man replied; "come in."

He stood aside as they entered, closed the door behind them, and then lifted a piece of old canvas thrown over a lighted lantern.

Chapter VI
Afloat

Jules Varlin held the lantern above his head and took a good look at his visitors. "You will pass very well for young fishermen, messieurs," he said, "when you have dirtied your faces and hands a bit, and rubbed your hair the wrong way all over your head. Well, come in here. My wife is waiting up to welcome you; it is her doing that you are here. I should not have agreed, but what can one do when a woman once sets her mind upon a thing?"

He opened the door. A woman rose from her seat; she was some years younger than her husband.

"Welcome, messieurs," she said; "we are pleased, indeed, to be able to return the kindness you showed to my brother."

The fisherman grunted.

"No, Jules," she said, "I won't have you say that you haven't gone willingly into this; you pretended not to, but I know very well that it was only because you like to be coaxed, and that you would have done it for Jacques's sake."

"Jacques is a good fellow," her husband replied, "and I say nothing against him; but I don't know that I should have consented if it had not been for you and your bothering me."

"Don't you believe him, monsieur. Jules has a good heart, though he likes pretending that he is a bear. Now, monsieur, I have some coffee ready for you."

"I need not say, madam," Terence said, "how truly thankful we both are for your and your husband's kindness, shown to us strangers, and I sincerely hope that you will have no cause to regret it. You may be sure of one thing, that if we are recaptured, we shall never say how our escape was effected, nor where we were sheltered afterwards; and if, after the war is over, we can find an opportunity of showing how grateful we are for your kindness, we shall not miss the chance."

"We are but paying the service you rendered to Jacques, monsieur. He tells me that, if it had not been for the aid the British prisoners gave them, probably those Spanish bandits would have captured the church during the night; and we know that they never show mercy to prisoners."

The coffee was placed on the table, and after drinking it the fisherman led them to a low shed in the yard.

"We could have done better for you," he said apologetically, "but it is likely that they may begin a search for you early in the morning. This yard can be seen from many houses round about, so that, were you to sleep upstairs, you might be noticed entering here in the morning, and it is better to run no risks. We have piled the nets on the top of other things; you will find two blankets for covering yourselves there. In the morning, I will come in and shift things, so as to hide you up snugly."

"We shall do just as well on the nets as if we were in bed," Terence laughed; "we are pretty well accustomed to sleep on the hard ground."

"I think we are going to have some bad weather," the man remarked, as they settled themselves on the nets. "I hope it will be so, for then none of the boats will put out, and there will be no comments on my staying at home instead of going out as usual. And now, good-night, and good sleep to you!"

"He is an honest-looking fellow," Terence said, when he had gone out, "and I have no doubt what his wife says of him is true; but it is not surprising that he held back at first. It is not everyone that is prepared to run the risk of heavy punishment for the sake of his wife's relations. This is not by any means bad; these nets make a very comfortable bed."

The next morning at daybreak the fisherman came in with a can containing hot coffee, two great slices of bread, and tin cups.

"Now, messieurs, when you have drunk that I will stow you away. We shifted most of the things yesterday, so as to make as comfortable a bed for you as may be."

The nets were pulled off, and a mass of sails, ropes, and other gear appeared underneath. One of the sails in the corner was pulled away, and showed a vacant space six feet long and four feet wide, extending down to the ground, which was covered by old nets.

"Now, messieurs, if you will get down there, I shall pile a couple of sacks over and throw the nets on the top, and there is no fear of your being disturbed. I will bring your meals in to you, and let you know what is doing in the town, but I shall not come in oftener than I can help. I shall leave the doors open as usual."

They took their places in the hole, and the fisherman piled sails and nets over the opening. There was no occasion to leave any apertures for air, for the shed was roughly built and there were plenty of openings between the planks of which it was constructed. They had, before he came in, divested themselves of their uniforms, and these the fisherman put into a kit-bag and carried indoors, where his wife at once proceeded to cut them up and thrust the pieces into the fire.

"It is a pity," she said regretfully; "but it would never do to leave them about. Think what a waistcoat I could have made for you, Jules, out of this scarlet cloth. With the gold buttons it would have been superb, and it would have been the envy of the quarter; but it would never do."

"I should think not, Marie. Burn the clothes up and give me the buttons and gold lace. I will put them in a bag with some stones and drop them into the river. The sooner we get rid of them the better."

As soon as the things were put into a bag he went out with them. The wind was blowing strongly, and, as he had predicted the night before, the clouds were flying fast, and there were many signs of dirty weather. He returned a couple of hours later.

"There is quite an excitement in the town, Marie," he said. "Everyone is talking about it. Two rascally English prisoners have escaped, and the soldiers say that they must be somewhere in the town, for that they could never have passed through the lines. Some *gendarmes* have been along the quays inquiring if a boat has been missed during the night, but they all seem to be safe. Written notices have been stuck up, warning every one, on pain of the severest punishment, not to give shelter to two young men, in whatever guise they may present themselves. The *gendarmes* say that the military authorities are convinced that they must have received assistance from without."

AFLOAT

For the next three days, indeed, an active search was kept up. Every house was visited by the *gendarmes*, but as there was no reason for suspecting one person more than another, there was no absolute search made of the houses, which, indeed, in so large a town as Bayonne, it would have been almost impossible to carry out effectually.

The fisherman reported each day what was going on.

"The soldiers are giving it up," he said, at the end of the third day. "I saw Jacques to-day for the first time. He tells me there was a tremendous row when your escape was discovered. The warder, and every soldier who had been on duty that night, were arrested and questioned. The warder was the first suspected, on the ground that you must have had assistance from without. He said that if you had he knew nothing about it, and that, as you knew all the soldiers of the prison guard, and as he had heard many of them say it was very hard, after fighting as you did, on their behalf, that you should be kept prisoner, any of them might have furnished you with tools for cutting the door and filing the bars. This was so clear that he was released at once. The soldiers were kept for two days under arrest. This morning the governor himself came down to the prison and the men under arrest were drawn up. He spoke to them very sharply to begin with.

"'One or more of you is assuredly concerned in this matter. A breach of trust of this kind is punishable with death.' Then he stopped and looked fiercely up and down the line, and went on in a different tone: 'At the same time I admit that some allowance is to be made for the crime, and I can understand that as soldiers you felt sympathy with soldiers who, although prisoners at the time, did not hesitate to cast in their lot with you and to fight side by side with you; still, a soldier should never allow private sentiments to interfere with his duty. I, myself, should have been glad, when you arrived here and I heard of what had happened, to have been able to place these British officers and soldiers in a ship and to have sent them back to their own country, but that would have been a breach of my duty, and I was forced to detain them here as prisoners. Of course, if I could find out which among you have been concerned in this affair, it would be my duty to punish them—for there must have been more than one—severely. However, although I have done my best to discover this, I am not sorry, men, that I have been unable to do so; for, although these men may have failed in their duties as soldiers, they have shown themselves true-hearted fellows to run the risk—not, I am sure, from any thought of reward, but to help those who have helped them. You can all return to your duty, and I hope that you will in future remember that duty is the first thing with a soldier, and that he should allow no other feeling to interfere with it.'

"Jacques and his comrades are all satisfied that, although the general felt it was his duty to reprimand them, he was at heart by no means sorry that you had got off.

"The *gendarmes* are still making their inquiries, but of course they have learned nothing. Nobody was about on the wharves at that time of night, and I don't think that they will trouble themselves much longer about it. They will come to believe that you must, somehow, have managed to get through the line of fortifications, and that you will be caught trying to make your way across the country. In another three or four days it will be quite safe for you to go down the river. For the first two days every boat that went down was stopped and examined, and some of the vessels were searched by a gun-boat and the hatches taken off, but I hear that no boats have been stopped to-day, so I fancy you will soon be able to go down without fear."

Although at night Terence and Ryan were able to emerge from their place of concealment and walk up and down the little yard for two or three hours, they were heartily glad when, a week after their confinement, Jules told them that he thought they might start at daybreak the next morning.

"Now, messieurs, if you tell me what you want, I will buy the things for you."

They had already made out a list; it consisted of a nine-gallon breaker for water, a dozen bottles of cheap wine, thirty pounds of biscuits, and fifteen pounds of salt meat, which Jules's wife was to cook. They calculated that this would be sufficient to last them easily until they had passed along the Spanish coast to a point well beyond the towns garrisoned by the French, if not to Corunna itself.

"But how about the boat?" Terence asked, after all the other arrangements had been decided upon. "As I told you, we don't wish to take a boat belonging to anyone who would feel its loss, and therefore it must be a ship's boat, and not one of the fishermen's. If we had money to pay for it, it would be another matter, but we have scarcely enough now to maintain us on our way through Spain, and there are no means of sending money here when we rejoin our army."

"I understand that, monsieur; and I have been along the quay this morning taking a look at the boats. There are at least a dozen we could choose from; I mean ships' boats. Of course, many of the craft keep their boats hauled up at the davits or on deck, but most of them keep one in the water, so that they can row off to another ship or to the stairs. Some simply leave them in the water, because they are too lazy to hoist them up. That is the case, I think, with one boat that belongs to a vessel that came in four days since from the West Indies. It's a good-sized ship's dinghy, such as is used for running out warps, or putting a sailor ashore to bring off anything required. The other boats are better suited for a voyage, but they are for the most part too large and heavy to be rowed by two oars, and, moreover, they have not a mast and sail on board as this has. Therefore that is the one that I fixed my eye on.

"The ship is lying alongside, and there is not another craft outside her. The boat is fastened to her bowsprit, and I can take off my boots and get on board and drop into her without difficulty, and push her along to the foot of some stairs which are but ten yards away. Of course, we will have the water and food and that bundle of old nets ready at the top of the stairs, and we can be out into the stream five minutes after I have cut her loose. We must start just before daylight is breaking, so as to be off before the fishermen put out, for if any of these were about they would at once notice that I have not got my own boat. At the same time I don't want to be far ahead of them, or to pass the gunboats at the mouth of the river in the dark, for that would look suspicious."

"And now, Jules, about yourself. Of course I know well that no money could repay you for the kindness you have shown us and your risking so much for strangers, and you know that we have not with us the means of making any return whatever for your services."

"I don't want any return, monsieur," the fisherman said. "I went into the matter a good deal against my will, because my wife had set her mind upon it; but since you came here I have got to have just as much interest in the matter as she has. I would not take a *sou* from you now; but if, some day, when these wars are over, you will send a letter to Marie with some little present to her, just to show her that you have not forgotten us, it would be a great pleasure to us."

"That I will certainly do, Jules. It may be some time before there will be an opportunity of doing it, but you may be sure that we shall not forget your kindnesses, and that directly peace is made, or there is a chance in any other way of sending a letter to you, we will do so."

That evening Jacques paid a visit to his sister. He had abstained from doing so before, because he thought that the soldiers who were suspected of being concerned in the escape might all be watched, and that if any of them were seen to enter a house, a visit might be paid to it by the *gendarmes*. He did not come until it was dark, and made a long detour in the town before venturing to approach it. Before he entered the lane he took good care that no one was in sight. When, after chatting for an hour, he rose to leave, Terence told him that when he wrote to his sister he should inclose a letter to him, as it would be impossible to write to him direct, for there would be no saying where he might be stationed. He begged him to convey the heartiest thanks of himself and Ryan to his comrades for the share they had taken in the matter.

On saying good-night, Terence insisted on Marie accepting as a parting gift his watch and chain. These were handsome ones, and of French manufacture, Terence having bought them from a soldier who had taken them from the body of a French officer, killed during Soult's retreat from Portugal. They could, therefore, be shown by her to her friends without exciting any suspicion that they had been obtained from an English source. Marie accepted them very unwillingly, and only after Terence declaring that he should feel very grieved if she would not take the one present he was capable of making. "Besides," he added, "no one can tell what fortune may bring about. Your husband might lose his boat or have a long illness, and it is well to have something that you can part with without discomfort in such a time of need."

Jules, although desiring no pay for his services and risks, was very much gratified at the present. "I, for my part, do not say no, monsieur," he said. "What you say is right. We are careful people, and I have laid by a little money; but, as you say, one cannot tell what may happen. And if the weather were bad and there were a risk of never getting back home again, it would be a consolation to me to know that, in addition to a few hundred francs we have laid by since we were married two years ago, there is something that would bring Marie, I should say, seven or eight hundred francs more at least. That would enable her to set up a shop or laundry, and to earn her own living. I thank you from my heart, monsieur, for her and for myself."

Terence and Ryan slept as soundly as usual until aroused by Jules; then they put on their sea-boots again, loaded themselves with the nets and the bags with the provisions and wine, while Jules took the water-barrel, and, after saying good-bye to Marie, started. There was not a soul on the wharf, and, putting the stores down at the top of the steps, they watched Jules, who, after taking off his boots, went across a plank to the ship, made his way noiselessly out on to the bow, swinging himself down into the boat, loosening the head-rope before he did so. A push with the oar against the ship's bow sent the boat alongside the quay, and he then worked her along with his hands against the wall until he reached the steps.

The stores were at once transferred to the boat, and they pushed it out into the stream. The tide had just turned to run out, and for half a mile they allowed her to drift down the river. By this time the light was broadening out in the sky. Jules stepped the mast and hoisted the sail, and then seated himself in the stern and put an oar out in the hole cut for it to steer with. Terence watched the operation carefully. The wind was nearly due aft, and the boat ran rapidly through the water.

"We are just right as to time," Jules said, as he looked back where the river made a bend. "There are two others coming down half a mile behind us, so that we shall only seem to be rather earlier than the rest."

Near the mouth of the river two gunboats were anchored. They passed within a short distance of one of these, and a solitary sailor, keeping anchor-watch on deck, remarked:

"You are going to have a fine day for your fishing, comrade."

"Yes, I think so, but maybe there will be more wind presently."

Some time before reaching the gunboat Ryan had lain down and the nets were thrown loosely over him, as it would be better that there should not seem to be more than the two hands that were generally carried in the small fishing-boats. Once out of the river they steered south, laying a course parallel to the shore and about a mile out. After an hour's sail Jules directed her head into a little bay, took out an empty basket that he had brought with him, and stepped ashore after a cordial shake of the hand. He had already advised them to bear very gradually to the south-west, and had left a small compass on board for their guidance.

"They are things we don't often carry," he said, "in boats of this size, but it will be well for you to take it. If you were blown out of sight of land you would find it useful. Keep well out from the Spanish coast, at any rate until you are well past Bilboa; after that you can keep close in if you like, for you will be taken for a fishing-boat from one of the small villages. I shall walk straight back now to the town. No questions are asked at the gates, and if anyone did happen to take notice of me they would suppose I had been round peddling fish at the farmhouses."

Coming along, he had given instructions to Terence as to sailing the boat. When running before the wind the sheet was to be loose, while it was to be tightened as much as might be necessary to make the sail stand just full when the wind was on the beam or forward of it.

"You will understand," he said, "that when the wind is right ahead you cannot sail against it. You must then get the sail in as flat as you can, and sail as near as you can to the wind. Then, when you have gone some distance, you must bring her head round till the sail goes over on the other side, and sail on that tack, and so make a zigzag course; but if the wind should come dead ahead I think your best course would be to lower the sail and row against it. However, at present, with the wind from the east, you will be able to sail free on your proper course."

Then he pushed the boat off. "You had better put an oar out and get her head round," he said, "before hoisting the sail again. Good-bye; *bon voyage!*"

Since leaving the river, Terence had been sailing under his instructions, and as soon as the boat was under way again he said to his companion: "Here we are free men again, Dicky."

"I call it splendid, Terence. She goes along well; I only hope she will keep on like this till we get to Corunna, or, better still, to the mouth of the Douro."

"We must not count our chickens before they are hatched, Dicky. There are storms and French privateers to be reckoned with. We are not out of the woods yet by a long way. However, we need not bother about them at present. It is quite enough that we have got a stout boat and a favouring wind."

"And plenty to eat and drink, Terence; don't forget that."

"No, that is a very important item, especially as we dare not land to buy anything for some days."

"What rate are we going through the water, do you think?"

"Jules said we were sailing about four knots an hour when we were going down the river, and about three when we had turned south and pulled the sail in. I suppose we are about half-way between the two now, so we can count it as three knots and a half."

"That would make," Ryan said, after making the calculation, "eighty-four miles in twenty-four hours."

"Bravo, Dicky! I doubted whether your mental powers were equal to so difficult a calculation. Well, Jules said that it was about four hundred miles to Corunna and about a hundred and fifty to Santander, beyond which he thought we could land safely at any village."

"Oh, let us stick to the boat as long as we can!" Ryan exclaimed.

"Certainly. I have no more desire to be tramping among those mountains and taking our chance with the peasants than you have, and if the wind keeps as it is now we should be at Corunna in something like five days; but that would be almost too much to hope for; so that, if it does but keep in its present direction till we are past Santander I shall be very well satisfied."

The mountains of Navarre and Biscay were within sight from the time they had left the river, and it did not need the compass to show them which way they should steer. There were many fishing-boats from Nivelle, Urumia, and St. Sebastian to be seen dotted over the sea on their left. They kept farther out than the majority of these, and did not pass any of them nearer than half a mile. After steering for a couple of hours Terence relinquished the oar to his companion.

"You must get accustomed to it as well as I," he said, "for we must take it in turns at night."

By twelve 'clock they were abreast of a town, which was, they had no doubt, San Sebastian. They were now some four miles from the Spanish coast. They were travelling at about the same rate as that at which they had started, but the wind came off the high land, and sometimes in such strong puffs that they had to loosen the sheet. The fisherman had shown them how to shorten sail by tying down the reef points and shifting the tack, and in the afternoon the squalls came so heavily that they thought it best to lower the sail and reef it. Towards nightfall the wind had risen so much that they made for the land, and when darkness came on threw out the little grapnel the boat carried, a hundred yards or so from the shore at a point where no village was visible. Here they were sheltered from the wind, and, spreading out the nets to form a bed, they laid themselves down in the bottom of the boat, pulling the sail partly over them.

"This is jolly enough," Ryan said. "It is certainly pleasanter to lie here and look at the stars than to be shut up in that hiding-place of Jules's."

"It is a great nuisance having to stop, though," Terence replied. "It is a loss of some forty miles."

"I don't mind how long this lasts," Ryan said cheerfully. "I could go on for a month at this work, providing the provisions would hold out."

"I don't much like the look of the weather, Dicky. There were clouds on the top of some of the hills; and though we can manage the boat well enough in such weather as we have had to-day, it will be a different thing altogether if bad weather sets in. I should not mind if I could talk Spanish as well as I can Portuguese, then we could land fearlessly if the weather was too bad to hold on; but you see the Spanish hate the Portuguese as much as they do the French, and would as likely as not hand us over at once at the nearest French post."

They slept fairly, and at daybreak got up the grapnel and hoisted the sail again. Inshore they scarcely felt the wind, but as soon as they made out a couple of miles from the land, they felt that it was blowing hard.

AFLOAT

"We won't go any farther out. Dick, lay the boat's head to the west again. I will hold the sheet while you steer, and then I can let the sail fly if a stronger gust than usual strikes us. Sit well over this side."

"She is walking along now," Ryan said joyously. "I had no idea that sailing was as jolly as it is."

They sped along all day, and before noon had passed Bilboa. As the afternoon wore on, the wind increased in force, and the clouds began to pass rapidly overhead from the south-east.

"We had better get her in to the shore," Terence said. "Even with this scrap of sail, we keep on taking the water in on that lower side. I expect Santander lies beyond that point that runs out ahead of us, and we will land somewhere this side of it."

But as soon as they turned the boat's head towards the shore, and hauled in the sheet as tightly as they could, they found that, try as they would, they could not get her to lie her course.

"We sha'n't make the point at all," Terence said, half an hour after they had changed the course. "Besides, we have been nearly over two or three times. I dare say fellows who understood a boat well could manage it, but if we hold on like this, we shall end by drowning ourselves. I think the best plan will be to lower the sail and mast and row straight to shore."

"I quite agree with you," Ryan said. "Sailing is pleasant enough in a fair wind, but I cannot say I care for it as it is now."

With some difficulty, for the sea was getting up, they lowered the sail and mast, and, getting out the oars, turned her head straight for the shore. Both were accustomed to rowing in still water, but they found that this was very different work. After struggling at the oars for a couple of hours they both agreed that they were a good deal farther away from the land than when they began.

"It is of no use, Dick," Terence said. "If we cannot make against the wind while we are fresh, we certainly cannot do so when we are tired, and my arms feel as if they would come out of their sockets."

"So do mine," Ryan said, with a groan. "I am aching all over, and both my hands are raw with this rough handle. What are we to do, then, Terence?"

"She is walking along now."

AFLOAT

"There is nothing to do that I can see but to get her head round and run before the wind. It is a nuisance, but perhaps the gale won't last long, and when it is over we can get up sail and make for the northwestern point of Spain. We have got provisions enough to last for a week. That is more comfortable," he added, as they got the boat in the required direction. "Now, you take the steering-oar, Dick, and see that you keep her straight as you can before the wind, while I set to and bale. She is nearly half-full of water."

It took half an hour's work with the little bowl they found in the boat before she was completely cleared of water. The relief given to her was very apparent, for she rose much more lightly on the waves.

"We will sit down at the bottom of the boat, and take it by turns to hold the steering-oar."

They had brought with them a lantern in which a lighted candle was kept burning, in order to be able to light their pipes. This was stowed away in a locker in the stern with their store of biscuit, and after eating some of these, dividing a bottle of wine, and lighting their pipes, they felt comparatively comfortable. They were, of course, drenched to the skin, and, as the wind was cold, they pulled the sail partly over them.

"She does not ship any water now, Terence. If she goes on like this, it will be all right."

"I expect it will be all right, Dick, though it is sure to be very much rougher than this when we get farther out; still, I fancy an open boat will live through almost anything, providing she is light in the water. I don't suppose she would have much chance if she had a dozen men on board, but with only us two I think there is every hope that she will get through it. It would be a different thing if the wind was from the west, and we had the great waves coming in from the Atlantic, as we had in that heavy gale when we came out from Ireland. As it is, nothing but a big wave breaking right over her stern could damage us very seriously; there is not the least fear of her capsizing, with us lying in the bottom."

They did not attempt to keep alternate watches that night, only changing occasionally at the stearing-oar, the one not occupied dozing off occasionally. The boat required but little steering, for, as both were lying in the stern, the tendency was to run straight before the wind. As the waves, however, became higher, she needed keeping straight when she was in a hollow between two seas. It seemed sometimes that the waves flowing behind the boat must break on to her and swamp her; but, as time after time she rose over them, their anxiety on this score lessened, and they grew more and more confident that she would go safely through it.

Occasionally the baler was used to keep her clear of the water which came in, in the shape of spray. At times they chatted cheerfully, for both were blessed with good spirits and the faculty of looking on the best side of things. They smoked their pipes in turns, getting fire from each other, so as to avoid the necessity of resorting to the lantern, which might very well blow out, in spite of the care they had at first exercised by getting under the sail with it when they wanted a light. They were heartily glad when morning broke. The scene was a wild one. They seemed to be in the centre of a circle of a mist which closed in at a distance of half a mile or so all round them. At times the rain fell, sweeping along with stinging force, but wet as they were, this mattered little to them.

"I would give something for a big glass of hot punch," Ryan said, as he munched a piece of biscuit.

"Yes, it would not be bad," Terence agreed; "but I would rather have a big bowl of hot coffee."

"I have changed my opinion of a seafaring life," Ryan said, after a pause. "It seemed delightful the morning we started, but it has its drawbacks, and to be at sea in an open boat during a strong gale in the Bay of Biscay is distinctly an unpleasant position."

"I fancy it is our own fault, Dicky. If we had known how to manage the boat I have no doubt that we should have been able to get to shore. When the wind first began to freshen we ought not to have waited so long as we did before we made for shelter."

"Well, we shall know better next time, Terence. I think that now that it is light we had better get some sleep by turns. Do you lie down for four hours and then I will take a turn."

"All right! But be sure you wake me up, and mind you don't go to sleep, for if you did we might get broadside on to these waves, and I have no doubt they would roll us over and over. So, mind, if before the four hours are up you feel you cannot keep your eyes open, wake me at once. Half an hour will do wonders for me, and I shall be perfectly ready to take the oar again."

Chapter VII
A French Privateer

Terence went off into a deep sleep as soon as he had pulled the sail over his head, but it seemed to him as if but a minute had elapsed when his companion began to stir him up with his foot.

"What is it?" he asked.

"I am awfully sorry to wake you," Ryan shouted, "but you have had two hours of it, and I really cannot keep my eyes open any longer. I have felt myself going off two or three times."

"You don't mean to say that I have been asleep for two hours?"

"You have, and a few minutes over. I looked at my watch as you lay down."

"All right! Give me the oar. I say, it is blowing hard!"

"I should think it is. It seems to me it is getting up rather than going down."

"Well, we are all right so far," Terence said cheerfully, for he was now wide awake again. "Besides, we are getting quite skilful mariners. You had better spend a few minutes at baling before you lie down, for the water is a good three inches over the boards."

All day the storm continued, and when darkness began to close in, it seemed to them that it was blowing harder than ever. Each had had two spells of sleep, and they agreed that they could now keep awake throughout the night. It was bad enough having no one to speak to all day, but at night they felt that companionship was absolutely needed. During the day they had lashed together the spars, sail, and the barrel of water, which was now nearly half empty, so that if the boat should be swamped they could cling to this support.

It was a terrible night, but towards the morning both were of opinion that the gale was somewhat abating. About eight o'clock there were breaks in the clouds, and by noon the sun was shining brightly. The wind was still blowing strong, but nothing to what it had been the evening before, and by nightfall the sea was beginning to go down. The waves were as high as before, but were no longer broken and created with heads of foam, and at ten o'clock they felt that they could both safely lie down till morning.

The steering-oar was lashed in its position, the sail spread over the whole of the stern of the boat, every drop of water was baled out, and, lying down side by side, they were soon fast asleep. When they woke the sun was high, the wind had dropped to a gentle breeze, and the boat was rising and falling gently on the smooth rollers.

"Hurrah!" Ryan shouted, as he stood up and looked round. "It is over. I vote, Terence, that we both strip and take a swim, then spread out our clothes to dry, after which we will breakfast comfortably, and then get up sail."

"That is a very good programme, Dicky; we will carry it out at once."

While they were eating their meal, Ryan asked:

"Where do you suppose we are, Terence?"

"Beyond the fact that we are right out in the Bay of Biscay, I have not the most remote idea. By the way the water went past us, I should say, that we had been going at pretty nearly the same rate as we did when we were sailing, say, four miles an hour. We have been running for forty-eight hours, so that we must have got nearly two hundred miles from Santander. The question is, would it be best to make for England now, or for Portugal? We have been going nearly north-west, so I should think that we are pretty nearly north of Finisterre, which may lie a hundred and twenty miles from us, and I suppose we are two or three times as much as that from England. The wind is pretty nearly due east again, now, so we can point her head either way. We must be nearly in the ship course, and are likely to be picked up long before we make land. Which do you vote for?"

"I vote for the nearest. We may get another storm, and one of them is quite enough. At any rate, Spain will be the shortest by a great deal, and if we are picked up, it is just as likely to be by a French privateer as by an English vessel."

"I am quite of your opinion, and am anxious to be back again as soon as I can. If we got to England and reported ourselves, we might be sent to the depot and not get out again for months; so here goes for the south."

A FRENCH PRIVATEER

The sail was hoisted, and the boat sped merrily along. In a couple of hours their clothes were dry.

"I think we had better put ourselves on short rations," Terence said. "We may be farther off than we calculate upon, and at any rate we had better hold on to the mouth of the Tagus if we can; there are sure to be some British officials there, and we shall be able to get money and rejoin our regiment without loss of time, while we might have all sorts of trouble with the Spaniards were we to land at Corunna or Vigo."

No sail appeared in sight during the day.

"I should think we cannot have come as far west as we calculated," Terence said, "or we ought to have seen vessels in the distance; however, we will keep due south. It will be better to strike the coast of Spain, and have to run along the shore round Cape Finisterre, than to risk missing land altogether."

That night they kept regular watches. The wind was very light now, and they were not going more than two knots an hour through the water. Ryan was steering when morning broke.

"Wake up, Terence!" he exclaimed suddenly. "Here is a ship within a mile or so of us; she is a lugger, I am afraid she is a French privateer.

"We have put our foot in it now, and no mistake," Ryan said; "it is another French prison, and this time without a friendly soldier to help us get out."

"It looks like it, Dicky. In another hour it will be broad daylight, and they cannot help seeing us. Still, there is a hope for us. We must give out that we are Spanish fishermen who have been blown off the coast. It is not likely they have anyone on board that speaks Spanish, and our Portuguese will sound all right in their ears; so, very likely, after overhauling us, they will let us go on our way. At any rate it is of no use trying to escape; we will hold on our course for another few minutes, and then head suddenly towards her. I will hail her in Portuguese, and they are sure to tell us to come on board, and then I will try to make them understand by signs, and by using a few French words, that we have been blown out to sea by the gale, and want to know the course for Santander; as the French have been there for some time, it would be natural enough for us to have picked up a little of their language."

In a few minutes they altered their course, and sailed towards the lugger, which soon turned towards them. When they approached within the vessel's length, Terence stood up, and shouted in Portuguese:

"What is the bearing of Santander?"

The reply was in French, "Come alongside!" given with a gesture of the arm explaining the words. They let the sail run down as they came alongside. Terence climbed up by the channels to the deck.

"*Español,*" he said to the captain, who was standing close to him as he jumped down on to the deck, "*Españoles, Capitaine; poisson, Santander; grand tempête,*" and he motioned with his arms to signify that they had been blown off-shore at Santander. Then he pointed in several directions towards the south, and looked interrogatively.

"They are Spanish fishermen who have been blown off the coast," the captain said to another officer. "They have been lucky in living it out. Well, we are short of hands, having so many away in prizes, and the boat will be useful in place of the one we had smashed up in the gale. Let a couple of men throw the nets and things overboard, and then run her up to the davits." Then he said to Terence: "Prisoners! Go forward and make yourself useful;" and he pointed towards the forecastle. Terence gave a yell of despair, threw his hat down on the deck, and, in a volley of Portuguese, begged the captain to let them go. The latter, however, only waved his hand angrily, and two sailors, coming up, seized Terence by the arms and dragged him forward. Ryan was called upon deck, and also ordered forward. He, too, remonstrated, but was cut short by a threatening gesture from the captain.

For a time they preserved an appearance of deep dejection, Terence tugging his hair as if in utter despair, till Ryan whispered: "For heaven's sake, Terence, don't go on like that or I shall break out in a shout of laughter."

"It is monstrous, it is inhuman!" Terence exclaimed in Portuguese. "Thus to seize harmless fisherman, who have so narrowly escaped drowning; the sea is less cruel than these men. They have taken our boat too, our dear good boat. What will our mothers think when we do not return? That we have been swallowed up by the sea. How they will watch for us, but in vain!"

A FRENCH PRIVATEER

Fortunately for the success of their story, the lugger hailed from a northern French port, and as not one on board understood either Spanish or Portuguese, they had no idea that the latter was the language in which the prisoners were speaking. After an hour of pretended despair, both rose from the deck on which they had been sitting, and on an order being given to trim the sails, went to the ropes and aided the privateersmen to haul at them, and before the end of the day were doing duty as regular members of the crew.

"They are active young fellows," the captain said to his first mate, as he watched the supposed Spaniards making themselves useful. "It was lucky for them that they had a fair store of provisions and water in their boat. We are very short-handed, and they will be useful. I would have let them go if it had not been for the boat, but as we have only one left that can swim, it was too lucky a find to give up."

The craft had been heading north when Ryan had first seen her and she held that course all day. Terence gathered from the talk of the sailors that they were bound for Brest, to which port she belonged. The Frenchmen were congratulating themselves that their cruise was so nearly over, and that it had been so successful a one. From time to time a sailor was sent up into the cross-trees and scanned the horizon to the north and west. In the afternoon he reported that he could make out the upper sails of a large ship going south. The captain went up to look at her.

"I think she is an English ship-of-war," he said when he descended to the deck, "but she is a long way off. With this light wind we could run away from her. She will not trouble herself about us; she would know well enough that she could not get within ten miles of us before it got dark."

This turned out to be the case, for the look-out from time to time reported that the distant sail was keeping on her course, and the slight feeling of hope that had been felt by Terence and Ryan faded away. They were placed in the same watch, and were below when, as daylight broke, they heard sudden exclamations, tramping of feet overhead, and a moment later the watch was summoned on deck.

"I hope that they have had the same luck that we had, and have run into the arms of one of our cruisers," Terence whispered in Portuguese to Ryan, as they ran up on deck together.

UNDER WELLINGTON'S COMMAND

As he reached the deck the boom of a cannon was heard, and at the same instant a ball passed through the mainsail. Half a mile away was a British sloop-of-war. She had evidently made out the lugger before the watch on board the latter had seen her. The captain was foaming with rage and shouting orders which the crew hurried to execute. On the deck near the foremast lay the man who had been on the look-out, and who had been felled with a handspike by the captain when he ran out on deck at the first alarm. Although at first flurried and alarmed, the crew speedily recovered themselves and executed with promptitude the orders which were given.

There was a haze on the water, but a light wind was stirring, and the vessel was moving through the water at some three knots an hour. As soon as her course had been changed so as to bring the wind forward of the beam, which was her best point of sailing, the men were sent to the guns, the first mate placing himself at a long eighteen-pounder which was mounted as a pivot-gun aft, a similar weapon being in her bows. All this took but four or five minutes, and shot after shot from the sloop hummed overhead. The firing now ceased, as the change of the lugger had placed the sloop dead astern of her, and the latter was unable, therefore, to fire even her bow-chasers without yawning. It was now the turn of the lugger. The gun in the stern was carefully trained, and as it was fired a patch of white splinters appeared in the sloop's bulwarks. A cheer broke from the French. The effect of the shot, which must have raked her from stem to stern, was at once evident. The sloop bore off the wind until her whole broadside could be seen.

"Flat on your faces!" the captain shouted.

There was a roar of ten guns and a storm of shot screamed overhead. Four of them passed through the sails; one ploughed up the deck, killing two sailors and injuring three others with the splinters. Two or three ropes of minor importance were cut, but no serious damage inflicted. The crew, as they leapt to their feet, gave a cheer. They knew that, with this light wind, their lugger could run away from the heavier craft, and that the latter could only hope for success by crippling her.

"Steady with the helm!" the captain went on, as the pivot-gun was again ready to deliver its fire. "Wait till her three masts show like one. Jacques, aim a little bit higher. See if you cannot knock away a spar."

The sloop was coming up again to the wind, and as she was nearly stem-on the gun cracked out again. A cheer broke from the lugger as her opponent's foretop-mast fell over her side, with all its hamper. Round the sloop came and delivered the other broadside. Two shots crashed through the bulwarks, one of them dismounting a gun, which in its fall crushed a man who had thrown himself down beside it. Another shot struck the yard of the foresail, cutting it asunder, and the lugger at once ran up into the wind.

"Lower the foresail!" the captain shouted. "Quick, men! And lash a spare spar to the yard. They are busy cutting away their topmast, but we shall be off again before they are ready to move. They have lost nearly a half a mile; we shall soon be out of range. Be sharp with that gun again!"

The sloop had indeed fallen greatly astern while delivering her broadsides, but her commander had evidently seen that, unless the wind sprang up, the lugger would get away from him unless he could cripple her, and that she might seriously damage him, and perhaps knock one of the masts out of him by her stern-chaser; his only chance, therefore, of capturing her was to take a spar out of her. He did not attempt to come about again after firing the second broadside, but kept up his fire as fast as his guns could be loaded. The lugger, however, was stealing rapidly away from him, and in ten minutes had increased her lead by another half-mile, without having suffered any serious damage; and the sloop soon ceased fire, as she was now almost out of range. Seven or eight crew had been more or less injured by splinters, but, with the exception of the three killed, none were badly hurt. The lugger was now put on her course, the guns lashed into their places again, and the three men killed sewn up in hammocks and laid between two of the guns, in order to be handed to their friends on arrival in port.

"That is another slip between the cup and the lip," Terence remarked to his companion as the sloop ceased firing. "I certainly thought when we came on deck that our troubles were over. I must say for our friend, the French captain, he showed himself a good sailor, and got out of the scrape uncommonly well."

"A good deal too well," Ryan grumbled; "it was very unpleasant while it lasted. It is all very well to be shot at by an enemy, but to be shot at by one's friends is more than one bargains for."

The coolness under fire displayed by the two Spaniards he had carried off pleased the captain, who patted them on the shoulder as he came along, his good temper being now completely restored by his escape.

"You are brave fellows," he said, "and will make good privateersmen. You cannot do better than stay with us. You will make as much money in a month as you would in a year's fishing."

Terence smiled vaguely as if he understood that the captain was pleased with them but did not otherwise catch his meaning. They arrived at Brest without further adventure. As they neared the port the captain asked Terence if he and his companion would enter upon the books of the privateer, and after much difficulty made, as he believed, Terence understand his question. The latter affected to consult Ryan, and then answered that they would be both willing to do so. The captain then put the names they gave him down on the ship's roll, and handed each of them a paper certifying that Juan Montes and Sebastian Peral belonged to the crew of the *Belle Jeanne,* naming the rate of wages that they were to receive, and their share in the value of the prizes taken. He then gave them eighty francs each as an advance on their pay from the date of their coming on board, and signified to them that they must buy clothes similar to those worn by the crew instead of the heavy fishermen's garments they had on.

"They will soon learn our language," he said to the mate, "and I am sure they will make good sailors. I have put down their wages and share of prize-money at half that of our own men, and I am sure they will be well worth it when they get to speak the language and learn their duties."

A FRENCH PRIVATEER

As soon as they were alongside, the greater portion of the men went ashore, and in the evening the boatswain landed with Terence and Ryan, and proceeded with them to a slop-shop, where he bought them clothes similar to those worn by the crew. Beyond the fact that these were of nautical appearance there was no distinctive dress. They then returned to the lugger, and changed their clothes at once, the boatswain telling them to stow away their boots and other things, as these would be useful to them in bad weather. The next day the privateer commenced to unload, for the most valuable portions of the cargoes of the captured ships had been taken on board, when the vessels themselves, with the greater portion of the goods they carried, had been sent into port under the charge of prize crews.

They remained on board for ten days, going freely into the town, sometimes with the sailors and sometimes alone. Terence pretended to make considerable progress in French, and was able, though with some difficulty, to make himself understood by the crew. The first mate had gone with them to the *mairie*, where the official stamp had been affixed to their ship-papers. They found that no questions were asked of persons entering or leaving the town on the land side, and twice strolled out and went some distance into the country. They had agreed that it would be better to defer any attempt to escape until the day before the lugger sailed, as there would then be but little time for the captain to make inquiries after them, or to institute a search. They bought a pocket-map of the north of France, and carefully studied the roads.

"It is plain enough what our best course is, Dick. We must go along this projecting point of Brittany through Dinan to Avranches, and then follow the coast up till we get to Coutances. You see it is nearly opposite Jersey, and that island does not look to be more than fifteen miles away, so that if we can get hold of a boat there we should be able to run across in three hours or so with favourable wind."

"That looks easy enough," Ryan agreed; "it seems to be about one hundred and twenty miles from here to Avaranches, and another thirty or forty up to Coutances, so we should do it in a week easily. What stories shall we make up if we are questioned?"

"I don't suppose the peasants we may meet on the road are likely to question us at all, for most of the Bretons speak only their own language. We had better always sleep out in the open. If we do run across an official we can show our papers and give out that we have been ill-treated on board the lugger and are going to St. Malo, where we mean to ship on another privateer; I know that is a port from which lots of them sail. I don't think we shall have any difficulty in buying provisions at small villages. My French will pass muster very well in such places, and I can easily remark that we are on our way to St. Malo to join a ship there, and if any village functionary questions us, these papers will be good enough for him. Or we can say that we got left ashore by accident when our craft sailed from Brest, and are going to rejoin her at St. Malo, where she was going to put in. I think, perhaps, that that would be a better story than that we had run away. I don't know that the authorities interest themselves in runaway seamen from privateers, but, at any rate, it is a likely tale; drunken seamen, no doubt, often do get left ashore."

"Yes, that would be a very good story, Terence, and I think that there would be no great fear even if we were to go boldly into a town."

"I don't think there would; still it is better to be on the safe side and avoid all risks."

Accordingly, the afternoon before the *Belle Jeanne* was to sail, they went ashore, brought enough bread and cold meat to last them for a couple of days, and two thick blankets, as it was now November and the nights were bitterly cold, and then left the town and followed the road for Dinan. On approaching the village of Landerneau they left the road and lay down until it was quite dark, then they made a detour through the fields, round the village, came down on the road again, walked all night, passing through Huelgoat, and then as morning was breaking they left the road again, and after going a quarter of a mile through the fields lay down in a dry ditch by the side of a thick hedge, ate a meal, and went to sleep. They did not start again until it was getting dusk, when they returned to the road, which they followed all night. In the morning they went boldly into a little village, and Terence went into a shop and bought a couple of loaves. His French was quite good enough for so simple an operation.

"I suppose you are going to St. Malo?" the woman said.

"Yes. We have had a holiday to see some friends at Brest, and are going to rejoin."

A FRENCH PRIVATEER

This was the only question asked, and after walking another two miles they lay up for the day as before. They had met several peasants on the road, and had exchanged salutations with them. They found by their map that they were now within twenty miles of Dinan, having made over thirty miles each night; and as both were somewhat footsore from their unaccustomed exercise, they travelled only some sixteen or seventeen miles the following night. The next evening, at about ten o'clock, they walked boldly through Dinan. Most of the inhabitants were already asleep, and the few who were still in the streets paid no heed to two sailors, going, they had no doubt, to St. Malo. Crossing the river Rance by the bridge, they took the road in the direction of the port, but after following it for a mile or two struck off to the east, and before morning arrived on the river running up from the bay of Mount St. Michaels. They lay down until late in the afternoon, and then crossed the river at a ferry, and kept along by the coast until they reached the Sebine river.

"We are getting on first-rate," Ryan said, as they lay down for a few hours' sleep. "We have only got Avranches to pass now."

"I hope we sha'n't be questioned at all, Dick, for we have now no good story to tell them, for we are going away from St. Malo instead of to it. Of course, as long as they don't question us we are all right. We are simply two sailors on our way home for a time, but if we have to show our papers with those Spanish names on them we should be in a fix. Of course we might have run away from our ship at St. Malo, but that would not explain our coming up this way. However, I hope my French is good enough to answer any casual questions without exciting attention. We will cross by the ferry-boat as soon as it begins to ply, and as Avranches stands some little distance up the river we can avoid it altogether by keeping along the coastline."

A score of peasants had assembled by the time the ferry boatsman made his appearance from his cottage, and Terence and his companion, who had been lying down 200 yards away, joined them just as they were going down to the boat.

"You are from St. Malo, I suppose?" an old peasant said to Terence.

The latter nodded.

"We have got a month's leave from our ship," he said. "She has been knocked about by an English cruiser, and will be in the shipwright's hands for five or six weeks before she is ready for sea again."

"You are not from this part of the country," the peasant, who was speaking in the patios of Normandy, remarked.

"No, we come from the south, but one of our comrades comes from Cherbourg, and as he cannot get away, we are going to see his friends and tell them that he is well. It is a holiday for us, and we may as well go there as anywhere else."

The explanation was simple enough for the peasant, and Terence continued chatting with him until they landed.

"You do not need to go through Avranches," the latter said. "Take the road by the coast through Granville to Coutances."

"How far is it to Coutances?"

"About twenty miles; at least so I have heard, for I have never been there."

After walking a few miles they went down on to the seashore and lay down among some rocks until evening. At eight o'clock they started again and walked boldly through Granville, where their sailor's dress would, they felt sure, attract no attention. It was about nine o'clock when they entered the place. Their reason for doing so at this hour was that they wished to lay in a stock of provisions, as they did not intend to enter Coutances until late at night, when they hoped to be able to get hold of a boat at once. They had just made their purchases when they met a fat little man with a red sash which showed him to be the Maire of the place, or some other public functionary.

"Where are you going, and what ship do you belong to?"

"We are sailors on our way from St. Malo to Cherbourg," Terence replied.

"You have papers, of course?"

"Of course, Monsieur le Maire."

"I must see them," the Maire said. "Come with me to my house close by."

There were several persons near, and a man in civil uniform was with the Maire. Therefore Terence gave an apparently willing assent, and, followed by the functionary, they went into a house close by. A lamp was burning on the table in the hall.

A FRENCH PRIVATEER

"Light these candles in my office," the Maire said. "The women have gone up to bed."

The man turned a key, went in, and, bringing out two candles, lighted them at the lamp, and they went into the room. The Maire seated himself in an arm-chair at the table. The minor functionary placed the two suspected persons on the side facing him, and took his place standing by their side. As they were going in, Terence whispered:

"If there is trouble, I will take this fellow, and you manage the Maire."

"Now," that functionary said, "let me see your papers. Why," he exclaimed, looking at the names, "you are not Frenchmen!"

"No," Terence said quietly. "We do not pretend to be; but, as you see, we are sailors who have done service on board a French privateer."

"But where is this privateer?"

"I don't know, Monsieur le Maire. We were not satisfied with our treatment, so we left her at Brest."

"This is very serious," the Maire said. "You are Spaniards. You have deserted your ship at Brest. You have travelled a hundred and fifty miles through France, and now what are you doing here?"

"We are, as you say, monsieur, travelling through France. We desire to see France. We have heard that it is the greatest country in the world. Frenchmen visit Spain in large numbers. Why should not Spaniards visit France?"

The tone of sarcasm in which Terence spoke was not lost upon the Maire, who rose from his seat purple with anger.

"You will take these men into custody," he said to his assistant. "This is a very grave business."

"Now, Dick!" Terence exclaimed; and, turning to the man who stood next to him, he grasped him suddenly by the throat. At the same moment Ryan caught up a heavy inkstand and threw it across the table at the Maire, striking that functionary in the stomach and doubling him completely up. Then he ran around the table and bound the man—who had not yet recovered his breath—tightly in his chair, and thrust his handkerchief into his mouth. The man whom Terence was holding had scarcely struggled. Terence, as he gripped him, had said, "Keep quiet or I will choke you!" and the prisoner felt that his assailant could do so in a moment if he chose. His hands were fastened tightly behind him with his own belt by Ryan. A short ruler was thrust between his teeth, and fastened there by a handkerchief going round the back of his head.

"So far so good, Dick. Now look round for something with which we can bind them more firmly." Several hanks of red tape lay upon the table; with a portion of one of these the back of the chair in which the Maire sat was lashed to the handle of a heavy bureau, then his feet were fastened to the two legs of the chair, so that he could neither kick nor upset himself. The other man was then fastened securely. This done, they blew out the candles, left the room, locked the door behind them, taking the key, and then sallied out into the street.

"That was a good shot of yours with the inkstand," Terence said.

"I had my eye on it all the time he was speaking," Ryan replied. "I saw that if I were to move to get round the table at him the little man would have the time to shout, but that if I could hit him in the wind it would be all right."

"Well, there must be no more stopping now. I don't know whether there is a Mrs. Maire; if not, there will certainly be no alarm until morning. If there is, it depends upon what sort of woman she is as to how long a start we shall get. If she is a sleepy woman she is probably dreaming by this time, and may not discover until morning that her lord and master is not by her side. If she is a bad-tempered woman, she will probably lie for an hour or two thinking over what she shall say to him when he comes in. If she is a nervous woman, she will get up and go downstairs.

"I left the lamp burning in the hall on purpose. Seeing it there she will naturally think that he has not come in, and will go upstairs again for an hour or two; then she will probably call up the servants, and may send them out to look for him; finally, she may go to the police office and wake up a constable. It is not probable there are many of them on night duty in a quiet place like this. Altogether, I calculate that it will be at least four hours before they think of breaking open the door of the office to see if he is there, so at the worst we have got four hours' start; at the best, ten hours. It is only half-past nine now; we shall be at the mouth of the Sienne in three hours or less. It does not look above nine or ten miles on the map, and directly we get fairly out of the town we will go as quickly as we can, for every minute is of importance.

"If we can get hold of a boat at once we ought to be at Jersey soon after daybreak, although I am not very sure of that, for I believe there are all sorts of strong currents along this coast. I remember one of the officers saying so as we came down the Channel on the voyage out. Of course, it will make a difference whether we can get a boat with a sail or not. If we cannot find a boat, we shall have to hide up, but you may be sure that there will be a hot search for us in the morning, and we must get off to-night if we can. Most likely there is a fishing village somewhere near the mouth of the river."

As soon as they were out of the town they broke into a trot, which they continued with scarcely any intermission until they approached a small village.

"I expect this stands on the bank of the river," Terence said. "There is no chance of anyone being up, so we can go through fearlessly."

A couple of hundred yards farther they reached the river. A large ferry-boat was moored here. Keeping the bank to the left, they were not long before they came upon several boats hauled up on the shore, while three or four others lay at their moorings a short distance out.

"Thank goodness!" Terence exclaimed. "We shall have no difficulty now."

They selected the boat lying nearest the water's edge. The moon was half full, but was now sinking towards the west. Its light, however, was of some assistance to them. There was a mast and sail in the boat, as well as a pair of oars. At first they were unable to move her down to the water, but getting some oars out of the other boats, they laid them down as rollers, and with these managed, after great exertions, to get her afloat.

Chapter VIII
A Smart Engagement

After pushing the boat out into the stream, Terence and his companion allowed it to drift quietly for some distance, and then, getting out the oars, rowed hard until they were beyond the mouth of the river. The tide was, they thought, by the level of the water where they had embarked, within an hour or two of flood. They therefore determined to shape their course to the north of the point where they believed Jersey to lie, so that, when tide turned, it would sweep them down upon it. The wind was too light to be any assistance, but the stars were bright, and the position of the north star served as a guide to the direction they should take.

It had taken them some considerable time to launch the boat, and they calculated that it was nearly midnight when they left the mouth of the river. There was no occasion to row hard, for until it became daylight and they could see the island of Jersey they would not shape their course with any certainty, and could only hope that by keeping to the north of it they would not find in the morning that the tide had taken them too far to the south.

"We are very lucky in our weather," Terence said, as, after labouring at the heavy oars for a couple of hours, they paused for a few minutes' rest. "If it had been a strong wind it would never have done for us to have started. I believe in bad weather there are tremendous currents about the islands, and desperately rough water. A fog would have been even worse for us. As it is, it seems to me we cannot go very far wrong. I suppose the tide is about turning now, but if by daylight we find that we have been carried a long way past the island, we shall soon have the tide turning again, which will take us back to it. I am more afraid of falling in with a French privateer than I am of missing the island. There are sure to be some of them at Granville, to say nothing of St. Malo. I don't suppose any of those at

A SMART ENGAGEMENT

Granville will put out in search of us merely to please the Maire, but if any were going to sea they would be sure to keep a look-out for us."

"If they did see us, we should have no chance of getting away, Terence. This boat is not as big as the one we stole at Bayonne, but it rows much heavier."

"There is one thing—even a privateer could not sail very fast in this light wind, and if it freshens in the morning we can get up the sail."

"Then I hope it will get up a bit," Ryan said, "for after another five or six hours' rowing with these beastly oars my hands will be raw, and I am sure my back and arms will be nearly broken."

"We must risk that, Dick; we calculated fifteen miles in a straight line across to Jersey, so that we must jog along at the rate of a couple of miles an hour to get far enough to the west. Now then, let us be moving again."

The night seemed interminable to them, and they felt relieved indeed when morning began to break. In another half-hour it would be light enough for them to see for a considerable distance. Upshipping their oars, they stood up and looked round.

"That must be Jersey," Terence exclaimed, pointing to the north. "The current must have taken us past it, as I was afraid it would. What time is it, Dick?"

"Nearly eight."

"Then the tide must be turning already. The island must be six miles away now. If we row hard we shall know in half an hour whether we are being carried north or south."

"But we must be going north if tide has turned, Terence?"

"I don't know—I remember that the mate of the *Sea Horse* said that in the Channel the course of the current did not change at high and low water, so there is no saying what way we are going at present. Well, there is a little more wind, and I suppose we had better get up our sail. There is Jersey, and whether we get there a little sooner or a little later cannot make much difference. I am sure we are both too tired to row her much faster then we can sail."

Ryan agreed, and they accordingly stepped the mast and hoisted the sail. At first the boat moved but slowly through the water, but the wind was refreshing, and in half an hour she was foaming along.

"Tide is against us still," Terence said presently. "I don't think we are any nearer Jersey than when we first saw it."

"Look there!" Ryan exclaimed, a few minutes later. "There is a lugger coming out from the direction of Granville."

"So there is, Dick, and, with the wind behind her, she won't be very long before she is here. I should say that she is about six or seven miles off, and an hour will bring her up to us."

"I will get out an oar, Terence. That will help us a bit. We can change about occasionally." Terence was steering with the other oar while he held the sheet. The boat was travelling at a good rate, but the lugger was fast running down towards them.

"There is a schooner coming out from Jersey!" Terence exclaimed joyously. "If she is a British privateer we may be saved yet. I had just made up my mind that we were in for another French prison."

Ryan looked over his shoulder. "She is farther off than the lugger," he said.

"Yes, but the current that is keeping us back is helping her on towards us. It will be a close thing; but I agree with you, I am afraid that the lugger will be here first. Change seats with me; I will have a spell at the oar."

He was a good deal stronger than Ryan, and he felt comparatively fresh after his hour's rest, so there was a perceptible increase in the boat's speed after the change had been effected. When the lugger was within a mile of them, and the schooner about double that distance, the former changed her course a little, and bore up as if to meet the schooner.

"Hurrah!" Ryan shouted. "The Frenchman is making for the schooner; and, if the Jersey boat don't turn and run, there will be a fight."

"The lugger looks to me the bigger boat," Terence said, as he stopped rowing for a moment. "However, we are likely to be able to slip off while they are at it."

Rapidly the two vessels approached each other, and when within a mile, a puff of smoke broke out from the lugger's bow, and was answered almost instantly by one from the schooner. Running fast through the water, the vessels were soon within a short distance of each other. Terence had ceased rowing, for there was no fear that the

A SMART ENGAGEMENT

lugger, which was now abeam of them, would give another thought to the small boat. The fight was going on in earnest, and the two vessels poured broadsides into each other as they passed, the lugger bearing round at once, and engaging the schooner broadside to broadside.

"The Frenchman has the heavier metal," Terence said. "I am afraid the schooner will get the worst of it. The lugger is crowded with men, too. What do you say, Dick? Shall we do our best to help the schooner?"

"I think we ought to," Ryan agreed at once. "She has certainly saved us, and I think we ought to do what we can."

Accordingly he brought the boat nearer to the wind. The two vessels were now close-hauled and were moving but slowly through the water. The boat passed two or three hundred yards astern of the lugger, sailed a little farther, and then, when able to lay her course for the schooner, went about, and bore down towards her. Just as they did so, the halliards of the schooner's mainsail were shot asunder, and the sail ran down the mast. There was a shout of triumph from the lugger, and she at once closed in towards her crippled adversary.

"They are going to try and carry the schooner by boarding." Terence exclaimed. "Keep her as close as she will go, Dick;" and, seizing his oar again, he began to row with all his might. By the time they came up, the two vessels were side by side, the guns had ceased fire, but there was a rattle of pistol shots, mingled with the clash of arms and the shouts of the combatants. Running up to the schooner's side, Terence and Ryan clambered on the channel, and sprung on to the deck of the schooner. A desperate fight was going on forward, where the two vessels touched each other. There was no one aft; here some fifteen or twenty feet of water separated the ships, and even the helmsman had left the wheel to join in the fight. About half of the lugger's crew had made their way on to the deck of the schooner, but the Jersey men were still fighting stoutly. The rest of the lugger's crew were gathered in the bow of their own vessel, waiting until there should be a clear enough space left for them to join their comrades.

"Things look bad," Terence exclaimed. "The French crew are a great deal stronger. Lend me a hand to turn two of these eight-pounders round. There are plenty of cartridges handy."

They drew the cannon back from their places, turned them round, loaded them with a charge of powder, and then rammed in two bags of bullets that were lying beside them. The schooner stood higher out of water than the lugger, and they were able to train the two cannon so that they bore upon the mass of Frenchmen in the latter's bow.

"Take steady aim," Terence said. "We are only just in time; our fellows are being beaten back."

A moment later the two pieces were fired. Their discharge took terrible effect among the French, sweeping away more than half of those gathered in the lugger's bow.

"Load again!" Terence exclaimed. "They are too strong for the Jersey men still."

For a moment the French boarders had paused, but now, with a shout of fury, they fell upon the crew of the schooner, driving them back foot by foot towards the stern. The cannon were now trained directly forward, and when the crowd of fighting men approached them, Terence shouted in French to the Jersey men to fall back on either side. The captain, turning round and, seeing the guns pointing forward, repeated the order in a stentorian shout. The Jersey men leapt to one side or the other, and the moment they were clear the two cannon poured their contents into the midst of the French, who had paused for a moment, surprised at the sudden cessation of resistance. Two clear lanes were swept through the crowd, and then, with a shout, the captain of the schooner and his crew fell upon the Frenchmen. Ryan was about to rush forward, when Terence said:

"No, no, Ryan, load again; better make sure."

The heavy loss they had suffered, however, so discouraged the French that many at once turned, and, running back, jumped on to the deck of the lugger, while the others, though still resisting, were driven after them. As soon as the guns were reloaded, they were trained as before to bear on the lugger's bow, and, as the French were driven back, they were again fired. This completed the discomfiture of the enemy, and with loud shouts the Jersey men followed them on to the deck of their own ship. Terence and Ryan now ran forward, snatched up a couple of cutlasses and joined their friends, and were soon fighting in the front line; but the French resistance was now almost over, their captain had fallen, and in five minutes the last of

A SMART ENGAGEMENT

them threw down their arms and surrendered, while a great shout went up from the crew of the schooner. The French flag was hauled down, and as soon as the prisoners had been sent below, an ensign was brought from the schooner, fixed to the flag halliards above the tricolor, and the two hoisted together. The captain had already turned to the two men who had come so opportunely to his assistance.

"I do not know who you are, or where you come from, men, but you have certainly saved us from capture. I did not know it was the *Annette* until it was too late to draw off, or I should not have engaged her, for she is the strongest lugger that sails out of Granville, and carries double our weight of metal, with twice as strong a crew; but, whoever you are, I thank you most heartily. I am half owner of the schooner, and should have lost all I was worth, to say nothing of perhaps having to pass the next five years in a French prison."

"We are two British officers," Terence said. "We have escaped from a French prison, and were making our way to Jersey, when we saw that lugger coming after us, and should certainly have been captured had you not come up, so we thought the least we could do was lend you a hand."

"Well, gentlemen, you have certainly saved us. Jacques Bontemps, the captain of the *Annette*, was an old acquaintance of mine; he commanded a smaller craft before he got the *Annette*, and we have had two or three fights together. So it was you whom I saw in that little boat! Of course, we made out that the lugger was chasing you, though why they should be doing so we could not tell, but we thought no more about you after the fight once began, and were as astonished as the Frenchmen when you swept their bow. I just glanced round and saw what looked like two French fishermen, and thought that you must be two of the lugger's crew, who, for some reason or other, had turned the guns against their own ship. It will be a triumph, indeed, for us when we enter St. Helier. The *Annette* has been the terror of our privateers. Fortunately she was generally away cruising, and many a prize has she taken into Granville. I have had the luck to recapture two of them myself, but when she is known to be at home we most of us keep in port, for she is a good deal more than a match for any craft that sails out from St. Helier. She only went into Granville yesterday, and I thought that there was no fear of her being out again for a week or so. When I saw her I took her for a smaller lugger that

A desperate fight was going on forward.

A SMART ENGAGEMENT

sails from that port, and which is no more than a match for us. The fact is, we were looking at her chasing you, and wondering if we should be in time, instead of noticing her size. It was not until she fired that first broadside that we found we had caught a tartar. We should have run if there had been a chance of getting away, but she is a wonderfully fast boat, and we knew that our only chance was to knock away one of her masts. And now we will be making sail again; you must excuse me for a few minutes."

In half an hour the main halliards had been repaired and the sail hoisted. When other damages were made good, the captain with half his crew went on board the lugger, and the two vessels sailed together for Jersey. Terence and his companion had accompanied the captain.

"Now, gentlemen, you may as well come down with me into the cabin. It is likely enough that you will be able to find some clothes in Bontemps's chest that will fit you; he was a dandy in his way. At any rate, his clothes will suit you better than those you have on."

They found, indeed, that the lugger's captain had so large a store of clothing that they had no difficulty whatever in rigging themselves out. While they were changing, the captain had left them. He returned presently with a beaming face.

"She is a more valuable prize than I hoped for," he said "She is full almost to the hatches with the plunder she had taken in her last cruise. I cannot make out what led her to come out of Granville unless it was in pursuit of you."

"I expect it was that," Terence said. "We were arrested by the Maire of Granville, and had to tie him and one of his officials up. He was a pompous little man, and no doubt when he got free went down to the port and persuaded the captain of the lugger to put out at once to endeavour to find us. I expect he told him that we were prisoners of importance, either English spies or French émigrés. Well, Captain, I am glad that the capture has turned out well for you."

"You certainly ought to share it," the captain said, "for if it had not been for you, matters would have gone all the other way, and we should have undoubtedly been captured."

"Oh, we don't want to share it! We have helped you to avoid a French prison, but you have certainly saved us from the same thing, so we are fairly quits."

"Well, we shall have time to talk about that when we get into port. In the meantime, we will search Jacques's lockers. Like enough there may be something worth having there. Of course, he may have taken it ashore directly he landed, but it is hardly likely, and as he has evidently captured several British merchantmen while he has been out, he is sure to have some gold and valuables in the lockers."

The search, indeed, brought to light four bags of money, each marked with the name of an English ship. They contained in all over L800, with several gold watches, rings, and other valuables.

"Now, gentlemen," the captain said, "at least you will divide this money with me. The *Annette* and the cargo below hatches are certainly worth ten times as much, and I must insist upon your going shares with me. I shall feel very hurt if you will not do so."

"I thank you, Captain," Terence said, "and will not refuse your offer. We shall have to provide ourselves with new uniforms and take a passage out to Portugal, which is where our regiments are at present, so the money will be very useful."

"And I see you have not a watch, monsieur. You had better take one of these."

"Thanks! I parted with mine to a good woman who helped me to escape from Bayonne, so I will accept that offer also."

In two hours the schooner entered the port of St. Helier, the lugger, under easy sail, following in her wake. They were greeted with enthusiastic cheers by the crowd that gathered on the quays as soon as it was seen that the prize was the dreaded *Annette*, which had for some months past been a terror to the privateers and fishermen of the place; and that she should have been captured by the *Cerf* seemed marvelous indeed. A British officer was on the quay when they got alongside. He came on board at once.

"The governor has sent me to congratulate you in his name, Captain Teniers," he said, "on having captured a vessel double your own size, which has for some time been the terror of these waters. He will be glad if you will give me some particulars of the action, and you will, when you can spare time afterwards, go up and give him a full report of it."

A SMART ENGAGEMENT

"I owe the capture entirely to these two gentlemen, who are officers in your army. They had escaped from a French prison, and were making for this port when I first saw them this morning, with the *Annette* in hot chase after them. It did not strike me that it was she, for it was only last night that the news came in that she had been seen yesterday sailing towards Granville; and I thought that she was the *Lionne*, which is a boat our own size. I came up before she had overhauled the boat, and directly the fight began I could see the mistake I had made. But as she was a good deal faster than we were, it was of no use running. There was just a chance that I might cripple her and get away."

He then related the incidents of the fight.

"Well, I congratulate you, gentlemen," the officer said heartily. "You have indeed done a good turn to Captain Teniers. To whom have I the pleasure of speaking?"

"My name is O'Connor," Terence replied. "I have the honour to be on Sir Arthur Wellesley's staff, and have the rank of captain in our army, but am a colonel in the Portuguese service. This is Lieutenant Ryan of His Majesty's Mayo Fusileers."

The officer looked a little doubtful while Terence was speaking. It was difficult to believe that the young fellow of one- or two-and-twenty at the outside could be a captain on Lord Wellington's staff—for Sir Arthur had been raised to the peerage after the battle of Talavera—still less that he should be a colonel in the Portuguese service. However, he bowed gravely, and said:

"My name is Major Chalmers, of the 35th. I am adjutant to the governor. If it will not be inconvenient, I shall be glad if you will return with me and report yourselves to him."

"We are quite ready," Terence said. "We have nothing to do in the way of packing up, for we have only the clothes we stand in, which were indeed the property of the captain of the lugger, who was killed in the action."

Telling Captain Teniers that they would be coming down again when they had seen the governor, the two friends accompanied the officer. Very few words were said on the way, for the major entertained strong doubts whether Terence had not been hoaxing him, and whether the account he had given of himself was not altogether fictitious. On arriving at the governor's, he left them for a few minutes in the anteroom, while he went in and gave the account he had received from the captain, and said that the two gentlemen who had played so important a part in the matter were, as they said, one of them an officer on the staff of Lord Wellington and a colonel in the Portuguese army, and the other a subaltern in the Mayo Fusileers.

"Why do you say, 'as they said,' major? Have you any doubt about it?"

"My only reason for doubting is that they are both young fellows of about twenty, which would accord well enough with the claim of one of them to be a lieutenant; but that the other should be a captain on Lord Wellington's staff and a colonel in the Portuguese service is quite incredible."

"It would seem so, certainly, major. However, it is evident that they have both behaved extraordinarily well in this fight with the *Annette*, and I cannot imagine that, whatever story a young fellow might tell to civilians, he would venture to assume a military station. Will you please ask them to come in? At any rate, their story will be worth hearing."

"Good day, gentlemen," he went on, as Terence and Ryan entered. "I have to congratulate you very heartily upon the very efficient manner in which you assisted in the capture of the French privateer that has for some time been doing great damage among the islands. She has been much more than a match for any of our privateers here, and although she has been chased several times by the cruisers, she has always managed to get away. And now, may I ask how you happened to be approaching the island in a small boat at the time that the encounter took place?"

"Certainly, sir. We were both prisoners at Bayonne. I myself had been captured by the French when endeavouring to cross the frontier into Portugal with my regiment, while Lieutenant Ryan was wounded at Talavera, and was in the hospital there when the Spaniards left the town and the French marched in."

"What is your regiment, Colonel O'Connor?"

"It is called the Minho regiment, sir, and consists of two battalions. We have had the honour of being mentioned in general orders more than once and were so on the day after the first attack of Victor upon Donkin's brigade stationed on the hill forming the left of the British position at Talavera."

A SMART ENGAGEMENT

The governor looked at his adjutant, who, rising, went to a table on which were a pile of official gazettes. Picking out one, he handed it to the governor, who glanced through it.

"Here is the general order of the day," he said, "and assuredly Lord Wellington speaks in the very highest terms of the service that Colonel O'Connor and the Minho regiment, under his command, rendered. Certainly very high praise indeed. You will understand, sir, that we are obliged to be cautious here; and it seemed so strange that so young an officer should have attained the rank of colonel, that I was curious to know how it could have occurred."

"I am by no means surprised that it should seem strange to you that I should hold the rank I claim. I was, like my friend Lieutenant Ryan, in the Mayo Fusileers, when I had the good fortune to be mentioned in despatches in connection with an affair in which the transport that took us out to Portugal was engaged with two French privateers. In consequence of the mention, General Fane appointed me one of his aides-de-camp, and I acted in that capacity during the campaign that ended at Corunna. I was left on the field insensible on the night after that battle. When I came to myself, the army was embarking, so I made my way through Galicia into Portugal, and on reaching Lisbon was appointed by Sir John Cradock to his staff, and was sent by him on a mission to the northern frontier of Portugal.

"On the way I took the command of a body of freshly-raised Portuguese levies, who were without an officer or leader of any kind. With the aid of a small escort with me I formed them into a reliable regiment, and had the good fortune to do some service with them. I was therefore confirmed in my command, and was given Portuguese rank. Sir Arthur Wellesley, on succeeding Sir John Cradock in the supreme command, still kept my name on the headquarters staff, thereby adding greatly to my authority, and continued me in the independent command of my regiment. After Talavera we were despatched to aid the Spaniards in holding the pass of Banos, but before we arrived there Soult had crossed the pass, and, being cut off by his force from rejoining the army, I determined to cross the mountains into Portugal. In doing so we came upon a French division on its march to Plasencia, and the company of my regiment with which I was, were cut off, and taken prisoners."

"Forgive me for having doubted you, Colonel O'Connor. I should, of course, have remembered your name. In his report of his operations, before and subsequent to the battle of Talavera, Lord Wellington mentions more than once that his left during his advance was covered by the partisan corps of Wilson and O'Connor, and mentions too that it was by messengers from Colonel O'Connor that he first learned how formidable a force was in his rear, and was therefore able to cross the Tagus and escape from his perilous position. Of course it never entered my mind that the officer who had rendered such valuable service was so young a man. There is only one mystery left. How is it, when you and Mr. Ryan escaped from Bayonne, that you are found in a boat in the Bay of St. Malo?"

"It does seem rather a roundabout way of rejoining," Terence said, with a smile. "We escaped in a boat, and made along the north coast of Spain, but when off Santander were blown out to sea in a gale and were picked up by a French privateer. We were supposed to be two Spanish fishermen, and, as the privateer was short of boats, they took ours and enrolled us among their crew. They were on their way to Brest, and we took an opportunity to desert, and made our way on foot until we reached the mouth of the river Sienne, and made off in a boat last night. This morning we saw the privateer in chase of us, and should certainly have been recaptured had not the *Cerf* come up and engaged her. While the fight was going on, we had gone on board the schooner unperceived by either party, and took what seemed to us the best way of aiding our friends, who were getting somewhat the worst of it, the crew of the lugger being very much stronger than the crew of the schooner."

"Well, I hope that you will both at once take up your quarters with me as long as you stay here, and I shall then have an opportunity of hearing of your adventures more in detail."

"Thank you very much, sir. We shall be very happy to accept your kind invitation; but I hope we shall not trespass upon your hospitality long, for we are anxious to be off as soon as possible, so as to rejoin without loss of time. I am particularly so, for, although it will be two or three months before there is any movement of the troops, I am afraid of finding someone else appointed to the command of my regiment, and I have been so long with it now that I should be sorry indeed to be put to any other work."

A SMART ENGAGEMENT

"That I can quite understand. Well, there is no regular communication from here, but there is not a week passes without some craft or other sailing from here to Weymouth."

"We would rather, if possible, be put on board some ship on her way to Portugal," Terence said. "If we landed in England, we should have to report ourselves, and might be sent to a depot, and be months before we got out there again. I spoke to the captain of the *Cerf* about it this morning, and he was good enough to promise that, as soon as he had repaired damages, he would run out into the Bay, and put us on board the first ship he overhauled bound for the Peninsula."

"That would be an excellent plan from your point of view," the governor said. "Teniers is one of the best sailors on the island, and has several times carried despatches for me to Weymouth. You could not be in better hands."

Four days later the schooner was ready to sail again. "This will be my last voyage in her," the captain said. "I have had an offer for her, and shall sell her as soon as I come back again, as I shall take command of the *Annette*. I ought to do well in her, for her rig and build are so evidently French that I shall be able to creep up close to any French vessel making along the coast or returning from abroad, without being suspected of being an enemy. Of course I shall have to carry a much stronger crew than at present, and I hope to clip the wings of some of these French privateers before long."

They had, on the day of their landing, ordered new uniforms, and had purchased a stock of underclothing. They were fortunate in being able to pick up swords and belts, and all were now ready for them, and on the fifth day after landing they said good-bye to the governor and sailed on board the *Cerf.* When twenty-four hours out, the vessel lay to, being now on the track of ships bound south. On the following day they overhauled six vessels, and, as the last of these was bound with military stores for Lisbon, Terence and Ryan were transferred to her. With a hearty adieu to the skipper they took their places in the boat and were rowed to the vessel, being greeted on their departure by a loud and hearty cheer from the crew of the privateer. There were no passengers on board the store-ship, and they had an uneventful voyage until she dropped anchor in the Tagus.

UNDER WELLINGTON'S COMMAND

After paying the captain the small sum he charged for their passage, they landed. They first went to a hotel and put up. On sallying out, Ryan had no difficulty in learning that the Mayo Fusileers were at Portalegre. Terence took his way to headquarters. The first person he met on entering was his old acquaintance Captain Nelson, now wearing the equipments of a major. The latter looked at him inquiringly, and then exclaimed:

"Why, it is O'Connor! Why, I thought you were a prisoner! I am delighted to see you. Where have you sprung from?"

"I escaped from Bayonne, and, after sundry adventures landed an hour ago. In the first place, what has been done with my regiment?"

"It is with Hill's division, which is at Abrantes and Portalegre."

"Who is in command?"

"Your friend Herrara. No British officer has been appointed in your place. There was some talk of handing it over to Trant in the spring, but, as nothing can be done before that, no one has yet been nominated."

"I am glad indeed to hear it. I have been fidgeting about it ever since I went away."

"Well, I will take you in to the adjutant-general at once. I heard him speak more than once of the services you rendered by sending news that Soult and Ney were both in the valley, and so enabling Lord Wellington to get safely across the Tagus. He said it was an invaluable service. Of course, Herrara reported your capture, and that you had sacrificed yourself and one of the companies to secure the safety of the rest. Now come in. This is Colonel O'Connor, sir," Major Nelson said, as he entered the adjutant-general's room. "I could not resist the pleasure of bringing him in to you. He has just escaped from Bayonne, and landed an hour ago."

"I am glad to see you, indeed," the adjutant-general said, rising and shaking Terence warmly by the hand. "The last time we met was on the day when Victor attacked us in the afternoon, after sending the Spaniards flying. You rendered us good service that evening, and still greater by acquainting the commander-in-chief of the large force that had gathered in his rear—a force at least three times as strong as we had reckoned on; a day later, and we should have been overwhelmed. As it was, we had just time to cross the Tagus before they were ready to fall upon us. I am sure Lord Wellington will be gratified indeed to hear that you are back again. I suppose you will like to return to your command of the Minho regiment?"

"I should prefer that to anything else," Terence said, "though, of course, I am ready to undertake any other duty that you might intrust to me."

"No, I think it would be for the good of the service that you should remain as you are. The difficulty of obtaining anything like accurate information of the strength and position of the enemy is one of the greatest we have to contend with; and, indeed, were it not for Trant's command and yours, we should be almost in the dark. Please sit down for a minute. I will inform Lord Wellington of your return."

Chapter IX
Rejoining

The adjutant-general returned in two or three minutes.

"Will you please come this way, Colonel O'Connor," he said, as he re-entered the room; "the commander-in-chief wishes to speak to you."

"I am glad to see you back, Colonel O'Connor," Lord Wellington said cordially, but in his usual quick short manner. "The last time I saw you was at Salamende. You did well at Talavera, and better still afterwards, when the information I received from you was the only trustworthy news obtained during the campaign, and was simply invaluable. Sir John Cradock did me no better service than by recognising your merits, and speaking so strongly to me in your favour that I retained you in command of the corps that you had raised. I shall be glad to know that you are again at their head when the campaign reopens, for I know that I can rely implicitly upon you for information. Of course, your name has been removed from the list of my staff since you were taken prisoner, but it shall appear in orders to-morrow again. I shall be glad if you will dine with me this evening."

"I wish I had a few more young officers like that," he said to the adjutant-general, when Terence had bowed and retired. "He is full of energy, and ready to undertake any wild adventure, and yet he is as prudent and thoughtful as most men double his age. I like his face. He has a right to be proud of the position he has won, but there is not the least nonsense about him, and he evidently has no idea that he has done anything out of the ordinary course. At first sight he looks a mere good-tempered lad, but the lower part of his face is marked by such resolution and firmness that it goes far to explain why he has succeeded."

REJOINING

There were but four other officers dining with the commander-in-chief that evening. Lord Wellington asked Terence several questions as to the route the convoy of prisoners had followed, the treatment they had received, and the nature of the roads, and whether the Spanish guerillas were in force. Terence gave a brief account of the attack that had been made on the French convoy, and the share that he and his fellow-prisoners had taken in the affair—at which Lord Wellington's usually impassive face lighted up with a smile.

"That was a somewhat irregular proceeding, Colonel O'Connor."

"I am afraid so, sir; but after their treatment by the Spaniards when in the hospital at Talavera, our men were so furious against them that I believe they would have fought them even had I endeavoured to hold them back, which, indeed, being a prisoner, I do not know that I should have had any authority to do."

"And how did you escape from Bayonne?" the general asked.

"Through the good offices of some of the soldiers who had been our escort, sir. They were on duty as a prison guard, and, being grateful for the help that we had given them in the affair with the guerillas, they aided me to escape."

"And how did you manage afterwards?"

Terence related very briefly the adventures that he and his companion had had before at last reaching Jersey.

On leaving, the adjutant-general requested him to call in the morning before starting to rejoin his regiment, as he expressed his intention of doing.

The talk was a long and friendly one, the adjutant-general asking many questions as to the constitution of his corps.

"There is one thing I should like very much, sir," Terence said, after he had finished. "It would be a great assistance to me if I had an English officer as adjutant."

"Do you mean one for each battalion, or one for the two?"

"I think that one for both battalions would answer the purpose, sir; it would certainly be of great assistance to me, and take a great many details off my hands."

"I certainly think that you do need assistance. Is there anyone you would specially wish to be appointed?"

"This is Colonel O' Connor, sir."

REJOINING

"I should be very glad to have Lieutenant Ryan, who has been with me on my late journey. We are old friends, as I was in the Mayo regiment with him; he speaks Portuguese very fairly. Of course, it would be useless for me to have an officer who did not do so. I should certainly prefer him to anyone else."

"That is easily managed," the officer replied. "I will put him in orders to-day as appointed adjutant to the Minho Portuguese regiment, with the acting rank of captain. I will send a note to Lord Beresford stating the reason for the appointment, for, as you and your officers owe your local rank to him, he may feel that he ought to have been specially informed of Ryan's appointment, although your corps is in no way under his orders, but acting with the British army."

"I am very much obliged to you, indeed, sir; it will be a great comfort to me to have an adjutant, and it will naturally be much more pleasant to have one upon whom I know I can depend absolutely. Indeed, I have been rather in an isolated position so far. The majors of the two battalions naturally associate with their own officers; consequently Colonel Herrara has been my only intimate friend, and although he is a very good fellow, one longs sometimes for the companionship of a brother Englishman."

Terence had not told Dick Ryan of his intention to ask for him as his adjutant. When he joined him at the hotel he saluted him with:

"Well, Captain Ryan, have you everything ready for the start?"

"I have, General," Dick replied with a grin, "or perhaps I ought to say Field-marshal."

"Not yet, Dicky, not yet; and, indeed, possibly I am premature myself in addressing you as captain."

"Rather; I should say I have a good many steps to make before I get my company."

"Well, Dick, I can tell you, that when the orders come out to-day you will see your name among them as appointed adjutant to the Minho Portuguese regiment, with acting rank as captain."

"Hurrah!" Ryan shouted. "You don't say that you have managed it, old fellow? I am delighted. This is glorious. I am awfully obliged to you."

"I think, Dick, we will make up our minds not to start until this evening. You know we had arranged to hire a vehicle, and that I should get a horse when I joined, but I think now we may as well buy the horses at once, for of course you will be mounted too. We might pay a little more for them, but we should save the expense of the carriage."

"That would be much better," Dick said. "Let us go and get them at once. There must be plenty of horses for sale in a place like this, and as we are both flush of money I should think that a couple of hours would do it."

"I hope it will. As I told them at headquarters that I was going to start to-day, I should not like any of them to run across me here this evening. No doubt the landlord of the hotel can tell us of some man who keeps the sort of animals we want. The saddlery we shall have no difficulty about."

Two hours later a couple of serviceable horses had been bought, with saddles, bridles, holsters and valises. In the last-named were packed necessaries for the journey, and each provided himself with a brace of double-barrelled pistols. The rest of their effects were packed in the trunks they had bought at Jersey, and were handed over to a Portuguese firm of carriers, to be sent up to the regiment. At two o'clock they mounted and rode to Sobral. The next day they rode to Santarem, and on the following evening to Abrantes.

They here learned that their corps was in camp with two other Portuguese regiments, four miles higher up the river. As it was dark when they arrived at Abrantes they agreed to sleep there and go on the next morning, as Terence wished to report himself to General Hill, to whose division the regiment was attached until operations should commence in the spring. They put up at an inn, and, having eaten a meal, walked out into the town, which was full of British soldiers. They were not long before they found the café that was set apart for the use of officers, and on entering, Terence at once joined a party of three, belonging to a regiment with all of whose officers he was acquainted, as they had encamped next to the Mayo Fusileers during the long months preceding the advance up the valley of the Tagus. Ryan was, of course, equally known to them, and the three officers rose with an exclamation of surprise as the newcomers walked up to the table.

REJOINING

"Why, O'Connor! How in the world did you get here? How are you, Ryan? I thought that you were both prisoners."

"So we were," Terence said, "but, as you see, we gave them the slip and here we are."

They drew up chairs to the little table. "You may consider yourself lucky in your regiment being on the river, O'Connor; you will be much better off than Ryan will be at Portalegre."

"I am seconded," Ryan said, "and have been appointed O'Connor's adjutant, with the temporary rank of captain."

"I congratulate you. The chances are you will have a much better time of it than if you were with your own regiment. I don't mean now, but when the campaign begins in the spring. O'Connor always seems to be in the thick of it, while our division may remain here while the fighting is going on somewhere else. Besides, he always manages to dine a good deal better than we do. His fellows, being Portuguese, are able to get supplies, when the peasants are all ready to take their oath that they have not so much as a loaf of bread or a fowl in their village. How will you manage to get on with them, Ryan, without speaking their language? Oh! I remember, you were grinding up Portuguese all the spring, so I suppose you can get on pretty well now."

"Yes; O'Connor promised that he would ask for me as soon as I could speak the language, so I stuck at it hard, and now you see I have got my reward."

"I can tell you that the troops here are a good deal better off than they are elsewhere. There is a fearful want of land carriage, but we get our supplies up by boats; that is why the Portuguese regiments are encamped on the river.

"Well, how did you get away from the French? It is curious that when I saw O'Grady last, which was a fortnight ago, when he came in to get a conveyance to take over sundry cases of whiskey that had come up the river for the use of his mess, he said, 'I expect that O'Connor and Dick Ryan will turn up here before the spring. I am sure they will if they have got together.'"

"It is too long a story to tell here," Ryan said. "It is full of hairbreadth escapes, dangers by sea and land, and ends up with a naval battle."

The officers laughed. "Well, will you come to our quarters?" one of them said. "We have got some decent wine and some really good cigars which came up from Lisbon last week, and there are lots of fellows who will be glad to see you."

They accordingly adjourned to a large building where the officers of the regiment were quartered, and in the apartment that had been turned into a mess-room they found a dozen officers, all of whom were known both to Terence and Ryan. After many questions were asked and answered on both sides, Ryan was requested to tell the story of their adventures after being taken prisoners. He told it in an exaggerated style that elicited roars of laughter, making the most of what he called the Battle of the Shirt-sleeves with the guerillas, exaggerating the dangers of his escape, and the horrors of their imprisonment for a week among the sails and nets.

"O'Connor," he said, "has hardly got back his sense of smell yet; the stink of tar mixed with fishy odours will be vivid in my remembrance for the rest of my life."

When he had at last finished, one of them said: "And now, how much of all this is true, Ryan?"

"Every fact is just as I have told it," he replied gravely. "You may think that I have exaggerated—for did an Irishman ever tell a story without exaggeration?—but I give you my honour that never did one keep nearer to the truth than I have done. I don't say that the fisherman's wife took quite such a strong fancy to me as I have stated, although she can hardly have been insensible to my personal advantages, but really, otherwise I don't know that I have diverged far from the narrow path of truth. I tell you, those two days that we were running before that gale was a thing I never wish to go through again."

"And you really tied up the Maire of Granville, Ryan?"

"We did so," Dicky said, "and a miserable object the poor little fat man looked as he sat in his chair trussed up like a fowl."

"And now, about the sea-fight, Ryan?"

"Every word was as it happened. O'Connor and I turned gunners, and very decent shots we made too, and a proof of it was, that if we would have taken it, I believe the captain of the schooner would have given us half the booty found in the lugger's hold; but we were modest and self-denying, and contented ourselves with a third each of the cash found in the captain's cabin, which we could not have refused if we wanted to, the captain made such a point of it. It came to nearly three hundred pounds apiece, and mighty useful it was, for we had, of course, to get new uniforms and rigs-out, and horses and saddlery at Lisbon. I don't know what I should have done without it, for my family's finances would not have stood my drawing upon them, and another mortgage would have ruined them entirely."

"Well, certainly, that is a substantial proof of the truth of that incident in your story; but I think that rather than have passed forty-eight hours in that storm, I would have stopped at Bayonne and taken my chance of exchange."

"Then I am afraid, Forester, that you are deficient in martial ardour," Terence said gravely. "Our desire to be back fighting the French was so great that no dangers would have appalled us."

There was a general laugh.

"Well, at any rate, you managed uncommonly well, Ryan, whether it was martial ardour that animated you or not, and O'Connor would creep out through a mouse's hole if there was no other way of doing."

"Now, what has been doing since we have been away?" Terence asked.

"Well, to begin with, all Andalusia has been captured by Soult, Suchet has occupied Valencia, Lerida was captured by him after a scandalously weak resistance, for there were over 9000 troops there, and the place surrendered after only 1000 had fallen. Gerona, on the other hand, was only captured by Augereau after a resistance as gallant as that of Saragossa. That is the extraordinary thing about these Spaniards. Sometimes they show themselves cowardly beyond expression, at others they fight like heroes. Just at present even the Juntas do not pretend that they have an army capable of driving the French out of the Pyrenees, which is a comfort, for we shall have to rely upon ourselves and not be humbugged by the Spaniards, the worthlessness of whose promises Lord Wellington has ascertained by bitter experience. The Portuguese government is as troublesome and as ruthless as that of Spain, but Wellington is able to hold his own with them, and there is little doubt that the regular regiments will fight and be really of valuable assistance to us, but these have been raised in spite of the constant opposition of the Junta at Lisbon.

UNDER WELLINGTON'S COMMAND

"There is no doubt that the next campaign will be a hot one, for now that Spain has been as completely subdued as such vainglorious, excitable people can be subdued, the French marshals are free to join against us, and it is hard to see how, with but 30,000 men, we are going to defend Portugal against ten times that number of French. Still, I suppose we shall do it somehow. The French have a large army on the other side of the Aqueda, and there is no doubt they will besiege Ciudad Rodrigo as soon as winter is over. I doubt whether we shall be strong enough to march to its relief, and I fancy that in that direction the Coa will be about our limit. At any rate it is likely to be a stirring campaign. The absurdity of the thing is, that we have an army in Sicily which might as well be at Jericho for any use it is. If it joined us here it would make all the differences in the world, though certainly till the campaign opens it would have to be quartered at Lisbon, for it is as much as the wretched transport can do to feed us. Now the truth is, Portugal is a miserably poor country at the best of times, and does not produce enough for the wants of the people. Of course it has been terribly impoverished by the war, the fields in most places have been untilled, and in fact the greater portion of the population, as well as our army, has to be fed from England. Altogether, Wellington must have enough worry to drive an ordinary man out of his mind. I never heard of such difficulties as those he has to meet. We come to help a people who won't help themselves, but want to dictate how we shall fight. Instead of being fed by the country, we have to feed it; and the whole object of the Juntas, both in Spain and Portugal, seems to be to throw every difficulty in our way and to thwart us at every turn. The first steps towards success would be to hang every member of every Junta in every place we occupy."

A general chorus of "Hear, hear!" showed how deeply was the feeling excited by the conduct of the Portuguese and Spanish authorities. After chatting until a late hour, Terence and his companion returned to their inn.

The next morning Terence reported himself to General Hill.

"I am glad to see you again, Colonel O'Connor," the general said. "The last time we met was when the surgeons were dressing my wounds on the heights near Talavera. That was a hot business for a time."

"Yes, sir; and I have to thank you very much for the very kind report you sent in as to the conduct of my regiment."

"They deserved it," the general said. "If they had not come up at the time they did, we should have had hard work to retake that hill. Your regiment has been behaving very well since they have been here. They, like the other Portuguese regiments, have often been on short rations, and their pay is very much in arrear, but there has been no grumbling. I know Herrara will be extremely glad to have you back again in command. He has said as much several times when he has been here. He is a good man, but not strong enough for his position, and I can see that he feels that himself, and is conscious that he is not equal to the responsibility. I intended to recommend that a British officer should be placed in command of the regiment before the campaign opens in the spring. Your two majors do their best, but they have scarcely sufficient weight, for their men know that they were but troopers when the regiment was first raised."

"I shall be glad to be back again, sir; and I am pleased to say that I have been given an adjutant—Lieutenant Ryan of the Mayo Fusileers. He has the acting rank of captain. He is an old friend of mine, and is a good officer. He has just effected an escape from Bayonne with me."

"Yes, that will be of great assistance to you," the general said. "With two battalions to command, you must want a right-hand man very much. I shall be glad if your regiment remains in my division when the campaign reopens, but I suppose that, as before, you will be sent ahead. At present it is only attached to my command for convenience of rationing and pay. I have inspected it twice, and it is by far the finest of the Portuguese regiments here. But I can see a certain deterioration, and I am sure that they want you back badly. Still, it is not your loss only that is telling on them. No soldiers like to go without their pay. Lord Wellington himself is always kept short of funds. The Portuguese Ministry declare that they have none. Of course that is all a lie; but, true or false, it is certain that all Portuguese regiments are greatly in arrears of pay, ill-provided with clothes, and, indeed, would be starved were it not that they are fed by our commissariat."

After his interview with the general, Terence went back to the inn, and five minutes later started with Ryan to join the regiment. The two battalions were engaged in drill when they rode up, but as the men recognised Terence there was a sudden movement, then a tremendous cheer, and, breaking their ranks, they ran towards him, waving their shakos and shouting loudly, while Herrara, Bull, and Macwitty galloped up to shake him by the hand.

"This is not a very military proceeding," Terence laughed, "but I cannot help being gratified."

He held up his hands for silence.

"Form the men into a hollow square," he said to the majors.

In a very short time the order was carried out, and then Terence addressed them.

"My men," he said, "I am deeply gratified by your hearty reception, and I can assure you that I am quite as glad to be back in the regiment as the regiment can be to have me with it again. While I was a prisoner one of the things that troubled me most was that when I returned I might find that someone else had been appointed your commander; and I was glad indeed when, upon landing at Lisbon, I heard that this had not been the case, and that I could resume my command of a body of men of whom I am proud, and at no time more proud than when you beat off the attacks of a whole brigade of French cavalry, and made good your escape to the mountains. I regret that some of your comrades failed to do this, but the manner in which they did their duty, and sacrificed themselves to cover your retreat, was worthy of all praise, and reflects the highest credit upon the regiment.

"I have been fortunate enough to make my escape from a French prison in company with my friend here, Captain Ryan, who has, at my request, been appointed by the commander-in-chief to be your adjutant. I am sorry to hear that there have been difficulties in the way of rations, and that your pay is in arrears. However, I know well that you are not serving for the sake of pay, but to defend your country from invasion by the French; and that, whether you get your pay day by day or receive it in a lump sum later on, will make no difference to you; and, indeed, in some respects, you will be better off for the delay, for, getting it daily, it is spent as soon as obtained, whereas, if it comes in a lump sum it will be useful to you when you return to your homes after your work is done. I am confident that, in this regiment at least, which has borne itself so well from the day that it was raised, there will be neither grumbling nor discontent, but that you will suffer any hardship or privation that may come in your way as trifling incidents in the great work that you have undertaken—to defend, at the cost of your lives if need be, your country from the invader. The regiment is dismissed drill for the day."

Loud cheers at once broke from the men, and, falling out, they proceeded to their tents.

"Well, Terence, there is no doubt about the enthusiasm of your fellows," Ryan remarked. "As you said, it was hardly military; but it was better, it was real affection, and I am sure the men would follow you anywhere."

Ryan shook hands with Herrara, Bull, and Macwitty, all of whom he knew well from his frequent visits to Terence in the spring.

"I am very glad that you have come to us, Captain Ryan," Bull said. "A regiment don't seem like a regiment without an adjutant, and it will take a lot of work off the Colonel's hands. I wish there could have been one for each battalion."

"How has the regiment been going on, Bull?"

"Nothing much to grumble about, sir; but I must say that it has been more slack than it was. We have all done our best, but we have missed you terribly, and the men don't seem to take quite as much pains with their drill as they used to do when you were in command. However, that will be all right now that you have come back again. I have always found that when the battalion was not working well the men have pulled themselves together at once when I said, 'This won't do, lads; the Colonel will be grievously disappointed when he comes back again if he finds that you have lost your smartness.' It was as much as we could do to hold them in hand when they saw you surrounded by the French. They would have rushed back again to a man if we would have let them. I own I felt it hard myself to be marching away and leaving you behind."

In a few minutes a couple of tents were erected by the side of that of Herrara, and while these were being got ready for occupation, Terence and Ryan, with the two majors, entered that of Herrara, and the latter produced two or three bottles of wine from his private store, and a box of cigars. So for some time they sat chatting, Terence giving an outline of the events that had happened since he had been away from the regiment. He and Ryan had ordered half-a-dozen small casks of wine and two cases of whiskey to be sent up with their trunks by water, and now asked regarding the rations of the men.

"They get their bread regularly," Herrara said. "They have put up some large bakeries at Abrantes, and as the flour is brought up in boats, there is no difficulty that way. They get their meat pretty regularly, and their wine always. There is no ground of complaint whatever as to rations here, though, from what I hear, it is very different at the stations where everything has to be taken up by waggons or mules. The difficulty is with the uniforms. Not one has been served out, and it is really difficult to get the men to look smart when many of them are dressed almost in rags. It is still worse in the matter of boots. A great many of them were badly cut when we were in the mountains, and especially in the rough march we had over the hills after you left us. The men themselves would greatly prefer sandals to boots, being more accustomed to them, and could certainly march farther in them than in stiff English boots. But, of course, it would be of no use sending in any requisition for them."

"I don't see why they should not wear sandals," Terence said; "at any rate, until there is an issue of boots. I suppose the men can make them themselves."

"In most cases, no doubt, they could. At any rate, those who could, would make them for the others. Of course they will all have to wear them of one colour, but as most of the cattle are black, there would be no difficulty about that."

"I have no doubt that we could get any number of hides at a nominal price from the commissariat. At any rate, I will see about it. I suppose they are made a good deal like Indian moccasins. I noticed that many of the Spanish troops wore them, but I did not examine them particularly."

"They are very easily made," Herrara said. "You put your foot on a piece of hide of the right size. It is drawn right up over the foot and laced. Another thickness of hide is sewn at the bottom to form the sole, and there it is. Of course, for work in the hills it might be well to use a double thickness of hide for the sole. The upper part is made of the thinnest portion of the hide, and if grease is rubbed well inside, so as to soften the leather as much as possible, it makes the most comfortable footgear possible."

"Well, we will try it, anyhow, " Terence said. "It may not look so soldierly, but at any rate it would look as well as boots with the toes out; and if any general inspects us and objects to them, we can say that we shall be perfectly ready to give them up as soon as boots are issued to us. But by using all black hides I really do not think that it will look bad; and there would certainly be the advantage that, for a night attack, the tread would be much more noiseless than that of a heavy boot. I really like the idea very much. The best plan will be to pick out two or three score of men who are shoemakers by trade, and pay them a trifle for the making of each pair. In that way we could get much greater uniformity than were each man to make his own. As to the clothes, I don't see that anything can be done about it beyond getting a supply of needles and thread, and seeing that every hole is mended as well as possible. I dare say new uniforms will be served out before the spring. It does not matter much in camp, and I suppose we are no worse than the other Portuguese regiments."

The next week was spent in steady drill, and by the end of that time the exercises were all done as smartly as before. Terence had already tried the experiment of sandals. The commissariat at Abrantes were glad enough to supply hides at a nominal price. He began by taking a dozen. These were first handed to a number of men relieved from their other duties, who, after scraping the under side, rubbed them with fat, and kneaded them until they were perfectly soft and pliable. The shoemakers then took them in hand, and after a few samples of various shapes were tried, one was fixed upon, in which the sandal was bound to the foot by straps of the same material, with a double thickness of sole. Terence tried these himself, and found them extremely comfortable for walking, and gave orders that one company should be entirely provided with them. As to appearance, they were vastly superior to the cracked and bulged boots the men were wearing.

UNDER WELLINGTON'S COMMAND

After a week of sharp drill Terence was satisfied, and proposed to Ryan that they should now ride over to Portalegre and pay a visit to their friends of the Fusileers, and accordingly the next day they went over. They were most heartily received.

"Sure, Terence, I knew well enough that you and Dicky Ryan would be back here before long. And so you have taken him from us! Well, it is a relief to the regiment, and I only hope that, now he is an adjutant, he will learn manners and behave with a little more discretion than he has ever shown before. How you could have saddled yourself with such a harebrained lad is more than I can imagine."

"That is all very well, O'Grady," Ryan laughed, "but it is a question of the pot calling the kettle black, only in this case the pot is a good deal blacker than the kettle. There may be some excuse for a subaltern like me, but none for a war-scarred veteran like yourself."

"Dick will do very well, O'Grady," Terence said. "I can tell you he sits in his tent and does his officer work as steadily as if he had been at it all his life, and if you had seen him drilling a battalion you would be delighted; it is just jealousy that makes you run him down, O'Grady—you were too lazy to learn Portuguese yourself."

"Is it lazy you say that I am, Terence? There is no more active officer in the regiment, and you know it; as for the heathen language, it is not fit for an honest tongue. They ought to have sent over a supply of grammars and dictionaries and taught the whole nation to speak English. When did you get back?"

"A week ago; but we have been too busy drilling the regiment to come over before. How are you getting on here, Colonel?"

"We are not getting on at all, O'Connor. It is worse than stationary we are. They ought to put on double the number of carts they allow us. Half the time we are on short rations, except wine, which, thank Heaven, the commissariat can buy in the country. It is evil times that we have fallen upon, and how we shall do when the snow begins to fall heavily is more than I can tell you."

"At any rate, Colonel, from what I hear, you are a good deal better off than the division at Guarda, for you are but a day's march from the river."

"The carts take two days over it," the colonel said, "and then bring next to nothing, for the poor bastes that draw them are half-starved, and it is as much as they can do to crawl along. They might just as well keep the whole division at Abrantes instead of sticking half of them out here, just as if the French were going to attack us now. There is the luncheon bugle. After we have done you may tell us how you and Ryan got out of the hands of the French, for I suppose you were not exchanged."

Chapter X
Almeida

The winter was long and tedious, but whenever the weather permitted, Terence set his men at work, taking them twice a week for long marches, so as to keep their powers in that direction unabated. The sandals turned out a great success. The men had no greatcoats, but they supplied the want by cutting a slit in the centre of their black blankets, and passing the head through it; this answered all the purposes, and hid the shabby condition of their uniforms. General Hill occasionally rode over to inspect this and the other Portuguese regiments encamped near them.

"That is a very good plan of yours, Colonel O'Connor," he said, the first time the whole regiment turned out in their sandals; "it is much more sensible footgear than the boots."

"I should not have adopted them, General, if the men had had any boots to put on, but those they had became absolutely unwearable. Some of the soles were completely off, the upper leathers were so cut and worn that they were literally of no use, and in many cases they were falling to pieces. The men like the sandals much better, and certainly march with greater ease. Yesterday they did thirty miles and came in comparatively fresh."

"I wish the whole army were shod so," the general said. "It would improve their marching powers, and we should not have so many men laid up footsore. I should say that the boots supplied to the army are the very worst that soldiers were ever cursed with; they are heavy, they are nearly as hard as iron when the weather is dry, and are as rotten as blotting-paper when it is wet. It is quite an accident if a man gets a pair to fit him properly. I believe it would be better if they were trained to march barefooted; their feet would soon get hardened, and at any rate it would be an improvement on the boots now served out to them.

"I wish the other Portuguese regiments were as well drilled and as well set up as your fellows. Of course, your men don't look smart at present, and would not make a good show on a parade-ground; but I hear that there are a large quantity of uniforms coming out shortly, and I hope, long before the campaign opens, they will all be served out. The British regiments are almost as badly off as the native ones. However, I suppose matters will right themselves before the spring, but they are almost as badly off now as they were when they marched into Corunna. The absurdity of the whole thing is that all the newly-raised Portuguese levies, who will certainly not be called upon to cross the frontier until next year, have got uniforms, while the men who have to do the work are almost in rags."

Two or three of the officers of the Fusileers rode over frequently to stop for a night or so with Terence; and the latter found time pass much more pleasantly then he had done before Ryan had joined him. During the day both their hands were full, but the evenings were very pleasant now that he had Dick as well as Herrara to talk to. The feeling of the responsibility on his shoulders steadied Ryan a good deal, and he was turning out a far more useful assistant than Terence had expected; but when work was over, his spirits were as high as ever, and the conversation in Terence's tent seldom languished.

Spring came, but there was no movement on the part of the troops. Ney, with 50,000 men, began the siege of Ciudad Rodrigo in earnest. The Agueda had now become fordable, and Crauford, with his light brigade, 2500 strong, was exposed to a sudden attack at any time. On the 1st of June, Terence received orders to march with his regiment to Guarda, where Wellington was concentrating the greater portion of his army, leaving Hill with 12,000 men to guard the southern portion of the frontier. Both the Spanish and Portuguese urged the general to relieve Ciudad Rodrigo, but Wellington refused steadily to hazard the whole fortune of the campaign on an enterprise which was unlikely to succeed. His total force was but 56,000 men, of whom 20,000 were untried Portuguese. Garrisons had to be placed at several points, and 8000 Portuguese were posted at Thomar, a day's march from Abrantes, as a reserve for Hill. It was not only the 50,000 infantry and 8000 cavalry of Massena, who now commanded, in front of Ciudad Rodrigo, that he had to reckon with. Regnier's division was at Coria, and could in three easy marches reach Guarda, or in four fall on Hill at Abrantes, and with but 26,000 men in line it would have been a desperate enterprise indeed to attack 60,000 veteran French soldiers merely for the sake of carrying off the 5000 undisciplined Portuguese besieged at Ciudad.

The Minho regiment had only received their new uniforms a month before the order came, and made a good show as they marched into Guarda, where Wellington's headquarters were now established. When Terence reported himself to the adjutant-general the latter said:

"At present, Colonel O'Connor, you cannot be employed in your former work of scouting. The French are altogether too powerful for a couple of battalions to approach them, and with 8000 cavalry they would make short work of you. Crauford must soon fall back behind the Coa; his position already is a very hazardous one. It has therefore been decided to place 1500 of your men along on this side of the Coa, and with half a battalion you will march at once to Almeida to strengthen the garrison of that place, which, as soon as Crauford retires, is certain to be besieged. It should be able to offer a long and stout resistance. You will, of course, be under the general orders of the commandant, but you will receive an authorization to take independent action should you think fit: that is to say, if you find the place can be no longer defended and the commandant is intending to surrender, you are at liberty to withdraw your command if you find it possible to do so."

On the following morning the corps left Guarda, and, leaving a battalion and a half on the Coa under Herrara, Terence, with 500 men, after a long march, entered Almeida that night. The town, which was fortified, was occupied only by Portuguese troops. It was capable of repulsing a sudden attack, but was in no condition to withstand a regular siege. It was deficient in magazines and bomb-proofs, and the powder, of which there was a large supply, was stored in an old castle in the middle of the town. On entering the place, Terence at once called upon Colonel Cox, who was in command.

"I am glad that you have come, Colonel O'Connor," the latter said. "I know that Lord Wellington expects me to make a long defence, and to keep Massena here for at least a month, but although I mean to do my best, I cannot conceal from myself that the defences are terribly defective. Then, too, more than half my force are newly-levied militia, in whom very little dependence can be placed. Your men will be invaluable in case of assault, but it is not assault I fear so much as having the place tumbled about our ears by their artillery, which can be so placed as to command it from several points. We are very short of artillery, and the guns are well-nigh as old as the fortifications."

"We will do our best, Colonel, in any direction you may point out, and I think that we could defend a breach against any reasonable force brought against it. I may say that I have been ordered, if the worst comes to the worst, to endeavour to make my way out of the town before it surrenders."

For a fortnight the place was left unmolested. Crauford's division still kept beyond the Coa, and his cavalry had had several engagements with French reconnoitring parties. On the 2nd of July, however, the news came that, after a most gallant resistance, Ciudad Rodrigo had surrendered, and it was now certain that the storm would roll westward in a very short time. Massena, however, delayed strangely, and it was not until daylight on the 24th that a sudden roll of musketry, followed almost immediately by a heavy artillery fire, told the garrison of Almeida that the light division was suddenly attacked by the enemy.

Crauford had received the strictest orders not to fight beyond Coa, but he was an obstinate man, and had so long maintained his position across the river that he believed that if attacked he should be able to withdraw over the bridge before any very strong force could be brought up to attack him. In this he was mistaken; the country was wooded, and the French march was unsuspected until they were close upon Crauford's force. The light division had, however, been well trained; indeed, it was composed of veteran regiments, and had been practised to get under arms with the least possible delay. They were, therefore, already drawn up when the French fell upon them, and, fighting hard and sternly, repelled all the efforts of the enemy's cavalry to cut them off from the bridge. Driving back the French light infantry, the light division crossed in safety, although with considerable loss, and repulsed with great slaughter every attempt of the French to cross the bridge.

Almeida was now left to its fate. Again Massena delayed, and it was not until the 18th of August that the siege was begun. On the 26th, sixty-five heavy guns that had been used in the siege of Ciudad

Rodrigo opened fire upon the town. The more Terence saw of the place the more convinced was he that it could not long be held after the French siege-guns had been placed in position. Moreover, there was great lukewarmness on the part of several of the Portuguese officers, while the rank and file were dispirited by the fate of Ciudad Rodrigo, and by the fact that they had, as it seemed to them, been deserted by the British army.

"I don't like the look of things at all," he had said to Bull and Ryan the evening before the siege-guns began their work. "In the first place, the defences will crumble in no time under the French fire; in the second place, I don't think that the Portuguese, with the exception of our own men, have any fight in them. Da Costa, the lieutenant-governor, openly declares that the place is indefensible, and that it is simply throwing away the lives of the men to resist. He is very intimate, I observe, with Bareiros, the chief of the artillery. Altogether, things look very bad. Of course we shall stay here as long as the place resists, but I am afraid that won't be for very long.

"I was speaking to Colonel Cox this afternoon. He is a brave man, and with trustworthy troops would, I am sure, hold the town until the last, but, unsupported as he is, he is in the hands of these rascally Portuguese officers. I told him that if he ordered me to do so, I would undertake with my men to arrest the whole of them, but he said that that would bring on a mutiny of all their troops, and this, bad as the situation already was, would only make matters much worse. I then suggested that, as the French are driving their trenches towards those two old redoubts outside the wall, I would, if he liked, place our force in them, and would undertake to hold them, pointing out that if they fell into the hands of the enemy they would soon mount their cannon there and bring down the whole wall facing in that direction. He quite agreed with that view of the case, but said that it would be a very exposed position; still, as our fellows were certainly the only trustworthy troops he had, he should be very glad if I would undertake the defence at once, as the French were pushing their approaches very fast towards them. I said that I was sure we could hold them for some little time, and that indeed it seemed to me that the French intended to bombard the town rather than to breach the walls, knowing the composition of the garrison, and perhaps having intelligence that their courage would be so shaken by a heavy fire that the place would surrender in a much shorter time than it would take to breach the walls.

"Accordingly he has given me leave to march our men up there at daybreak to-morrow, taking with us ten days' provisions. I said that if he had trouble with the other Portuguese regiments I would, on his hoisting a red flag on the church steeple, march in at once to seize and shoot the leaders of the mutiny if he wished it. Of course, one of my reasons for wanting to take charge of the redoubts was that we should have more chance of withdrawing from them than we should of getting out of the town itself in the confusion and panic of an approaching surrender."

Bull and Ryan both agreed with Terence, and at daybreak the next morning the half-battalion marched out, relieved the Portuguese troops holding the two redoubts, and established themselves there. They had brought with them a number of intrenching tools, and were accompanied by an engineer officer. So, as soon as they reached the redoubts several parties of men were set to work to begin to sink pits for driving galleries in the direction of the approaches that the French were pushing forward, while others assisted a party of artillerymen to work the guns. Some of the best shots in the corps took their places on the rampart, and were directed to maintain a steady fire on the French working parties.

The roar of cannon when the French batteries opened fire on the town was prodigious, and it was not long before it was evident that there was no present design on the part of the French to effect a breach.

"I expect they have lots of friends in the town," Terence said to Dick Ryan, as they watched the result of the fire, "and they make sure that the garrison will very soon lose heart. Do you see how many shots are striking the old castle? That looks as if the French knew that it was the magazine. They are dropping shell there, too, and that alone is enough to cause a scare in the town, for if one of them dropped into the magazine the consequences would be terrific. They are not pushing on the trenches against us with anything like the energy with which they have been working for the past week, and it is certainly curious that they should not keep up a heavier fire from their batteries upon us, for it is evident that they cannot make an assault on this side of the town at any rate until they have captured our redoubts."

"I wish we were well out of it," Ryan exclaimed. "It is quite certain that the place must fall sooner or later, and though we might beat the French back several times, it must come to the same in the end. The thing I am most concerned about at present is how we are to get away."

"I quite agree with you, Dick; and you know we have had several looks at the French lines from the roof of the church. Their batteries are chiefly on this side, so as to be in readiness to meet any attempt of Wellington to succour the place, and also to show the garrison that there is no chance whatever of their being able to draw off. We agreed that the chances would be much better of getting out on this side than on the other."

"Yes; but we also agreed, Terence, that there would be a good deal more difficulty in getting safely back, for practically the whole of their army would be between us and Wellington."

"It will be a difficult business, Dicky, whichever way we go, and I suppose that, at last, we shall have to be guided by circumstances."

In a very short time fires broke out at several points in the town. The guns on the walls made but a very feeble reply to the French batteries, and one or two bastions, where alone a brisk fire was at first maintained, drew upon themselves such a storm of missiles from the French guns that they were soon silenced.

"It is quite evident that the Portuguese gunners have not much fight in them," Bull said.

"I am afraid it is the disaffection among their officers that is paralysing them," Terence said. "But I quite admit that it may be good policy to keep the men under cover. They really could do no good against the French batteries, which have all the advantage of position as well as numbers and weight of metal; and it would certainly be well to reserve the troops till the French drive their trenches close up. If I thought that the silence of the guns on the walls were due to that, I should be well content, but I am afraid it is nothing of the sort. If the French keep up their fire as at present for another forty-eight hours, the place will throw open its gates. The inhabitants must be suffering frightfully. Of course, if Colonel Cox had men he could thoroughly rely upon, he would be obliged to harden his heart and disregard the clamour of the townspeople for surrender; but as the garrison is pretty certain to make common cause with them, it seems to me that the place is lost if the bombardment continues."

In a short time, seeing that the working parties in the enemy's trenches made no attempt to push them farther forward, Terence withdrew the men from their exposed position on the ramparts, leaving only a few there on the look-out, and told the rest to lie down on the inner slopes, so as to be in shelter from the French fire. Bull was in command of the force in the other redoubt, which was a quarter of a mile away. The redoubts were, however, connected by a deep ditch, so that communication could be kept up between them, or reinforcements sent from one to the other, unobserved by the enemy except by those on one or two elevated spots. All day the roar of the cannon continued; from a dozen points smoke and flame rose from the city, and towards these the French batteries chiefly directed their fire in order to hinder the efforts of the garrison to check the progress of the conflagration.

Just after dark, as Ryan and Terence were sitting down in an angle of the bastion to eat their supper, there was a tremendous roar, accompanied by so terrible a shock that both were thrown prostrate upon the ground with a force that, for the moment, half-stunned them. A broad glare of light illuminated the sky; there was the rumble and roar of falling buildings and walls, and then came dull, crashing sounds as masses of brickwork, hurled high up into the air, fell over the town and the surrounding country. Then came a dead silence, which was speedily broken by the sound of loud screams and shouts from the town.

"It is just as we feared," Terence said, as, bruised and bewildered, he struggled to his feet. "The magazine in the castle has exploded."

He ordered the bugler to sound the assembly, and, as the men gathered, it was found that although many of them had been hurt severely by the violence with which they had been thrown down, none had been killed either by the shock or the falling fragments. An officer was at once sent to the other redoubt to inquire how they had fared, and to give orders to Bull to keep his men under arms, lest the French should take advantage of the catastrophe and make a sudden attack.

"Ryan, do you take the command of the men here until I come back. I will go into the town and see Colonel Cox. I fear that the damage will be so great that the town will be really no longer defensible, and, even if it were, the Portuguese troops will be so cowed that there will be no more fight left in them."

It was but five hundred yards to the wall. Terence was unchallenged as he ran up. The gate was open, and on entering he saw that the disaster greatly exceeded his expectations. The castle had been shattered into fragments, the church levelled to the ground, and of the whole town only six houses remained standing. Five hundred people had been killed, the wildest confusion prevailed, the soldiers were running about without object or purpose, apparently scared out of their senses; women were shrieking and wringing their hands by the ruins of their houses; men were frantically tugging at beams and masses of brickwork to endeavour to rescue their friends buried under the ruins. Presently he came upon Colonel Cox, who had just been joined by Captain Hewitt, the only British officer with him, who had instantly gone off to see the amount of damage done to the defences, and had brought back news that the walls had been levelled in several places, and the guns thrown into the ditch.

Da Costa, Bareiros, and several other Portuguese officers were loudly clamouring for instant surrender, and the French shells again beginning to fall into the town added to the prevailing terror. In vain the commandant endeavoured to still the tumult, and to assure those around him that the defence might yet be continued for a short time, and better terms be obtained than if they were at once to surrender.

"Can I do anything, Colonel?" Terence said. "My men are still available."

The officer shook his head. "Massena will see in the morning," he said, "that he has but to march in. If these men would fight, we could still perhaps defend the breaches for a day or two. But it would only be useless slaughter. However, as they won't fight, I must send a flag of truce out and endeavour to make terms. At any rate, Colonel O'Connor, if you can manage to get off with your command, by all means do so. Of course, I shall endeavour to obtain terms for the garrison to march out, but I fear that Massena will hear of nothing but unconditional surrender."

"Thank you, Colonel. Then I shall at once return to my corps and endeavour to make my way through."

On returning to the redoubt, Terence sent a message to Bull to come to him at once, and when he arrived, told him and Ryan the state of things in the town, and the certainty that it would surrender at once.

"The Portuguese are so clamorous," he said, "that a flag of truce may be despatched to Massena in half an hour's time. The Portuguese are right so far that if the place must be surrendered, there is no reason for any longer exposing the troops and the townsfolk to the French bombardment. Therefore, it is imperative that, if we are to make our way out, we must do so before the place surrenders. We agreed yesterday as to the best line to take; the French force here is by no means considerable, their main body being between this and the Coa. Massena, knowing the composition of the garrison here, did not deem it requisite to send a larger force than was necessary to protect the batteries, and the major portion of these are on the heights behind the city. Between the road leading to Escalon and that through Fort Conception there is no French camp, and it is by that line we must make our escape.

"We know that there are considerable forces somewhere near Villa Puerca, but when we reach the river Turones we can follow its banks down with very little fear. It is probable that they have a force at the bridge near S. Felices; but I believe the river is fordable in many places now. At any rate, they are not likely to be keeping a sharp watch anywhere to-night. They must all know that that tremendous explosion will have rendered the place untenable, and except at the batteries which are still firing there will be no great vigilance, especially on this side, for it would hardly be supposed that, even if the garrison did attempt to escape, they would take the road to the east, and so cut themselves off from their allies and enter a country wholly French. Of course with us the case is different. We can march farther and faster than any French infantry. The woods afford abundant places of concealment, and we are perfectly capable of driving off any small bodies of cavalry that we may meet.

Fortunately we have eight days' provision of biscuit. Of course it was with a view to this that I proposed that we should bring out so large a supply with us. Now I think we had better start at once."

"I quite agree with you, Colonel," Bull said. "I will return to the other redoubt and form the men up at once. I shall be ready in a quarter of an hour."

"Very well, Bull. I will move out from here in a quarter of an hour from the present time, and march across and join you as you come out. We must round between your redoubt and the town. In that way we shall avoid the enemy's trenches altogether."

The men were at once ordered to fall in. Fortunately, none were so seriously disabled as to be unfit to take their places in the ranks. The necessity for absolute silence was impressed upon them, and they were told to march very carefully, as a fall over a stone and the crash of a musket on the rocks might at once call the attention of a French sentinel. As the troops filed out through the entrance of the redoubt, Terence congratulated himself upon their all having sandals, for the sound of their tread was faint indeed to what it would have been had they been marching in heavy boots. At the other redoubt they were joined by Bull with his party. There was a momentary halt, while six men, picked for their intelligence, went on ahead, under the command of Ryan.

They were to move twenty paces apart. If they came upon any solitary sentinel one man was to be sent back instantly to stop the column, while two others crawled forward and surprised and silenced the sentry. Should their way be arrested by a strong picket they were to reconnoitre the ground on either side, and then one was to be sent back to guide the column so as to avoid the picket.

When he calculated that Ryan must be nearly a quarter of a mile in advance, Terence gave the orders for the column to move forward. When a short distance had been traversed, one of the scouts came in with the news that there was a cordon of sentries across their path. They were some fifty paces apart, and some must be silenced before the march could be continued.

Ten minutes later another scout brought in news that four of the French sentries had been surprised and killed without any alarm being given, and the column resumed its way, the necessity for silence being again impressed upon the men. As they went forward they

ALMEIDA

received news that two more of the sentries had been killed, and that there was in consequence a gap of 350 yards between them. A scout led the way through the opening thus formed. It was an anxious ten minutes, but the passage was effected without any alarm being given, the booming of the guns engaged in bombarding the town helping to cover the sound of their footsteps. It had been settled that Ryan and the column were both to march straight for a star low down on the horizon, so that there was no fear of either taking the wrong direction. In another half-hour they were sure that they were well beyond the French lines, whose position, indeed, could be made out by the light of their bivouac fires.

For three hours they continued their march at a rapid pace without a check, then they halted for half an hour, and then held on their way till daybreak, when they entered a large village. They had left the redoubts at nine o'clock, and it was now five, so that they had marched at least twenty-five miles, and were within some ten miles of the Aqueda. Sentries were posted at the edge of the wood, and the troops then lay down to sleep. Several times during the day parties of French cavalry were seen moving about, but they were going at a leisurely pace, and there was no appearance of their being engaged in any search. At nightfall the troops got under arms again, and made their way to the Aqueda.

A peasant, whom they fell in with soon after they started, had undertaken to show them a ford. It was breast-deep, but the stream was not strong and they crossed without difficulty, holding their arms and ammunition well above the water. They learned that there was, indeed, a French brigade at the bridge of S. Felices. Marching north now they came before daybreak upon the Douro. Here they again lay up during the day, and that evening obtained two boats at a village near the mouth of the Tormes, and crossed into the Portuguese province of Tras os Montes.

The 500 men joined in a hearty cheer on finding themselves safe in their own country. After halting for a couple of days Terence marched to Castel Rodrigo, and then, learning that the main body of the regiment was at Pinhel, marched there and joined them, for it had been supposed that he and the half-battalion had been captured at the fall of Almeida. The Portuguese regular troops at that place had, at the surrender at daybreak after the explosion, all taken service with the French, while the militia regiments had been disbanded by Massena and allowed to return to their homes.

From here Terence sent off his report to headquarters, and asked for orders. The adjutant-general wrote back, congratulating him on having successfully brought off his command, and ordering the corps to take post at Linares. He found that another disaster similar to that at Almeida had taken place, the magazine at Albuquerque having been blown up by lightning, causing the loss of four hundred men. The French army were still behind the Coa, occupied in restoring the fortifications of Almeida and Ciudad Rodrigo, and it was not until the 17th of September that Massena crossed the Coa and began the invasion of Portugal in earnest, his march being directed towards Coimbra, by taking which line he hoped to prevent Hill, in the south, from effecting a junction with Wellington.

The latter, however, had made every preparation for retreat, and as soon as he found that Massena was in earnest he sent word to Hill to join him on the Alva, and fell back in that direction himself.

Terence received orders to co-operate with 10,000 of the Portuguese militia, under the command of Trant. Wilson and Miller were to harass Massena's right flank and rear. Had Wellington's orders been carried out, Massena would have found the country deserted by its inhabitants and entirely destitute of provisions, but as usual his orders had been thwarted by the Portuguese government, who sent secret instructions to the local authorities to take no steps to carry them out; and the result was that Massena, as he advanced, found ample stores for provisioning his army.

The speed with which Wellington fell back baffled his calculations, and by the time he approached Viseu, the whole British army was united near Coimbra. His march had been delayed two days by an attack made by Trant and Terence upon the advanced guard as it was making its way through a defile. A hundred prisoners were taken, with some baggage, and a serious blow would have been struck at the French had not the Portuguese levies been seized with panic and fled in confusion; Trant was, consequently, obliged to draw off. The attack, however, had been so resolute and well-directed that

ALMEIDA

Massena, not knowing the strength of the force opposing him, halted for two days until the whole army came up, and thus afforded time for the British to concentrate and make their arrangements.

The ground chosen by Wellington to oppose Massena's advance was on the edge of the Sierra Busaco, which was separated by a deep and narrow valley from the series of hills across which the French were marching. There were four roads by which the French could advance; the one from Mortagao, which was narrow and little used, passed through Royalva, the other three led to the position occupied by the British force between the village of Busaco and Pena Cova. Trant's command was posted at Royalva. Terence with his regiment took post with a Portuguese brigade of cavalry on the heights above S. Marcella, where the road leading south to Espinel forked, a branch leading from it across the Mondego, in the rear of the British position, to Coimbra. Here he could be aided, if necessary, by the guns at Pena Cova, on the opposite side of the river.

While the British were taking up their ground between Busaco and Pena Cova, Ney and Regnier arrived on the crest of the opposite hill. Had they attacked at once, as Ney wished, they might have succeeded, for the divisions of Spenser, Leith, and Hill had not yet arrived. But Massena was ten miles in the rear, and did not come up until next day with Junot's corps, by which time the whole of the British army was ranged along the opposite heights.

Their force could be plainly made out from the French position, and so formidable were the heights that had to be scaled by an attacking force, that Ney, impetuous and brave as he was, no longer advocated an attack. Massena, however, was bent upon fighting. He had every confidence in the valour of his troops, and was averse to retiring from Portugal baffled, by the long and rugged road he had travelled; therefore dispositions were at once made for the attack. Ney and Regnier were to storm the British position, while Junot's corps was to be held in reserve.

At daybreak on the 29th the French descended the hill, Ney's troops, in three columns of attack, moving against a large convent towards the British left centre, while Regnier, in two columns, advanced against the centre.

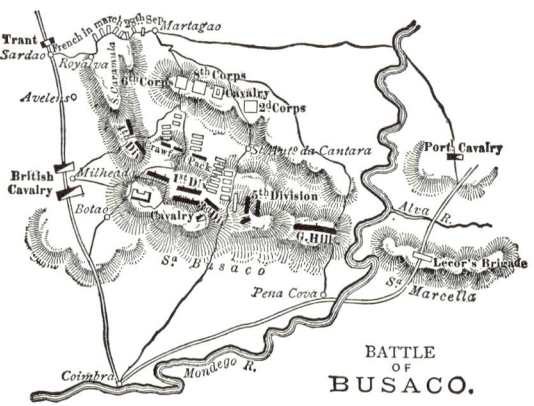

Regnier's men were the first engaged, and, mounting the hill with great gallantry and resolution, pushed the skirmishers of Picton's division before them, and in spite of the grape fire of a battery of six guns, almost gained the summit of the hill—the leading battalions establishing themselves among the rocks there, while those behind wheeled to the right. Wellington, who was on the spot, swept the flank of this force with grape, and the 88th and a wing of the 45th charged down upon them furiously. The French, exhausted by their efforts in climbing the hill, were unable to resist the onslaught, and the English and French, mixed up together, went down the hill, the French still resisting, but unable to check their opponents, who, favoured by the steep descent, swept all before them.

In the meantime the battalions that had gained the crest held their own against the rest of the third division; and had they been followed by the troops who had wheeled off towards their right, the British position would have been cut in two. General Leith, seeing the critical state of affairs, had, as soon as he saw the third division pressed back, despatched a brigade to its assistance. It had to make a considerable detour round a ravine, but it now arrived, and, attacking with fury, drove the French grenadiers from the rocks, and pursued them with a continuous fire of musketry until they were out of range. The rest of Leith's division soon arrived, and General Hill moved his division to the position before occupied by Leith. Thus, so formidable a force was concentrated at the point where Regnier made his effort, that, having no reserves, he did not venture to renew the attack.

On their right the French had met with no better success. In front of the convent, but on lower ground, was a plateau, and on this Crauford posted the 43rd and 52nd regiments of the line in a slight dip, which concealed them from observation by the French. A quarter of a mile behind them, on the high ground close to the convent, was a regiment of German infantry. These were in full sight of the enemy. The other regiment of the light division was placed lower down the hill and supported by the guns of a battery. Two of Ney's columns advanced up the hill with great speed and gallantry, never pausing for a moment, although their ranks were swept by grape from the artillery, and a heavy musketry fire by the light troops. The latter were forced to fall back before the advance, the guns were withdrawn, and the French were within a few yards of the edge of the plateau, when Crauford launched the 43rd and 52nd regiments against them.

Wholly unprepared for such an attack, the French were hurled down the hill. Only one of their columns attempted to retrieve the disaster and advanced against the right of the light division. Here, however, they met Pack's brigade, while Crauford's artillery swept the wood through which they were ascending. Finally they were forced to retire down the hill, and the action came to an end. Never did the French fight more bravely, but the position, held by determined troops, was practically impregnable. The French loss in killed and wounded was 4500, that of the allies only 1300, the difference being caused by the fact that the French ranks throughout the action were swept with grape by the British batteries, while the French artillery could do nothing to aid their infantry.

Chapter XI
The French Advance

As there were no signs of any French force approaching the position held by the Portuguese, Terence moved his regiment a short distance forward to a point which enabled them to obtain a view right down the valley in which the conflict was taking place. He then allowed them to fall out of their ranks, knowing that in less than a minute from the call being sounded they would be under arms again, and in readiness to move in any direction required. Then, with Herrara and his three English officers, he moved a short distance away and watched the scene. As soon as Regnier's columns had crossed the bottom of the ravine, their guns along the crest opened fire on the British position facing them.

"They are too far off for grape," Terence said. "You remember, Ryan, at Corunna, how those French batteries pounded us from the crest and how little real damage they did us? A round shot does not do much more harm than a bullet, unless it strikes a column in motion or troops massed in solid formation. Those fellows are mounting the hill very fast."

"They are indeed," Ryan agreed. "You can see how the line of smoke of our skirmishers on the hillside gets higher and higher."

"I wish our regiment was there, Colonel," Bull said. "We might do some good, while here we are of no more use than if we were a hundred miles away."

"No, no, Bull, that is not the case. If the French had not seen that this position was strongly held they might have moved a division by this road, and if they had done so they would have turned the main position altogether, and forced Wellington to fall back at once. So you see we are doing good here, though I do not say that I should not like to be over there."

"The French will soon be at the top of the hill," Herrara exclaimed. "See how they are pushing upwards."

"They certainly are gaining ground fast," Macwitty said. "They are within a hundred yards of the top. Our men don't seem to be able to make any stand against them at all. See, Colonel, the lower column is turning off more towards their left."

"They had better have kept together, Macwitty. It is evident that Picton's division is hard pressed as it is, and if those two columns had united and thrown themselves upon him, they would have broken right through our line. As it is, the second party will have Leith's division to deal with. Do you see one of his brigades marching swiftly to meet them, and some guns sweeping the French flank? I wish we were nearer."

The scene had become too exciting for further conversation, and they watched almost breathlessly. The line of smoke on the top of the crest showed that the head of the column had made good its footing there, while the quick puffs of smoke and the rattle of musketry denoted that the other column was also within a short distance of the summit, but Leith's regiments were approaching the spot at the double. Presently there was a crash of a tremendous volley, and then the leading regiment disappeared over the brow of the hill and into brushwood. The roar of musketry was heavy and continuous, and then Ryan gave a joyous shout, as it could be seen that the two long smoke wreaths were becoming mixed together, and that the movement was downwards, and ere long the dark masses of troops could be seen descending the hill even more rapidly than they had climbed it. Leith's second brigade was now approaching the scene of the struggle, and was near at hand; Hill's division was seen in motion towards the same spot.

"That is all right now," Terence said; "but there is another big fight going on further up the valley."

It was too far off to make out the movements of the troops, but even at that distance the smoke rolling up from the hillside gave some idea of the course of the fight. Here, too, after mounting more than half-way up the slope, it could be seen that the tide of war was rolling down again, though more slowly, and with harder fighting

THE FRENCH ADVANCE

than it had done in the struggle nearer to them. And when at last the firing gradually ceased, they knew that the French had been repulsed all along the line.

"The men had better open their haversacks and eat a meal," Terence said. "We may get an order to move at any moment."

No orders came, however, and the troops remained in the positions that they occupied until the following morning; then a heavy skirmishing fire broke out, and for some time it seemed as if the battle was to be renewed. No heavy masses of the French, however, came down from the hill on their side to support the light troops in the valley, and in the afternoon the firing died away. Towards evening a staff-officer rode up at full speed, and handed a note to Terence.

"The French have turned our left by the Royalva Pass. Trant has failed to check them, and the whole army must fall back. These are your instructions."

The mishap had not been Trant's fault. He had been sent by the Portuguese general on a tremendous detour, and when he arrived at the position assigned to him, his troops were utterly exhausted by their long and fatiguing march. A large proportion had deserted or fallen out, and with but 1500 wearied and dispirited men, he could offer but little resistance to the French advance, and, being attacked by their cavalry, had been driven away with loss. Terence opened the note.

You will march at once. Keep along on this side of the Mondego, breaking up your command into small parties, who will visit every village within reach. All of their inhabitants who have not obeyed the proclamations and retired are to leave at once. Destroy all provisions that you can find. Set fire to the mills, and where this is not practicable, smash the machinery; and, bearing south as you go, spread out over the country between the Zezere and the sea, and continue to carry on the duty assigned to you, compelling the peasants to drive their animals before them along the roads to Lisbon.

"I understand, sir," Terence said, after reading the note, "and will carry out the orders to the best of my ability."

Five minutes later the regiment was under arms. Terence called the whole of the officers together, and explained the instructions that he had received. The two battalions were broken up into half-companies, which, as they marched along the Mondego, were to be left behind one by one, each party, when left, turning south, and proceeding to carry out the orders received. In a few cases only were companies to keep intact, as, although a hundred men would be ample for the duty at the large villages, two hundred would not be too much in a town like Leiria. On reaching Foz d'Aronce, half a battalion moved to the east to work down by the river Zezere, the rest turned to the right to follow the course of the Mondego down to the sea. For convenience, and in order to keep the troops in hand, Bull, Macwitty, Ryan, and Herrara each took the command of half a battalion, with orders to supervise the work of the companies belonging to it, and to keep in touch with the nearest company of the next battalion, so that the two thousand men could advance to a certain extent abreast of each other.

Foz d'Aronce had already been evacuated by its inhabitants, but in all other villages the orders were carried out. By daybreak the last company in the two battalions reached the sea-coast, and after two hours' rest began its march south. The others had long been at work. It was a painful duty. The frightened villagers had to be roused in the darkness, and told that the French were approaching, and that they must fly at once, taking their animals and what they could carry off in carts away with them. While the terrified people were harnessing horses to their carts, piling their few valuables into them and packing their children on the top, the troops went from house to house searching for and destroying provisions, setting fire to barns stored with corn, and burning or disabling any flour-mills they met with.

Then, as soon as work was done, they forced the villagers to take the southern road. There was no difficulty in doing this, for, although they had stolidly opposed all the measures ordered by Wellington, trusting that the French would not come, now that they had heard they were near, a wild panic seized them. Had an orderly retreat been made before, almost all their belongings might have been saved. Now, but little could be taken even by the most fortunate. The children, the sick, the aged had to be carried in carts, and in their haste and terror they left behind many things that might well have been saved.

The peasantry in the villages suffered less than the townspeople, as their horses and carts afforded means of transport, but even here the scenes were most painful. In the towns, however, they were vastly

THE FRENCH ADVANCE

more so; the means for carriage for such a large number of people being wanting, the greater number of the inhabitants were forced to make their way on foot, along roads so crowded with vehicles of every kind that the British divisions were frequently brought to a standstill for hours, where the nature of the country prevented their quitting the road and making their way across the fields.

On the 29th the greater portion of the British troops passed the Mondego. Hill retired upon Thomar, and the rest of the troops were concentrated at Milheada. The commissariat stores followed the coast road down to Reniche, and were embarked there. The light division and the cavalry remained, after the main body had been drawn across the Mondego, north of that river.

Soon after starting on his work Terence learned that the British troops had passed through Pombal, Leiria, and Thomar. It was consequently unnecessary for him to endeavour to clear those towns.

The delays caused at every village rendered the work slow as well as arduous. The French drove the light division through Coimbra, and, following, pressed so hotly that a number of minor combats took place between their cavalry and the British rear-guards. Before Leiria the rear-guards had to fight strongly to enable the guns to quit the town before the French entered it. Terence presently received orders to collect his regiment again, and, crossing the Zezere, to endeavour to join Trant and the other leaders of irregular bands, and to harass Massena's rear. He had already, knowing that great bodies of French cavalry had crossed the Mondego, called in the companies that were working Leiria and the coast, as they might otherwise have been cut up in detail by the French cavalry.

With these he marched east, picking up the other companies as he went, and on the same evening the regiment was collected on the Zezere. Having followed the river up, he reached Foz d'Aronce, and then, finding that several bodies of French troops had already passed through that village, he turned to the left and camped close to the Mondego, sending ten of his men over the river in peasants' clothes to ascertain the movements of the enemy. One of them returned with news that he had come upon a party of Trant's men, who told him that their main body were but two miles away, and that there were no French north of Coimbra.

The regiment had made a march of upwards of forty miles that day. Therefore, leaving them to rest, Terence forded the Mondego and rode with Ryan to Trant's village.

"I am glad indeed to see you, O'Connor," the partisan leader said, as Terence entered the cottage where he had established himself. "Is your regiment with you?"

"Yes, it is three miles away on the other side of the river. We have marched something like eighty miles in two days. We have been busy burning mills and destroying provisions, but the French cavalry are all over the country, so I was ordered to join you and aid you to harass the French line of communication, and to do them what damage we could."

"There is not much to be done in the way of cutting their communications; at least, there is nothing to be done to the north and east of this place, for Massena brought all his baggage and everything else with him, and cut himself loose altogether from his base at Ciudad. If the people had but carried out Wellington's orders, Massena would have suffered a fearful disaster. We have learned from stragglers we have taken that the fourteen days' provisions with which they marched were altogether exhausted, and that they had been unable to obtain any here. They would have had to retreat instantly, but I hear that in Coimbra alone there is enough food for their whole army for at least two months."

"But could we not have destroyed it as we retreated?"

"Of course, we ought to have done so," Trant said; "but from what I hear the affair was very badly managed. Instead of the first division that went through burning all the magazines and stores, it was left to Crauford to do so, and he, as usual, stopped so long facing the enemy that at last he was regularly chased through Coimbra, and, the roads being blocked with carts, his brigade would have been destroyed had the French infantry pushed strongly after him.

"Things are just as bad in the way of provisions on the other side of the river. We have done a great deal in the way of destroying mills and magazines. I am afraid Massena will find enough provisions to last his army all the winter."

"That is bad."

THE FRENCH ADVANCE

"Had it only been Coimbra, no very great harm would have been done, for the French troops got altogether out of hand when they entered, plundered the place, and, as I hear, destroyed enough provisions to have lasted them a month."

"Of course they hold the town?"

"Oh, yes! It is full of their sick and wounded."

"What force have you?" Terence asked.

"I have 1500 men of my own. Miller and Wilson, with some of the northern militias, will be here shortly, and I expect in a few days we shall have 8000 men."

"The great thing would be to act before the French know that there is so strong a force in the neighbourhood," Terence said, "because as soon as they hear that, they are sure to send a strong force back to Coimbra."

"How do you mean to act?" Trant asked in some surprise.

"I propose that we should capture Coimbra at once. I have 2000 men and you have 1500. I don't suppose they have left above a couple of thousand in the town, perhaps even less, and if we take them by surprise I should think we ought to be able to manage that number without difficulty. I certainly consider my own men to be a match for an equal number of French."

"It is a grand idea," Trant said, "and I don't see why we should not carry it out. As you say, the sooner the better. They may know that I am here, but they will never dream of my making such attempt with a force which, I must own, is not always to be relied upon. They are always shifting and changing. After a long march, half of them will desert, then in a few days the ranks swell again, consequently the men have little discipline and no confidence in each other, and are little better than raw levies, but for rough street fighting I have no doubt they would be all right, especially when backed by good troops like yours. How would you proceed? As yours is the real fighting body, you should have the command."

"Not at all," Terence said warmly. "You are my senior officer, not only in rank but in age and experience. My orders were to assist you as far as I could, and while we are together I am ready to carry out your orders in any way."

"Will your men be able to attack in the morning?"

"Certainly. They will have a good night's rest and will be quite ready for work, say, at four o'clock in the morning. It is not more than two hours' march to Coimbra, so that we shall be there by daybreak. Have they any troops between us and the town?"

"They have a post at a village a mile this side, O'Connor. Do you know how far their army is on the other side of the river?"

"I know that they had a division close to Leiria the day before yesterday, but whether they have any large body just across the Mondego I cannot say."

"Then we will first surprise their post. I will undertake that. Will you march your force down the river close to the town? I have a hundred cavalry, and as soon as I have captured the post I will send them on at a gallop with orders to ride straight through to the bridge and prevent any mounted messengers passing across it. As soon as you hear them come along the road do you at once enter the town. I will bring my men on at the double, and we shall not be many minutes after you. It would be as well for you to enter it by several streets, as that will cause greater confusion than if you were in a solid body. The principal point is the great convent of Santa Clara, which has been converted into a hospital. No doubt a portion of the garrison are there; the rest will be scattered about in the public buildings, and can be overpowered in detail. I think we are certain of success. I hope you will stop for a time and take supper with me, and in the meantime I will send down orders for my men to be under arms here at half-past three."

Terence and Ryan remained for an hour, and then rode back to the regiment. The men were all sound asleep, but Herrara and the two majors were sitting round a camp-fire.

"What news, Colonel?" the former asked, as Terence rode up.

"Good news. We are going to take Coimbra to-morrow morning. All Massena's sick and wounded and his heavy baggage are there. They have no suspicion that any force is yet assembled in the neighbourhood, and I expect we shall have easy work of it. They have a post a mile out of the town. Trant will surprise and capture that at five in the morning. Just before daybreak we shall enter the town. We must march from here at half-past three."

THE FRENCH ADVANCE

"That is something like news, Colonel," Macwitty exclaimed. "It will cut the French off from this line of retreat altogether, and they must either fall back by the line of the Tagus or through Badajoz and Merida."

Terence laughed. "You are counting your chickens before they are hatched, Macwitty. At the present it seems more likely that Wellington will have to embark his troops, than that Massena will have to retreat. He must have nearly a hundred thousand men, counting those who fought with him at Busaco and the two divisions that marched down through Foz d'Aronce, while Wellington, all told, cannot have above 40,000. Certainly, some of the peasants told me they had heard that a great many men were employed in fortifying the heights of Torres Vedras, and Wellington may be able to make a stand there, but as we have never heard anything about them before, I am afraid that they cannot be anything very formidable. However, just at present we have nothing to do with that; if we can take Coimbra it will certainly hamper Massena, and, if the worst comes to the worst, we can fall back across the Douro. Don't let the bugles sound in the morning. It is not likely, but it is possible, that the French may send out cavalry patrols at night. If a bugle were heard they might ride back and report that a force was in the neighbourhood, and we should find the garrison prepared for us. Now we had better do no more talking. It is past eleven, and we have but four and a half hours to sleep."

At half-past three the troops were roused. They were surprised at the early call, for they had expected two or three days' rest after the heavy work of the last eight days, but the company officers soon learned the news from their majors, and as it quickly spread through the ranks, the men were at once alert and ready. Fording the river, they marched at a rapid pace by the road to Coimbra, and soon after five o'clock arrived within a few hundred yards of the town. Then they were halted and broken up into four columns, which were to enter the town at different points. The signal for moving was to be the sound of a body of cavalry galloping along the road. Terence listened attentively for the rattle of musketry in the distance, but all was quiet, and he had little doubt that the French had been surprised and captured without a shot being fired.

Soon after half-past five he heard a dull sound, which before long grew louder, and in five minutes a body of horsemen swept past at a gallop. The troops at once got into motion and entered the town; there was no longer any motive for concealment; the bugles sounded, and with loud shouts the Portuguese ran forward. French officers ran out of private houses and were at once seized and captured. Several bodies of troops were taken in public buildings before they were fairly awake. Some of the inhabitants, of whom many, unable to make their escape, had remained behind or who had returned from the villages to which they had at first fled, came out and acted as guides to the various buildings where the French troops were quartered, and in little over a quarter of an hour the whole town, with the exception of the convent of Santa Clara, was in their hands.

By this time Trant had come up with his command. The troops rapidly formed up again, and, issuing from several streets, advanced against the convent. The astonished enemy fired a few shots, then, on being formally summoned to surrender, laid down their arms. Thus on the third day after Massena quitted the Mondego, his hospitals, depots, and nearly 6000 prisoners, wounded and unwounded, among them a company of the Imperial Guard, fell into the hands of the Portuguese.

The next day Miller and Wilson came up, and their men, crossing the bridge and spreading over the country, gathered in 300 more prisoners, while Trant marched with those he had captured to Oporto.

On the 10th of October the whole of Wellington's army was safely posted on the tremendously strong position that he had, unknown to the army, carefully prepared and fortified for the protection of Lisbon. It consisted of three lines of batteries and intrenchments. The second was the most formidable; but the first was so strong also that Wellington determined to defend this instead of falling back to the stronger line. At the foot of the line of mountains on which the army was posted, stretching from the Tagus to the sea, ran two streams; the Zandre, a deep river, which extended nearly half-way along the twenty-nine miles of lines, covered the left of the position, while a stream running into the Tagus protected the right.

THE FRENCH ADVANCE

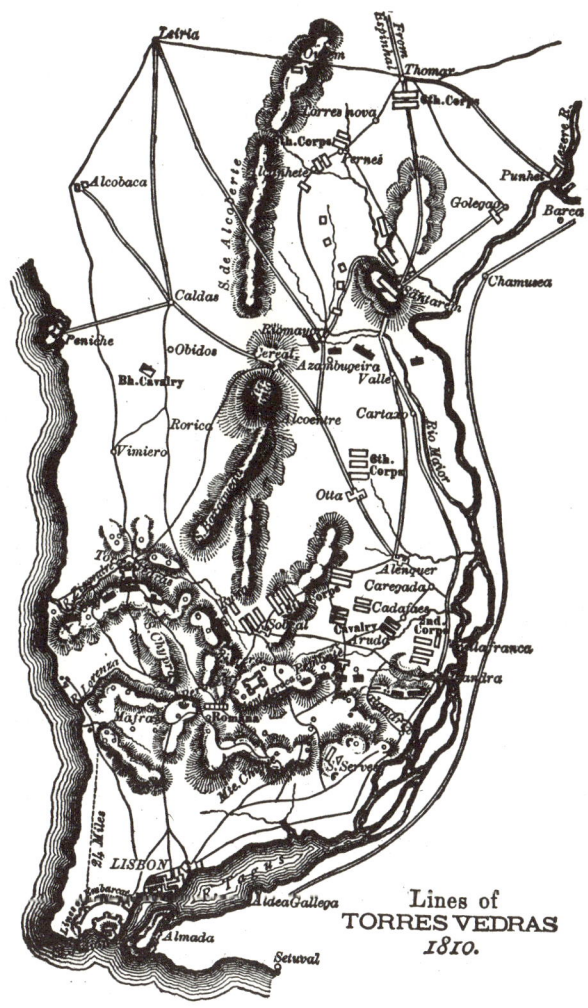

Lines of
TORRES VEDRAS
1810.

The centre, therefore, was almost the only part at which the line could be attacked with any chance of success, and this was defended by such tremendous fortifications as to be almost impregnable.

Massena, who had only heard vague rumours of the existence of these fortifications four days before, was astounded at the unexpected obstacle which barred his way. The British troops, as soon as they arrived, were set to work to strengthen the intrenchments. Trees were felled, and every accessible point was covered by formidable abattis. The faces of the rocks were scarped, so that an enemy who won his way partly up the hill would find his farther progress arrested by a perpendicular wall of rock. Soon the eminences on the crest bristled with guns, and Massena, after carefully reconnoitring the whole position, came to the conclusion that it could not be attacked, and disposed his troops in permanent positions facing the British centre and right from Sobral to Villafranca on the Tagus, and sent his cavalry out over the country to bring in provisions.

To lessen the district available for this operation, Wellington sent orders for the northern militia to advance, and, crossing the Mondego, to drive in the foraging parties. Trant, Wilson, and the other partisan corps were also employed in the work. A strong force took up its position between Castello Branco and Abrantes, while the militia and partisans occupied the whole country north of Leiria, and the French were thus completely surrounded. Nevertheless, the store of provisions left behind in the towns and villages was so large that the French cavalry were able to bring in sufficient supplies for the army.

During the week that followed, the Minho regiment was engaged in watching the defiles by which Massena might communicate with Ciudad Rodrigo, or through which reinforcements might reach him. Wilson and Trant were both engaged on similar service, the one farther to the north, while the other, who was on the south bank of the Tagus with a number of Portuguese militia and irregulars, endeavoured to prevent the French from crossing the river and carrying off the flocks, herds, and corn, which, in spite of Wellington's entreaties and orders, the Portuguese government had permitted to remain, as if in handiness for the French foraging parties.

THE FRENCH ADVANCE

Owing to the exhausted state of both the British and Portuguese treasuries, it was impossible to supply the corps acting in rear of the French with money for the purchase of food. But Terence had received authority to take what provisions were absolutely necessary for the troops, and to give orders that would at some time or other be honoured by the military chest. A comparatively small proportion of his men were needed to guard the defiles against such bodies of troops as would be likely to traverse them in order to keep up Massena's communications. Leaving therefore, a hundred men in each of the principal defiles, and ordering them to entrench themselves in places where they commanded the road, and could only be attacked with the greatest difficulty, while the road was barred by trees felled across it so as to form an impassable abattis, behind which twenty men were stationed, Terence marched with 1500 men towards the frontier.

Five hundred of these were placed along the Coa, guarding the roads, and with the remainder he forded the river, and placed himself in the woods, in the plain between Almeida and Ciudad Rodrigo. Here he captured several convoys of wagons proceeding with provisions for the garrison of the former place. A portion of these he despatched under guard for the use of the troops on the Coa and for those in the passes, thus rendering it unnecessary to harass the people, who had returned to their villages after Massena had advanced against Lisbon. Growing bolder with success he crossed the Aqueda, and, marching round to the rear of Ciudad Rodrigo, cut off and destroyed convoys intended for that town, causing great alarm to the garrison.

These were absolutely ignorant of the operations of Massena, for so active were the partisans in the French rear that no single messenger succeeded in getting through, and even when accompanied by strong escorts the opposition encountered was so determined that the French were obliged to fall back without having accomplished their purpose. Thus, then, the garrison at Ciudad Rodrigo were ignorant both of Massena's whereabouts and of the nature of the force that had thrown itself in his rear. Several times strong parties of troops were sent out. When these were composed of cavalry only, they were boldly met and driven in. When it was a mixed force of cavalry, infantry, and artillery, they searched in vain for the foe.

"Good news. We are going to take Coimbra."

THE FRENCH ADVANCE

So seriously alarmed and annoyed was the governor that 3000 troops were withdrawn from Salamanca to strengthen the garrison. In December, Massena, having exhausted the country round, fell back to a very strong position at Santarem, and Terence withdrew his whole force, save those guarding the defiles, to the neighbourhood of Abrantes, so that he could assist the force stationed there, should Massena retire up the Tagus, and prevent his messengers passing through the country between the river and the range of mountains south of the Alva, by Castello Branco or Velha; posting strong parties to guard the fords of the Zezere.

So thoroughly was the service of watching the frontier line carried out that it was not until General Foy himself was sent off by Massena that Napoleon was informed of the state of things. He was accompanied by a strong cavalry force and 4000 French infantry across the Zezere, and ravaged the country for a considerable distance. Before such strength Terence was obliged to fall back. Foy was accompanied by his cavalry until he had passed through Castello Branco, and was then able to ride without further opposition to Ciudad Rodrigo.

Beresford was guarding the line of the Tagus between the mouth of the Zezere and the point occupied on the opposite bank by Wellington, sending a portion of his force up the Zezere, and these harassed the French marauding parties extending their devastations along the line of the Mondego.

Although the Minho regiment had suffered some loss during these operations, their ranks were kept up to the full strength without difficulty. Great numbers of the Portuguese army deserted during the winter, owing to the hardships they endured from want of food and the irregularity of their pay. Many of these made for the Minho regiment, which they had learned was well fed and received their pay with some degree of regularity, the latter circumstance being due to the fact that Terence had the good luck to capture with one of the convoys behind Ciudad Rodrigo a considerable sum of money intended for the pay of the garrison. From this he had without hesitation paid his men the arrears due to them, and had still 30,000 dollars, with which he was able to continue to feed and pay them after moving to the line of the Zezere.

He only enrolled sufficient recruits to fill the gaps made by war and disease, refusing to raise the number above 2000, as this was as many as could be readily handled, for he had found that the larger number had but increased the difficulties of rationing and paying them.

Chapter XII
Fuentes d'Onoro

In the early spring, Soult, who was besieging Cadiz, received orders from Napoleon to co-operate with Massena, and although ignorant of the latter's plans, and even of his position, prepared to do so at once. He crushed the Spanish force on the Gebora, captured Badajoz, owing to the treachery and cowardice of its commander, and was moving north when the news reached him that Massena was falling back. The latter's position had indeed become untenable. His army was wasted by sickness, and famine threatened it, for the supplies obtainable from the country round had now been exhausted. Wellington was, as he knew from his agents in the Portuguese government, receiving reinforcements, and would shortly be in a position to assume the offensive.

The discipline in the French army under Massena had been greatly injured by its long inactivity. The only news he received as to Soult's movements was that he was near Badajoz; therefore, the first week in March he began his retreat by sending off 10,000 sick and all his stores to Thomar. Then he began to fall back. Thick weather favoured him, and Ney assembled a large force near Leiria, as if to advance against the British position. Two other corps left Santarem on the night of the fifth and retired to Thomar. The rest of the army moved by other routes.

For four days Wellington, although discovering that a retreat was in progress, was unable to ascertain by which line Massena was really retiring. As soon as this point was cleared up he ordered Beresford to concentrate near Abrantes, while he himself followed the line the main body of the French army seemed to be taking. It was soon found that they were concentrating at Pombal, with the apparent intention of crossing the Mondego at Coimbra, whereby they would have obtained a fresh and formidable position behind the Mondego, with the rich and untouched country between the river and the Douro, upon which they could have subsisted for a long time. Therefore, calling back the troops that were already on the march to relieve Badajoz, which had not yet surrendered, he advanced with all speed upon Pombal, his object being to force the French to take the line of retreat through Miranda for the frontier, and so prevent him from crossing the Mondego.

Ney commanded the rear-guard, and carried out the operation with the same mixture of vigour, valour, and prudence with which he afterwards performed the same duty to the French army on its retreat from Moscow. He fought at Pombal and at Redinha, and that so strenuously that, had it not been for Trant, Wilson, and other partisans who defended all the fords and bridges, Massena would have been able to have crossed the Mondego. Wellington, however, turned one by one the positions occupied by Ney; and Massena, believing that the force at Coimbra was far stronger than it really was, changed his plans and took up a position at Cazal Nova.

Here he left Ney and marched for Miranda, but although Ney covered the movement with admirable skill, disputing every ridge and post of vantage, the British pressed forward so hotly that Massena was obliged to destroy all his baggage and ammunition. Ney rashly remained on the east side of the river Cerra, in front of the village of Foz d'Aronce, and being attacked suddenly, was driven across the river with a loss of 500 men, many being drowned by missing the fords, and others crushed to death in the passage. However, Ney held the line of the river, blew up the bridge, and his division withdrew in good order. Massena tarnished the reputation gained by the manner in which he had drawn off his army from its dangerous position, by the ruthless spirit with which the operation was conducted, covering his retreat by burning every village through which he passed, and even ordering the town of Leiria to be destroyed, although altogether out of the line he was following.

After this fight the British pursuit slackened somewhat, for Wellington received the news of the surrender of Badajoz, and seeing that Portugal was thus open to invasion by Soult on the south, despatched Cole's division to join that of Beresford, although this left him inferior in force to the army he was pursuing. The advance was retarded by the necessity of making bridges across the Cerra,

FUENTES D'ONORO

which was now in flood, and the delay enabled Massena to fall back unmolested to Guarda, where he intended to halt and then to move to Coria, whence he could have marched to the Tagus, effected a junction with Soult, and be in a position to advance again upon Lisbon with a larger force than ever. He had, however, throughout been thwarted by the factious disobedience of his lieutenants Ney, Regnier, Brouet, Montbrun, and Junot, and this feeling now broke into open disobedience, and while Ney absolutely defied his authority, the others were so disobedient that fierce and angry personal altercations took place.

Massena removed Ney from his command. His own movements were, however, altogether disarranged by two British divisions marching over the mountains by paths deemed altogether impassable for troops, which compelled him to abandon his intention of marching south, and to retire to Sabuga on the Coa. Here he was attacked. Regnier's corps, which covered the position, was beaten with heavy loss; but owing to the combinations, which would have cut Massena off from Ciudad Rodrigo, failing, from some of the columns going altogether astray in a thick fog, Massena gained that town with his army. He had lost in battle, from disease, or taken prisoners, 30,000 men since the day when, confident that he was going to drive Wellington to take refuge on board his ships, he had advanced from that town.

Even now he did not feel safe, though rejoined by a large number of convalescents; and, drawing rations for his troops from the stores of the citadel, he retired with the army to Salamanca. Having reorganised his force, procured fresh horses for his guns, and rested the troops for a few days, Massena advanced to cover Ciudad Rodrigo and to raise the siege of Almeida, which Wellington had begun without loss of time, and with upwards of 50,000 men Massena attacked the British at Fuentes d'Onoro. The fight was long and obstinate and the French succeeded in driving back the British right, but failed in a series of desperate attempts to carry the village of Fuentes.

Both sides claimed the battle as a victory, but the British with the greater ground, for Massena fell back across the Aqueda, having failed to relieve Almeida, whose garrison, by a well-planned night-march, succeeded in passing through the besieging force, and effected their retreat with but small loss, the town falling into the possession of the British.

Terence had come up, after a series of long marches, on the day before the battle. His arrival was very opportune, for the Portuguese troops with Wellington were completely demoralised and exhausted by the failure of their government to supply them with food, pay, or clothes. So deplorable was their state that Wellington had been obliged to disband the militia regiments, and great numbers of desertions had taken place from the regular troops.

The regiment had been stationed on the British right. Here the fighting had been very severe. The French cavalry force was enormously superior to the British, who had but a thousand troops in the field. These were driven back by the French, and Ramsay's battery of horse-artillery was cut off. But Ramsay placed himself at the head of his battery, and at full gallop dashed through the French infantry and cavalry, and succeeded in regaining his friends. The two battalions of the Minho regiment, who were posted in a wood, defended themselves with the greatest resolution against an attack by vastly superior numbers, until the French advancing on each side of the wood had cut them off from the rest of the division. Then a bugle-call summoned the men to assemble at the rear of the wood, and, forming squares, the two battalions marched out.

Twelve French guns played upon them, and time after time masses of cavalry swept down on them, but, filling up the gaps in their ranks, they pressed on, charged two French regiments at the double, that endeavoured to block their way, burst a path through them, and succeeded in rejoining the retiring division, which received them with a burst of hearty cheering. Two hundred had fallen in the short time that had elapsed since they left the wood.

Terence had been in the centre of one of the squares, but just as they were breaking through the French ranks he had ridden to the rear face and called upon the men to turn and repulse a body of French cavalry that was charging down upon them.

At this moment a bullet struck his horse in the flank. Maddened with the sudden pain, the animal sprang forward, broke through the ranks of the Portuguese in front of it, and, before Terence could recover its command, dashed at full speed among the French cavalry. Before

FUENTES D'ONORO

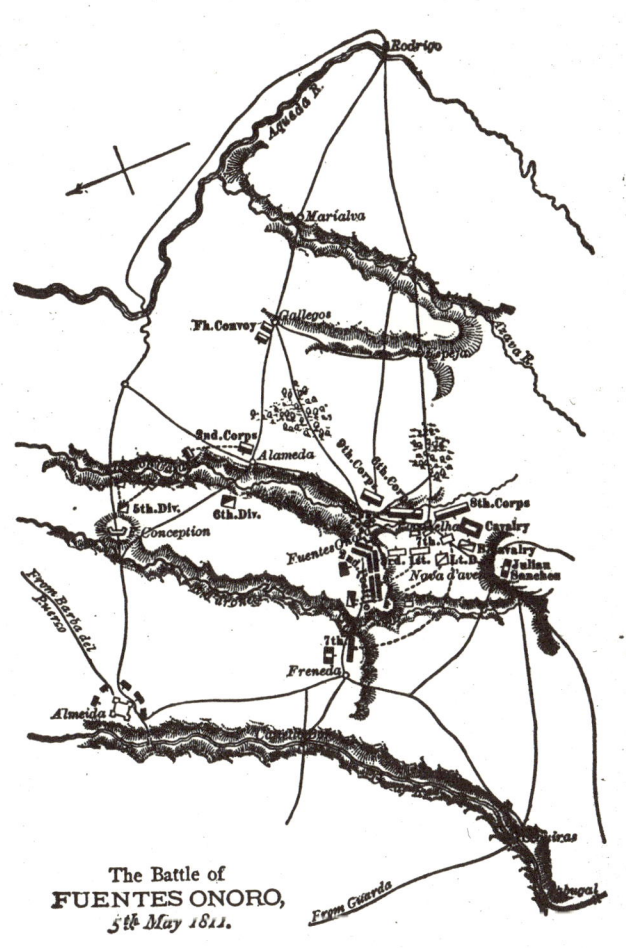

The Battle of
FUENTES ONORO,
5th May 1811.

he could strike a blow in defence, Terence was cut down. As he fell, the cavalry passed over him; but, fortunately, the impetus of his charge had carried him nearly through their ranks before he fell, and the horses of the rear rank leapt over his body without touching him. It was the force of the blow that had felled him, for, in the hurry of striking, the trooper's sword had partly turned, and it was with the flat rather than the edge that he was struck.

Although half-stunned with the blow and the heavy fall, he did not altogether lose consciousness. He heard, as he lay, a crashing volley, which would, he felt sure, repulse the horsemen; and fearing that in their retreat they might ride over him, trampling him to death, he struggled to his feet. The French, however, though repulsed, did not retire far, but followed upon the retreating regiment until it joined the British, when a battery opened upon them, and their commander called upon them to fall back. This was done in good order and at a steady trot. On seeing Terence standing in their path, an officer rode up to him.

"I surrender," Terence said.

A trooper was called out and ordered to conduct him to the rear, where many other prisoners, who had been taken during the French advance, were gathered. Here an English soldier bound up Terence's wound, from which the blood was streaming freely, a portion of the scalp having been shorn clean off.

"That was a narrow escape, sir," the man said.

"Yes; I don't know how it was that it did not sever my skull, but I suppose that it was a hasty blow, and the sword must have turned. It might have been worse by a good deal. I am afraid things are going badly with us."

"Badly enough here," the soldier said, "but I think we are holding our own in the centre. There is a tremendous roar of fire going on round that village there. I was captured half an hour ago, and it has been growing louder and louder ever since."

For another two hours the battle continued, and, as it still centered round the village, the spirits of the prisoners rose, for it was evident that, although the right had been driven back, the centre was at least holding its position against all the efforts of the French. In the afternoon the fire slackened, and only a few shots were fired. The next morning at daybreak the prisoners, 300 in number, were marched away under a strong escort. Both armies still occupied the same positions they had held the day before, and there seemed every probability of the battle being renewed. When, however, they had marched several miles, and no sound of heavy firing was heard, the prisoners concluded that either Wellington had retired, or that Massena, seeing his inability to drive the British from their position, intended himself to fall back upon Ciudad.

The convoy marched twenty miles and then halted for the night. Two hours after they did so a great train of waggons containing wounded came up and halted at the same place. The wounded were lifted out and laid on the ground, where the surgeons attended to the more serious cases.

"*Pardon, monsieur,*" Terence said in French to one of the doctors who was near him, "are there any of our countrymen among the wounded?"

"No, sir, they are all French," the doctor replied.

"That is a good sign," Terence said to an English officer who was standing by him when he asked the question.

"Why so, Colonel?"

"Because, if Massena intended to attack again to-morrow, he would have sent the British wounded back as well as his own men. The French, like ourselves, make no distinction between friends and foes, and that he has not sent them seems to me to show that he intends himself to fall back, and to leave the British wounded to the care of their own surgeons rather than embarrass himself with them."

"Yes, I have no doubt that is the case," the officer said. "It seems then that we must have won the day after all. That is some comfort, anyhow, and I shall sleep more soundly than I expected. If we had been beaten there would have been nothing for it but for the army to fall back again to the lines of Torres Vedras, and Wellington would have had to fight very hard to regain them. If Massena does fall back, Almeida will have to surrender."

"I was inside last time it surrendered," Terence said, "but I managed to make my way out with my regiment after the explosion."

"I wonder whether Massena means to leave us at Ciudad or to send us on to Salamanca?"

"I should think that he would send us on," Terence replied; "he will not want to have 300 men eating up the stores at Ciudad, besides requiring a certain portion of the garrison to look after them."

Terence's ideas proved correct, and, without stopping at Ciudad, the convoy of prisoners and wounded continued their march until they arrived at Salamanca. Terence could not help smiling as he was marched through the street, and thought of the wild panic that he and Dicky Ryan had caused when he was last in that town. The convent which the Mayo Fusileers had occupied was now turned into a prison, and here the prisoners taken at Fuentes d'Onoro were marched, and joined those who had fallen into the hands of the French during Massena's retreat. Among these were several officers of his acquaintance, and as discipline was not very strict, they were able to make themselves fairly comfortable together.

The French, indeed, along the whole of the Portuguese frontier, had their hands full, and the force at Salamanca was so small that but few men could be spared for prison duties, and, so long as their captives showed no signs of giving trouble, their guards were satisfied to leave them a good deal to their own devices, watching the gate carefully, but leaving much of the interior work of the prison to be done by Spanish warders; for, violent as the natives were in their expressions of hatred for the French, they were always ready to serve under them in any capacity in which money could be earned.

"There can be no difficulty whatever in making one's escape from here," Terence said to a party of four or five officers who were lodged with him in a room, from whose window a view over the city was obtainable. "It is not the getting out of this convent that is difficult, but the making one's way across this country to rejoin. I have no doubt that one could bribe one of those Spaniards to bring in a rope, and, even if that could not be obtained, we might manage to make one from our blankets; but the question is, what to do when we have got out? Massena lies between us and Ciudad, and from what I hear the French soldiers say, the whole line is guarded down to Badajoz, where Soult's army is lying. Victor is somewhere farther to the south, and their convoys and cavalry will be traversing the whole country. I speak Portuguese well, and know enough of Spanish to pass as a Spaniard among Frenchmen, but to any one who does not speak either language it would be next to impossible to get along."

FUENTES D'ONORO

"I quite see that," one of the officers said, "and for my part I would rather stay where I am than run the risk of such an attempt. I don't know a word of Spanish, and should be recaptured before I had been out an hour. If I got away from the town I should be no better off, for I could not obtain a disguise. As to making one's way from here to Almeida, it would be altogether hopeless."

The others agreed, and one of them said, "But don't let us be any hindrance to you, O'Connor. If you are disposed to try, by all means do so, and if we can help you in any way we will."

"I shall certainly try," Terence said, "but I shall wait a little to see how things go. It may be by this time Wellington has fallen back again, and in that case no doubt Massena will advance. We heard, as we came along, that Marmont, with six divisions, is approaching the frontier, and even if Wellington could maintain himself on the Aqueda, Soult is likely to crush Beresford, and may advance from Badajoz towards Lisbon, when the British will be obliged to retire at once. To make one's way across the open country between this and Ciudad would be easy enough, while it would be dangerous in the extreme to enter the passes while the French troops are passing through them on Wellington's rear. My Portuguese would, of course, be a hindrance rather than a benefit to me on this side of the frontier, for the Spaniards hate the Portuguese very much more heartily than they do the French. You know that when they were supplying our army with grain the Spanish muleteers would not bring any for the use of the Portuguese brigades, and it was only by taking it as if for the British divisions, and distributing it afterwards to the Portuguese, that the latter could be kept alive. As a British officer I should feel quite safe if I fell into the hands of Spanish guerillas, but as a Portuguese officer my life would not be worth an hour's purchase."

Two days later came the news that a desperate battle had been fought by Beresford at Albuera, near Badajoz. He had been attacked by Soult, but after tremendous fighting, in which the French first obtained great advantages, they had been at last beaten off by the British troops, and it ended a drawn battle, the losses on both sides being extraordinarily heavy. It was not until some time afterwards that Terence learned the particulars of this desperate engagement.

Beresford had 30,000 infantry, 2000 cavalry, and 38 guns, but the British infantry did not exceed 7000. Soult had 4000 veteran cavalry, 19,000 infantry, and 40 guns.

The battle began badly. Blake with his Spaniards were soon disposed of by the French, and in half an hour the battle was all but lost, a brigade of the British infantry being involved in the confusion caused by the Spanish retreat, and two-thirds of its number being destroyed. The whole brunt of the battle now fell upon the small British force remaining. French columns pushed up the hill held by them, the cannon on both sides swept the ground with grape. The heavy French columns suffered terribly from the fire from the English lines, but they pressed forward, gained the crest of the rise, and, confident of victory, were still advancing, when Cole and Houghton's brigades came up and restored the battle; and the British line, charging through a storm of grape and musketry, fell upon the French columns and drove them down the hill again in confusion.

The Portuguese battalions had fought well, as had the German regiment, but it was upon the British that the whole brunt of the fight had fallen. In the four hours that the combat lasted, 7000 of the allies and over 8000 of the French had been killed or wounded. Of the 6000 British infantry only 1800 remained standing when the battle was over, 4200 being killed or wounded; 600 Germans and Portuguese were placed *hors de combat;* while of the Spaniards, who formed the great mass of the army, 2000 were killed or wounded by the French artillery and musketry, or cut down while in disorder by the French cavalry.

Never was the indomitable valour of British infantry more markedly shown than at the battle of Albuera. The battle had been brought on in no small degree by their anxiety for action. The regiments had been disappointed that, while their comrades were sharing in Wellington's pursuit of Massena, they were far away from the scene of conflict, and when Beresford would have fallen back, as it would have been prudent to do, they became so insubordinate that he gave way to their desire to meet the French, and so fought a battle where defeat would have upset all Wellington's plans for the campaign, and victory would have brought no advantages with it. Like Inkerman, it was a soldiers' battle. Beresford's dispositions were faulty in the extreme, and tactically the day was lost before the fighting began.

FUENTES D'ONORO

The Spanish portion of the army did no real fighting, and in their confusion involved the loss of nearly the whole of a British brigade, and it was only by the unconquerable valour of the remainder of the British force that victory was gained against enormous odds, and that against some of the best troops of France.

Terence was in the habit of often going down and chatting with the French guard at the gate. Their duties were tedious, and they were glad of a talk with this young British officer, who was the only prisoner in their keeping who spoke their language fluently, and from them he obtained what news they had of what was going on. A fortnight later he gathered that the British force on the Aqueda had been greatly weakened, that there was no intention of laying siege to Ciudad, and it was believed that Wellington's main body had marched south to join Beresford.

This was indeed the only operation left open to the British general. Regnier's division of Marmont's army had joined Massena, and it would be impossible to besiege Ciudad while a force greatly superior to his own was within easy striking distance. On the other hand, Beresford was in no position to fight another battle, and as long as Badajoz remained in the hands of the French they could at any time advance into Portugal, and its possession was therefore of paramount importance. Marmont had succeeded Massena in command, the latter marshal having been recalled to France, and the great bulk of the French army was now concentrated round Salamanca, from which it could either march against the British force at Ciudad or unite with Soult, and, in overwhelming strength, either move against Cadiz or advance into Portugal.

Wellington therefore left Spenser to guard the line of the Coa and make demonstrations against Ciudad, while with the main body of his army he marched south. The news decided Terence to attempt to make his escape in that direction. He did not know whether his own regiment would be with Spenser or Wellington, but it was clear that more important events would be likely to take place near Badajoz than on the Coa. The French would be unlikely to choose the latter route for an advance into Portugal. The country had been stripped bare by the two armies that had marched across it, the roads were extremely bad, and it would be next to impossible for an army to carry with it sustenance for the march, still less for maintaining itself after it had traversed the passes. Moreover, Spenser, falling back before them, would retire to the lines of Torres Vedras, and the invaders would find themselves, as Massena had done, baffled by that tremendous line of fortifications, where they might find also Wellington and his army, who would have shorter roads to follow, established before they arrived.

Some of the townspeople were allowed to pass in and out of the convent to sell fruit and other articles to the British prisoners, and Terence thought it better to open negotiations with one of these rather than one of the warders in French pay. He was not long in fixing upon one of them as an ally. She was a good-looking peasant girl, who came regularly with grapes and fruit. From the first Terence had made his purchases from her, and had stood chatting with her for some time.

"I want to get away from here, Nita," he said on the day he received the news of Wellington's march to the south.

"I dare say, señor," she laughed. "I suppose all the other prisoners want the same."

"No doubt; but you see, they would not have much chance of getting away, because none of them understand Spanish. I talk it a little, as you see. So if I got out and had a disguise I might very well make my way across the country."

"There are many brigands about," she said, "and it is not safe for a single man to travel anywhere. What do you want me to do?"

"I want a rope fifty feet long, not a very thick one, but strong enough to bear my weight. That is the first thing. Then I want a disguise; but that I could get if a friend would be in readiness to give it to me after I had slid down the rope into the street."

"How could I give you a rope, señor, with all these people about?"

"You could put it into the bottom of your basket and cover it over with fruit. You could take your stand near the door at the foot of the stairs leading up to my room. Then I could, in the hearing of the rest, say that it was my fête day, and that I was going to give the others a treat, so that I would buy all your grapes. After we had bargained for them I could hand you the money, and say, 'Give me your basket. I will run upstairs, empty it, and bring it down to you.' As this would save my making five or six journeys upstairs, there would be nothing suspicious about that."

"I will think it over," the girl said gravely. "I do not see that there would be much danger. I will give you an answer to-morrow."

The next day she said, when Terence went up to her, "I will do it, señor. I have a lover who is a muleteer; I spoke to him last night, and he will help you. To-morrow I will give you a rope. In the afternoon you are to hang something out of your window, not far, but so that it can be just seen from the street. That red sash of yours will do very well. Do not let it go more than an inch or two beyond the window-sill, so that it will not attract any attention. When the clock strikes ten, Garcia and I will be in the street below that window. This is a quiet neighbourhood, and no one is likely to be about. Garcia will have a suit of muleteer's clothes for you, and you can change at once. I will carry those you have on to our house and destroy them. Garcia will take you to his lodging. He starts at daybreak with his mules, and you can travel with them."

"Thank you most heartily, Nita. Here are five gold pieces for the purchase of the ropes and clothes."

"Oh, they will not cost anything like as much as that!" the girl said.

"If they don't, you must buy yourself a little keepsake, Nita, in remembrance of me; but I will send you something better worth having, by Garcia, when I reach our army and am able to get money with which I can pay him for his labour and loss of time."

"I don't want money," the girl said, drawing herself up proudly. "I am helping you because I like you, and because you have come here to drive the French away."

"I should not think of offering you money, Nita. I know that it is out of pure kindness that you are doing it, but you could not refuse some little trinket to wear on your wedding-day."

"I may never get married," the girl said with a pout.

"Oh, I know better than that, Nita! A girl with as pretty a face as yours would never remain single, and I should not be surprised if you were to tell me that the day is fixed already."

"It is not fixed, and is not likely to be, señor. I have told Garcia that I will never marry as long as the French are here. He may go out with one of the partisan forces. He often talks about doing so, and might get shot any day by these brigands. When I am married I am not going to stay at home by myself while he is away among the mountains."

"Ah! Well, the war cannot last for ever. You may have Wellington here before the year is out. Give me your address, so that when we come I may find you out."

"Callao San Salvador, No.10. It is one of my uncles I am living with there. My home is in Burda, six miles away. It is a little village, and there are so many French bands ranging over the country, that a month ago my father sent me in here to stay with my uncle, thinking that I should be safer in the city than in the little village. He brings fruit in for me to sell twice a week."

"Very well. If we come here I shall go to your uncle's and inquire for you, and if you have left him I will go out to your village and find you."

All passed off as arranged without the slightest hitch. Terence took the girl's basket and ran upstairs with it, emptied the fruit out on the table, thrust the rope under his bed, and ran down again and gave Nita the basket. At ten o'clock at night he slung himself from the window, after a hearty good-bye to his fellow-prisoners, several of whom, now that it was too late, would gladly have shared in his adventure.

"I should be very glad if you were going with me, but at the same time I own that I do not think we should get through. I question, indeed, if the muleteer would take anyone who did not understand enough Spanish to pass if he were questioned by French soldiers; and if he would do so it would greatly increase the risk. At the same time, if one of you would like to take my place, I will relinquish it to you, and will, after you have gone off with the muleteer, go in another direction, and take my chance of getting hold of a disguise somehow and of making my way out."

None of the others would hear of this, and after extinguishing the light, so as to obviate the risk of anyone noticing him getting out of the window, Terence slipped down to the ground just as the clock struck ten.

"I want to get away from here, Nita."

"Good evening, señor!" a voice said, as his feet touched the ground. "Here is your disguise. Nita is watching a short distance away, and will give us notice if anyone approaches. You had best change at once."

Terence took off his uniform, and, with the assistance of the muleteer, donned the garments that he had brought for him; then he rolled the others into a bundle, and the muleteer gave a low whistle, whereupon Nita came running up.

"Thanks be to the saints that no one has come along!" she said, as the rope, which Terence had forgotten, fell at their feet, his companions having, as agreed, untied the upper end.

"That will come in useful," Garcia said, coiling it up on his arm. "Now, señor, do not let us stand talking. Nita will take the uniform and burn it."

"I will hide it if you like," the girl said. "There can be no reason for their searching our house."

"Thank you, Nita, but it would be better to destroy it at once. It may be a long time before I come this way again; besides, the things have seen their best days, and I have another suit I can put on when I join my regiment. Thanks very much for your kindness, which I shall always remember."

"Good-bye, señor! May the saints protect you!" and, without giving him time to say more, she took the bundle from Garcia's hand and sped away down the street.

"Now, señor, follow me," he said, and turned to go in the other direction.

"You had best call me Juan, and begin at once," Terence said. "If by accident you were to say señor in the hearing of anyone, there would be trouble at once."

"I shall be careful, never fear," the man said. "However, there would only be harm done if there happened to be a Frenchman or one of their Spaniards, who are worse, present; as to my own comrades, it would not matter at all. We muleteers are all heart and soul against the French, and will do anything to injure them. We are all obliged to work for them, for all trade is at an end, and we must live. Many have joined the partisans, but those who have good mules cannot go away and give up their only means of earning a living, for although the French pay for carriage by mules or carts, if they come upon animals that are not being used they take them without a single scruple. Besides, there are not many partisans in this part of Spain. The French have been too long in the valley here, and are too strong in the Castiles for their operations. It is different in Navarre, Aragon, and Catalonia, and in Valencia and Mercia. There the French have never had a firm footing, and most of the strong places are still in Spanish hands. In all the mountainous parts, in fact, there are guerillas, but here it is too dangerous. There are bands all over the country, but these are really but robbers, and no honest man would join them.

"This is the house." He turned in at a small doorway and unlocked the door, closing it after them. "Put your hand on my shoulder, Juan," he said. "I have a light upstairs."

He led the way in darkness up a stone staircase, then unlocked another door and entered a small room, where a candle was burning. "This is my home when I am here," he said. "Most of us sleep at the stables where our mules are put up, but I like having a place to myself, and my mate looks after the mules."

Nothing could have been simpler than the furniture of the room. It consisted of a low pallet, a small table, and a single chair. In a corner were a pair of saddle-bags and two or three coloured blankets; a thick coat lined with sheepskin hung against the wall; in a corner was a brightly-coloured picture of a saint, with two sconces for candles by the side of it. The muleteer had crossed himself and bowed to it as he came in, and Terence doubted not that it was the picture of a saint who was supposed to take special interest in muleteers. From a small cupboard the man brought out a flask of wine and two drinking-cups.

"It is good," he said, as he placed them on the table. "I go down to Xeres sometimes, and always bring up a half-octave of something special for my friends here."

After pouring out the two cups, he handed the chair politely to Terence, and sat himself down on the edge of the pallet; then, taking out a tobacco bag and a roll of paper, he made a cigarette and handed it to Terence, and then rolled one for himself.

Chapter XIII
From Salamanca to Cadiz

"Now let us talk about our journey," the muleteer said, when he had taken two or three whiffs at his cigarette. "Nita tells me that you wish, if possible, to join your army near Badajoz. That suits me well, for I have orders from a merchant here to fetch him twelve mule-loads of sherry from Xeres, and Badajoz is, therefore, on my way. The merchant has a permit signed by Marmot for me to pass unmolested by any French troops, saying that the wine is intended for his use and that of his staff. If it were not for that, there would be small chance, indeed, of his ever getting it. There is so little trade now that it is scarce possible to buy a flask of the white wine of the south here. Of course the pass will be equally useful going down to fetch it, for without it my mules would be certain to be impressed for service by the French.

"So, you see, nothing could have happened more fortunately, for anywhere between the Tagus and Badajoz we can turn off from Estremadura into Portugal. It would not be safe to try near Badajoz, for Soult's army is scattered all over there, and though the pass would be doubtless respected by superior officers, if we fell in with foraging parties they would have no hesitation in shooting me, tearing up the pass, and carrying off my mules. For your sake as well as my own, therefore, I would turn off and cross the mountains, say, to Portalegre, and go down to Elvas; there you would be with your friends, and I could cross again farther south and make my way down to Xeres."

"They say that two of Marmont's divisions started south yesterday."

FROM SALAMANCA TO CADIZ

"That is unfortunate, for they will leave little behind them in the way of food and drink, and we shall find it better to travel by by-roads. I should not mind being impressed if it were only for the march down to Badajoz, but once with an army, there is no saying how long one may be kept."

"If we find any difficulty in crossing into Portugal this side of Badajoz, I shall not mind going down to Cadiz. I should have no difficulty there in getting a ship to Lisbon."

"Well, we shall see," the muleteer said. "We will go the short way if we can. I hate the Portuguese, and they are no fonder of us; but with you with me, of course, I should not be afraid of interference from them."

"But the Portuguese are fighting on our side, and aiding us to help you."

"Yes, because they think it is better that the war should be carried on here than in their own country; besides, from what I hear, it is with no good-will that they fight under your British general, but only because he tells them that unless they furnish so many troops he will have nothing more to do with them, but will sail away with his army to England."

"That may be true, Garcia; but you know that when we were here, for I was with the British army that marched through Salamanca, the Spanish authorities were no more willing to assist than were the Portuguese, and not a single soldier, with the exception of two or three thousand half-armed men under Romana, joined, from the day we crossed the frontier to that on which we embarked to Corunna."

"The authorities are all bad," Garcia said scornfully. "They only think of feathering their own nests and of quarrelling among themselves. The people are patriots, but what can they do when the Juntas keep the arms the English have sent us in their magazines, and divide the money among themselves? Then our generals know nothing of their business, and have their own ambitions and rivalries. We are all ready to fight; and when the drum is beaten and we are called out, we go willingly enough. But what do we do when we go out? We are marched backwards and forwards without motive, the officers are no good, and when at last we do see the French, we are always beaten, and the generals and the officers are the first to run away. We ought, in the first place, to rise, not against the French, but against the Juntas, and the councillors, and the hidalgos; then, when we have done with them, we ought to choose officers from among ourselves, men that have done good service as leaders of partisans; then we could meet the French. We are brave enough when we are well led. See how the people fought at Saragossa, and since then at Gerona, and many other places. We are not afraid of being killed, but we have no confidence in our chiefs."

"I have no doubt that is so, Garcia, and that if the regiments were trained by British officers, as some of the Portuguese now are, you would fight well. Unfortunately, as you say, your generals and officers are chosen, not for their merits, but from their influence with the Juntas, whose object is to have the army filled with men who will be subservient to their orders. Then there is another thing against you: that is, the jealousy of the various provinces; there is no common effort. When Valencia is invaded, for example, the Valencians fight, but they have no idea of going out from their homes to assist Castile or Catalona, and so one after another the provinces are conquered by the French."

"That is so," Garcia said thoughtfully. "If they were to rise here, I would fight, and take my chance of being killed, but I should not care to risk my life in defence of Valencia, with which I have nothing whatever to do. I don't see how you are to get over that so long as we are divided into provinces."

"Nor do I, Garcia. In times of peace these various governments may work well enough, but nothing could be worse than the system when a country is invaded. What time do you start to-morrow?"

"As soon as the gates are open; that will be five o'clock. It is eleven now, so we had better get some sleep. In the morning I must see that your dress is all right. Nita has given me a bottle of walnut juice to stain your face and hands. Do you lie down on the bed, señor; I will wrap myself up in this cloak. I am more accustomed to sleep on that than on the bed."

Terence removed his outer garments, and in a few minutes was sound asleep. At four o'clock Garcia roused him. The morning was breaking, and with the assistance of the muleteer he made his toilet and stained his face, neck, and hands, and darkened his hair; then they each ate a piece of bread with a bunch of grapes, took a drink of red wine, and then sallied out, Garcia carrying his sheepskin cloak and Terence the three coloured blankets. A quarter of a mile farther they came to an inn frequented by muleteers.

"I have told my mate about you," Garcia said, "so you need not be afraid of him, nor indeed of any of us. There is not a muleteer who would not do what he could to aid the escape of a British officer."

Most of the mules were already saddled, and Garcia went up with Terence to a man who was buckling a strap.

"Sanchez," he said, "this is our new comrade, Juan, who I told you would accompany us this journey."

The man nodded.

"It will be all the better," he said; "twelve mules are rather too much for two men to manage when we get among the mountains."

Garcia and Terence at once set to work to assist, and in ten minutes the cavalcade started. Garcia rode the leading mule, three others being tied in single file behind it. Terence came next, and Sanchez brought up the rear. The animals were fine ones, and Garcia was evidently proud of them, showing their good points to Terence, and telling him their names. The mules were all very fond of their master, turning their heads at once when addressed by name, and flapping their long ears in enjoyment as he rubbed their heads or patted their necks. The town was already astir, and as they reached the gates, country carts were pouring in, laden with fruits and vegetables for the market. Garcia stopped for a moment as an old man came along with a cart.

"How are you, father?"

"How are you, Garcia? Off again?"

"Yes; I am going to Xeres for wine for the French general."

"I see that you have got a new comrade."

"Yes; the journey is a long one, and I thought that it was as well to have another mate."

"Yes, it is dangerous travelling," the old man said. "Well, good-bye, and good fortune to you!"

Garcia put his mules in motion again, and they passed through the gate and soon left Salamanca behind. There was little conversation on the way. The two Spaniards made and smoked cigarettes continually, and Terence endeavoured to imitate them by addressing the endearing words they used to their animals, having learned the names of the four of which he was in charge. At first they did not respond to this strange voice, but as they became accustomed to it each answered when its name was called by quickening its pace and by a sharp whisk of the tail, that showed it understood that it was addressed.

Terence knew that his escape would not be discovered until eight o'clock, when the doors were opened and the prisoners assembled in the yard for the roll-call. Should any pursuit be organised, which was unlikely, it would be in the direction of Ciudad, as it might be supposed that an escaped prisoner would naturally make for the nearest spot where he could join his friends. One prisoner more or less would, however, make but little difference, and the authorities would probably content themselves with sending a message by a trooper to all the towns and villages on that road to arrest any suspicious persons travelling without proper papers. On the line they were pursuing, the risk of interference was very small. The marshal's pass would be certainly respected by the officers of the corps under his command, and it was not until they fell in with parties of Soult's troops that any unpleasantness was to be apprehended, though even here the worst that could be looked for, if they met any large body of troops, would be that the mules might be taken for a time for service in the army. After a long day's journey they halted for the night at a village. Here they found that the troops marching south had encamped close at hand for the night, and the resources of the place had been completely exhausted. This mattered but little, as they carried a week's store of bread, black sausage, cheese, onions, garlic, and capsicums. The landlord of the little inn furnished them with a cooking-pot, and a sort of stew, which Terence found by no means unpalatable, was concocted. The mules were hobbled and turned out on to the plain to graze, for the whole of the forage of the village had been requisitioned for the use of the cavalry and baggage animals of the French column.

On the following morning they struck off from the road they had been following, and, travelling for sixteen hours, came down on it again at the foot of the pass of Bejar, and learned from some peasants that they had got ahead of the French column, which was encamped two or three miles down the road. Before daybreak they were on their way again, and reached Banos in the afternoon. There were but few inhabitants remaining here, for the requisitions for food and forage made by the troops that had so frequently passed through the defiles were such that the position of the inhabitants had become intolerable; and when they learned from Garcia that two divisions of French troops would most probably arrive that evening, and that Marmont's whole army would follow, most of the inhabitants who remained hastily packed their most valuable belongings in carts and drove away into the hills.

The landlord of the largest inn, however, stood his ground. He was doing well, and the principal officers of troops passing through always took up their quarters with him, paid him fairly for their meals, and saw that, whatever exactions were placed upon the town, he was exempted from them. Therefore the muleteers were able to obtain a comfortable meal, and after resting their animals for three hours, and giving them a good feed of corn, went on for a few miles farther, and then, turning off, encamped among the hills. They were about to wrap themselves in their cloaks and blankets, and to lie down for the night, when a number of armed men suddenly appeared.

"Who are you, and whither are you going?" one who appeared to be their leader asked.

"We are bound for Xeres," Garcia replied, rising to his feet; "we are commissioned by Señor Moldeno, the well-known wine merchant of Salamanca, to procure for him as much good Xeres wine as our mules will carry."

"It is a pity that we did not meet you on the way back instead of on your journey there; we should appreciate the wine quite as thoroughly as his customers would do. But how do you propose to bring your wine back when the whole country south swarms with Soult's cavalry?"

"Don Moldeno obtained a pass for us from Marmont, who, I suppose, is one of his customers."

"We could not think of allowing wine to pass for the use of a French marshal," the man said.

"It is not likely that he will drink it for some time," Garcia said carelessly, "for he is marching in this direction himself. Two of his divisions have probably by this time reached Banos, and we heard at Salamanca that he himself, with the rest of them, will follow in a day or two."

"That is bad news," the man said. "There will be no travellers along here while the army is on its march. Are your mules carrying nothing now?"

"Nothing at all. The mules would have been requisitioned two days ago, as were most of the others in Salamanca, but Marmont's pass saved us."

"Are you carrying the money to buy the wine with?"

"No, Don Moldeno knew better than that. I have only a letter from him to the house of Simon Peron at Xeres. He told me that that would be sufficient, and they would furnish me with the wine at once on my handing the letter to them."

"Well, comrades," the man said to the others gathered round, "it is evident that we shall get no booty to-night, and may as well be off to our own fires, where supper is waiting for us, and move away from here at daybreak. The French may have parties of horse all over the hills to-morrow, searching for provisions, cattle, and sheep."

"That was a narrow escape," Garcia said, as the brigands moved off. "I wonder they did not take our mules; but I suppose they had as many as they want—three or four would be sufficient to carry their food and anything they may have stolen—more than that would only be a hindrance to them in moving about, especially now they know that the French may be in the neighbourhood in a few hours, if they have not arrived already. Well, señor, what is the next thing to be done?"

Terence did not answer for some little time.

"It is not easy to say," he replied at length. "Seeing that Marmont and Soult are practically united, there can be no doubt that our troops will have to fall back again to Portugal. The whole country is covered with French cavalry, and in addition we have to run risks from these brigands, who may not always prove so easy to deal with as the men who have just left us. What do you think yourself? You know the country, and can judge far better than I can as to our chance of getting through."

"I don't think it will be possible, señor, to carry out the plan of trying to cross into Portugal in this direction. It seems to me, now that Soult is engaged, and there can be no large bodies of French near

Seville, our best plan would be to make for that town, whence, so far as we know, the country is clear of the enemy down to Cadiz; and when we reach that port, you can take ship to Lisbon."

"But in that case I shall not be able to get the money to pay you, for I shall not be known; and although I could doubtless get a passage, I do not think that I could obtain any funds."

"Do not speak of it, señor. The British will be in Salamanca one of these days, and then you will be able to pay me; or, if I should not be there at the time, you can leave the money for me with Nita or her father. It was for her sake that I undertook the business, and I have no doubt whatever that you will discharge the debt when you enter Salamanca."

"That I certainly will, and to make it more certain I will ask one of the officers of my old regiment to undertake to find her out, and to pay the money, in case I may be with my own men in some other part of the country."

"That will be quite enough, señor. Do not trouble yourself further on the matter. We will start for Seville at daybreak."

Travelling rapidly, the little party kept along the range of the Sierras, and then proceeded by the valley of the Tagus and crossed the river at Talavera, and then, keeping nearly due south, struck the Guadiana at Ciudad Real, and crossing La Mancha gained the Sierra Morena, held west for some distance along the southern slopes, and then turned south and struck the Guadalquivir between Cordova and Seville, and arrived safely at the latter town. They had been obliged to make a great number of detours to avoid bodies of the enemy, but the muleteer had no difficulty in obtaining information from the peasants as to the whereabouts of the French, and after reaching the plains always travelled at night. They fell in twice with large parties of guerillas, but these were not brigands, for as the country was still unconquered, and the French only held the ground they occupied, the bands had not degenerated into brigandage, but were in communication with the local authorities, and acted in conformity with their instructions in concert with the Spanish troops. It was, however, nearly a month from the date of their leaving Salamanca before they arrived at Cadiz. Terence had during the journey greatly improved his knowledge of Spanish by his conversation with the muleteers, and as the language was so similar to the Portuguese, he soon acquired facility in speaking it. They put up at a small *fonda,* or inn, frequented by muleteers, and Terence at once made his way to the house where he heard that the British agent resided. The latter, on hearing his story, was surprised indeed that he should have made his way through Spain from a point so far away as Salamanca, and occupied for the greater portion of the distance by the French.

"A sloop-of-war is sailing to-morrow for the Tagus," he said, "and I will give you a letter to her captain, who will of course give you passage." Terence informed him of the great services the muleteer had rendered him, and asked him if he could advance him sufficient money to repay the man.

"I certainly have no funds at my disposal for such a purpose, Captain O'Connor,"—for Terence had said nothing about his Portuguese rank, finding that its announcement always caused a certain amount of doubt,—"but I will strain a point and grant you thirty pounds on your bill upon your agent at Lisbon. I have no doubt that it will be met on presentation. But should, for example, your vessel be wrecked or captured, which I am by no means contemplating as likely, the amount must go down among subsidies to Spaniards who have rendered good service."

"Thank you, sir. That will be sufficient, not to reward the man for the risk he has run and the fidelity that he has shown, but it will at least pay him for the service of his mule. I do not suppose that he would earn more, and it will be a satisfaction to me to know that he is at least not out of pocket."

The agent at once handed him a bag of silver, together with a letter to the officer in command of the *Daphne*. He hired a boat and was rowed off to the ship, which was lying with several other small British war-ships in the port. When he ascended the side, the officer on duty asked him somewhat roughly in bad Spanish what he wanted.

"I have a letter for Captain Fry," he replied in English, to the surprise of the lieutenant. "I am a British officer who was taken prisoner at the battle of Fuentes d'Onoro."

"You must not blame me for having taken you for a Spaniard," the lieutenant said in surprise as he handed the letter Terence held out, to the midshipman, with a request to deliver it to the captain.

"Your disguise is certainly excellent, and if you speak Spanish as well as you look the part, I can quite understand your getting safely through the country."

"Unfortunately I do not. I speak it quite well enough for ordinary purposes, but not well enough to pass as a native. I travelled with a muleteer, who did all the talking that was necessary. I have been a month on the journey, which has greatly improved my Spanish. I knew little of it when I started, but I should not have got on so quickly had I not been thoroughly up in Portuguese, which, of course, helped me immensely."

The midshipman now came up and requested Terence to follow him to the captain's cabin. The captain smiled as he entered.

"It is well that Mr. Bromhead vouched for you, Captain O'Connor, for I certainly should have had difficulty in bringing myself to believe that you were a British officer. I shall, of course, be very glad to give you a passage, and to hear the story of your adventures, which ought to be very interesting."

"I have had very few adventures," Terence replied. "The muleteer knew the country perfectly, and had no difficulty in obtaining from the peasants news of the movements of the French. When I started I had no idea of making such a long journey, but had intended to join Lord Beresford in front of Badajoz if I could not manage to cross the frontier higher up; but Marmont's march south rendered that impossible, and I thought that the safer plan would be to keep well away from the frontier, as of course things are much more settled in the interior, and two or three muleteers with their animals would excite little attention, even if we passed through a town with a large French garrison, except that the mules might have been impressed; and as I had no means of recompensing my guide in that case, I was anxious to avoid all risk. When do you sail, sir?"

"At eight o'clock to-morrow. You cannot very well go in that attire," the captain said, smiling. "I shall be glad to advance any sum that you may require to procure clothes. You can, no doubt, pay me on your arrival at Lisbon."

Terence gladly accepted a loan of ten pounds, and with it returned to shore. On reaching the little inn, he at once handed thirty pounds to Garcia. The man, however, absolutely refused to accept it.

"No, señor, since you have got money I will take fifty dollars to pay for food and forage on my way back, although really you have cost me nothing, for I had to make the journey on business. But even did you owe me the money I would not take it now. I may not be so lucky on my way back as we have been in coming, and might be seized by brigands, therefore I would in any case rather that you left the matter until you come to Salamanca."

"But that may not be for a long time. It is quite as likely that we may be obliged to quit Portugal and embark for England as that we shall ever get to Salamanca."

"Who knows, señor! Luck may turn. However, I would rather that it were so. I have had the pleasure of your having made the journey with me, and I shall have pleased Nita. If you come, well and good; if not, it cannot be helped, and I shall not grieve over it. If I had money with me I might lose it, and it might cost me my life."

Terence had again gone out and purchased a suit of clothes befitting a Spanish gentleman. He took the muleteer with him. They had no longer any reason for concealing their identity, and should he find it necessary to announce himself to be a British officer, it might be useful to have corroboration of his story. He also laid in a fresh stock of linen, of which he was greatly in need, and the next morning, after a hearty farewell to Garcia, he went down to the port in his new attire, and, carrying a small valise containing his purchases, took a boat to the ship. The evening before, he had called in at the agent's to thank him again, when the latter told him that he had some urgent despatches from the junta of Cadiz to that of Seville, and some despatches of his own to persons at Cordova, and others in Madrid, who were in communication with the British government, and he offered a sum for their safe delivery that would recompense the muleteer for the whole of his journey. This Garcia had gladly acceded to, on condition that he might stop for a day to get the wine at Xeres.

The voyage to Lisbon lasted three days, and was a very pleasant one to Terence. On his arrival there he at once repaid the captain the loan he had received from him, having over thirty pounds still in hand. He next saw the agent, and requested him to pay the bill when presented, and after waiting three days to obtain a fresh uniform, started up the country and rejoined Wellington, who had been compelled to fall back again behind Coa. He reported himself to the adjutant-general.

"You have just arrived in time, Captain O'Connor," the latter said, "for your regiment is under orders to start to-morrow to join the force of the guerilla Moras, who with two thousand men is in the mountains on our frontier near Miranda, and intends to threaten Zamora, and so compel Marmont to draw off some of his troops facing us here. Your regiment is at present on the Douro, fifteen miles away. How have you come here?"

"I travelled by a country conveyance, sir. I am at present without a horse, but no doubt I can pick one up when I have obtained funds from the paymaster."

"I will give you an order on him for fifty pounds," the adjutant said. "Of course there is a great deal more owing to you, but it will save trouble to give you an order for that sum on account; I don't suppose you will want more. I will have inquiries made about a horse. If you return here in an hour I dare say I shall hear of one for sale. Your regiment has not done much fighting since you left it, but they behaved well at Banos, where we had a very sharp fight. They came up just at the critical moment, and they materially assisted us in beating off the attack of the French, who were in greatly superior force, and nearly succeeded in capturing or exterminating the light division."

On his return Terence found that one of the officers on the adjutant-general's staff knew of a horse that had been captured by a trooper in a skirmish with French dragoons three days before. It was a serviceable animal; and as the soldier was glad to take ten pounds for it, Terence at once purchased it. The adjutant told him that, on mentioning his return, Lord Wellington had requested him to dine with him, and to come half an hour before the usual time, as he wished to question him with reference to the state of the country he had passed through, and of the strength and probable movements of the French troops in those districts.

"I am glad to see you back again, Colonel O'Connor," the general said when he entered. "Of course I heard how you had been captured, and have regretted your absence. Colonel Herrara is a good officer in many ways, and the regiment has maintained its state of efficiency, but he does not possess your energy and enterprise, nor the readiness to assume responsibilities and to act solely upon his own initiative—a most valuable quality," he said, with one of his rare smiles, "when combined with sound judgement, for an officer commanding a partisan corps like your own, but which, if general, would in a very short time put an end to all military combinations and render the office of a commander-in-chief a sinecure. Now, sir, will you be good enough to point out on this map exactly the line you followed in travelling from Salamanca to Cadiz, and give me any information you gained concerning the roads, the disposition of the people, and the position and movements of the French troops."

Terence had anticipated that such information would be required of him, and had, every evening when they halted, jotted down every fact that he thought could be useful, and on the voyage to Lisbon had written from them a full report both of the matters which the general now inquired about and of the amount of supplies which could probably be obtained in each locality, the number of houses and accommodation available for troops, the state and strength of the passes, and the information that Garcia had obtained for him of mountain-tracks by which these passages could be turned by infantry and cavalry in single file.

"I have brought my report, sir," he said, producing it. "I endeavoured to make the most of my opportunities to gain all the information possible that might be useful to myself or the commander of any column moving across the same country. I fear that it is far from being perfect; but as I wrote it from my notes made at the end of each day, I think it will answer its purpose as far as it goes."

Attached to each day's journey was a rough sketch-map showing the cross-roads, rivers, bridges, and other particulars. The general took the bulky report, sat down and read a page here and there, and glanced at the maps. He looked up approvingly.

"Very good, indeed, Colonel O'Connor. If all officers would take advantage of their opportunities as you have done, the drudgery my staff have to do would be very much lightened, and they would not be constantly working in the dark." He handed the report to the adjutant-general. "This may be of great utility when an advance begins," he said. "You had better have two or three copies of it made. It will be useful to the quartermaster's department as well as to yourself, and of great assistance to the officers in command of any detached parties that may be despatched to gather in supplies or to keep in check an enemy advancing on our flank. Some day, when I can find time, I will read the whole report myself. It will be well to have a dozen copies made of the first five or six pages and the maps, for the perusal of any officer sent out with a detachment on scouting duty, as a model of the sort of report that an officer should send in of his work when on such duty."

The party at dinner was a small one, consisting only of some five or six officers of the headquarter staff and two generals of divisions. After dinner Lord Wellington asked Terence how he escaped from Salamanca, and the latter briefly related the particulars of his evasion.

"This is the second time you have escaped from a French prison," Lord Wellington said, when he had finished. "The last time, if I remember rightly, you escaped from Bayonne in a boat."

"But you did not get to England in that boat, surely, Colonel O'Connor?" one of the generals laughed.

"No, sir; we were driven off shore by a gale and picked up by a French privateer. We escaped from her as she was lying in port at Brest, made our way to the mouth of the river Sienne, about nine miles north of Granville, and then, stealing another boat, started for Jersey. We were chased by a French privateer, but before she came up to us a Jersey privateer arrived and engaged her. While the fight was going on we got on board the Jersey boat, which finally captured the Frenchman and took her into port."

"And from there, I suppose, you found your way to England, and enjoyed a short rest from your labours?"

"No, sir. The captain of the privateer, who thought that we had rendered him valuable assistance in the fight, sailed out with us on to the ship track, and put us on board a transport bound for Lisbon."

"Well, you are more heart and soul in it than I am," the general laughed. "I should not have been able to deny myself a short run in England."

"I was anxious to get back to my regiment, sir, as I was afraid that if I did not return before the next campaign opened, some other officer might be appointed to its command."

"You need not trouble yourself on that score in the future, Colonel O'Connor," Lord Wellington said. "If you have the bad luck to be captured again, I shall know that your absence will be temporary; and if it became necessary to appoint anyone else to your command, it would only be until your return."

On leaving the commander-in-chief's quarters, the adjutant-general asked Terence when he thought of rejoining his regiment.

"I am going to start at once, sir. I ordered my horse to be saddled and in readiness at ten o'clock."

"You must not think of doing so," the adjutant said. "The road is very bad and not at all fit to be traversed on a dark night like this. Besides, you would really gain nothing by it. If you leave at daybreak, you will overtake your regiment before it has marched many miles."

Chapter XIV
Effecting A Diversion

At twelve o'clock the next day Terence rode up to his regiment just as it had halted for two hours' rest. As soon as he was recognised the men leapt to their feet, cheering vociferously, and gathered round him, while a minute or two later Herrara, Ryan, and the two majors ran up to greet him.

"I have been expecting you for the last month," Ryan exclaimed, "though how you were to get through the French lines was more than I could imagine. Still, I made sure you would do it somehow."

"You gave me credit for more sharpness than I possess, Dick. I felt sure it could not be done, and so I had to go right down to Cadiz and back to Lisbon by ship. It was a very much easier affair than ours was, and I met with no adventures and no difficulties on the way. Well, Herrara, I heard at headquarters that the regiment is going on well, and they fought stoutly at Banos. Your loss was not heavy, I hope?"

"We had fifty-three killed and a hundred more or less seriously wounded; more than half of them have rejoined; the vacancies have been filled up, and the two battalions are both at their full strength. Two of the captains, Fernandez and Panza, were killed. I have appointed two of the sergeants temporarily, pending your confirmation on your return."

"It is well that it is no worse. They were both good men, and will be a loss to us. Whom have you appointed in their places?"

"Gomes and Mendoza, the two sergeant-majors. They are both men of good family and thoroughly know their duty. Of course I filled their places for the time with two of the colour-sergeants."

"I suppose you have ridden from headquarters, Terence," Ryan put in, "and must be as hungry as a hunter. We were just going to sit down to a couple of chickens and a ham, so come along."

While they were taking their meal, Terence gave them an account of the manner in which he had escaped from Salamanca.

"So you were in our old quarters, Terence! Well, you certainly have a marvellous knack of getting out of scrapes. When we saw your horse carrying you into the middle of the French cavalry, I thought for a moment that the Minho regiment had lost its colonel, but it was not for long, and soon I was sure that somehow or other you would give them the slip again. Of course, I have been thinking of you as a prisoner at Ciudad, and I was afraid that they would keep a sharper watch over you there than they did at Bayonne. Still, I felt sure that you would manage it somehow, even without the help we had. What are your orders?"

"I have none, save that we are to march to Miranda, where we shall find a guerilla force under Moras, and we are to operate with him and do all we can to attract the attention of the French. That is all I know, for I have not had time to look at the written instructions I received from the adjutant-general when I said good-bye to him last night, but I don't think there are any precise orders. What were yours, Herrrara?"

"They are that I was to consult with Moras; to operate carefully, and not to be drawn into any combat with superior or nearly equal forces; which I took to mean equal to the strength of the regiment, for the guerillas are not to be depended upon to the smallest extent in anything like a pitched combat."

"There is no doubt about that," Terence agreed. "For cutting off small parties, harassing convoys, or anything of that sort, they are excellent, but for down-right hard fighting the guerillas are not worth their salt. The great advantage of them is that they render it necessary for the French to send very strong guards with their baggage and convoys, and occasionally, when they are particularly bold and numerous, to despatch columns in pursuit of them. If it were not for these bands, they would be able to concentrate all their troops, and would soon capture Andalusia and Valencia, and then turn their attention to other work. As it is, they have to keep the roads clear, to leave strong garrisons everywhere, and to keep a sufficient force in each province to make head against the guerillas; for if they did not do so, all their friends would be speedily killed, and the peasantry be constantly incited to rise."

EFFECTING A DIVERSION

The men leapt to their feet, cheering vociferously.

"Do you know anything of the Moras?"

"He is said to be a good leader," Herrara replied, "and to have gathered under him a number of other bands. He has the reputation of being less savage and cruel than the greater part of these partisan leaders; and though, no doubt, he kills prisoners—for in that he could hardly restrain his men—he does not permit the barbarous cruelties that are a disgrace to the Spanish people. In fact, I believe his orders are that no prisoners are to be taken."

"I will look at my instructions," Terence said, drawing out the paper he had received the night before. "Yes," he said, when he had read them; "my instructions are a good deal like yours, but they leave my hands somewhat more free. I am to consult with Moras, to operate with him when I think it advisable, and in all respects to act entirely upon my own judgement and discretion, the main object being to compel the French to detach as many men as possible from this neighbourhood, in order to oppose me, and I am to take every advantage the nature of the country may afford to inflict heavy blows upon them."

"That is all right," Ryan said cheerfully. "I had quite made up my mind that we should always be dependent upon Moras, and be kept inactive owing to his refusal to carry out anything Herrara might propose; but as you can act independently of him, we are sure to have plenty of fun."

"We will make it as hot for them as we can, Dick; and if we cannot do more, we can certainly oblige the French to keep something like a division idle to hold us in check. With the two battalions, and Moras's irregulars, we ought to be able to harass them amazingly, and to hold any of these mountain passes against a considerable force."

After two hours' halt the march was renewed, and two days later the regiment arrived at Miranda. The frontier ran close to this town, the Douro separating the two countries. They learned that Moras was lying four miles farther to the north, and across the frontier line, doubtless preferring to remain in Spain, in order to prevent a quarrel between his followers and the Portuguese. The next morning Terence, accompanied by Ryan and four mounted orderlies, rode into the glen where he and his followers were lying. They had erected a great number of small arbours of boughs and bushes; and as Terence rode up to one of these, which was larger and better finished than the rest, Moras himself came to the entrance to meet them.

He did not at all correspond with Terence's ideas of a guerilla chief. He was a young man of three- or four-and-twenty, of slim figure and with a handsome, thoughtful face. He had been a student of divinity at Salamanca, but had killed a French officer in a duel brought on by the insolence of the latter, and had been compelled to fly. A few men had gathered round him, and he had at once raised his standard as a guerilla chief. At first his operations had been on a very small scale, but the success that had attended these enterprises, and the reports of his reckless bravery, had speedily swelled the number of his followers; and although as a rule he kept only a hundred with him, he could at any time, by sending round a summons, collect five times that number in a few hours. When Terence introduced himself as the colonel of the two battalions that had arrived at Miranda to operate in conjunction with him, Moras held out his hand frankly.

"I am very glad indeed to meet you, Colonel O'Connor," he said. "I received a despatch four days ago from your general, saying that the Minho regiment would shortly arrive at Miranda to act in concert with me. I was glad indeed when I heard of this, for the name of the regiment is well known on this side of the frontier as well as on the other, having been engaged in many gallant actions, and your name is equally well known in connection with it; but I hardly expected to meet you, for the despatch said the Minho regiment under Lieutenant-colonel Herrara."

"Yes. I only rejoined it two days ago, having been taken prisoner at Fuentes d'Onoro, and having made my escape from Salamanca."

"Your aid will be invaluable, señor. My own men are brave enough, but they are irregulars in the full sense of the word;" and he smiled. "And although they can be relied upon for a sudden attack, or for the defence of a pass, they could not stand against a French force of a quarter of their strength in the plain. We want backbone, and no better one could be found than your regiment. I am the more glad that you are in command, because you know, unhappily, we and the Portuguese do not get on well together; and while my men would hesitate to obey a Portuguese commander, and would have no confidence in him, they would gladly accept your leadership."

"I hope that there will be no difficulties on the ground of race," Terence said. "We are fighting in a common cause against a common enemy, and dissensions between ourselves are as absurd as they are dangerous. Let me introduce Captain Ryan, adjutant of the regiment."

Moras shook hands with Ryan, who had been looking on with some surprise at the colloquy between him and Terence. Moras then asked them into his arbour.

"I have little to offer you," he said with a smile, "save black bread and wine; the latter, however, is good. I obtained a large supply of it from a convoy we captured a few days since."

The wine was indeed excellent, and, accustomed as they were to the coarse bread of the country, Terence and Ryan were able to eat it with satisfaction.

"Now, Colonel," Moras said, "beyond the fact that we are to act in concert, I know nothing of the plans. Please to remember that while it is said that we are to discuss our plans of operations together, I place myself unreservedly under your orders. Of irregular warfare I have learned something; but of military science and anything like extensive operations I am as ignorant as a child, while you have shown your capacity for command. I may be of advantage to you from my knowledge of the country; and indeed there is not a village track that someone or other of my followers is not well acquainted with."

"That, of course, will be of great advantage to us," Terence replied courteously, "and I thank you much for what you have said; but I am sure, from what I have heard, you underrate your abilities. Beyond regimental drill I knew very little of warfare until I, quite by accident, came to assume the command of my regiment: and it was only because I drilled and disciplined it thoroughly that I had the good fortune to obtain some successes with it. Your acquaintance with the country will be fully a set-off to any superior knowledge that I may have of military matters, and I have no doubt that we shall get on well together. The instructions that I have received are to the effect that we are to make incursions and attacks in various directions, concealing, as far as possible, our strength, and so to oblige the French to detach a considerable number of troops to hold us in check. This would relieve the pressure upon Lord Wellington's army, and would

EFFECTING A DIVERSION

deter the enemy from making any offensive movement into Portugal until our general has received the reinforcements expected shortly, and is in a position to take the offensive."

"It will be just the work to suit us," the guerilla chief said. "And as I received a subsidy from your political agent at Lisbon a few days since, I am in a position to keep the whole force I have together, which is more than I can do generally, for even if successful in an attack on a convoy, the greater portion of the men scatter and return to their homes; and as long as their share of the booty lasts, they do not care to come out again."

Terence now produced a map with which he had been supplied, and a considerable time was spent in obtaining full particulars of the country through which the troops might have to march, ascertaining the best spots for resistance when retreating, or for attacking columns who might be despatched in pursuit of them, and in discussing the manner and direction in which their operations would most alarm and annoy the enemy. It was finally agreed that Terence should break up his battalions into three parties. Two of these consisted each of half a battalion, 500 strong, and would be under the command of Bull and Macwitty. Each of them would be accompanied by 300 guerillas, who would act as scouts, and in case opportunity should offer, join in any fighting that might take place.

The other two half-battalions formed the third body under the command of Terence himself, and would, with the main force of the guerillas, occupy the roads between Zamora, Salamanca, and Valladolid. In this way the French would be harassed at several points, and would find it so difficult to obtain information as to the real strength of the foe that was threatening them, that they would be obliged to send up a considerable force to oppose them, and would hesitate to undertake any serious advance into Portugal until the question was cleared up and their lines of communication assured again. It was agreed, in the first place, that the forces should unite in the mountains west of Braganza, between the river Esla on the east and Tera on the north, affording a strong position, from which, in case of any very large force mustering against them, they could retire across the frontier into Portugal.

Terence had been supplied with money and an authority to give orders on the paymaster's department for such purchases as were absolutely necessary. Moras was also well supplied, having not only the money that had been sent him, but the proceeds of a successful attack upon a convoy proceeding to Salamanca, in which he had captured a commissariat chest with a considerable sum of money, besides a large number of cattle and several waggon loads of flour. All these provisions, with some that Terence had authority to draw from the stores at Miranda, were to be taken to the spot they had chosen as their headquarters in the hills.

"You beat me altogether, Terence," Ryan said, as, after all these matters had been arranged, they rode out from the guerilla's camp. "It is only about three months since I saw you. Then you could only just get along in Spanish. Now you are chattering away in it as if you had never spoken anything else all your life."

"Well, you see, Dick, I knew just enough when I was taken prisoner to be able to, as you say, get along in it, and that made all the difference to me. If I had known nothing at all of it I should not have been able to benefit by my trip with the muleteers in Spain. As it was, I was able to talk with them, and as we rode side by side all day, and sat together by a fire for hours after we had halted when the day's journey was over, we did a tremendous lot of talking, and, as you see, I came out at the end of the month able to get along really fluently. I, no doubt, make a good many mistakes, and mix a good many Portuguese words with my Spanish, but that does not matter in the least so long as one is with friends; although it would matter a good deal if I were trying to pass as a Spaniard among people who might betray me if they found out that I was English. I see that you have improved in Portuguese almost as much as I have in Spanish. It is really only the first drudgery that is difficult in learning a language. When once one makes a start one gets on very fast, especially if one is not afraid of making mistakes. I never care a rap whether I make blunders or not so that I can but make myself understood."

Three days later the two bodies were assembled in a valley about equally distant from Miranda and Braganza. It had the advantage of being entered from the east only through a narrow gorge, which could be defended against a very superior force, while there were two mountain tracks leading from it, by which the force there could be

EFFECTING A DIVERSION

withdrawn should the entrance be forced. A day was spent by the leaders in making their final arrangements, while the men worked at the erection of a great wall of rocks, twelve feet high and as many thick, across the mouth of the gorge, collecting quantities of stones and rocks on the heights on either side to roll down upon any enemy who might endeavour to scale them, while another very strong party built a wall six feet high in a great semicircle round the upper mouth of the gorge, so that a column forcing its way through thus far would be met by so heavy a fire that they could only debouch into the valley with immense loss.

Two hundred men of the Minho regiment, drawn from Terence's party, were to occupy the valley with three hundred of the guerillas, who would be able to do good service by occupying the heights while the regular infantry held the newly-erected walls. One of Moras' most trusted lieutenants was to command them, while after some discussion it was arranged that Herrara should be in general command of the garrison. The brave fellow was reluctant to remain inactive, but he had been for some time seriously unwell, having been laid up for some time with a severe attack of dysentery, and was really unfit for any continued exertion, although he had made light of his illness, and refused to go on the sick-list. Terence pointed out to him that the command was a very important one. Here all the plunder that they might obtain from the enemy would be carried, and if by means of spies or traitors the French obtained news of the situation of the post, he might be attacked in great force before the other detachments could arrive to his assistance.

As there were four thousand French troops at Zamora, it was agreed that no direct attack could be made upon the town. Bull with his force was to watch the garrison, attack any detachments that might be sent out, leaving them severely alone when they sallied out in force, and to content himself with outmarching their infantry, and beating off any cavalry attacks. He was, if necessary, to retreat in the direction of their stronghold. Macwitty was to occupy the road between Zamora and Valladolid, while the main body held the roads between both the latter town and Zamora to Salamanca. Frequent communication was to be kept up between them, so that either column might speedily be reinforced if necessary.

UNDER WELLINGTON'S COMMAND

In the course of a week the whole country was in a state of alarm, bridges were broken down, roads blocked by deep cuttings across them, convoys attacked, small French posts at Tordesillas, Fuentelapena, and Valparaiso captured, the French soldiers being disarmed and then taken under an escort to within ten miles of Salamanca. Toro was entered suddenly, and a garrison of three hundred men taken by surprise and forced to lay down their arms. The powder, bullocks, and waggons with their stores were sent by circuitous routes to the bridge across the Douro at Miranda, and then up to their stronghold. So vigilant a watch was kept on the roads that no single courier was able to make his way from Valladolid to Salamanca or Zamora, and beyond the fact that the whole country seemed swarming with enemies, the French commanders were in absolute ignorance of the strength of the force that had so suddenly invaded Leon.

One day a messenger rode in from Macwitty to Fuentelapena, where Terence had his headquarters, saying that a body of 4000 French infantry with 1000 cavalry were on the march from Valladolid towards Zamora. Strong positions had already been selected for the defence, and a bridge broken down at a point where the road crossed a tributary of the Douro. Terence at once sent Ryan with 200 men to reinforce Macwitty, and despatched several mounted messengers to find Bull, and to tell him to join him on the road four miles to the east of the point where Macwitty was defending the passage of the river. He himself marched directly on that point, crossing the river at Tordesillas. He arrived there early in the morning, and found that the French column had passed late the evening before.

At this point the road ran between two hills, several times crossing a stream that wound along the valley. A large number of men were at once set to work breaking down the bridges, and throwing up a breastwork along the bank where the river made a sharp bend, crossing the valley from the foot of the hills on one side to that of those on the other. While this work was being done, cannon shots were heard, then a distant rattle of musketry. Terence knew that by this time Ryan would have joined Macwitty, and Moras at once started with his men and 400 of the Portuguese to threaten the French rear, and make a dash upon their baggage. Terence's orders to the officers in command of these two companies were that they were to keep

EFFECTING A DIVERSION

their men well together, and to cover the retreat of the guerillas from cavalry attacks. The firing continued for the next hour and a half, then it suddenly swelled in volume, and amid the rattle could be heard the sound of heavy volleys of musketry.

Terence had, half an hour before, ridden forward at full speed with four mounted orderlies. When he arrived at a spot where he could survey the scene of combat, he saw that it was more serious than he had anticipated. The guerillas were falling back rapidly, but as soon as they gained the high ground they halted and opened fire upon the cavalry, who, scattered over the plain, were pursuing them. His own men were retreating steadily and in good order, facing round and pouring heavy volleys into the French cavalry as they charged them. The French attack on Macwitty had ceased, and Terence saw bodies of infantry moving towards the right, where on rising ground a body of troops about a thousand strong were showing themselves menacingly.

He had no doubt for a moment that this was Bull's command, who, hearing the firing, and supposing that Terence was engaged there, had led his command straight to the scene of action. He at once sent an orderly back at full gallop to order the men in the valley to come on at the top of their speed, and then rode along the hillside and joined Bull, who was now closely engaged with the advancing columns of French. So hot was the fire from Bull's own men and the guerillas that the two French battalions wavered and came to a halt, and then, breaking into skirmishing order, advanced up the hill.

"Don't wait too long, Bull," Terence said. "There is a steeper slope behind you. However, I don't think they will come up very far—not at least until they are reinforced. There is another body just starting, and I think we can hold on here until they join the skirmishing line. As soon as they do so, sound the order for the men to fall back."

"Where are your men, sir?"

"They are four miles away, at the spot where I told you to join me. However, the mistake is of no importance. I have sent off for them, and as soon as they arrive and show themselves, I fancy the French will retreat."

He tore out a leaf from his pocket-book and wrote out an order to Macwitty:

UNDER WELLINGTON'S COMMAND

Leave Captain Ryan with his command to hold the river, and march at once with the rest of your men to the ford which we heard of a mile down the river, cross there, and ascend the hills on the French right, scattering your men so as to make as much show as possible, and menacing the French with attack. Tell Captain Ryan to redouble his fire, so as to prevent the French noticing the withdrawal of your force.

This he gave to one of his orderlies, and told him to swim the river and deliver it to Major Macwitty. When Terence had done this, he was able to give his attention to what was passing. Across the valley his men had now ascended the hill and joined the guerillas. The French cavalry, unable to charge up the heights, had fallen back. A column of French, some fifteen hundred strong, were marching in that direction. As he had expected, the skirmishers in front of him were making but little way, evidently halting for the arrival of the reinforcement, which was still more than half a mile distant. The French gunners had been withdrawn from the bank of the river, and were taking up positions to cover the advance of their infantry, and their shot presently came singing overhead, doing no harm, however, to the Portuguese, who were lying down on the crest of the swell, and keeping up a steady fire on the French skirmishers.

Ten minutes later the column was within a short distance of the line of defenders. Terence gave the word, and his men retired up another and steeper slope behind, while the guerillas were ordered to remain to keep up a brisk fire, until the French were within thirty yards of the crest, and were then to run back at full speed, and join him above. The Portuguese had scarcely taken up their position when a tremendous fire broke out below. A minute later the guerillas were seen rushing up the hill, and close behind them came the French line, cheering loudly. As they appeared, the Portuguese opened fire, and with such steadiness and precision that the leading files of the French were almost annihilated. But the wave swept upwards, and, encouraged by the shouts of their officers, they advanced against the second position. For half an hour an obstinate fight was maintained, the strength of the position neutralising the effect of the superior numbers of the French. The Spaniards fought well, imitating the steadiness of the Portuguese, and, being for the most part good marksmen, their fire was very deadly, and several determined attacks of the French were beaten off with heavy loss. Then from the valley below was heard the sound of a bugle. The call was repeated by the bugles of the assailants, and slowly and reluctantly the French began to fall back. Terence looked round. He had from time to time glanced across to the hills opposite, and had seen his men there retiring steadily, and in good order, before the assault of the French, and now he saw that his force from the valley was marching rapidly along the hill-top to their assistance, while away on the French right, Macwitty's command, spread out to appear of much greater strength than it really possessed, was moving down the slope as if to the assault.

Below, in the valley, a battalion of French infantry with their cavalry and artillery were drawn up, and were evidently only waiting for the return of the two assaulting columns to join in their retreat.

The French commander doubtless supposed that he was caught in a trap; unable to effect the passage of the river, and seeing the stubborn resistance his troops were meeting with on the hills, the arrival of two fresh bodies of the enemy on the scene induced him to believe that the foe were in great force, and that ere long he might be completely surrounded. He moved forward slowly by the road he had come, and was presently joined by the two detached parties. As soon as they moved on, Terence sent an orderly at a gallop across the valley to order Macwitty and Moras to follow the French along on the hills on their side of the valley, and to harass them as much as possible, while he, with Bull's command, kept parallel with them on his side.

The French cavalry kept ahead of their column; the leading battalion was thrown out as skirmishers on the lower slopes of the hills, while the artillery, in the rear, kept up a heavy fire upon the Portuguese and Spanish as soon as they were made out on the hills above them. Terence kept his men on the crest, and signalled to Macwitty to do the same; but the guerillas swarmed down the hillside and maintained a galling fire on the French column. Terence took his men along at the double, and, heading the column, descended into the valley at the point they had fortified. Here there was a sharp fight. The French cavalry fell back after suffering heavily; their infantry advanced gallantly, and after a fierce fight drove the Portuguese from their wall and up the hillside.

Here they maintained a heavy fire until the column opened out and the French artillery came to the front, when Terence at once ordered the men to scatter, and climb the hill at full speed. Without attempting to repair the broken bridges, the French infantry crossed the stream breast-high, and the cavalry and artillery followed; and Terence, seeing that their retreat could not be seriously molested, and that if he attempted to do so he should suffer very heavily from their artillery, sounded a halt, and the French continued their retreat to Valladolid, leaving behind them all their baggage, which they had been unable to get across the stream.

Terence's force came down from the hills and assembled in the valley. Congratulations were exchanged on the success that had attended their efforts, then the roll was at once called, and it was found that a hundred and three men of the Minho regiment were missing. There was no roll among the guerillas, but Moras's estimate, after counting the number assembled, was, that upwards of two hundred were absent from the ranks, fully half of these having been overtaken and killed by the French cavalry. Terence at once sent off two parties of his own men to the points where the fight had been fiercest; they were to collect the wounded, including those of the French, and to carry them down into the valley, while parties of guerillas searched the hillsides down to the scene of action for their comrades who had fallen from the fire of the French artillery and musketry.

When the wounded were collected it was found there were upwards of two hundred French infantry, fifty-nine guerillas, and twenty-four Portuguese; the smaller proportion of wounded of the latter being accounted for by the fact that so many had been shot through the head while lying down to fire at the French as they climbed the hill. Two hundred and thirty French soldiers had been killed. Terence at once set his men to dig wide trenches, in which the soldiers of the three nationalities were laid side by side. A considerable amount of reserve ammunition being captured in the waggons, the men's cartridge-boxes were filled up again, and the rest was packed in a waggon. Some of the drivers had cut their traces, but others had neglected to do this, and there were sufficient waggons to carry all the wounded, both friends and enemies, together with a considerable amount of flour.

EFFECTING A DIVERSION

The French wounded were taken to the ford by which Macwitty had crossed, and then some of them who had been wounded in the leg, and although unable to walk were fit to drive, were given the reins and told to take the waggons to Zamora, a distance of twelve miles. Fifty men were told off to march with them until within sight of the town, as otherwise they would have assuredly been attacked, and the whole of the wounded massacred by the Spanish peasants. The force then broke up again, each column taking as much flour and meat as the men could carry; the remaining waggons and stores were heaped together and set on fire. Long before this was done they had been rejoined by Ryan and his command; he had remained guarding the river until the French had disappeared up the valley, and had then crossed at the ford, but, though using all haste, he did not rejoin the force until the whole of the fighting was over.

"This has been a good day's work, Terence," he said, when that evening the force had entered Tordesillas and quartered themselves there for the night. "You may be sure that the general at Valladolid will send messengers to Salamanca giving a greatly exaggerated account of our force, and begging them to send down to Marmont at once for a large reinforcement. If the couriers make a detour in the first place we shall not be able to cut them off."

"No, Dick, and we wouldn't if we could. I have no doubt that he will report the force with which his column was engaged as being nearly double what it really is. Besides, sharp as we have been, I expect some messengers will by this time have got through from Zamora. The commandant there will report that a large force is in the neighbourhood of that town, and that, without leaving the place entirely undefended, he has not strength enough to sally out against them. They cannot know that this force and ours have joined hands in the attack on the Valladolid column, nor that this represented anything like the whole of the force that have been harrying the country and cutting off detached posts. The fact, too, that this gathering was not a mere collection of guerillas or of the revolted peasantry, but that there were regular troops among them in considerable numbers, will have a great effect, and Marmont will feel himself obliged, when he gets the news, to send some fifteen or twenty thousand troops up here to clear the country. Now, the first thing to do is to draw up a report of the engagement and send it off to

Wellington. I think that it will be a good thing, Dick, for you to carry it yourself. I don't think that there is any fear of your being interrupted on your way to Miranda, and as an officer you will be able to get fresh horses and take the news quicker than an orderly could do, and it is of great importance that the chief should know, as soon as possible, what has taken place here. I shall speak very strongly of your services during the past week, and it is always a good thing for an officer selected to carry the news of a success; and, lastly, you can give a much better account of our operations since we crossed the frontier than an orderly could do, and Wellington may want to send orders back for our future work."

"I am game," Ryan said, "and thank you for the offer. How long will you be?"

"Well, it is eight o'clock now, and if you start at midnight it will be soon enough; so if you have finished your supper you had better lie down on that bed in the next room and get a sleep, for you were marching all last night and will want some rest before starting on such a journey."

Chapter XV
Dick Ryan's Capture

Terence wrote two despatches, one giving a full account of the engagement, the other a detail of the work that had been performed since they crossed the frontier. He wrote them in duplicate, so that he might send off another messenger three hours later, in case by any chance Ryan failed to reach Miranda. He carefully abstained from giving any real account of the strength of the various columns, in each case putting the number at five times their actual strength, so that if the despatches should miscarry, not only would no information be conveyed to the French, but they would be led to believe that the invading force was vastly stronger than they had hitherto supposed. Ryan was, of course, to explain when he delivered the despatches that the figures must in all cases be divided by five, and the reason why false numbers had been inserted.

Terence let him sleep until one o'clock, and then roused him. Several French horses had been found straying riderless along the valley, and the best of these was picked out for him. A few minutes later, Dick was on his way to Miranda. The road by which he was to travel would take him some six miles south of Zamora, and the distance to be ridden was between fifty and sixty miles. He knew that he could not do this at a gallop, and went along at a steady pace, sometimes trotting and sometimes cantering. It was now late in September, and at half-past five it was still dark when Ryan approached the spot where the road he was following crossed the main road between Zamora and Salamanca.

He was riding at a canter, when suddenly, to his surprise and consternation, he rode into the midst of a body of cavalry halted on the main road. The sound of his horse's feet had been heard, and before he could even draw his sword he was seized and taken prisoner. A French officer rode down the line.

"What is the matter? " he asked.

"We have taken a prisoner, sir," the sergeant answered. "We heard him coming by this cross-road, and seized him as he rode in among us. He is a soldier—an officer, I should think, from what I can see of him."

"Who are you, sir?" the French officer said to Ryan.

The latter saw that concealment was useless. It would soon be light enough for his scarlet uniform to be seen. He therefore replied in broken French: " My name is Ryan. I hold the rank of captain. I was riding to Miranda when, unfortunately, I fell in with your troopers as they were halted. I did not hear, and, of course, could not see them until I was among them."

"Riding with despatches, no doubt," the officer said. "Search him at once, men. He might destroy them."

"Here they are, sir," Ryan said, taking the despatches from inside his jacket. "You need not have me searched. I give you my word of honour as a British officer that I have no others on me."

"Put him in the middle of the troop, sergeant," the officer said. "Put a trooper in special charge of him, on each side. Unbuckle his reins and buckle them on to those of the troopers. Do you ride behind him and keep a sharp look-out upon him. It is an important capture."

Five minutes later the squadron again started on their way south. Ryan, after silently cursing his bad luck at having arrived at the spot just as this body of cavalry were crossing, wondered what evil fortune had sent them there at that precise moment. He was not long in arriving at a conclusion. The convoy of the French wounded had arrived at Zamora late in the evening, and the commandant, thinking it likely that the enemy, who had hitherto blocked the roads, might have concentrated for the attack on the column, had decided upon sending off a squadron of cavalry to carry the important news he had learned from the wounded, of the defeat of the column, five thousand strong, coming to his relief from Valladolid. The party proceeded at a brisk trot, and, meeting with no resistance, arrived at Salamanca by ten o'clock in the morning.

"Search him at once."

The officer in command at once rode with Ryan, the latter guarded by four troopers, to the residence of the general. Leaving Dick with his escort outside, he entered the house, and sent in his name and the duty with which he was charged to the general. He was at once shown into his room.

"I congratulate you on having got through, Captain D'Estrelles," the general said as he entered. "It is ten days since we heard from Zamora; we have sent off six messengers. I don't know whether any of them have arrived."

"No, sir, none of them. The commandant sent off one or two every day, and I suppose they, like those you sent, were all stopped."

"The whole country seems on fire," the general said.

"We have had five or six parties come in here disarmed, who had been captured by the enemy, and it would seem that all our posts on the road to Zamora and on that to Valladolid have been captured. The men could only report that they were suddenly attacked by such overwhelming forces that resistance was impossible. They say that the whole country seems to swarm with guerillas, but there are certainly a considerable number of regular troops among them. What has happened at Zamora?"

"These despatches will inform you, sir; but I may tell you that we are virtually beleaguered. The country round swarms with the enemy. Two or three reconnaissances in force met with the most determined opposition."

"Are you in communication with Valladolid?"

"No, sir. Our communications were stopped at the same time as those to this town; but I am sorry to say that you will see by the general's despatch that a severe disaster has happened to the column coming from Valladolid to our relief."

The general took the despatch and rapidly perused its contents.

"A column five thousand strong, with cavalry and guns, repulsed! The enemy must be in force indeed. From the estimates we have received from prisoners they released, I thought they must be fully ten thousand strong. I see that the wounded who were sent by Moras estimate those engaged with him at twelve thousand, and it is hardly probable that they could, at such short notice, have assembled in anything like their full strength."

DICK RYAN'S CAPTURE

"I have also to report, general, that we, this morning before daybreak, captured a British officer on his way to Miranda with despatches. We were fortunately halted for the moment, so that he was unaware of our presence until he rode into the midst of us. These are his despatches. I have not opened them."

"It is an important capture, indeed," the general said. "That is, if the report contains details of the fighting; its contents may enable us to form a clearer idea than we can at present, of their numbers."

He broke the seal and read the account of the battle. "It is signed T. O'Connor, Colonel," he said. "The name is well-known to us as that of a very active partisan leader. Three of the columns appear to have been commanded by British officers. Here we have them: Major Bull, Major Macwitty, and Captain Ryan."

"It is Captain Ryan whom we have made prisoner, sir."

"Their dispositions appear to have been good and ably worked out. The bridge across the river had been destroyed, and our crossing was opposed by one column. While we were attempting to force the passage, three more columns attacked us, one on each flank and rear; while a fourth, composed of a portion of the force defending the passage, who, as soon as we were fairly engaged with the other columns, crossed the ford lower down, leaving a thousand men to face us on the river bank—advanced against our left. Finding themselves thus greatly outnumbered, the column fell back, leaving behind them some five hundred dead and wounded. Their passage was closed by the enemy, who had broken down some bridges and thrown a breastwork across the valley, but after sharp fighting they made their way through."

He then turned to the other despatch. "This is still more useful," he said. "It is a general report of their proceedings since they crossed the frontier, and gives the number of each column. They total up to twenty-five thousand men, of which some ten thousand seem to be regular troops, the rest guerilas."

"Do you wish to see the prisoner, sir? He is waiting with the guard outside."

"Yes, I might as well see him, though, as a point of fact, he can give us no more information than that contained in these reports, which are very full and detailed."

"So, sir," he said when Ryan was brought in, "you are a British officer."

"I am, sir," Dick replied quietly. "At present on detached duty, serving on the staff of Colonel O'Connor."

"Who is with the guerilla chief Moras," the general said.

"Yes, sir. The troops under Colonel O'Connor have been acting in concert with Moras and other forces, much to the advantage of such of your soldiers as fell into our hands, not one of whom has suffered insult or injury, and all have been permitted to go free after being deprived of their arms. Colonel O'Connor also sent away all the French wounded who fell into our hands after the battle, in waggons, escorted by a strong body of his troops, to within a mile of Zamora, in order to protect them from massacre by the peasants."

"He behaved, sir, as a British officer would be expected to behave," the general said warmly. "Were the war always conducted on the same principle, it would be better for both armies and for the people of this country. I will place you on parole if you choose."

"I thank you, General, but I would rather have my hands free should I see any opportunity of escaping."

"That you are not likely to do," the general said, "for if you refuse to be bound by your parole I must take measures against your having any of these opportunities that you speak of, until the country is cleared and you can be sent with a convoy to France. I am sorry that you refuse, but as I should do so myself under similar circumstances, I cannot blame you."

Accordingly, Ryan was taken to a strong prison in the heart of the city, where, however, he was assigned comfortable quarters, a sentry being placed at his door, and, as the window that looked into the courtyard was strongly barred, his chances of escape seemed slight indeed, and he was almost inclined to regret that he had not accepted the general's offer and given his parole not to attempt to escape.

Two days later, one of Moras's men, who belonged to Salamanca, went into the town to see some friends, and brought back the news that a British officer had been captured by a party of French dragoons coming from Zamora. He had been seen by many of the townspeople as he sat on his horse, with four troopers round him, at the door of

DICK RYAN'S CAPTURE

the governor's house. He had been lodged in the city prison. A comparison of dates showed that there could be no doubt that the prisoner was Dick Ryan, and Terence was greatly vexed at his loss.

"So far as the despatches go," he said to Herrara, who had on the day before arrived from their stronghold, which was now safe from attack, "there can be no doubt that it is fortunate rather than otherwise that they have fallen into the hands of the French, for they will give them an altogether exaggerated impression of our strength, and I have no doubt that the orderly who left two hours later has got through in safety. Still, I am greatly annoyed that Ryan has been made prisoner. I miss his services and companionship very much, and if I can possibly get him out, I will do so. I will see Moras, and ask him to send the man, who brought the news, back again to gather further particulars. I would take the matter in hand myself, but being in command here I must consider the duty with which I am intrusted before a question of private friendship."

Moras presently came in to see Terence, and when the latter told him what he wanted, he undertook at once to obtain every detail possible as to the place of Ryan's confinement.

"A number of my men come from the town," he said, "and I will cause inquiries to be made among them at once, and choose half a dozen, with connections who may be able to assist, and send them into Salamanca, with instructions to act in concert, to ascertain whether it is possible to do anything by bribery, to endeavour to communicate with the prisoner, and to devise some plan for his escape from the gaol.

"It was a strong place before the French came. It was the city prison, but they took it over, and have used it not only for prisoners of war, but for persons suspected of being in communication with your people, and even for officers of their own army who have been convicted of insubordination or disobedience of orders, or other offences. One of the men I will send, and to whom I shall intrust the general arrangement of the matter, is one of my lieutenants, Leon Gonzales. He has been a friend of mine since boyhood, and entered as a law student when I went into the college for divinity. He is daring and fearless. He has an excellent head, and a large acquaintance among the young men at the university, and, indeed, in all classes of society. He belongs to one of our best families."

"Yes, of course I know him," Terence said. "He has several times come with you when you have ridden over, and was in command of the detachment that was with me when we captured the French garrison at Tordesillas. I was much pleased with him, and, although too occupied to see much of him, I conceived a great liking for him. I should say that he is just the man to manage this business successfully, if it is possible to do so."

"At all events I will despatch him with six other men, whom he may choose himself, this afternoon," Moras said. "I had intended him to remain in command of the party we leave here when we march to-night, but I will hand that over to another."

That night the force, with the exception of 500 guerillas and as many of the Minho regiment, marched away from the station they occupied to take up a new position between Valladolid and Palencia. Herrara was to remain behind in command of the 500 Portuguese. These, in conjunction with the guerillas, were to occupy their old positions, stopping all lines of communication, showing themselves in villages and towns hitherto unvisited, and, divided into parties of two or three hundred, march rapidly about the country, so that the fact that the main body had moved elsewhere should be unknown to the French authorities, who would therefore believe that the force that was to cut the road north of Valladolid was a newly-arrived one.

Thirty-six hours later Terence, with a battalion and a half of his regiment and 1500 of Moras's guerillas, took up their position in the mountains lying to the east of Palencia, between the rivers Esqueva and Arlanza. From this position they could with equal facility come down on the road between Valladolid and Palencia, or between the latter town and Burgos. Here for some weeks they maintained themselves, in the first place falling upon convoys from Valladolid south, and when these only moved forward under escorts too strong to be attacked, carrying on their operations on the road to Burgos. In these raids they obtained an abundance of provisions, a considerable number of arms and much ammunition, and in two or three instances a large amount of treasure that was being taken forward for the payment of the troops.

The provisions and wine were amply sufficient for the support of the force. Half the money was set aside for future needs, being divided between the regimental chest of Moras and that of the Minho regiment. The other half was similarly divided as prize-money among the men, a proportion being sent down to Herrara for his command. The operations of the band caused immense annoyance and difficulty to the French. It was no longer possible to travel by the main road from France between Burgos and Valladolid, and thence down to Salamanca or Zamora, without the convoys being accompanied by strong bodies of troops. Several incursions into the mountains were organized from Burgos, which was always a great military centre, aided by detachments from Palencia, but these met with no success whatever. On entering the passes they were assailed by a heavy fire from invisible foes, great rocks were rolled down upon them, and when after much loss they succeeded in forcing their way up to the hills, no traces of their foe could be discovered.

As among Moras's guerillas were natives of both Burgos and Palencia, and these had put themselves in communication with their friends, the band was kept well informed of every movement of the French, and received early intelligence when a convoy, or an expedition into the hills, was on the point of setting out, and of the exact strength of the military force employed. They were therefore always prepared either to sally out for an attack on the convoy or to oppose an expedition as soon as it entered the mountains. Their stores were hidden away among rocks, being divided into several portions, so that should the French by fortune or treachery discover one of these the loss would not cripple them. Their greatest enemy was cold. It was now the end of October, and several times snow had fallen, and it was necessary to keep up large fires.

This was a double inconvenience. In the first place, the smoke by day and the flames by night might betray the position of their camp; and in the second place, their tracks in the snow, which would speedily cover the hills, would enable the enemy to follow them wherever they moved. It was therefore determined that they could no longer maintain their position there, but must return to the plains. Frequent communication had been kept up with Herrara, who reported that Salamanca was now occupied by so large a force that he was no longer able to maintain his position, and that he had fallen back across the Douro, and had established himself in the stronghold, from which he made frequent excursions towards Zamora and Benavente.

To Dick Ryan in his prison the first fortnight had passed slowly. That Terence would, as soon as he learned of his capture, make every effort to free him he knew well, but he could not see how he could give him any material aid. The French force at Salamanca was far too strong to admit of a possibility of any attempt to rescue him by force, and the barred windows and the sentry seemed to close every chance of communication from without.

On the tenth day of his imprisonment he noticed that the sergeant who brought his food had been changed.

"What has become of Sergeant Pipon?" he asked the non-commissioned officer who filled his place.

"He was killed yesterday evening in the streets," the man replied. "It was not an ordinary broil, for he had half a dozen dagger stabs. It is some time since those dogs of Spaniards have killed a French soldier in the town, and there is a great fuss over it. The municipality will have to pay 10,000 dollars if they cannot produce his murderer. It is curious, too, for Pipon was not a man to get drunk. He did not speak a word of the language, and therefore could not have had a dispute with a Spaniard. We have been ordered to be more vigilant than before. I suppose the authorities think that perhaps there was some attempt to bribe him, and on his seizing the man who made it, some of the fellow's comrades rushed upon him and killed him."

Ryan wondered whether the supposition was a correct one, and whether the men concerned had been set at work by Terence in order to effect his release. Two days later, on cutting the loaf that formed his day's ration of bread, he found a small piece of paper in its centre. It had evidently been put there before the bread was baked, for although he examined it very closely he could find no sign in the crust of an incision by which the note might have been inserted. It contained only the words: *Keep your eyes open and be in readiness. Friends are working for your release.*

So Terence was at work. Evidently the baker had been gained over, but how it had been contrived that this special loaf should have been handed to him he could not imagine, unless one of the men in charge of the distribution of the prison rations had been bribed. That something of the sort must have taken place he was certain, and although he was still unable to imagine how he could be got out of the prison, he felt that in some way or another Terence would manage

DICK RYAN'S CAPTURE

it. He thought over the means by which the latter had escaped from the convent, but the laxity that had there prevailed in allowing people to come in to sell their goods to the prisoners was not permitted in the prison where he was confined. The prisoners were indeed allowed to take exercise for an hour in the court-yard, but no civilian ever entered it, and twelve French soldiers watched every movement of those in the yard, and did not permit a single word to be exchanged.

Another week passed, and Ryan began to fear that his friends outside had abandoned the scheme as impossible, when one day he received another message: *Do not undress to-night. On reaching the court-yard take the first passage to the right, follow it to the end. The bars of the window there have been nearly sawn through. Inclosed with this is a saw. Finish the work on the middle bars. You will find a cord hanging down outside. Friends will be awaiting you.*

With the note was a very fine steel saw, coiled round and round, and a tiny phial of oil. Ryan gave a cry of delight as he read it, and then hid the saw and the oil-bottle in his bed, made up the tiny note into a pellet, and swallowed it. As he ate his dinner he pondered over how so much could have been managed. The court-yard of the prison was, he knew, some ten feet higher than the ground outside. Some one must after nightfall have climbed up to the passage window and sawn the bars almost asunder with a saw as fine as the one he had received. The cuts could hardly have been perceptible, and had probably been filled in with dust or black-lead each night after the work was done. The difficulty must have been great, for be had learned that sentries patrolled the street outside the prison, and the work could only have been carried on for two or three minutes at a time. How he was to get down to the court-yard he knew not, but probably a sentry had been found more amenable to a bribe than the old sergeant had been.

To his bitter disappointment the night passed without anything unusual taking place, and the scheme had evidently failed. He broke up his loaf eagerly the next morning, and found, as he expected, another message: *Authorities suspicious. Sentries changed. Must wait till vigilance subsides. Keep yourself in readiness.*

A fortnight passed, and then, in the middle of the night, he leapt suddenly from the bed on which he had thrown himself without undressing, as he heard the key grating in the door. For a minute or two the sound continued, and his heart sank again.

"They have got a key, but it won't fit," he muttered. Suddenly he heard the bolt shoot back, and the door quietly opened.

"Are you ready?" a voice asked in a whisper.

"Quite ready."

"Then follow me."

Ryan had caught up his boots as he leapt from the bed. The man outside had evidently taken the precaution to remove his, for his step was perfectly noiseless. Dick followed him down-stairs and out into the court-yard. He could then see that the man was not, as he had expected, in uniform, but wore a long cloak and a sombrero, like those in general use among the peasantry. He turned in at the passage that had been indicated to Ryan, and stopped at the grated opening at the end. Ryan at once took out the saw, poured some oil on it, and passed his nail down the bar until he found a fine nick. Clearing this out with the saw, he began to cut. The task was far easier than he had expected, for the bar bad been already almost sawn through, and in five minutes the cut was completed.

A couple of feet higher up he found the other incision, and completed it as quietly as before. Then he removed the piece cut out, and handed it to the man, who laid it quietly down on the pavement of the passage.

In ten minutes the other bar was removed.

"I have the cord," the man said, and unwound some ten feet of stout rope from his waist. Ryan put his head out through the hole and looked down. In the darkness he could see nothing, but he heard the heavy tread of two sentries. As the sound of their footsteps faded away in the distance he heard a sudden exclamation and a slight movement, and a few seconds later a voice below asked in a whisper, "Are you there?"

"Yes," Ryan replied joyfully.

Putting a noose which was at one end of the rope over the stump of one of the bars, he at once slid down. A moment later the other man descended after him.

DICK RYAN'S CAPTURE

"This way, señor," the voice said, and, taking his hand, led him across the street, and then after a quarter of a mile's walk stopped at the door of a large house. He opened this with a key, and led the way up the stairs to the second floor, opened another door, and said, "Enter, señor, you are at home."

Ryan had noticed that the man who bad released him had not followed them, but had turned away as soon as they left the prison.

"You are most welcome, señor," his guide said, as, opening another door, he led the way into a handsome apartment where a lamp was burning on the table. "First let me introduce myself," he said. "My name is Alonzo Santobel, by profession an advocate. I am a friend of Don Leon Gonzales, one of Moras's officers, whom I believe you know. He will be here in a minute or two. He has followed us at a distance, to be sure that we were not watched. He enlisted me in this enterprise, and I have gladly given my assistance, which indeed was confined to bringing you here. All the rest he has managed himself, with the aid of six of his men who accompanied him here. He has been longer over it than he had expected, but we had difficulties that we did not anticipate." He spoke in French, but added: "I understand sufficient Portuguese to follow anything that you say, señor."

"I am indeed grateful to you all," Ryan said warmly. "It is good of you indeed to run so great a risk for a stranger."

"Not exactly a stranger, señor, since you are a friend of my friend, Leon Gonzales."

At this moment the door of the room opened, and the officer named entered and warmly shook hands with Ryan, and congratulated him cordially on his release.

"Thanks to you, señor," Dick said gratefully.

"It has been a matter of duty as well as pleasure," the other replied courteously, "for Moras committed the task of freeing you to my hands."

"I have just been telling Señor Ryan," the other said, "that you found it somewhat more difficult than you expected."

"Yes, indeed. In the first place, my face is known to so many here, and, unhappily, so many Spaniards are friends of the French, that I dared not show myself in the streets in the daytime. And before I tell my story, Alonzo, please open a bottle of wine and produce a box of cigars. Our friend has not had a chance of a decent smoke since he has been shut up.

"Now, señor, I will tell you all about it," he went on, as soon as the glasses were filled and the cigars lighted. "In the first place, one of the men with me has a cousin who works for the baker who contracts for the supply of bread to the prison, and, fortunately, it was one of his duties to go with the bread to hand it over and see it weighed. That simplified affairs amazingly. In the next place, it was necessary to get hold of the soldier who usually handed the bread to the non-commissioned officers, who each took the rations for the prisoners under their special charge. I had been well provided with money, and when the soldier came out one evening I got into conversation with him. He assented willingly enough to my offer to have a bottle of good wine together. Then I opened the subject.

"'I believe you distribute the bread rations to the prisoners?' I said.

He nodded.

"'I want one special loaf which is rather better bread than the rest, though it looks the same, to reach a prisoner who is a friend of mine. It may be that I shall want two or three such loaves to reach him, and I will not mind paying a hundred francs for each loaf.

"'A hundred francs is a good sum,' he said, 'especially as our pay is generally some months in arrear; and there can be no harm in a prisoner getting one loaf more than another. But how am I to know which is the loaf?'

"'It will be the last the baker's man will deliver to you, my friend. He will give you a wink as he hands it to you, and you will only have to put it on the tray intended for the English prisoner, Ryan, when the sergeant comes down to the kitchen for it. But, mind, don't make any mistake and put it on the wrong tray.'

"'I will be careful,' the soldier said, 'and I don't mind how many loaves you send in at the same price.'

"'Very well,' I said. 'Here are the hundred francs for the first loaf, which will come not to-morrow morning, but the day after.'

"So that part of the business was arranged easily enough; but another attempt, which I had set on foot at the same time, had already failed. My men had discovered who was the sergeant under whose charge you were. He was an old soldier, and I had my doubts whether he could be bribed. One of the men who spoke a little French undertook it, but took the precaution of having three of the others near him when he attempted it.

"It was two or three evenings before he could get speech with him in a quiet place, but he managed at last to do so.

"'Sergeant,' he said, 'do you want to earn as much money in a day as your pay would amount to in a year?'

"'It depends how it would have to be earned,' the sergeant said cautiously.

"'We want to get a friend of ours out of that prison,' the man said, 'and would pay a thousand francs for your assistance.'

"The sergeant at once grasped him by the throat.

"'You attempt to bribe me!' he exclaimed. 'Parbleu! We will hear what the governor says about it;' and he began to drag him along.

"There was nothing to be done, and the three other men, who had been standing hidden in a doorway, ran out and poniarded the Frenchman before he had time to give the alarm. It was unfortunate, but it was unavoidable. However, two days later the loaf got safely to you; at least we were assured that it had done so by the soldier in the kitchen. In the meantime I learned from a man who had been a warder in the prison before the French took possession of it, that the passage close to the bottom of your staircase terminated at the barred window in the street behind. Two of my men undertook to cut the bars. It was no easy matter, for there were sentries outside, and one came along the back every two or three minutes. The men had a light ladder, and, directly he had passed, ran across the street, placed it in position, and fell to work. But the constant interferences by the passing of the sentinel annoyed them, and greatly hindered the work.

"You see the sentry had to patrol the lane down one side of the prison, then along behind, and back, so they had only the time taken by him from the corner to the end of the lane and back, to work. They were so annoyed at this that one night, when the sentry came to be relieved, he was found stabbed to the heart, and as this misfortune happened just after he went on duty, the men managed to file one of the bars that night. Curiously enough, the same accident happened two nights later, just as I had arranged with a Spaniard who had enlisted in the French army that he would aid you to escape. He was a sharp fellow, and had managed to get the key of your room from the peg where it hung, and to take an impression of it in wax, from which we had a key made.

Everything was now ready. The other bar was sawn on the night the accident happened to the second sentry. The next night the Spaniard was to be on guard on your staircase, and I sent you a loaf with a message to be in readiness. Unfortunately, the second accident aroused the suspicion of the authorities that these affairs had something to do with the escape of a prisoner. Accordingly, the sentries outside were doubled, two men patrolling together, and that evening the guards were suddenly changed.

"It was evident that for a time nothing could be done. For nearly a fortnight this dodging about of the guard continued, then, as all was quiet, things went back to their old course; four sentries were taken off, the others going about two together, each pair taking two sides of the prison. This morning my Spaniard, who, as he was on duty at night, was able to come out into the town early, told the man who had arranged the affair with him that he would be on night duty, and would manage to take his place among the guards, so that when they arrived at your door he should be the one to be left there. As the bread had been already sent in I had no opportunity to warn you."

"I suppose the Spanish soldier you bribed has deserted?"

"Certainly. There was nothing else for him to do. He had that long cloak under his military greatcoat, and the sombrero flattened inside it, so that before opening your door he had only to stand his musket in the corner, laying his great-coat and shako by it, and he was in a position to go through the streets anywhere as a civilian. He has been well paid, and as he was already heartily tired of the French service, he jumped at the offer we made him."

After chatting for some time longer and obtaining some more details of the proceedings of the rescue party, Ryan and Gonzales lay down for a few hours' sleep on the couches in the room, while their host turned into his bed, which he had vainly attempted to persuade one or other to accept.

Chapter XVI
Back with the Army

Ryan remained four days in the flat occupied by Don Alonzo Santobel. Leon Gonzales had left before daybreak, to regain the house where he was staying with one of his friends before the discovery of the escape of a prisoner was made. The affair was certain to cause great excitement, and there was no doubt that everyone leaving the town would be strictly examined at the gates, and not improbably every house would be searched, and an order issued that no one would be allowed to be out at night after ten o'clock without a military pass. Three soldiers had been in turn assassinated, and one had deserted, a prisoner had been released, and there were evidently several persons concerned in the matter, and it would not improbably be guessed by the authorities that the actors in the plot were agents of the British officer in command of the troops that had given them such trouble over the whole province between Burgos and Salamanca.

Don Alonzo gave his man-servant, on whose fidelity he could rely, permission to go into the country for ten days to visit his relations, and Ryan was installed in his place and dressed in a suit of his clothes, but was not to open the door to visitors, the Spaniard himself doing so, and mentioning to those who called that his servant had gone on his holiday. The French indeed instituted a strict search among the poorer quarters. But the men who had accompanied Don Leon were all dressed as villagers who had come into the town from fear of being attacked by the guerillas and their allies, and as the people with whom they stayed all vouched for their story, and declared with truth that they were relatives, none of them were molested. For four days all persons passing out of the gates were examined, but at the end of that time matters resumed their ordinary course, and Don Leon and his followers all quitted the town soon after the market closed, carrying with them empty baskets as if they were countrymen who had disposed of the produce they had brought in.

Clothes of the same kind were procured for Ryan, and the day after his friends had left, he, too, went through the gate, going out with several peasants who were returning home. One of Leon's followers had taken out his uniform in his basket with a cloth thrown over it, on which were placed some articles of crockery which he had apparently bought for his use at home. Ryan had been carefully instructed as to the road he should follow, and four miles out from the city he turned down a by-path. He kept on for a mile and a half, and then came to a farmhouse standing alone. As he approached, Leon came out to meet him and shook him warmly by the hand.

"I have been feeling very anxious about you," he said. "We got through yesterday unquestioned, but the officer at the gate to-day might have been a more particular sort of fellow, and might have taken it into his head to question any of those who came out. The others all went on at once, but we will keep quiet until nightfall. I left my horse here when I came in, which I could do safely, for the farm belongs to me, and the farmer has been our tenant for the last thirty years. There is a horse for you here also.

"I have got the latest intelligence as to where the French are lying. They have a strong force at Tordesillas, but this won't matter to us, for I got a message from Moras yesterday saying that the hills are now all covered with snow, and that the whole force would march to-day for their old quarters in the valley near Miranda, so we sha'n't have to cross the river to the north, but will keep on this side and cross it at Miranda or at some ford near. The column that was operating round Zamora fell back behind the Esla a fortnight since, for four thousand of the French reinforcements from the south had reached Zamora, and strong parties of their cavalry were scouting over the whole of the country round."

Ryan had already heard how the road between Valladolid and Burgos had been interrupted, and several convoys cut off and captured. He was glad to find, however, that no serious fighting had taken place while he had been a prisoner.

BACK WITH THE ARMY

After nightfall they started on their journey. They travelled sixty miles that night. The farmer's son, a young fellow of twenty, who knew the country thoroughly, accompanied them on horseback for the first twenty miles to set them on their way. The road they followed ran almost parallel to the Tormes, all the bridges over that river being, as they learned, held by strong parties of French troops, posted there to prevent any bodies of the Spaniards crossing it and placing themselves between Salamanca and Ciudad Rodrigo.

When morning broke they were within five miles of the Douro, and entered the wood where they intended to pass the day, as they were unaware whether any French troops were stationed along the river. Both were still dressed as countrymen, and Leon went in the afternoon to a little hamlet half a mile from the wood. There he learned that 2000 French were encamped at a village a mile from the bridge at Miranda. But one of the peasants, on Leon's telling him that he was a lieutenant of Moras, offered to guide them to a ford, of whose existence he did not think the French were aware.

It was seldom used, as it could only be forded in very dry seasons, but as the water now was, it would only be necessary to swim their horses a distance of a few yards. The two friends slept a great part of the day, and, as the sun set, finished the provisions they had brought with them, and were ready to start when, two hours later, their guide arrived from the village. His information proved correct. He led them straight to the ford, which they found unguarded, and, rewarding him handsomely for his trouble, swam across, and an hour later entered Miranda and put up at a small inn.

They mounted early the next morning, and in the afternoon, after a three hours' ride across the mountains, came down into the valley, where their arrival excited much enthusiasm among the troops, the garrison having been joined by Macwitty's column.

"I cannot say that I was not expecting to see you, Captain Ryan," Macwitty said, as he shook hands heartily, "for I heard from the colonel that Don Leon had started with a party to try and get you out of prison, and that he was sure he would accomplish it if it were at all possible. I am expecting him here in a day or two with the rest of the regiment, for I had a message two days ago from him, saying that it was too cold to remain on the hills any longer, and that he should start on the day after the messenger left. Of course the messenger was mounted, but our men can march as far in a day as a man can ride, and are sure to lose no time. They would take the Leon road for some distance, then strike off and cross the upper Esla at Maylorga, follow the road down, avoiding Benavente, cross the Tera at Vega, take the track across the mountains, and come down into the valley from above. He said that he should only bring such stores as they would be able to carry on the march, and that he hoped to get here before the French were aware that he had left the mountains."

Late in the afternoon Leon's followers arrived. They had travelled at night so as to avoid being questioned by the French cavalry, who were scattered all over the country. Ryan was glad to see the men who had risked so much for him, and very pleased to be able to exchange his peasant's clothes for his uniform. The next morning he and Leon mounted and rode by the track by which Terence would arrive, and met him halfway between Vega and the camp. The greeting was a hearty one, indeed, and as Ryan shook hands with Moras, he said:

"I cannot tell you, señor, how much I am indebted to Don Leon for the splendid way in which he managed my rescue. Nothing could have been more admirably contrived, or better carried out. It certainly seemed to me, after I had been there a day or two, that a rescue was simply impossible, though I knew that Colonel O'Connor would do his best to get me out as soon as he learned that I was captured."

"I gave you credit for better sense, Dick, than to ride right into the hands of the French," Terence said, as he and Ryan rode on together at the head of the column.

"I think you would have done it yourself, Terence. The night was dark, and I could not see ten yards ahead of me. If they had been on the march, of course I should have heard them, but by bad luck they had halted just across the road I was following. It was very fortunate that you put all the numbers wrong in your despatches, and I can tell you it was a mighty comfort to me to know that you had done so, for I should have been half-mad at the thought that they had got at your real strength, which would have entirely defeated the object of our expedition. As it was, I had the satisfaction of knowing that the capture of the despatches would do more good than harm. Did the man who followed me get through?"

BACK WITH THE ARMY

"Yes, he kept his eyes open, Dicky," Terence said. "He returned ten days later with a letter from the adjutant-general, saying that the commander-in-chief was highly satisfied with my reports, and that the forward movement of the French had ceased, and at several points their advanced troops had been called in. Spies had brought news that ten thousand men under General Drouet had marched for Salamanca, and that reports were current in the French camp that a very large force had crossed the frontier at the north-eastern corner of Portugal, with the evident design of recovering the north of Leon, and of cutting the main line of communication with France.

"He added that he trusted that I should be able to still further harass the enemy, and cause him to send more reinforcements. He said that doubtless I should be very shortly driven back into Portugal again, but that he left the matter entirely to my judgment, but pointed out that if I could but maintain myself for another fortnight the winter would be at hand, when the passes would be blocked with snow, and Marmont could no longer think of invading Portugal in force. As it is now more than a month since that letter was written, and certainly further reinforcements have arrived, I think the chief will be well satisfied with what we have done. I have sent off two letters since then, fully reporting on the work we have been at between Burgos and Valladolid, but whether they have reached him I cannot tell."

"Macwitty has one despatch for you. He tells me it came nearly a fortnight ago, but that he had at that time been compelled to fall back behind the Esla, and that as the country beyond swarmed with parties of the French cavalry, he thought that no messenger could get through, and that great harm might result were the despatches to fall into the hands of the enemy.

"Well, I daresay it will keep, Dick, and that no harm will have been done by my not receiving it sooner. Now tell me all about your escape; were you lodged in our old convent?"

"I had no such luck, Terence. I was in the city prison in the centre of the town, and my window, instead of looking out into the street, was on the side of the court-yard. The window was strongly barred, no civilians were allowed to enter the prison, and I think that even you, who have a sort of genius for escapes, would have found it, as I did, simply impossible to get away."

"No, the look-out was certainly bad, and you had none of the advantages we had at Bayonne, of being guarded by friendly soldiers. If I had at Salamanca not been able to make friends with a Spanish girl—Well, tell me all about it."

Ryan gave full details of the manner in which Don Gonzales had contrived his escape.

"That was well managed indeed," Terence said. "Splendidly done. Leon is a trump; he ought to have been born an Irishman, and to have been in our regiment. I don't know that I can give him higher praise than that."

On their arrival in the valley, they found that another courier had returned half an hour before. Both despatches expressed the commander-in-chief's extreme satisfaction with the manner in which Terence had carried out his instructions.

The employment of your force in cutting the main road between Valladolid and Palencia and between the latter place and Burgos, while at the same time you maintained a hold on the country south of the Douro, thus blocking the roads from Salamanca both to Zamora and Valladolid, was in the highest degree deserving of commendation. The garrisons of all the towns named were kept in a state of constant watchfulness, and so great was the alarm produced, that another division followed that of Drouet. This has paralyzed Marmont. As snow has already begun to fall among the mountains, it is probable that he will soon go into winter quarters. Your work, therefore, may be considered as done, and as your position in the mountains must soon become untenable, it would be well if you at once withdraw all your forces into Portugal.

Moras also received a despatch signed by Lord Wellington himself, thanking him warmly for the services he had rendered.

I may say, sir, that yours is the first case, since I have had the honour to command the British force in the Peninsula, that I have received really valuable assistance from a body of irregular troops, and that I am highly sensible of the zeal and ability which you have shown in co-operating with Colonel O'Connor, a service which has been of extreme value to my army. I must also express my high gratification, not only with the conduct of the men under your command when in action, but at the clemency shown to French prisoners, a clemency, unfortunately, very rare during the present war. I shall not fail to express to the central Spanish authorities my high appreciation of your services. I have given orders to the officer

BACK WITH THE ARMY

commanding the detachment of British troops at Miranda that should you keep your force together near the frontier, he will, as far as possible, comply with any request you may make for supplies for their use.

Moras was highly gratified with this despatch. "I shall," he said, "stay in this valley for the winter, but I shall not keep more than a hundred or a hundred and fifty men with me. The peasants will disperse to their homes. Those remaining with me will be the inhabitants of the towns, who could not safely return, as they might be denounced by the Spanish spies in French pay as having been out with me. We have plenty of supplies stored up here to last us through the winter."

Terence at once sent off a report of his return, and an acknowledgment of the receipt of the despatches from headquarters, and the next day, in obedience to his orders, marched with his regiment across the frontier and established himself in Miranda. The answer came in five days. It was brief.

On receipt of this, Colonel O'Connor will march with the regiment under his command to Pinhel, and there report himself to General Crauford.

Terence had ridden over the afternoon before to the valley, where he found that but two hundred of the guerillas remained; fifty of these were on the point of leaving, the rest would remain with Moras through the winter.

On arrival at Pinhel after three days' marching, he reported himself to General Crauford. The general himself was absent, but from the head of his staff he received an order on the quartermaster's department. Tents for his men were at once given him, and a spot pointed out for their encampment. Six regiments were, he heard, in the immediate neighbourhood, and among them he found, to his great joy, were the Mayo Fusiliers. As soon as the tents were erected, rations drawn, and a party despatched to obtain straw for bedding from the quartermaster's department, Terence left Herrara and the two majors to see that the troops were made comfortable, and then rode over with Ryan to the camp of the Fusiliers.

They were received with the heartiest welcome by the colonel and officers, in whose ranks, however, there were several gaps, for the regiment had suffered heavily at Fuentes d'Onoro.

"So you have been taken prisoner again, Terence!" Captain O'Grady exclaimed. "Sure it must be on purpose you did it. Anyone may get taken prisoner once, but when it happens twice, it begins to look as if he was fonder of French rations than of French guns."

"I didn't think of it in that light, O'Grady; but now you put it so, I will try and not get caught for the third time."

"We heard of your return, of course, and that you had gone straight with your regiment to Miranda. We had a line from Dicky the day before he started, and mighty unkind we have thought it that neither of you have sent us a word since then, and you with nothing to do at all, at all, while we have been marching and countermarching, now here and now there, now backwards and now forwards, ever since Fuentes d'Onoro, till one's legs were ready to drop off one."

"Give someone else a chance to put in a word, O'Grady," the colonel said. "Here we are all dying to know how O'Connor slipped through the hands of the French again, and sorra a word can anyone get in when your tongue is once loosened. If you are not quiet I will take him away with me to my own quarters, and just ask two or three men who know how to hold their tongue to come up and listen to his story."

"I will be as silent as a mouse, Colonel dear," O'Grady said humbly, "though I would point out that O'Connor, being a colonel like yourself, and in no way under your orders, might take it into his head to prefer to stop with us here, instead of going with you. Now, Terence, we are all waiting for your story, why don't you go on?"

"Because, as you see, I am hard at work eating, just at present. We have marched twenty miles this morning, with nothing but a crust of bread at starting, and the story will keep much better than luncheon."

Terence did not hurry himself over his meal, but when he had finished he gave them particulars of his escape from Salamanca, his journey down to Cadiz, and then round by Lisbon.

"I thought there would be a woman in it, Terence," O'Grady exclaimed. "With a soft tongue, and a presentable sort of face, and impudence enough for a whole regiment, it was aisy for you to put the comhether on a poor Spanish girl who had never had the good luck to meet an officer of the Mayo Fusiliers before. Sure I have always said to meself that if I was ever taken prisoner, it would not be long before some good-looking girl would take a fancy to me, and get me out of the French clutches. Sure if a young fellow like yourself, without any special recommendations except a bigger share of impudence than usual, could manage it, it would be aisy indeed for a man like meself, with all the advantages of having lost an arm in battle, to get round them."

There was a shout of laughter round the table, for O'Grady had as usual spoken with an air of earnest simplicity, as if the propositions he was laying down were beyond question.

"You must have had a weary time at Miranda since you came back, O'Connor," the colonel said, "with no one there but a wing of the 65th."

"I don't suppose they were to be pitied, Colonel," Doctor O'Flaherty laughed. "You may be sure that they kept Miranda lively in some way or other; trust them for getting into mischief of some sort."

"There is no saying what we might have done if we had, as you suppose, been staying for the last two months at Miranda, but in point of fact that has not been the case. We have been across the frontier, and have been having a pretty lively time of it—at least I have, for Dick has spent a month of it inside a French prison."

"What!" the major exclaimed. "Were you with that force that has been puzzling us all, and has been keeping the French in such hot water that, as we hear, Marmont was obliged to give up his idea of invading Portugal, and had to hurry off twenty thousand men to save Salamanca and Valladolid from being captured? Nobody has been able to understand where the army sprung from or how it was composed. The general idea was that a division from England must have landed at either Oporto or Vigo, or that it must have been brought round from Sicily, for none of our letters or papers said a word about any large force having sailed from England. Not a soul seemed to know anything about it. I know a man on Crauford's staff, and he assured me that none of them were in the secret.

"A French officer who was brought in a prisoner a few days since put their numbers down at twenty-five thousand at least, including, he said, a large guerilla force. He said that Zamora had been cut off for a long time, that the country had been ravaged, and posts captured almost at the gates of Salamanca; and that communications had been interrupted and large convoys captured between Burgos and Valladolid, and that one column five thousand strong had been very severely mauled and forced to fall back. This confirmed the statements that we had before heard from the peasantry and the French deserters. Now there is a chance of penetrating the mystery, which has been a profound puzzle to us here, and indeed to the whole army.

"The officer taken seemed to consider that the regular soldiers were Portuguese, but of course that was nonsense. Beresford's troops were all with him down south, and as to any other Portuguese army, unless Wellington has got one together as secretly as he got up the lines of Torres Vedras, the thing is absurd. Besides, who had ever heard of Portuguese carrying on such operations as these without having a lot of our men to stiffen them, and to set them a good example?"

Terence did not at once answer. Looking round the table he saw that in place of the expressions of amusement with which the previous conversation had been listened to, there was now on every face a deep and serious interest. He glanced at Ryan, who was apparently absorbed in the occupation of watching the smoke curling up from his cigar. At last he said:

"I fear, major, that I cannot answer your question. I may say that I have had no specific orders to keep silence, but as it seems that the whole matter has been kept a profound secret, I do not think that, unless it comes out in some other way, I should be justified in saying anything about it. I think that you will agree with me, Ryan."

Dick nodded.

"Yes, I agree with you that it would be best to say nothing about it till we hear that the facts are known. What has been done once may be done again."

"Quite so, Dick; I am glad that you agree with me. However, there can be no objection to your giving an account of your gallant charge into the middle of the French cavalry, and the story of your imprisonment and escape. I am sure, Colonel, that it will be a source of gratification to you to know that one of your officers dashed single-handed right into the midst of a French squadron."

Ryan laughed.

BACK WITH THE ARMY

"I am afraid the interest in the matter will be diminished, Colonel, when I mention that the charge was executed at night, and that I was ignorant of the vicinity of the French until I rode into the middle of them."

There was again a general laugh.

"I was on my way with despatches for Lord Wellington," he went on, "when this unfortunate business happened."

"That was unfortunate indeed, Ryan," the colonel said. "They did not capture your despatches, I hope?"

"Indeed and they did, Colonel. They had fast hold of me before I could as much as draw my sword. They, however, gained very little by them, for knowing that it was possible I might be captured, the despatches had been so worded that they would deceive rather than inform anyone into whose hands they might fall, though, of course, I had instructions to explain the matter when I delivered them safely."

Then he proceeded to give a full account of his rescue from the prison of Salamanca. This was listened to with great interest.

"It was splendidly managed," the colonel said, when he had brought his story to an end. "It was splendidly managed. Terence himself could not have done it better. Well, you are certainly wonderfully handy at getting into scrapes. Why, you have both been captured twice, and both times got away safely. When I gave you your commission, Terence, I thought that you and Ryan would keep things alive, but I certainly did not anticipate that you would be so successful that way as you have been."

"I have had very little to do with it, Colonel," Ryan said.

"No, I know that at Athlone, Terence was the ringleader of all the mischief that went on. Still, you were a good second, Ryan; that is, if that position does not really belong to O'Grady."

"Is it me, Colonel?" O'Grady said in extreme surprise, and looking round the table with an air of earnest protest. "When I was always lecturing the boys."

"I think, O'Grady, your manner of lecturing was akin to the well-known cry, 'Don't throw him into the pond, boys.'"

At this moment there was a sound of horses drawing up in front of the house.

"It is the general and his staff," one of the ensigns said, as he glanced through the window. The table had been cleared, but there was a sudden and instant rush to carry away bottles and glasses to hiding-places. Newspapers were scattered along the table, and when the door opened half a minute later and the general entered, followed by his staff, the officers of the Mayo Fusiliers presented an orderly and even studious appearance. They all rose and saluted as the general entered.

"I hope I am not disturbing you, gentlemen," General Crauford said gravely, but with a sly look of amusement stealing across his rugged face. "I am glad to see you all so well employed. There is no doubt that the Irish regiments are greatly maligned. On two or three occasions when I have happened to call upon their officers, I have uniformly found them studying the contents of the newspapers. Your cigars too, must be of unusually good quality, for their odour seems mingled with a faint scent of, what shall I say—it certainly reminds me of whisky, though, as I see, that must be but fancy on my part. However, gentlemen, I have not come in to inspect your mess-room, but to speak to Colonel O'Connor;" and he looked inquiringly round.

Terence at once stepped forward and again saluted. The general, whom Terence had not before met, looked him up and down, and then held out his hand.

"I have heard of you many times, Colonel O'Connor. General Hill has talked to me frequently of you; and not long since, when I was at headquarters, Lord Wellington himself spoke to me for some time about you, and from his staff I learned other particulars. That you were young, I knew, but I was not prepared to find one who might well pass as a junior lieutenant or even as an ensign. This was the regiment that you formerly belonged to, and as, on sending across to your corps, I learned that you were here, I thought it as well to come myself to tell you before your comrades and friends that I have received from headquarters this morning a request from the adjutant-general to tell you personally, when you arrived, the extreme satisfaction that the commander-in-chief feels at the services that you have rendered.

"When I was at headquarters the other day I was shown the reports that you have during the last six weeks sent in, and am therefore in a position to appreciate the work you have done. It is not too much to say that you have saved Portugal from invasion, have paralyzed the movements of the French, and have given to the commander-in-chief some months in which to make his preparations for taking the field in earnest in the spring. Has Colonel O'Connor told you what he has been doing?" he said suddenly, turning to Colonel Corcoran.

"No, General. In answer to our questions he said that, as it seemed the matter had been kept a secret, he did not feel justified in saying anything on the subject until he received a distinct intimation that there was no further occasion for remaining silent."

"You did well, sir," the general said, again turning to Terence, "and acted with the prudence and discretion that has, with much dash and bravery, distinguished your conduct. As, however, the armies have now gone into winter quarters, and as a general order will appear to-day speaking of your services, and I have been commissioned purposely to convey to you Lord Wellington's approval, there is no occasion for further mystery on the subject. The force whose doings have paralyzed the French, broken up their communications, and compelled Marmont to detach twenty thousand men to assist at least an equal force in Salamanca, Zamora, Valladolid, and Palencia, has consisted solely of the men of Colonel O'Connor's regiment and about an equal number of guerillas, commanded by the partisan Moras. I need not tell you that a supreme amount of activity, energy, and prudence united must have been employed thus to disarrange the plans of a French general commanding an army of one hundred thousand men by a band of two battalions of Portuguese and a couple of thousand undisciplined guerillas. It is a feat that I myself or any other general in the British army might well be proud to have performed, and too much praise cannot be bestowed upon Colonel O'Connor and the three British officers acting under his command, of all whose services, together with those of his Portuguese officers, he has most warmly spoken in his reports. And now, Colonel, I see that there are on your mess-table some dark rings that may possibly have been caused by glasses. These, doubtless, are not very far away, and I have no doubt that when I have left, you will very heartily drink the health of your former comrade—I should say comrades, for I hear that Captain Ryan is among you. Which is he?"

Ryan stepped forward.

"I congratulate you also, sir," he said. "Colonel O'Connor has reported that you have rendered great services since you were attached to him as adjutant, and have introduced many changes which have added to the efficiency and discipline of the regiment. My staff, as well as myself, will be very pleased to make the personal acquaintance of Colonel O'Connor and yourself, and I shall be glad if you will both dine with me to-day, and if you, Colonel Corcoran, will accompany them. To-morrow I will inspect the Minho regiment at eleven o'clock, and you will then introduce to me your lieutenant-colonel and your two majors, who have all so well carried out your instructions."

So saying, he shook hands with the colonel, Terence, and Ryan, and with an acknowledgment of the salutes of the other officers, left the room with his staff.

"If a bullet does not cut short his career in some of his adventures," he said to Colonel Corcoran, who had accompanied him, "O'Connor has an extraordinary future before him. His face is a singular mixture of good temper, energy, and resolute determination. There are many gallant young officers in the army, but it is seldom that reckless bravery and enterprise are joined, as in his case, with prudence and a head to plan. He cannot be more than one-and-twenty, so there is no saying what he may be when he reaches forty. Trant is an excellent leader, but he has never accomplished a tithe of what has been done by that lad."

The general having left the room, the officers crowded round Terence. But few words were said, for they were still so surprised at what they had heard as to be incapable of doing more than shake him warmly by the hand and pat him on the shoulder. Ryan came in for a share in this demonstration.

The colonel returned at once after having seen the general ride off.

"Faith, Terence," he said, "if justice were done they would make me a general for putting you into the army. I have half a mind to write to Lord Wellington and put in a claim for promotion on that ground. What are you doing, O'Grady?" he broke off, as that officer walked round and round Terence, scrutinizing him attentively as if he had been some unknown animal.

BACK WITH THE ARMY

"I am trying to make sure, Colonel, that this is really Terence O'Connor, whom I have cuffed many a time when he was a bit of a spalpeen with no respect for rank, as you yourself discovered, Colonel, in the matter of that bird he fastened in the plume of your shako. He looks like him, and yet I have me doubts. Is it yerself, Terence O'Connor? Will you swear to it on the testiments?"

"I think I can do that, O'Grady," Terence laughed. "You see I have done credit to your instructions."

"You have that. I always told you that I would make a man of you, and it is my instruction that has done it. How I wish, lad," he went on with a sudden change of voice, "that your dear father had been here this day! Faith, he would have been a proud man. Ah! It was a cruel bullet that hit him at Vimiera."

"Ay, you may well say that, O'Grady," the colonel agreed. "Have you heard from him lately, Terence?"

"No, Colonel. It's more than four months since I have had a letter from him. Of course he always writes to me to headquarters; but as I only stopped there a few hours on my way from Lisbon to join the regiment, I stupidly forgot to ask if there were any letters for me; and of course there has been no opportunity for them to be forwarded to me since. However, they will know in a day or two that I have arrived here, and will be sure to send them on at once."

"Now, let's hear all about it, O'Connor, for at present we have heard nothing but vague rumours about the doings of this northern army of yours beyond what the general has just said."

"But first, Colonel, if you will permit me to say so," O'Grady put in, "I would propose that General Crauford's suggestion as to the first thing to be done should be carried out, and that the whisky keg should be produced again. We have a good stock, Terence, enough to carry us nearly through the winter."

"Then it must be a good stock, indeed, O'Grady," Terence laughed. "You see the general was too sharp for us."

"That he was, but, as a Scotchman, he has naturally a good nose for whisky. He is a capital fellow; hot-tempered and obstinate as he undoubtedly is, he is as popular with his division as any general out here. They know that if there is any fighting to be done, they are sure to have their share and more, and except when roused, he is cheery and pleasant. He takes a great interest in his men's welfare, and does all that he can to make them as comfortable as possible, though, as they generally form the advanced guard of the army, they necessarily suffer more than the rest of us."

By this time the tumblers were brought out from the cup-boards, into which they had been so hastily placed on the general's arrival. Half a dozen black bottles were produced, and some jugs of water, and Terence's health was drunk with all the honours. Three cheers were added for Dicky Ryan, and then all sat down to listen to Terence's story.

Chapter XVII
Ciudad Rodrigo

"Before O'Connor begins," the colonel said, "you had better lay on the table in front of you the pocket maps I got from Lisbon for you last year, after O'Connor had lectured us on the advantages of knowing the country. I can tell you, Terence, they have been of no small use to us since we left Torres Vedras, and I think that even O'Grady could pass an examination as to the roads and positions along the frontier with credit to himself. I think, gentlemen, that you who have not got your maps with you would do well to fetch them. You will then be able to follow Colonel O'Connor's story, and get to know a good deal more about the country, where I hope we shall be fighting next spring, than we should in any other way."

Several of the officers left the room and soon returned with their maps.

"I feel almost like a schoolmaster," Terence laughed. "But, indeed, as our work consisted almost entirely of rapid marching, which you would scarcely be able to follow without maps, it may really be useful, if we campaign across there, to know something of the roads and the position of the towns and villages."

Then he proceeded to relate all that had taken place, first describing the incidents of the battle and their work among the mountains.

"You understand," he said, "that my orders were, not so much to do injury to the enemy as to deceive them as to the amount of our force, and to lead them to believe it to be very much stronger than it really was. This could only be done by rapid marches, and, as you will see, the main object was to cut all his lines of communication, and at the same time to show ourselves in force at points a considerable distance apart. To effect this, we, on several occasions, marched upwards of sixty miles in a day, and upwards of forty several days in succession, a feat that could hardly be accomplished except by men at once robust and well accustomed to mountain work, and trained to long marches, as those of my regiment have been since they were first raised."

Then, taking out a copy of his report, he gave in much fuller detail than in the report itself an account of the movements of the various columns and flying parties during the first ten days, and then, more briefly, their operations between Burgos and Valladolid, ending up by saying:

"You see, Colonel, there was really nothing out of the way in all this. We had the advantage of having a great number of men who knew the country intimately; and the cutting of all their communications, the exaggerated reports brought to them by the peasants, and the maintenance of our posts round Salamanca and Zamora while we were operating near Burgos and Valladolid, impressed the commanders of these towns with such an idea of our strength, and such uneasiness as to their communications, that after the reverse to their column none of them ever ventured to attack us in earnest."

"That is no doubt true," the colonel said, "but to have done all this when—with the reinforcements sent up, and the very strong garrisons at four of the towns, to say nothing of the division of Burgos—they had forty thousand men disposable, is a task that wanted a head well screwed on. I can see how you did it, but that would be a very different thing to doing it oneself. However, you have taught us a great deal of the geography of the country between the frontier and Burgos, and it ought to be useful. If I had received an order this afternoon to march with the regiment to Tordesillas, for example, I should have known no more where the place stood or by what road I was to go to it than if they had ordered me to march to Jericho. Now, I should cross the roads at points at which we were not likely to be attacked, and throw out strong parties to protect our flanks till we had passed, and should feel that I was not stumbling along in the dark and just trusting to luck."

"Now, Colonel, we must be off to our own quarters," Terence said. "We have been too long away now, and if I had not known that Herrara and the majors were to be trusted to do their work—and in fact they did it well without my assistance all the time I was away prisoner—I could not have left them, as I did, half an hour after they had encamped."

The next morning Terence received a copy of the orders of the day, of the division at present under General Crauford's command, together with the general orders of the whole army from headquarters. In the latter, to which Terence first turned, was a paragraph: *Lord Wellington expresses his great satisfaction at the exceptional services rendered by the Minho Portuguese regiment, under its commander, Captain T. O'Connor, of the headquarter staff, bearing the rank of colonel in the Portuguese army. He has had great pleasure in recommending him to the commander-in-chief for promotion in the British army. He has also to report very favourably the conduct of Lieutenant Ryan of the Mayo Fusileers, and Ensigns Bull and Macwitty, all attached for service to the Minho regiment, and shall bring before General Lord Beresford that of Lieutenant-colonel Herrara of same regiment.*

In the divisional orders of the day appeared the words: *In noticing the arrival of the Minho Portuguese regiment, under the command of Colonel Terence O'Connor, to join the division temporarily under his command, General Crauford takes this opportunity of congratulating Colonel O'Connor on the most brilliant services that his regiment has performed in a series of operations upon the Spanish side of the frontier.*

Four days later Terence received two letters from home. These were written after the receipt of that sent off by him on his arrival at Cadiz, narrating his escape. His father wrote:

My dear Terence,—*Your letter, received this morning, has taken a heavy load off our minds. Of course we saw the despatches giving particulars of the battle of Fuentes d'Onoro, which by the way seems to have been rather a confused sort of affair, and the enemy must have blundered into it just as we did, only as they were all there, and we only came up piecemeal, they should have thrashed us handsomely if they had known their business. Well, luck is everything, and, as you have had a good deal more than your share of it since you joined, one must not grumble if the jade has done you a bad turn this time.*

However, as you have got safely out of their hands, you have no reason for complaint. Still, you had best not try the thing too often. Next time you may not find a good-looking girl to help you out. By the way, you don't tell us whether she was good-looking. Mention it in your next; Mary is very curious about it. We are getting on capitally here, and I can tell you the old place looks quite imposing, and I was never so comfortable in my life. We have as much company as I care for, and scarce a day passes but some young fellow or other rides over on the pretence of talking over the war news with me. But I am too old a soldier to be taken in, and know well enough that Mary is the real attraction.

My leg has now so far recovered that I can sit a horse; but though I ride with your cousin when the hounds meet anywhere near, I cannot venture to follow, for if I got a spill, it might bring on the old trouble again and lay me up for a couple of years. I used to hope that I should get well enough to be able to apply to be put on full pay again. But I feel myself too comfortable here to think of it; and indeed, until I have handed Mary to someone else's keeping, it would of course be impossible, and I have quite made up my mind to be moored here for the rest of my life. But to return. Of course, as soon as I saw you were missing, I wrote to an old friend on the general staff at Dublin, and asked him to write to the Horse Guards.

The answer came back that it was known that you had been taken prisoner, and that you were wounded, but not severely. You were commanding the rear face of the square into which your regiment had been thrown, when your horse, which was probably hit by a bullet, ran away with you into the ranks of the enemy's cavalry. After that we were, of course, more comfortable about you, and Mary maintained that you would very soon be turning up again like a bad penny. I need not say that we are constantly talking about you. Now, take care of yourself, Terence. Bear in mind that if you get yourself killed, there will be no more adventures for you—at least none over which you will have any control.

Your cousin has just expressed the opinion that she does not think you were born to be shot; she thinks that a rope is more likely than a bullet to cut short your career. She is writing to you herself: and as her tongue runs a good deal faster than mine, I have no doubt that her pen will do so also. As you say, with your Portuguese pay and your own, you are doing well; but if you should get pinched at any time, be sure to draw on me up to any reasonable amount. It seems to me that things are not going on very well on the frontier, and I should not be surprised to hear that Wellington is in full retreat again for Torres Vedras. Remember me to the colonel, O'Driscoll, and all the others. I see by the Gazette *that Stokes, who was junior ensign when the regiment went into action at Vimiera, has just got his step. That shows the changes that have taken place, and how many good fellows have fallen out of the ranks. Again I say, take care of yourself.—Your affectionate* FATHER..

His cousin's letter was, as usual, long and chatty, telling him about his father, their pursuits and amusements, and their neighbours.

You don't deserve so long a letter, she said, *when she was approaching the conclusion, for although I admit your letters are long, you never seem to tell one just the things one wants to know. For example, you tell us exactly the road you travelled down to Cadiz, with the names of the villages, and so on, just as if you were writing an official report. Your father says it is very interesting, and has been working it all out on the map. It is very interesting to me to know that you have got safely to Cadiz, but as there were no adventures by the way, I don't care a snap about the names of the villages you passed through, or the exact road you traversed.*

Now, on the other hand, I should like to know all about this young woman who helped you to get out of prison. You don't say a word about what she is like, whether she is pretty or plain. You don't even mention her name, or say whether she fell in love with you or you with her, though I admit that you do say that she was engaged to the muleteer Garcia. I think if I had been in his place I should have managed to let you fall into the hands of the French again. I should say a man was a great fool to help to rescue anyone his girl had taken all sorts of pains to get out of prison. At any rate, sir, I expect you to give me a fair and honest description of her the next time you write, for I consider your silence about her to be in the highest degree suspicious. However, I have the satisfaction of knowing that you are not likely to be in Salamanca again for a very long time. Your father says he does not think anything will be done until the present Ministry are kicked out here, and Wellington hangs the principal members of all the Juntas in Portugal, and all that he can get at in Spain.

He is the most bloodthirsty man that I have ever come across, according to his own account, but in reality he would not hurt a fly. He is always doing kind actions among the peasantry, and the "Major" is quite the most popular man in this part of the country. I have not yet forgiven you for having gone straight back to Spain instead of running home for a short time when you were so close to us at Jersey. I told you when I wrote that I should never forgive you, and I am still of the same opinion. It was too bad. Your father has just called to ask if I am going on writing all night, and it is quite time to close, that it may go with his own letter, which a boy is waiting to carry on horseback to the post-office four miles away, so good-bye.—Your very affectionate cousin, MARY

The next two months passed quietly at Pinhel. Operations continued to be carried on at various points, but although several encounters of minor importance took place, the combatants were engaged rather in endeavouring to feel each other's positions, and to divine each other's intentions, than to bring about a serious battle. Marmont believed Wellington to be stronger than he was, while the latter rather underestimated the French strength. Thus there were on both sides movements of advance and retirement.

During the time that had elapsed since the battles of Fuentes d'Onoro and Albuera, Badajos had been again besieged by the British, but ineffectually; and in August, Wellington, taking advantage of Marmont's absence in the south, advanced and established a blockade of Ciudad Rodrigo. This had led to some fighting. The activity of General Hill, and the serious menace to the communications effected by Terence's Portuguese and the guerillas, had prevented the French from gathering in sufficient strength, either to drive the blockading force across the frontier again, or from carrying out Napoleon's plans for the invasion of Portugal. Wellington, on his part, was still unable to move, owing to the absence of transport, and the manner in which the Portuguese government thwarted him at every point, leaving all his demands, that the roads should be kept in good order, unattended to, starving their own troops to such an extent that they were altogether unfit for action, placing every obstacle to the calling out of new levies, and in every way hindering his plans.

He obtained but little assistance or encouragement at home. His military chest was empty, the muleteers who kept up the supply of food for the army were six months in arrears of pay. The British troops were also unpaid, badly supplied with clothes and shoes, while money and stores were still being sent in unlimited quantities to the

CIUDAD RODRIGO

Spanish Juntas, where they did no good whatever, and might as well have been thrown into the sea. But in spite of all these difficulties, the army was daily improving in efficiency; the men were now inured to hardships of all kinds, they had in three pitched battles proved themselves superior to the French, and they had an absolute confidence in their commander.

Much was due to the efforts of Lord Fitzroy Somerset, Wellington's military secretary, who, by entering into communication with the commanders of brigades and regiments, most of whom were quite young men—for the greater part of the army was but of recent creation—was enabled not only to learn something of the state of discipline in each regiment, but greatly to encourage and stimulate the efforts of its officers, who felt that the doings of their regiment were observed at headquarters, that merit would be recognized without favouritism, and that any failure in the discipline or morale of those under their orders would be noted against them. Twice, during the two months, Terence had been sent for to headquarters in order that he might give Lord Fitzroy minute information concerning the various roads and localities, point out natural obstacles where an obstinate defence might be made by an enemy, or which could be turned to advantage by an advancing army. The route maps that he had sent were frequently turned to and fully explained.

The second visit took place in the last week in November, and on his arrival the military secretary began the conversation by handing a *Gazette* to him.

"This arrived yesterday, Colonel O'Connor, and I congratulate you that upon the very strong recommendation of Lord Wellington you are gazetted to a majority. Now that your position is so well assured, there will be no longer occasion for you to remain nominally attached to the headquarter staff. Of course it was before I came out that this was done, and I learned that the intention was that you would not act upon the staff, but it was to be merely an honorary position, without pay, in order to add to your authority and independence when you happen to come in contact with Portuguese officers of a higher rank."

"That was so, sir. I was very grateful for the kindness that Lord Wellington showed in thus enabling me to wear the uniform of his staff, which was of great assistance to me at the time, and indeed I am deeply conscious of the kindness with which he has on every occasion treated me, and for his recommending me for promotion."

"I should have been personally glad," Lord Fitzroy went on, "to have had you permanently attached to our staff, as your knowledge of the country might at times be of great value, and of your zeal and energy you have given more than ample proofs. I spoke of the matter to the general this morning. He agreed with me that you would be a great addition to the staff, but, upon the other hand, such a step would very seriously diminish the efficiency of the regiment that you raised and have since commanded. The regiment has lately rendered quite exceptional services, and under your command we reckon it to be as valuable in the fighting line as if it were one of our own, which is more than can be said for any other Portuguese battalion, although some of them have of late fought remarkably well. I do not say that Colonel Herrara, aided by his three English officers—who, by the way, are all promoted in this *Gazette,* the two ensigns to the rank of lieutenants, and Mr. Ryan to that of captain—would not keep the regiment in a state of efficiency so far as fighting is concerned, but without your leading it could not be relied upon to act for detached service such as it has performed under you."

"Thank you, sir. Of course it would be a great honour to me to be on the general's staff, but I should be very sorry to leave the regiment; and, frankly, I do not think that it would get on well without me. Colonel Herrara is ready to bestow infinite pains on his work, but I do not think that he would do things on his own responsibility. Bull and Macwitty have both proved themselves zealous and active, and I can always rely upon them to carry out my orders to the letter, but I doubt if they would get on as well with Herrara as they do with me. I am very glad to hear that they and Mr. Ryan have got their steps. The latter makes an admirable adjutant, and if I had to choose one of the four for the command I should select him, but he has not been very long with the regiment, is not known personally, and would not, I think, have the same influence with the Portuguese officers and men. Moreover, I am afraid that, having been in command so long, I should miss my independence if I had only to carry out the orders of others."

"I can quite understand that," the military secretary said with a smile. "I can quite realize the fascination of the life of a partisan leader, especially when he has, which Trant and the others have not, a body of men whom he has trained himself, and upon whom he can absolutely rely. You can still, of course, wear the uniform of a field-officer on the general's staff, and so will have very little alteration to make save by adding the proper insignia of your rank. I will write you a line authorizing you to do so. Now, let us have a turn at your maps. I may tell you in confidence that, if an opportunity offers, we shall at once convert the blockade of Ciudad into a siege, and hope to carry it before the enemy can march with sufficient force to its relief.

"To do so he would naturally collect all his available forces from Salamanca, Zamora, and Valladolid, and would probably obtain reinforcements from Madrid and Estremadura, and I want to ascertain, as far as possible, the best means of checking the advance of some of these troops by the blowing up of bridges or the throwing forward of such a force as your regiment to seize any defile or other point that could be held for a day or two and an enemy's column thus delayed; even twenty-four hours might be of importance."

"I understand, sir. Of course, the passes between Madrid and Avila might be retained for some little time, especially if the defenders had a few guns, but they would be liable to be taken in the rear by a force at Avila, where there were, when I went down south, over five thousand men. As to the troops coming from the north, they would doubtless march on Salamanca. From that town they would cross the Huebra and Yeltes so near their sources that no difficulty would be caused by the blowing up of bridges, if any exist, but the pass over the Sierra de Gatta on the south of Ciudad might be defended by a small force without difficulty."

The maps were now got out, and the matter gone into minutely. After an hour's conversation, Lord Fitzroy said:

"Thank you, Colonel O'Connor. Some of the information that you have given me will assuredly be very useful if we besiege Ciudad. From what we hear there are a good many changes being made in the

French command. Napoleon seems about to engage in a campaign with Russia, and is likely to draw off a certain portion of the forces here, and while these changes are being made it would seem to offer a good opportunity for us to strike a blow."

On the last day of December, Terence received the following order:—

Colonel O'Connor will draw six days' rations from the commissariat, and at daybreak to-morrow march to the river Aqueda, and on the following day will ford that river and will post himself along the line of the Yeltes from its junction with the Huebra to the mountains, and will prevent any person or parties crossing from this side. It is of the highest importance that no intelligence of the movements of the army should be sent either by the garrison of Ciudad or by the peasantry to Salamanca. When his provisions are exhausted, he is authorised to hire carts and send in to the army round Ciudad, but, if possible, he should obtain supplies from the country near him, and is authorised to purchase provisions and to send in accounts and vouchers for such purchases to the paymaster's department.

"Hurrah, Ryan!" he exclaimed on reading the order. "Things are going to move at last! This means, of course, that the army is going to besiege Ciudad at once, and that we are to prevent the French from getting any news of it until it is too late for them to relieve it. For the last month guns and ammunition have been arriving at Almeida, and I thought that this weary time of waiting was drawing to an end."

"I am glad indeed, Terence. I must say that I was afraid that we should not be moving until the spring. Shall we go in and say good-bye to our fellows?"

"Yes, we may as well; but mind, don't say where we are going to, only that we are ordered away. I don't suppose that the regiments will know anything about it till within an hour of the time they march. There can be no doubt that it is a serious business. Ciudad held out for weeks against Massena, and with Marmont within a few days' march, with an army at least as strong as ours, it will be a tough business, indeed, to take it before he can come up to its relief; and I can well understand that it is all-important that he shall know nothing about the siege till it is too late for him to arrive in time."

"We have come in to say good-bye, Colonel," Terence said, as he and Ryan entered the mess-room of the Mayo Fusileers that evening.

"And where are you off to, O'Connor?"

"Well, sir, I don't mind mentioning it in here, but it must go no further. The chief, knowing what we are capable of, proposes that I shall make a rapid march to Madrid, seize the city, and bring King Joseph back a prisoner."

There was a roar of laughter.

"Terence, my boy," Captain O'Grady said, "that is hardly a mission worthy of a fighting man like yourself. I expect that you are hiding something from us, and that the real idea is that you should traverse Spain and France, enter Germany, and seize Boney, and carry him off with you to England."

"I dare not tell you whether you are right or not, O'Grady. Things of this sort must not even be whispered about. It is a wonderfully good guess that you have made, and when it is all over you will be able to take credit for having divined what was up, but for mercy's sake don't talk about it. Keep as silent as the grave, and if anyone should ask you what has become of us, pretend that you know nothing about it."

"But you are going, O'Connor?" the colonel said, when the laughter had subsided.

"Yes, Colonel. We march to-morrow morning. I dare say you will hear of us before many days are over, and may perhaps be able to make even a closer guess than O'Grady, as to what we are doing. I am heartily glad that we are off. We are now at our full strength again; most of the wounded have rejoined, and I could have filled up the vacancies a dozen times over. The Portuguese know that I always manage to get food for my men somehow, which is more than can be said for the other Portuguese regiments, though those of Trant and Pack are better off than Beresford's regulars. Then, too, I think they like fighting now that they feel that they are a match for the French, man for man. They get a fair share of it, at any rate. The three months that we have been idle have been useful, as the new recruits know their work as well as the others."

"Then you don't know how much longer we are going to stop in this bastely hole?" O'Grady asked.

"Well, I will tell you this much, O'Grady; I fancy that before this day week you will all have work to do, and that it is likely to be hot."

"That is a comfort, Terence. But, my dear boy, have a little pity on us and don't finish off the business by yourselves. Remember that we have come a long way, and that it will be mighty hard for us if you were to clear the French out of Spain and leave nothing for us to do but to bury their dead and escort their army as prisoners to the port."

"I will bear it in mind, O'Grady; but don't you forget the past. You know how desperately you grumbled at Rolica because the regiment was not in it, and how you got your wish at Vimiera, and lost an arm in consequence; so, even if I do, as you say, push the French out of Spain, you will have the consolation of knowing that you will be able to go back to Ireland without leaving any more pieces of you behind."

"There is something in that, Terence," O'Grady said gravely. "I think that when this is over I shall go on half-pay, and there may as well be as much of me left as possible to enjoy it. It's an ungrateful country I am serving. In spite of all that I have done for it, and the loss of my arm into the bargain, here am I, still a captain, though may be I am near the top of the list; still, it is but a captain I am, and here are two gossoons like yourself and Dick Ryan, the one of you marching about a field-officer and the other a captain. It is heart-breaking entirely, and me one of the most zealous officers in the service. But it is never any luck I have had from the day I was born."

"It will come some day, never fear, O'Grady, and perhaps it may not be so far off as you fear.

"Well, Colonel, we will just take a glass with you for luck and then say good-night, for I have a good many things to see after, and must be up very early so as to get our tents packed and handed over, to draw our rations, eat our breakfast, and be off by seven."

CIUDAD RODRIGO

It was close upon that hour when the regiment marched. It was known that there were no French troops west of the Huebra, but after fording the Aqueda the force halted until nightfall, and then moved forward and reached the Huebra at midnight, lay down to sleep until daybreak, and then extended along the bank of the Yeltes as far as its source among the mountains, thus cutting the roads from Ciudad to Salamanca and the North. The distance to be watched was some twenty miles, but as the river was in many places unfordable it was necessary only to place patrols here, while strong parties were posted, not only on the main roads, but at all points where by-roads or peasants' tracks led down to the bank.

On that day a bridge was thrown across the Aqueda six miles below Ciudad for the passage of artillery, but, owing to the difficulties of carriage, it was five days later before the artillery and ammunition could be brought over, and this was only done by the aid of 800 carts, which Wellington had caused to be quietly constructed during the preceding three months.

On the 8th the light division and Pack's Portuguese contingent forded the Aqueda three miles above Ciudad, and, making a long detour, took up their position behind a hill called the Great Teson. They remained quiet during the day, and, the garrison believing that they had only arrived to enable the force that had long blockaded the town to render the investment more complete, no measures of defence were taken; but at night the light division fell suddenly on the redoubt of San Francisco on the Great Teson. The assault was completely successful. The garrison was a small one, and had not been reinforced. A few of them were killed, and the remainder taken, with a loss to the assailants of only twenty-four men and officers. A Portuguese regiment, commanded by Colonel Elder, then set to work; and these, in spite of a heavy fire kept up all night by the French forts, completed a parallel 600 yards in length before day broke.

Chapter XVIII
The Sack of a City

For the next four days the troops worked night and day, the operations being carried on under a tremendous fire from the French batteries. The trenches being carried along the whole line of the Small Teson, on the night of the 13th the convent of Santa Cruz was captured, and on the 14th the batteries opened fire against the town, and before morning the 40th Regiment carried the convent of San Francisco, and thus established itself within the suburb, which was inclosed by an entrenchment that the Spanish had thrown up there during the last siege. The French artillery was very powerful, and at times overpowered that of the besiegers. Some gallant sorties were also made, but, by the 19th, two breaches were effected in the ramparts, and preparations were made for an assault.

That evening Terence received an order to march at once to the place and to join Pack's Portuguese. The assault was to be made by the 3rd and light divisions, aided by Pack's command, and Colonel O'Toole's Portuguese riflemen. The main British army lay along the Coa in readiness to advance at once and give battle should Marmont come up to the assistance of the besieged town. On the 19th both the breaches were pronounced practicable, and during the day the guns of the besiegers were directed against the artillery on the ramparts, while the storming parties prepared for their work. The third division was to attack the great breach; the light division was to make for the small breach; and upon entering the inclosure known as the *fausse braye,* a portion were to turn and enter the town by the Salamanca gate, while the others were to penetrate by the breach.

Colonel O'Toole, with his Portuguese, was to cross the river and to aid the right attack, while Pack's Portuguese were to make a false attack on the San Jago gate on the other side of the town, and to convert this into a real assault if the defence should prove feeble.

THE SACK OF A CITY

The French scarcely appeared conscious that the critical moment was at hand, but they had raised breastworks along the tops of both breaches and were perfectly prepared for the assault. When the signal was given, the attack was begun on the right. The 5th, 77th, and 94th regiments rushed from the convent of Santa Cruz, leapt down into the *fausse braye,* and made their way to the foot of the great breach, which they reached at the same moment as the rest of the third division, who had run down from the Small Teson. A terrible fire was opened upon them, but, undismayed by shell, grape, and musketry from the ramparts and houses, they drove the French behind their new work. Here, however, the enemy stood so stoutly that no progress could be made; unable to cross the obstacle, the troops nevertheless maintained their position, although suffering terrible losses from the French fire.

Equally furious was the attack on the small breach by the light division. After a few minutes' fighting they succeeded in bursting through the ranks of the defenders, and then, turning to the right, fought their way along the ramparts until they reached the top of the great breach. The French there wavered, on finding that their flank was turned, and the third division, seizing the opportunity, hurled themselves upon them, and this breach was also won. O'Toole's attack was successful; and on the other side of the town, Pack's Portuguese, meeting with no resistance, had blown open the gate of San Jago, and had also entered the town.

Here a terrible scene took place, and the British troops sullied their victory by the wildest and most horrible excesses. They had neither forgotten nor forgiven the treatment they had experienced at the hands of the Spaniards, both before and after the battle of Talavera, when they were almost starved, while the Spaniards had abundant supplies, and yet left the British wounded unattended to die of starvation in the hospitals when they evacuated the city. From that time their animosity against the Spaniards had been vastly greater than their feeling against the French, who had always behaved as gallant enemies, and had treated their wounded and prisoners with the greatest kindness.

Now this long-pent-up feeling burst out, and murder, rapine, and violence of all sorts raged for some hours wholly without check. Officers who endeavoured to protect the hapless inhabitants were shot down, all commands were unheeded, and abominable atrocities were perpetrated. Some share of the blame rests with Wellington and his staff, who had taken no measures whatever for maintaining order in the town when possession should be gained of it, a provision which should never be omitted in the case of an assault. The Portuguese, whose animosity against the Spaniards was equally bitter, imitated the example of the British comrades. Fires broke out in several places, which added to the horror of the scene. The castle was still held by the French, the troops having retreated there as soon as the breach had been carried. There was not, therefore, even the excuse of the excitement of street fighting to be made for the conduct of the victors.

In vain Terence and his officers endeavoured to keep their men together. By threes and fours these scattered down the side streets, to join the searchers for plunder, until at last he remained alone with his British and Portuguese officers.

"This is horrible," he said to Ryan, as the shouts, shrieks, and screams told that the work of murder as well as plunder was being carried on. "It is evident that, single-handed, nothing can be done. I propose that we divide into two parties, and take these two houses standing together under our protection. We will have two English officers with each, as there is no chance of the soldiers listening to a Portuguese officer. How many are there of us?"

There were the twelve captains and twenty subalterns.

"Bull and Macwitty, do you take half of them; Colonel Herrara, Ryan, and I will take the other half. When you have once obtained admission, barricade the door and lower windows with furniture. When the rioters arrive, show yourselves at the windows, and say that you have orders to protect the houses from insult, and if any attack is made you will carry out your orders at whatever cost. When they see four British officers at the windows they will suppose that special instructions have been given us with respect to these two houses. If they attack, we must each defend ourselves to the last, holding the stairs if they break in. If only our house is attacked, come with half your force to our assistance, and we will do the same to you. We can get along by those balconies without coming down into the street."

THE SACK OF A CITY

The force was at once divided. Terence knocked at the door of one house, and his majors at that of the other. No answer was received, but as they continued to knock with such violence that it seemed as if they were about to break down the doors, these were presently opened. Terence entered. A Spanish gentleman, behind whom stood a number of trembling servants, advanced.

"What would you have, señor?" he asked. "I see that you are an officer. Surely you cannot menace with violence those who are your allies?"

"You are right, señor; but unfortunately our troops have shaken off all discipline, and are pillaging and, I am afraid, murdering. The men of my own regiment have joined the rest, and I with my officers, finding ourselves powerless, have resolved at least to protect your mansion and the next from our maddened troops. I can give you my word of honour that I and these gentlemen, who are all my officers, have come as friends, and are determined to defend until the last your mansion, which happened to be the first we came to. A similar party is taking charge of the next house, and if necessary we can join forces."

"I thank you indeed, sir. I am the Count de Montego. I have my wife and daughters here, and in their name as well as my own I thank you most cordially. I have some twenty men, sir. Alone we could do nothing, but they will aid you in every way, if you will but give orders."

"In the first place, count, we will move as many articles of heavy furniture as possible against the doors. I see that your lower windows are all barred. We had better place mattresses behind them to prevent shot from penetrating. I hope, however, that it will not come to that, and that I shall be able to persuade any that may come along that these houses are under special protection."

The count at once ordered his servants to carry out the British officer's instructions, and the whole party were soon engaged in piling heavy furniture against the door. The count had gone up to allay the fears of his wife and daughters, who, with the female servants, were gathered in terrible anxiety in the drawing-room above. As soon as the preparations were completed, Terence, Ryan, and Herrara went upstairs, and after being introduced to the ladies, who were now to some extent reassured, Terence went out on to the balcony with Ryan, leaving Herrara in the drawing-room, as he thought it was best that only British officers should show themselves. Terrible as the scene had been before, it was even worse now. The soldiers had everywhere broken into the cellars, and numbers of them were already drunk, many discharged their muskets recklessly, some quarreled among themselves as to the spoil they had taken, and fierce fights occurred.

In two or three minutes Bull and Macwitty appeared on the balcony of the next house.

"I see it is too far to get across," Terence said. "If you cannot find a plank, set half a dozen men to prise up a couple from the floor."

Presently a number of soldiers came running along down the street.

"Here are two big houses," one shouted. "There ought to be plenty of plunder here."

"Halt!" Terence shouted. "These houses are under special protection, and, as you see, I myself and three other British officers are placed here to see that no one enters. I have a strong force under my orders, and anyone attempting to break down the doors will be shot instantly, and all who aid him will be subsequently tried and hung."

The men, on seeing the four British officers, three of them in the dress of field-officers, and one, the speaker, in the uniform of the staff, at once drew back.

"Come on, mates," one said, as they stood indecisive; "we shall only lose time here, while others are getting as much plunder as they can carry. Let us go on."

But as the wine took effect, others who came along were less disposed to listen to orders. Gradually gathering until they were in considerable numbers, several shots were fired at the officers, and one man, advancing up the steps, began to hammer at the door with the butt-end of his musket. Terence leaned over the balcony, and, drawing his pistol and taking a steady aim, fired, and the man fell with a sharp cry. A number of shots were fired from below, but the men were too unsteady to take aim, and Terence was uninjured. Again he stood up.

THE SACK OF A CITY

"Men," he shouted, "you have shown yourselves to be brave soldiers to-day. Are you now going to disgrace yourselves by mutiny against officers who are doing their duty, thereby running the risk of being tried and hung? I tell you again that these houses are both defended by a strong force, and that we shall protect them at all hazard. Go elsewhere, where booty is to be more easily obtained."

His words, however, were unheeded. Some more shots were fired, and then there was a general rush at the doors, while another party attacked that of the next house. The officers were all provided with pistols, and Terence hurried below with Ryan.

"Do not fire," he said to the others, "until they break down the door. It will take them some time, and at any moment fresh troops may be marched in to restore order."

The door was a strong one, and, backed as it was, it resisted for a considerable time. Those who first attacked it speedily broke the stocks of their guns, and had to make way for others. Presently the attack ceased suddenly.

"Run upstairs, Dicky, and see what they are doing, and how things are going on next door."

Ryan soon returned.

"They are bringing furniture and a lot of straw from houses opposite; they have broken down the next door, but they have not got in yet."

"Let the servants at once set to work to draw pails of water from the well in the court-yard, and carry them upstairs. Ryan, you had better go into the next house and see if they are pressed. Tell them that they must hold out without my help for a short time. I am going to send six officers out by the back of the house to collect some of our men together. Another will be in readiness to open the back-door as soon as they return. I shall keep them from firing the pile as long as I can. The count has two double-barrelled guns; I don't want to use them if I can help it, but they shall not get in here. Do you stop, and help next door. There can be no fighting here yet, for if they do burn the door it will be a long time before they can get in."

The native officers started at once. They were of opinion that they would soon be able to bring in a good many of their men, for the Portuguese are a sober race, and few would have got intoxicated. Most of the men would soon find that there was not much booty to be obtained, and that even what they got would probably be snatched from them by the English soldiers, and would consequently be glad to return to their duty again. An officer took his place at the back door in readiness to remove the bars, another went up with Terence to the first floor, and the remainder stopped in the hall with six of the men-servants. Terence went upstairs and looked down into the street. There was a lot of furniture with bundles of faggots and straw piled there.

"Now," he said to the officer, "empty these pails at once; the servants will soon bring some more up. I will stand here with these guns and fire at any one who interferes with you. Just come out into the balcony, empty your pails over, and go back at once. You need scarcely show yourself, and there is not much chance of your being hit by those drunken rascals."

Yells and shouts of rage were heard below as the water was thrown over. As fast as the pails were emptied the servants carried them off and refilled them. At last two soldiers appeared from a house opposite with blazing torches. The guns had been loaded by the count with small-shot, as Terence was anxious not to take life. As soon as the two men appeared he raised the fowling-piece to his shoulder and fired both barrels in quick succession. With a yell of pain the soldiers dropped their torches. One fell to the ground, the other clapped his hands to his face and ran down the street in an agony, as if half mad. Half a dozen muskets were discharged, but Terence had stepped back the moment he had fired, and handed the gun to the count, who was standing behind him, to recharge.

Two other soldiers picked up the torches, but dropped them as Terence again fired. Another man snatched up one of them, and flung it across the street. It fell upon some straw that had been thoroughly soaked by the water, and burned out there harmlessly. It was not long before the servants began to arrive with the full buckets, and when these also had been emptied, Terence, glancing over, had little fear that the pile could now be lighted. The pails were sent down again, and he waited for the next move. The fighting had ceased at the other door, the soldiers having drawn back from the barricade to see the effect of the fire. Ryan ran across the plank and rejoined Terence.

"Things are quiet there for the present," he said. "There has not been much harm done. When they had partly broken down the door, they began firing through it. Bull and Macwitty kept the others back from the line of fire, and not a pistol has been discharged yet. Bull cut down one fellow who tried to climb over the barricade, but otherwise no blood has been shed on either side."

Help was coming now. One of the Portuguese officers was admitted with twenty-four men that he had picked up. The others came in rapidly, and within a quarter of an hour three hundred men were assembled. All were sober, and looked thoroughly ashamed of themselves as they were formed up in the court-yard. Terence went down to them. He said no word of blame.

"Now, men," he said, "you have to retrieve your characters. Half of you will post yourselves at the windows, from the ground-floor to the top of the house. You are not to show yourselves till you receive orders to do so. You are not to load your guns, but as you appear at the windows, point them down into the street. The officers will post you five at each window. The rest of you are at once to clear away the furniture in the hall; and, when you receive the order, throw open the door and pour out, forming across the street as you do so. Captain Ryan will be in command of you. You are not to load, but to clear the streets with your bayonets. If any of the soldiers are too drunk to get out of your way, knock them down with the butt-end of your muskets; but if they rush at you, use your bayonets."

He went round the house and saw that five men were in readiness at each window looking into the street. He ordered them to leave the doors open.

"A pistol will be fired from the first landing," he said; "that will be the signal, then show yourselves at once."

He waited until Ryan's party had cleared away the furniture. He then went out on to the balcony and addressed the crowd of soldiers, who were standing uncertain what step to take next, many of them having already gone off in search of plunder elsewhere.

"Listen to me, men!" he shouted. "Hitherto I have refrained from employing force against men who, after behaving as heroes, are now acting like madmen; but I shall do so no longer. I will give you two minutes to clear off, and anyone who remains at the end of that time will have to take his chance."

The man fell, with a sharp cry.

THE SACK OF A CITY

Derisive shouts and threats arose in reply. He turned round and nodded to the count, who was standing at the door of the room with a pistol in his hand. He raised it and fired, and in a moment soldiers appeared at every window, menacing the crowd below with their rifles. At the same moment the door opened, and the Portuguese poured out, with Ryan at their head, trampling over the pile raised in front of it. There was a moment of stupefied dismay amongst the soldiers. Hitherto none had believed that there were any in the houses, with the exception of a few officers, and the sudden appearance of a hundred men at the windows and a number pouring out through the door took them so completely by surprise that there was not even a thought of resistance.

Men who had faced the terrors of the deadly breaches turned and fled, and, save a few leaning stupidly against the opposite wall, none remained by the time Ryan had formed up the two lines across the street. Each of these advanced a short distance, and were at once joined by the defenders of the other house, and by those at the windows.

"Do you take command of one line, Bull, and you of the other, Macwitty. I don't think that we shall be meddled with, but should any of them return and attack you, you will first try and persuade them to go away quietly. If they still attack, you will at once fire upon them. Herrara, will you send out all your officers and bring the men in at the back-doors, as before. We shall soon have the greater part of the regiment here, and with them we can hold the street, if necessary, against any force that is likely to attack it."

In half an hour, indeed, more than fifteen hundred men had been rallied, and while two lines, each a hundred strong, were formed across the street, some eighty yards apart, the rest were drawn up in a solid body in the centre, Terence's order being that, if attacked in force, half of them were to at once enter the houses on both sides of the street and to man the windows. He felt sure, however, that the sight of so strong a force would be sufficient to prevent the rioters interfering with them, the soldiers being, for the most part, too drunk to act together or with a common object.

This, indeed, proved to be the case. Parties at times came down the street, but, on seeing the dark lines of troops drawn up, they retired immediately on being hailed by the English officers, and slunk off under the belief that a large body of fresh troops had entered the town. An hour later a mounted officer, followed by some five or six others and some orderlies, rode up.

"What troops are these?" the officer asked.

"The Minho Portuguese regiment, General," Bull answered, "commanded by Colonel O'Connor."

The general rode on, the line opened, and he and his staff passed through. Terence, who had posted himself in the balcony, so as to have a view of the whole street, at once ran down. Two of the men with torches followed him. On approaching he at once recognised the officer as General Barnard, who commanded one of the brigades of the light division.

"So your regiment has remained firm, Colonel O'Connor?" the general said.

"I am sorry to say, sir, that it did not at first, but scattered like the rest of the troops. My officers and myself for some time defended these two large houses from the attack of the soldiery. Matters became very serious, and I then sent out some of my officers, who soon collected three hundred men, which sufficed to disperse the rioters without our being obliged to fire a shot. The officers then again went out, and now between fifteen and sixteen hundred men are here. I am glad that you have come, sir, for I felt in a great difficulty. It was hard to stay here inactive when I was aware that the town was being sacked and atrocities of every kind perpetrated; but, upon the other hand, I dared not undertake the responsibility of attempting to clear the streets. Such an attempt would probably end in desperate fighting. It might have resulted in heavy loss on both sides, and have caused such ill-feeling between the British and Portuguese troops as to seriously interfere with the general dispositions for the campaign."

"No doubt you have taken the best course that could be pursued, Colonel O'Connor; but I must take on myself the responsibility of doing something. My appearance at the head of your regiment will have some effect upon the men of the light division, and those who are sober will, no doubt, rally round me, though hitherto my efforts have been altogether powerless. All the officers will, of course, join us at once. I fear that many have been killed in trying to protect the inhabitants; but now that we have at least got a nucleus of good troops, I have no doubt that we shall be successful. Have you any torches?"

"There is a supply of them in the house, sir."

"Get them all lighted, and divide them among the men. As soon as you have done this, form the regiment into column."

"Are they to load, sir?"

"Yes," the general said shortly; "but instruct your officers that no one is to fire without orders, and that the sound of firing at the head of the column is not to be considered as a signal for the rest to open fire, though it may be necessary to shoot some of these insubordinate scoundrels. By the way, I think it will be best that only the leading company should load. The rest have their bayonets, and can use them if attacked."

Some forty torches were handed over by the count. These were lighted and distributed along the line, ten being carried by the leading company.

"You have bugles, Colonel?"

"Yes, sir. There is one to each company."

"Let them all come to the front and play the Assembly as they march on. Now will you ride at their head by my side, sir? Dismount one of my orderlies and take his horse."

By the time all the preparations were completed, they had been joined by nearly two hundred more men. Just before they started, Terence said:

"Would it not be well, General, if I were to tell off a dozen parties of twenty men, each under the command of a steady non-commissioned officer, to enter the houses on each side of the road as we go along, and to clear out any soldiers they may find there?"

"Certainly. But I think that when they see the regiment marching along, and hear the bugles, they will clear out fast enough of their own accord."

With bugles blowing, the regiment started. Twenty men with an officer had been left behind at each of the houses they had defended, in case parties of marauders should arrive and endeavour to obtain an entrance. As they marched by, men appeared at the windows. Most of these were soldiers, who with an exclamation of alarm when they saw the general, followed by two battalions in perfect order, hastily ran down and made their escape by the backs of the houses, or came quietly out, and, forming in some sort of order, accompanied the regiment. Several shots were heard behind as the search parties cleared out those who had remained in the houses, and presently the force entered the main square of the town and halted in its centre, the bugles still blowing the Assembly. Numbers of officers at once ran up, and many of the more sober soldiers.

"Form them up as they arrive," the general said to the officers. In a few minutes some five hundred men had gathered. "Do you break your regiment up into four columns, Colonel O'Connor. A fourth of these men shall go with each, with a strong party of officers. The soldiers will be the less inclined to resist if they see their own comrades and officers with your troops, than if the latter were alone. I will take the command of one column myself, do you take that of another. Colonel Strong, will you join one of the majors of Colonel O'Connor's regiment, and will you, Major Hughes, join the other. All soldiers who do not at once obey your summons to fall in will be taken prisoners, and those who use violence you will shoot without hesitation. All drunken men are to be picked up and sent back here. Place a strong guard over them, and see that they do not make off again."

Five minutes later the four columns started in different directions. A few soldiers who, inflamed by drink, fired at those who summoned them to surrender, were instantly shot, and in half an hour the terrible din that had filled the air had quietened down. Morning was breaking now. In the great square, officers were busy drawing up the men who had been brought in, in order of their regiments. The inhabitants issued from their houses, collected the bodies of those who had been killed in the streets, and carried them into their homes, and sounds of wailing and lamentation rose from every house. Lord Wellington now rode in with his staff. The regiments that had disgraced themselves were at once marched out of the town, and their places taken by those of other divisions.

But nothing could repair the damage that had been done, and the doings of that night excited throughout Spain a feeling of hostility to the British that has scarcely subsided to this day, and was heightened by the equally bad conduct of the troops at the storming of Badajoz.

THE SACK OF A CITY

Long before the arrival of Lord Wellington the whole of the Minho regiment had rejoined. Terence ordered that the late comers should not be permitted to fall in with their companies, but should remain as a separate body. He marched the regiment to a quiet spot in the suburbs, and ordered them to form in a hollow square, with the men who had last joined in the centre. These he addressed sternly.

"For the first time," he said, "since this regiment was formed, I am ashamed of my men. I had thought that I could rely upon you under all circumstances. I find that this is not so, and that the greed for plunder has at once broken down the bonds of discipline. Those who, the moment they were called upon, returned to their colours, I can forgive, seeing that the British regiments set them so bad an example, but you men, who to the last remained insubordinate, I cannot forgive. You have disgraced not only yourselves, but your regiment, and I shall request Lord Wellington to attach you to some other force. I only want to command men I can rely upon."

A loud chorus of lament and entreaty rose from the men.

"It is as painful to me as it is to you," Terence went on, raising his hands for silence. "How proud I should have been if this morning I could have met the general and said that the regiment he had been good enough to praise so highly several times, had proved trustworthy, instead of having to report that every man deserted his officers, and that many continued the evil work of pillage, and worse, to the end."

Many of the men wept loudly, others dropped upon their knees and implored Terence to forgive them. He had already instructed his two majors what was to be done, and they and the twelve captains now stepped forward.

"Colonel," Bull said, in a loud voice that could be heard all over the square, "we, the officers of the Minho regiment, thoroughly agree with you in all that you have said, and feel deeply the disgrace the conduct of these men has brought upon it, but we trust that you will have mercy on them; and we are ready to promise in their name that never again will they so offend, and that their future conduct will show how deeply they repent of their error."

There was a general cry from the men of, "Indeed we do. Punish us as you like, Colonel, but don't send us away from the regiment!"

Terence stood as if hesitating for some time; then he said: "I cannot resist the prayer of your officers, men, and I am willing to believe that you deeply regret the disgrace you have brought upon us all. Of one thing I am determined upon; not one man in the regiment shall be any the better for his share in this night's work, and that this accursed plunder shall not be retained. A blanket will be spread out here in front of me, and the regiment will pass along before me by twos. Each man, as he files by, will empty out the contents of his pockets and swear solemnly that he has retained no object of spoil whatever. After that is over I shall have an inspection of kits, and if any article of value is found concealed, I will hand over its owner to the provost-marshal to be shot forthwith."

The operation took upwards of two hours. At Herrara's suggestion a table was brought out, a crucifix placed upon it, and each man as he came up, after emptying out his pockets, swore solemnly, laying his hand upon the table, that he had given up all the spoil he had collected. Terence could not help smiling at the scene the regiment presented before the men began to file past. No small proportion of the men stripped off their coats and unwound from their bodies rolls of silk, costly veils, and other stuffs of which they had taken possession. All these were laid down by the side of the blanket, on which a pile of gold and silver coins, a great number of rings, brooches, and bracelets, had accumulated by the time the whole had passed by.

"The money cannot be restored," Terence said to Herrara, "therefore set four non-commissioned officers to count it out. Have the jewels all placed in a bag; let all the stuffs and garments be made into bundles. I shall be obliged if you will take a sufficient number of men to carry them, and go down yourself with a guard of twenty men to the syndic, or whatever they call their head men to carry them, and hand them over to him. Say that the Minho regiment returns the spoil it had captured, and deeply regrets its conduct. Will you say that I beg him to divide the money among the sufferers most in need of it, and to dispose the jewels and other things where they can be seen, and to issue a notice to the inhabitants that all can come and inspect them, and those who can bring proof that any of the articles belong to them can take them away."

THE SACK OF A CITY

The regiment was by this time formed up again, and Terence, addressing them, told them of the orders that he had given, saying that, as the regiment had made all the compensation in their power, and had rid itself of the spoils of a people whom they had professedly come to aid, it could now look the Spaniards in the face again. Just as he concluded, a staff-officer rode up.

"Lord Wellington wishes to speak to you, Colonel," he said. "We have been looking about for you everywhere, but your regiment seemed to have vanished."

"Then I must leave the work of inspecting the kits to you, Herrara. You will see that every article is unfolded and closely examined, and place every man in whose kit anything is discovered under arrest at once. I trust that you will not find anything, but if you do, place a strong guard over the prisoners, with loaded muskets, and orders to shoot any one of them who tries to escape."

Walking by the side of the staff-officer—for he had returned the horse lent him by General Barnard—he accompanied him to a house in the great square, where Lord Wellington had taken up his quarters.

Chapter XIX
Gratitude

"Your regiment has been distinguishing itself again, Colonel O'Connor, I have heard from three sources. First, General Barnard reported to me that he and the other officers were wholly unable to restrain the troops from their villainous work last night until he found you and your regiment drawn up in perfect order, and was able with it to put an end to the disorder everywhere reigning. In the second place, the Count de Montego and the Marquis de Valoroso, two of the wealthiest nobles in the province, have called upon me to return thanks for the inestimable service, as they expressed it, rendered by Colonel O'Connor and his officers in defending their houses and protecting the lives and honour of their families from the assaults of the soldiers. They said that the defenders consisted entirely of officers. How was that?"

"I am sorry to say that my men were at first infected by the general spirit of disorder. Left alone by ourselves, I thought that we could not do anything better than save from spoliation two fine mansions that happened to be at the spot where we had been left. We had to stand a sharp siege for two or three hours, but we abstained as far as possible from using our arms, and I think that only two or three of the soldiers were wounded. However, we should have had to use our pistols in earnest in a short time had I not sent out several of my officers by the back entrance of the house, and these were not long in finding, and persuading to return to their duties, a couple of hundred men. As soon as we sallied out, the affair was at an end, and the soldiers fled. The officers were sent out again, and when an hour later General Barnard came up, we had some seventeen hundred in readiness for action, and his arrival relieved me of the heavy responsibility of deciding what course had better be adopted."

GRATITUDE

"Yes, he told me so, and I think that you acted very wisely in holding your men back till he arrived, for nothing could have been more unfortunate than a conflict in the streets between British and Portuguese troops. There is no doubt that had it not been for your regiment the disgraceful scenes of last night would have been very much worse than they were. I should be glad if you will convey my thanks to them."

"Thank you, sir; but I shall be obliged if you will allow me to say that you regret to hear that a regiment in which you placed confidence should have at first behaved so badly, but that they had retrieved their conduct by their subsequent behaviour, and had acted as you would have expected of them. I have been speaking very severely to them this morning, and I am afraid that the effect of my words would be altogether lost were I to report your commendation of their conduct without any expression of blame."

Lord Wellington smiled.

"Do it as you like, Colonel O'Connor. However, your regiment will be placed in orders to-day as an exception to the severe censure passed upon the troops who entered the town last night. And do you really think that they will behave better another time?"

"I am sure they will, sir. I threatened to have the three hundred who had not joined when General Barnard arrived transferred to another regiment, and it was only upon their solemn promise, and by the whole of the officers guaranteeing their conduct in the future, that I forgave them. Moreover, every article taken in money, jewels, or dress, has been given up, and I have sent them to the syndic—the money for distribution among the sufferers, the jewellery and other things to be reclaimed by those from whom they were taken. Their kits were being examined thoroughly when I came away, but I think that I can say with certainty that no single stolen article will be found in them."

"You have done very well, sir, very well, and your influence with your men is surprising. Your regiment will be quartered in the convent of San Jose. Other divisions will move in this afternoon, and take the place of the 1st and 3rd brigades; your regiment, therefore, may consider it a high honour that they will be retained here. I dare say that it will not be long before I find work for you to do again. Lord Somerset will give you an order at once to take possession of the convent."

Terence returned to the regiment in high spirits. The work of inspection was still going on. At its conclusion Colonel Herrara reported that no single article of plunder had been found.

"I am gratified that it is so, Herrara," he said; "now let the regiment form up in a hollow square again.

"Men," he went on, "I have a message for you from Lord Wellington;" and he repeated that which he had suggested. "Thus you see, men, that the conduct of those who at once obeyed orders and returned to their ranks has caused the misconduct of the others to be forgiven, and Lord Wellington has still confidence that the regiment will behave well in future. The fact that all plunder has been given up to be restored to its owners had, of course, some effect in inducing him to believe this. I hope that every man will take the lesson to heart, that the misdeeds of a few may bring disgrace on a whole regiment, and that you will in future do nothing to forfeit the name that the Minho regiment has gained for good conduct as well as for bravery."

A loud cheer broke from the regiment, which then marched to the convent of San Jose and took up its quarters there. Two hours later the two Spanish nobles called upon Terence. The Count de Montego introduced his companion.

"We have only just heard where you were quartered," he went on. "We have both been trying in vain all the morning to find you; not a soldier of your regiment was to be seen in the streets, and, although we questioned many officers, none could say where you were. You went off so suddenly last night that I had no opportunity of expressing our gratitude to you and your officers."

"You said enough, and more than enough, last night, Count," Terence replied, "and we are all glad indeed that we were able to protect both your houses. Lord Wellington informed me that you had called upon him and spoken highly of the service we had been able to render you. Pray say no more about it. I can quite understand what you feel, and I can assure you that no thanks are due to me for having done my duty as a British officer and a gentleman on so lamentable and, I admit, disgraceful an occasion."

GRATITUDE

"My wife and daughters and those of the Marquis of Valoroso are all most anxious to see you and thank you and your officers. They were too frightened and agitated last night to say aught, and, indeed, as they say, they scarcely noticed your features. Can you bring your officers round now?"

"I am sorry to say I cannot do that, señor. They have to see after the arrangements and comfort of the men, the getting of the rations, the cooking, and so on. To-morrow they will, I am sure, be glad to pay you a visit."

"But you can come, can you not, Colonel?"

"Yes, I am at liberty now, Count, and shall be happy to pay my respects to the señoras."

"The more I hear," the marquis said, as they walked along together, "of the events of last night, the more deeply I feel the service that you have rendered us. I am unable to understand how it is that your soldiers should behave with such outrageous violence to allies."

"It is very disgraceful, and greatly to be regretted, señor; but I am bound to say that as I have now gone through four campaigns, and remember the conduct of the Spanish authorities to our troops during our march to Talavera, our stay there, and on our retreat, I am by no means surprised that among the soldiers, who are unable to draw a distinction between the people and the authorities, there should be a deep and lasting hatred. There is no such hatred for the French. Our men fought the battle of Talavera when weak with hunger, while the Spaniards, who engaged to supply them with provisions, were feasting. Our men were neglected and starved in the hospitals, and would have died to a man had not, happily for them, the French arrived and treated them with the greatest humanity and kindness. Soldiers do not forget this sort of thing; they know that for the last three years the promises of the Spanish authorities have never once been kept, and that they have had to suffer greatly from the want of transport and stores promised. We can, of course, discriminate between the people at large and their authorities, but the soldiers can make no such distinction, and, deeply as I deplore what has happened here, I must own that the soldiers have at least some excuse for their conduct."

The two Spaniards were silent.

"I cannot gainsay your statement," the Count de Montego said. "Indeed, no words can be too strong for the conduct of both the central and all the provincial juntas."

"Then, señor, how is it that the people do not rise and sweep them away, and choose honest and resolute men in their place?"

"That is a difficult question to answer, Colonel. It may be said, Why do not all people, when ill governed, destroy their tyrants?"

"Possibly because as a rule the tyrants have armies at their backs; but here, such armies as there are, although nominally under the orders of the juntas, are practically led by their own generals, and would obey them rather than the juntas. However, that is a matter for the Spanish people alone. Although we have suffered cruelly by the effects of your system, please remember that I am not in the smallest degree defending the conduct of our troops, but only trying to show that they had at least some excuse for regarding the Spaniards as foes rather than as allies, and that they had, as they considered, a long list of wrongs to avenge."

"There is truth in all you say, Colonel. Unfortunately, men like ourselves, who are the natural leaders of the people, hold aloof from these petty provincial struggles, and leave all the public offices to be filled with greedy adventurers, and have been accustomed to consider work of any kind beneath us. The country is paying dearly for it now. I trust, when the war is over, seeing how the country has suffered by our abstention from politics and from the affairs of our provinces, we shall put ourselves forward to aid in the regeneration of Spain."

By this time they had arrived at the door of the count's house. The street had been to some extent cleared, but shattered doors, broken windows, portions of costly furniture, and household articles of all sorts still showed how terrible had been the destruction of the previous night. Large numbers of the poorer class were at work clearing the roads, as the city authorities had been ordered by Lord Wellington to restore order in all the thoroughfares.

The count led the way up to the drawing-room. The countess and her three daughters rose.

GRATITUDE

"I introduced our brave defender to you last night," the count said, "but in the half-darkened room, and in the confusion and alarm that prevailed, you could have had but so slight a view of him that I doubt whether you would know him again."

"I should not, indeed," the countess said. "We have been speaking of him ever since, but could not agree as to his appearance. Oh, señor, no word can tell you how grateful we feel to you for your defence of us last night. What horrors we should have suffered had it not been for your interposition!"

"I am delighted to have been of service to you, señora. It was my duty, and it was a very pleasurable one, I can assure you, and I pray you to say no more about it."

"How is it that you speak Spanish so well, señor?" the countess asked, after her daughters had shyly expressed their gratitude to Terence.

"I owe it chiefly to a muleteer of Salamanca. I was a prisoner there last year, and he accompanied me for a month after I had made my escape from the prison. Also, I owe much to the guerilla chief Moras, with whom I acted for six weeks last autumn. I had learned a little of your language before, and, speaking Portuguese fluently, I naturally picked it up without any great difficulty."

"Your name is not unknown to us, Colonel," the count said. "Living so close to the frontier as we do, we naturally know much of what passes in Portugal, and heard you spoken of as a famous leader of a strong Portuguese regiment, that seems to have been in the thick of all the fighting; but we heard that you had been taken prisoner by the French at the battle of Fuentes d'Onoro."

"Yes, I had the misfortune to be captured by them, and was sent to Salamanca, but I escaped by the aid of a girl who sold fruit in the prison. A muleteer took me with him on a journey to Cadiz, and thence I came round to Lisbon by ship."

"You seem very young to have seen so much service, if you will excuse my saying so, Colonel."

Terence smiled.

"I have had great luck, señor; extraordinary luck."

"Ah, Colonel! We know how well you have deserved that luck, as you call it, and would never have been in command of such a regiment if you had not done something very much out of the way to attract the attention of your commanders."

"I was not appointed to the regiment, I raised it myself; that is to say, I came upon a number of Portuguese who had been called out for service, but who had neither leader nor arms. Being anxious to fight for their country, they asked me to be their leader, and I accepted the offer. I found them docile and obedient, and with the aid of two British troopers with me, a Spanish officer, and twelve of his troopers, I established something like order and discipline; and as we were fortunate in our first affair with the enemy, they had faith in me, and I was able to raise them to a point of discipline which is, I think, now quite equal to that of our own regiments. Seeing that I made myself useful with my corps, I was confirmed in my command, and obtained the rank of colonel in the Portuguese service, and am now a major in our own."

"I hope, señor, that later on you will tell us the story of some of your adventures. Be assured that the house and all in it are yours, and that it is not for mere curiosity that we would hear your story, but that, as we shall ever retain a grateful memory of what you have done for us, everything relating to you is of deep interest to us."

After chatting for another quarter of an hour, Terence went with the Count de Montego to the house next door. Here he received an equally warm welcome from the wife and son and daughter of the marquis.

At both houses he was warmly urged to take up his quarters there during his stay at Ciudad, but explained that his place was with his regiment. He promised that he would call frequently when his duties permitted him to do so.

The next day the two Spanish noblemen came to him, and after parade was over, carried off the greater portion of the officers to be also introduced to their families. From that time three or four of the officers were always invited to dinner at each house. Terence and Ryan frequently spent their evenings there, and their hosts introduced them to many of the leading people in the town.

GRATITUDE

The Spanish general, Carlos d'Espana, was appointed governor of Ciudad. Papers having been discovered showing that many of the inhabitants had acted as French emissaries, these he executed without mercy. So rigorous, however, were his measures that it was felt that more than sufficient blood had been shed, and accordingly several British deserters found in the town were pardoned. Many others of these men had fallen, fighting desperately in the breach, believing that there was no hope of mercy being extended to them if taken prisoners. In the siege the allies lost 1200 men and 90 officers, among whom were Generals Crauford and MacKinnon, both killed, and General Vandeleur badly wounded. Lord Wellington was created Duke of Ciudad Rodrigo by the Spaniards, and Earl of Wellington by the English. The French loss was 300 killed and wounded, 1500 prisoners, an immense store of ammunition, and 150 guns.

Thanks to the vigilance with which the Minho regiment had guarded the line of the fords of the Yeltes, no news of the siege was received by Marmont in time for him to interfere with it. The bridge over the Aqueda had been thrown across on the 1st of January, and the siege began on the 8th, but even on the 12th nothing was known at Salamanca of the advance of the British army, and it was not until the 15th, three days after the town had fallen, that news that the siege had begun reached Marmont at Valladolid. He had ordered his army to concentrate on Salamanca, but it was not until the 25th that 35,000 men were collected there, and on the following day the news arrived of the fall of Ciudad. In the meantime large numbers of labourers were being employed in repairing and strengthening the fortifications of that town, while Wellington laboured in making preparations for the siege of Badajoz.

These, however, progressed but slowly, owing to the refusal of the Portuguese government to supply transport for the guns, or to furnish any facilities whatever for the supply of food for the army. Wellington maintained his headquarters on the Coa until the first week in March, and then moved south with the greater part of the army, Ciudad being left entirely in the hands of the Spaniards, the general supplying the governor with provisions and stores, and explaining to him the object and intention of the new works. A very strong force was left to guard the frontier of Portugal from an invasion by Marmont, 50,000 men, of whom 20,000 were Portuguese, being scattered along the line and guarding all the passes, the Minho regiment being ordered to take post again at Pinhel.

Terence left Ciudad with reluctance. He had all along been treated as a dear friend in the houses of the two Spanish noblemen, and spent most of his evenings at one or other of them. He had been obliged to tell in full detail all his adventures since he joined the army. The rescue of his cousin from the convent at Oporto had particularly excited the interest of the ladies, who asked innumerable questions about her. Ryan frequently accompanied him, but his very slight knowledge of Spanish prevented him from feeling the same pleasure at the familiar intercourse. Bull and Macwitty were absolutely ignorant of the language, and although Herrara now and then accepted invitations to dinner, Terence and Ryan were the only two officers of the regiment who felt at home among the Spaniards.

Before the regiment marched off, each of the Portuguese officers was presented with a handsome gold watch bearing an inscription expressing the gratitude of the two Spanish noblemen and their families. Bull, Macwitty, and Herrara received, in addition, heavy gold chains. Ryan received a splendid horse, with saddle, holsters, and a brace of finely-finished pistols; and a similar present was made to Terence. On the day when he went to say good-bye he found the ladies of both families assembled at the Count de Montego's. His host said:

"You must consider the horses and equipment as a special present from myself and the marquis, Colonel O'Connor; but the ladies of our two families wish to give you a little memorial of their gratitude."

"They are memorials only," his wife said, "and are feeble testimonies indeed of what we feel. These are the joint presents of the marquise and her daughter, and of myself and my girls," and she gave him a small case containing a superb diamond ring of great value, and then a large case containing a magnificent parure of diamonds and emeralds.

"This, señor, is for your future wife. She will value it, I am sure, not so much for what it may be worth, but as a testimony of the gratitude of six Spanish ladies for the inestimable services that you rendered them. Perhaps they will have a special value in her eyes, inasmuch as the stones all formed a small part of the jewels of the

GRATITUDE

two families that you saved from plunder. We have, of course, had them reset, and there was no difficulty in getting this done, for at present ours are, I believe, the only jewels in Ciudad."

"My dear countess," Terence said, much moved, "I do not like taking so valuable a present."

"What is it in comparison to what you have done for us, señor? And please do not suppose that we have seriously diminished our store. Nowhere, I believe, have ladies such jewels as they have in Spain, and few families can boast of finer ones than those of the marquise and myself. And I can assure you that we shall value our jewels all the more when we think that some of their companions will be worn by the wife of the gentleman who has preserved more than our lives."

"That is a royal gift, indeed," Herrara said, when Terence showed him the jewels. "I should be afraid to say what they are worth. Many of the old Spanish families possess marvelous jewels, relics of the day when the Spaniards owned the wealth of the Indies and the spoils of half Europe, and I should imagine that these must have been among the finest stones in the possession of both families. If I were you, Colonel, I should take the very first opportunity that occurs of sending them to England."

"You may be sure that I shall do so, Herrara. They are not the sort of things to be carried about in a cavalry wallet, and I have no other place to stow them. As soon as we arrive at Pinhel I will get a strong box made to hold the two cases, and hand them over to the paymaster there, to be sent down to Lisbon by the next convoy. He sent home all the money that I did not want to keep by me when we were at Pinhel last."

Two other Portuguese regiments and a brigade of British infantry were stationed at Pinhel in readiness at any moment to march to Almeida or Guarda, should Marmont make a forward movement, which was probable enough; for it was evident, by the concentration of his troops at Salamanca and Valladolid, that he had no intention of marching south, but intended to leave it to Soult, with the armies of Estremadura, Castile, and Andalusia, to relieve Badajoz. From time to time news came from that town. The siege had begun on the 17th of March, the attack being made on a fortified hill called the Picurina, but at first the progress was slow. Incessant rain fell, the ground became a swamp, and all operations had several times to be suspended, while Phillipon, the brave officer who commanded the garrison, made numerous sorties from the town with more or less success.

On the night of the 25th an assault was made on the strong fort on the Picurina, which was captured after desperate fighting and the loss of 19 officers and 300 men killed and wounded. On the following day the trenches were opened for the attack upon the town itself. The assailants laboured night and day, and on the 6th a breach had been effected in the work called the Trinadad, and this was to be attacked by the 4th and light divisions. The castle was at the same time to be assailed by Picton's division, while General Power's Portuguese were to make a feint on the other side of the Guadiana, and San Roque was to be stormed by the forces employed in the trenches.

The enterprise was well-nigh desperate. The breaches had not been sufficiently cleared, and it was known that the enemy had thrown up strong intrenchments behind them. Most of the guns were still in position to sweep the breaches, and another week at least should have been occupied in preparing the way for an assault. But Wellington was forced here, as at Ciudad, to fight against time. Soult was close at hand, and the British had not sufficient force to give him battle and at the same time to continue the siege of the town; and it was therefore necessary either to carry at once, at whatever cost of life, or to abandon the fruits of all the efforts that had been made. Had Wellington's instructions been carried out, there would have been no occasion whatever for the assault to have been delivered until the breaches were greatly extended, the intrenchments destroyed, and the guns silenced. The Portuguese ministry, however, had thwarted him at every turn, and the siege could not be commenced until a fortnight after the date fixed by Wellington. This fortnight's delay cost the lives of 4000 British soldiers.

Four of the assaults on the breaches failed. On the crest of these Phillipon had erected a massive stockade, thickly bristling with sabre-blades. On the upper part of the breach, planks, similarly studded, had been laid; while on either side a vast number of shells, barrels of powder, faggots soaked in oil, and other missiles and

GRATITUDE

combustibles, were piled in readiness for hurling down on the assailants; while the soldiers behind the defences had been supplied with four muskets each.

Never did British soldiers fight with such dogged bravery as was here evinced. Again and again they dashed up the breach, the centre of a volcano of fire; shells burst among them, cannon poured volleys of grape through their ranks, the French plied them with musketry, fire-balls lit up the scene as if by day, mines exploded under their feet; yet again and again they reached the terrible breastwork. But all efforts to climb it were fruitless. Numbers of those in front were pressed to death against the sabres by the eager efforts of those behind to get up, and for hours the assault continued. At last, seeing the impossibility of success, and scorning to retreat, the men gathered at the foot of the breach, and there endured, sternly and silently, the murderous fire that was maintained by the enemy.

Picton, however, had gained possession of the castle. Walker with his command had captured the bastion of San Vincenti, and part of his command fought their way along the battlement towards the breaches, while another marched through the town. Finding that the town had been entered at several points, the defenders of the breach gave way, and the soldiers poured into the town. Here even more hideous scenes of murder and rapine were perpetrated than at Ciudad Rodrigo, and went on for two days and nights absolutely unchecked. It has never been satisfactorily explained why, after the events in the former town, no precautions were taken by the general commanding to prevent the recurrence of scenes that brought disgrace on the British army, and for which he cannot be held blameless. Five thousand men and officers were killed or wounded in the siege, of these, 3500 fell in the assault.

The next three months passed without any action of importance. The discipline of the army had, as might have been expected, deteriorated greatly as a consequence of the unbridled license permitted to the soldiers after the capture of the two fortresses, and the absence of any punishment whatever for the excesses there committed. Lord Wellington complained bitterly in his letters home of the insubordination of the troops, of the outrages committed upon the peasantry, especially by detached parties, and of the general disobedience of orders. But he who had permitted the license and excesses to be carried on unchecked and unpunished, cannot but be considered largely responsible for the natural consequences of such laxity.

In May heavy rains prevented any movement on either side, except that the town of Almaraz, a most important position at the bridge across the Tagus, permitting Soult and Marmont to join hands, was captured by surprise by General Hill, the works, which had been considered almost impregnable, being carried by assault in the course of an hour. This was one of the most brilliant exploits of the war. Wellington had moved north and was again on the Aqueda, and on the 13th of June, rain having ceased, he crossed the river, and on the 16th arrived within six miles of Salamanca, and drove a French division across the Tormes. On the 17th the river was crossed both above and below the town, and the forts defending it were at once invested. Marmont had that day retired with two divisions of infantry and some cavalry, and was followed immediately by a strong British division.

The Minho regiment had been one of the first to take post on the Aqueda after Wellington's arrival on the Coa, and moved forward in advance of the army, which was composed of 24,000 British troops, with a Spanish division, and several Portuguese regiments.

As soon as Marmont had retired, Salamanca went wild with joy, although the circle of forts still prevented the British from entering. The chief of these was San Vincenti, which stood on a perpendicular cliff overhanging the Tormes. It was flanked by two other strong forts, from which, however, it was divided by a ravine. The battering-train brought with the army was altogether inadequate—only four eighteen-pounders and three twenty-four-pound howitzers were available—and the forts were far stronger than Wellington had been led to expect.

A few guns had been sent forward by General Hill, and on the 18th seven pieces opened fire on San Vincenti. The next day some more howitzers arrived, and a breach was made in the wall of the convent, but the ammunition was exhausted, and the fire ceased until more could be brought up. That day, however, Marmont, with a force of 20,000 men, was seen advancing to the relief of the forts. The British army at once withdrew from the neighbourhood of the convent, and took up its position in order of battle on the heights of

GRATITUDE

San Christoval. On the 21st three divisions of infantry and a brigade of cavalry joined Marmont, raising his force to 40,000 men. The French the next night sent a portion of their force across the Tormes, and when daylight broke, the German cavalry, which had been placed to guard the ford, was seen retiring before 12,000 French infantry, with twenty guns.

Graham was also sent across the Tormes with his division, which was of about the same strength as the French force, and as the light division was also following, the French retired, recrossed the ford, and rejoined the main body of their army. The next night the batteries again opened fire on San Vincenti, and on the 27th the fort was breached, and both surrendered just as the storming parties were advancing to the assault, and Marmont retreated the same night across the Douro, by the roads to Tordesillas and Toro.

As soon as it was possible to enter Salamanca, Terence rode down into the town, accompanied by Ryan. The forts had not yet surrendered, but their hands were so full that they had no time to devote to annoying small parties of British officers passing into the town.

Terence had noted down the address that Nita had given him, and at once rode there, after having with some difficulty discovered the lane in which the house was situated. An old man came to the door. Terence dismounted.

"What can I do for you, señor?"

"I wanted to ask you if your niece, Nita, is still staying with you?"

The man looked greatly surprised at the question.

"She has done no harm, I hope?" he asked.

"Not at all, but I wish to speak to her. Is she married yet to Garcia, the muleteer?"

The old man looked still more surprised.

"No, señor; Garcia is away; he is no longer a muleteer."

"Well, you have not answered me if your niece is here."

"She is here, señor, but she is not in the house at this moment. She returned here from her father's last autumn. The country was so disturbed that it was not right that young women should remain in the villages."

"Will you tell her that a British officer will call to see her in half an hour, and beg her to remain in until I come?"

"I will tell her, señor."

Terence went at once to a silversmith's, and bought the handsomest set of silver jewellery, such as the peasants wore, that he had in his shop, including bracelets, necklaces, large filigree hairpin and earrings, and various other ornaments.

Chapter XX
Salamanca

"She is a lucky girl, Terence," Ryan said, as they quitted the shop. "She will be the envy of all the peasant girls in the neighbourhood when she goes to church in all that finery to be married to her muleteer."

"It has only cost about twenty pounds, and I value my freedom at a very much higher price than that, Dick. If I had not escaped I should not have been in that affair with Moras that got me my promotion, and at the present time should be in some prison in France."

"You would not have got your majority, I grant, Terence, but wherever they shut you up, it is morally certain that you would have been out of it long before this. I don't think anything less than being chained hand and foot and kept in an underground dungeon would suffice to hold you."

"I hope that I shall never have to try that experiment, Dicky," Terence laughed; "and now, I think you had better go into this hotel and order lunch for us both. It is just as well not to attract attention by two of us riding to that lane. We have not done with Marmont yet, and it may be that the French will be masters of Salamanca again before long, and it is just as well not to get the old man or the girl talked about. I will leave my horse here too. See that both of them get a good feed; they have not had overmuch since we crossed the Aqueda."

As there were a good many British officers in the town, no special attention was given to Terence as he walked along through the street, which was gay with flags. When he reached the house in the lane the old man was standing at the door.

"Nita is in now, señor. She has not told me why you wanted to see her. She said it was better that she should not do so, but she thought she knew who it was."

The girl clapped her hands as he entered the room to which the old man pointed.

"Then it is you, Señor Colonello. I wondered, when we heard the English were coming, if you would be with them. Of course I heard from Garcia that you had gone safely on board a ship at Cadiz. Then I wondered whether, if you did come here, you would remember me."

"Then that was very bad of you, Nita. You ought to have been quite sure that I should remember you. If I had not done so I should have been an ungrateful rascal, and should have deserved to die in the next French prison I got into."

"How well you speak Spanish now, señor!"

"Yes: that was principally due to Garcia, but partly from having been in Spain for six weeks last autumn. I was with Moras, and we gave the French a regular scare."

"Then it was you, señor! We heard that an English officer was in command of the troops who cut all the roads and took numbers of French prisoners, and defeated 5000 of their troops, and, as they said, nearly captured Valladolid and Burgos."

"That was an exaggeration, Nita. Still, we managed to do them a good deal of damage, and kept the French in this part of the country pretty busy. And now, Nita, I have came to fulfil my promise;" and he handed her the box in which the jeweller had packed up his purchases.

"These are for your wedding, Nita, and if it comes off while we are in this part of the country I shall come and dance at it."

The girl uttered cries of delight as she opened parcel after parcel.

"Oh, señor, it is too much, too much altogether!" she cried, as she laid them all out on the table before her.

"Not a bit of it," Terence said. "But for you I should be in prison now. If they had been ten times as many and ten times as costly, I should still have felt your debtor all my life. And where is Garcia now?"

"He has gone to join Morillo," she said. "He always said that as soon as the English came to our help he should go out, so six weeks ago he sold all his mules and bought a gun and went off."

"I am sorry not to have seen him," Terence said. "And now, Nita, when he returns you are to give him this little box. It contains a present to help you both to start housekeeping in good style. You see that I have put your name and his both on it. No one can say what may happen in war. Remember that this is your joint property, and if by ill fortune he should not come back again, then it becomes yours."

"Oh, señor, you are altogether too good! Oh, I am a lucky girl! I am sure that no maid ever went to church before with such splendid ornaments. How envious all the girls will be of me!"

"And I expect the men will be equally envious of Garcia, Nita. Now, if you will take my advice you will not show these things to anyone at present, but will hide them in the box in some very safe place until you are quite sure that the French will never come back again. If your neighbours saw them, some ill-natured person might tell the French that you had received them from an English officer, and then it might be supposed that you had been acting as a spy for us, so it is better that you should tell no one, not even your uncle—that is, if you have not already mentioned it to him."

"I have never told him," the girl said. "He is a good man and very kind, but he is very timid and afraid of getting into trouble. If he asks me who you are and what you wanted, I shall tell him that you are an English officer who was in prison in the convent, that you always bought your fruit of me, and said if you ever came to Salamanca again you would find me out."

"That will do very well. Now I will say good-bye, Nita. If we remain here after the French have retreated I will come and see you again, for there will be so many English officers here that I would not be noticed. But there may be a battle any day, or Marmont may fall back, and we should follow him, so that I may not get an opportunity again."

"I hope you will come, I do hope you will come! I will bury all these things this evening in the ground in the kitchen after my uncle has gone to bed."

"Well, good-bye, Nita. I must be off now, as I have a friend with me. When you see Garcia you can tell him that you have given me a kiss. I am sure he won't mind."

"I should not care if he did," the girl said saucily, as she held up her face. "Good-bye, señor. I shall always think of you and pray the Virgin to watch over you."

After Marmont fell back across the Douro there was a pause in the operations, and as the British army was quartered in and around Salamanca, the city soon swarmed with British soldiers, and presented a scene exactly similar to that which it had worn when occupied by Moore's army nearly four years before.

"What fun it was, Terence," Ryan said, "when we frightened the place out of its very senses by the report that the French were entering town!"

"That is all very well, Dick, but I think that you and I were just as much frightened as the Spaniards were when we saw how the thing had succeeded and that all our troops were called out. There is no saying what they would have done to us had they found out who started the report. The very least thing that would have happened would have been to be tried by court-martial and dismissed from the service, and I am by no means sure that worse than that would not have befallen us."

"Yes, it would have been an awful business if we had been found out. Still, it was a game, wasn't it? What an awful funk they were in! It was the funniest thing I ever saw. Things have changed since then, Terence, and I am afraid we have quite done with jokes of that sort."

"I should hope so, Dick. I think that I can answer for myself, but I am by no means sure as to you."

"I like that," Ryan said indignantly. "You were always the leader in mischief. I believe you would be now if you had the chance."

"I don't know," Terence replied, a little more seriously than he had before spoken. "I have been through a wonderful number of adventures since then, and I don't pretend that I have not enjoyed them in something of the same spirit in which we enjoyed the fun we used to have together, but, you see, I have had an immense deal of responsibility. I have two thousand men under me, and though Bull and Macwitty are good men so far as the carrying out of orders goes, they are still too much troopers, seldom make a suggestion, and never

SALAMANCA

really discuss any plan I suggest, so that the responsibility of the lives of all these men really rests entirely upon my shoulders. It has been only when I have been separated from them, as when I was a prisoner, that I have been able to enjoy an adventure in the same sort of way that we used to do together."

"I little thought then, Terence, that in three years and a half, for that is about what it is, I should be a captain and you a major—for I don't count your Portuguese rank one way or the other."

"Of course you have had two more years' regimental work than I have had. It would have been much better for me if I had had a longer spell of it too. Of course, I have been extraordinarily fortunate, and it has been very jolly, but I am sure it would have been better for me to have had more experience as a subaltern before all this began."

"Well, I cannot say I see it, Terence. At any rate, you have had a lot more regimental work than most officers, for you had to form your regiment, teach them discipline, and everything else, and I don't think that you would have done it so well if you had been ground down into the regular regimental pattern, and had come to think that powder and pipe-clay were actual indispensables in turning out soldiers."

The quiet time at Salamanca lasted a little over a fortnight, for in the beginning of July, Lord Wellington heard that, in obedience to King Joseph's reiterated orders, Marmont, having received reinforcements, was preparing to recross the Douro, that Soult was on the point of advancing into Portugal, and that the king himself, with a large army, was on the way to join Marmont.

The latter, indeed, was not to have moved till the king joined him, but, believing that his own army was ample for the purpose, and eager to gain a victory, unhampered by the king's presence, he suddenly crossed at Tordesillas, and it was only by his masterly movements and a sharp fight at Castile that Wellington succeeded in concentrating his army on the Aqueda. The British general drew up his army in order of battle on the heights of Vallesa, but the position was a strong one, Marmont knew the country perfectly, and instead of advancing to the attack, he started at daybreak on the 20th, marched rapidly up the river, and crossed it before any opposition could be offered, and then marched for the Tormes.

By this movement he had turned Wellington's right flank, was as near Salamanca as were the British, and had it in his power, unless checked, to place himself on the road between Salamanca and Ciudad, and so to cut their line of retreat. Seeing his position thus turned, Wellington made a corresponding movement, and the two armies marched along lines of hills parallel with each other, the guns on both sides occasionally firing. All day long they were but a short distance apart, and at any moment the battle might have been brought on. But Wellington had no opportunity for fighting except at a disadvantage, and Marmont, having gained the object for which he had manoeuvred, was well content to maintain his advantage. At nightfall the British were on the heights of Cabeca and Aldea Rubia, and so secured their former position at San Christoval.

Marmont, however, had reached a point that gave him the command of the ford at Huerta, and had it in his power to cross the Tormes when he pleased, and either to recross at Salamanca or to cut the road to Ciudad. He had proved, too, that his army could outmarch the British, for although they had already made a march of some distance when the race began, he had gained ground throughout the day in spite of the efforts of the British to keep abreast of him. Moreover, Marmont now had his junction with the king's army approaching from Madrid securely established, and could either wait for his arrival or give battle if he saw a favourable opportunity. Wellington's position was grave. He had not only to consider his adversary's force but the whole course of the war, which a disaster would imperil. He had the safety of the whole Peninsula to consider, and a defeat would not only entail the loss of the advantage he had gained in Spain, but would probably decide the fate of Portugal also. He determined, however, to cover Salamanca till the last moment in hopes that Marmont might make some error that would afford him an opportunity of dealing a heavy blow.

The next morning the allies occupied their old position at San Christoval, while the French took possession of Alba, whence the Spaniards had been withdrawn without notice to Wellington. The evening before, the British general had sent a despatch to the Spanish commander, saying that he feared that he should be unable to hold his position. The messenger was captured by the French cavalry, and Marmont, believing that Wellington was about to retreat, and fearing that he might escape him, determined to fight rather than wait for the arrival of the king. The French crossed the Tormes by the fords of Huerta and Alba, the British by other fords above Salamanca. This movement was performed while a terrible storm raged. Many men and horses of the 5th Dragoon Guards were killed by the lightening, while hundreds of the picketed horses broke their ropes and galloped wildly about.

The position of the British army in the morning was very similar to that occupied by a portion of it when besieging the forts of Salamanca, extending from the ford of St. Marta to the heights near the village of Arapiles. This line covered Salamanca, but it was open to Marmont to march round Wellington's right, and so cut his communications with Ciudad. During the night Wellington heard that the French would be joined in the course of two days by twenty guns and 2000 cavalry, and resolved to retire before these came up unless Marmont afforded him some opportunity of fighting to advantage. The latter, however, was too confident of victory to wait for the arrival of this reinforcement, still less for that of the king, and at daybreak he took possession of a village close to the British, thereby showing that he was resolved to force on a battle.

Near this were two detached hills, called the Arapiles or Hermanitos. They were steep and rugged. As the French were seen approaching, a Portuguese regiment was sent to seize them, and these gained the one nearest to them, while the French took possession of the second. The 7th division assailed the height first, and gained and captured half of it. Had Wellington now wished to retire, it would have been at once difficult and dangerous to attempt the movement. His line was a long one, and it would have been impossible to withdraw without running the risk of being attacked while in movement and driven back upon the Tormes. Ignorant of Marmont's precise intentions, for the main body of the French army was almost hidden in the woods, Wellington could only wait until their plans were developed. He therefore contented himself with placing the 4th division on a slope behind the village of Arapiles, which was held by the light companies of the Guards.

The 5th and 6th divisions were massed behind the hill, where a deep depression hid them from the sight of the enemy. For some time things remained quiet, except that the French and British batteries, on the top of the two Hermanitos, kept up a duel with each other. During the pause the French cavalry had again crossed the Tormes, by one of the fords used in the night by the British, and had taken post at Aldea Tejarda, thus placing themselves between the British army and the road to Ciudad. This movement, however, had been covered by the woods. About twelve o'clock, fearing that Wellington would assail the Hermanito held by him, Marmont brought up two divisions to that point, and stood ready to oppose an attack which Wellington, indeed, had been preparing, but had abandoned the idea, fearing that such a movement would draw the whole army into a battle on a disadvantageous line.

The French marshal, however, fearing that Wellington would retreat by the Ciudad road before he could place a sufficient force on that line to oppose the movement, sent General Maucune with two divisions covered by fifty guns and supported by cavalry, to move along the southern ridge of the basin and menace that road, holding in hand six divisions in readiness to fall upon the village of Arapiles should the British interfere with Maucune's movement. The British line had now pivoted round until its position extended from the Hermanito to near Aldea Tejarda.

In order to occupy the attention of the British, and prevent them from moving, the French force attacked the village of Arapiles, and a fierce struggle took place. Had Marmont waited until Clausel's division, still behind, came up, and occupied the ridge so as to connect the French main army with Maucune's division, their position would have been unassailable; but the fear that Wellington might escape had overcome his prudence, and as Maucune advanced, a great gap was left between his division and that of Marmont. As soon as Wellington perceived the mistake, he saw that his opportunity had come. Orders were despatched in all directions, and suddenly the two divisions, hidden from the sight of the French behind the Hermanito, dashed down into the valley, where two other divisions joined them.

The 4th and 5th were in front with Bradford's Portuguese, and the 6th and 7th formed the second line, while the Spanish troops marched between them and the 3rd division, forming the extreme right at Aldea Tejarda. The light divisions of Pack's Portuguese and the heavy cavalry remained in reserve on high ground behind them.

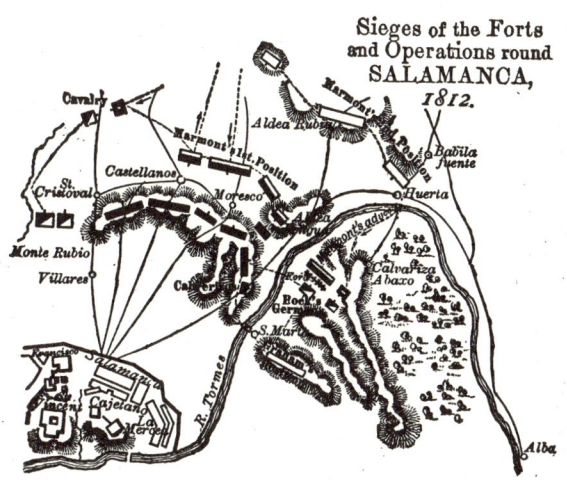

In spite of a storm of bullets from Maucune's guns, the leading divisions marched steadily forward, and while the third division dashed across the valley, and, climbing the ridge, barred his progress, the main line advanced to attack his flank. Marmont, seeing the terrible danger in which Maucune was involved, sent officer after officer to hasten up the troops from the forest, and with his centre prepared to attack the English Hermanito, and to drive them from that portion of the village they still held, but as he was hurrying to join Maucune, a shell exploded near him, hurling him to the ground with a broken arm and two deep wounds in his side. This misfortune was fatal to the French chances. Confusion ensued, and the movements of the troops were paralysed.

It was about five o'clock when the third division, under Pakenham, fell upon Maucune's leading division, and two batteries of artillery suddenly opened fire on their flank from the opposite height. Having no expectation of such a stroke, and believing that the British were ere this in full retreat along the Ciudad road, the French were hurrying forward, lengthening out into a long straggling line. The onslaught of Pakenham's division was irresistible, supported as it was by guns and cavalry. Nevertheless, the French bore themselves gallantly, forming line as they marched forward, while their guns poured showers of grape into the approaching infantry.

Nothing, however, could stop them. Pressing forward, they broke the half-formed lines into fragments, and drove them back in confusion upon the columns behind. The French cavalry endeavoured to check the British advance by a charge on their flank, but were repulsed by the infantry, and the British light horsemen charged and drove them off the field. Pushing forward, Pakenham came upon the second half of the division they had defeated, formed up on the wooded heights, one face being opposed to him, and the other to the 5th division, Bradford's Portuguese, and a mass of cavalry moving across the basin. The French had been already driven out of Arapiles, and were engaged in action with the 4th division, but the battle was to some extent retrieved, for Clausel's division had arrived from the forest and reinforced Maucune, and spread across the basin, joining hands with the divisions massed near the French Hermanito.

SALAMANCA

Marmont had been carried off the field. Bonnet, who had succeeded him, was disabled, and the chief command devolved on Clausel, a general of talent, possessing great coolness and presence of mind. His dispositions were excellent, but his troops were broken up into lines, columns, and squares. A strong wind raised the sandy soil in clouds of dust, the sinking sun shone full in the faces of his troops and at once concealed the movements of their enemies from them, and prevented them from acting with any unity. Suddenly, two heavy bodies of light and heavy cavalry broke from the cloud of dust and fell upon them. Twelve hundred Frenchmen were trampled down, and as the cavalry rode on, the third division ran forward at the double through the gap that they had formed. Line after line of the French infantry was broken and scattered, and five of their guns captured by one of the squadrons. Two thousand prisoners were taken, and three divisions that Maucune had commanded were a mass of fugitives.

In the meantime a terrible battle was raging in the centre. Here Clausel had gathered three fresh divisions, and behind these the fugitives from the left rallied; he placed three others, supported by the whole of the cavalry, to cover the retreat, while yet another remained behind the French Hermanito. Pack's Portuguese were advancing against it, and arrived nearly at the summit when the French reserves leapt from the rocks, and opened a tremendous fire on their front and left flank, and the Portuguese were driven down the hill with much loss. Almost at the same moment one of the regiments of the 14th division was suddenly charged by 1200 French soldiers, hidden behind a declivity, and driven back with heavy loss.

For a moment it seemed that the fate of the battle might yet be changed, but Wellington had the strongest reserve; the sixth division was brought up, and though the French fought obstinately, Clausel was obliged to abandon the Hermanito, and the army began to fall back, the movement being covered by their guns and the gallant charges of their cavalry. The whole of the British reserves were now brought into action, and hotly pressed them; but, for the most part maintaining their order, the French fell back into the woods, and, favoured by the darkness, and nobly covered by Maucune, who had been strongly reinforced, they drew off with comparatively little loss, thanks to the Spaniards' abandonment of the fort guarding the ford at Alba. Believing that the French must make for the ford of Huerta, Wellington had greatly strengthened his force on that side, and after a long march to the ford, was bitterly disappointed on arriving there at midnight to find that there was no sign of the enemy, although it was not until morning that he learned that they had passed unmolested over the ford of Alba. Had it not been for the Spanish disobedience and folly, Marmont's whole army would have had no resource but to surrender.

Marmont's strength when the fight began was 42,000 infantry and cavalry, and 74 guns; Wellington had 46,000 infantry and cavalry, and 60 pieces, but this included a considerable Spanish force and one of their batteries, and 10,000 Portuguese, who, however, could not be reckoned as good troops. The pursuit of the French was taken up hotly next morning, and they were chased for 40 miles that day, but the next morning they eluded their pursuers, marched to Valladolid, drew off the garrison there, and left it to be occupied by the British the following day.

The Minho regiment had been, two days before the battle, attached to the 6th division. For a time, being in the second line, they looked on, impatient spectators of the fight, but at the crisis of the battle they were brought up to check Clausel's impetuous counter-attack, and nowhere was the struggle fiercer. Hulse's brigade, to which they were attached, bore more than its share of the fighting, and the 11th and the 61st together had but 160 men and officers left when the battle was over. The Portuguese fought valiantly, and the fact that their countrymen had been defeated in their attempt to capture the French Hermanito, inspired them with a fierce determination to show that Portuguese troops could fight as well as their allies. They pushed forward well abreast of the other regiments of the brigade, and suffered equally. In vain the French attempted to check their advance. Showers of grape swept their ranks, volleys of musketry, at a distance of but a few yards, withered up their front lines, and for a time a hand-to-hand fight with bayonets raged. In the terrible roar of artillery and musketry, words of command were unheard, but the men mechanically filled up the gaps in their ranks, and the one thought of all was to press forward, until at length the French yielded, and fell sullenly back, disputing every yard of the ground, and a fresh division took up the pursuit.

SALAMANCA

The order to halt was given. The men looked round confused and dazed, as if waking from a dream. Grimed with powder, soaked with perspiration, breathless and haggard, many seemed scarcely able to keep their feet, and every limb trembled at the sudden cessation of the terrible strain. Then as they looked round their ranks and to the ground they had passed over, now so thickly dotted with the dark uniforms, hoarse sobs broke from them, and men who had gone unflinchingly through the terrible struggle burst into tears. The regiment had gone into action over 2000 strong, scarce 1200 remained unwounded. Of the officers, Bull had fallen desperately wounded; Macwitty had been shot through the head; a shell had struck Terence's horse, and, bursting, had carried off the rider's leg above the knee. The men near him uttered a simultaneous cry as he fell, and, regardless of the fight, oblivious to the storm of shot and shell, had knelt beside him. Terence was perfectly sensible.

"Do one of you give me my flask out of my holster," he said, "and another cut off the leg of my trousers as high as you can above the wound. That is right. Now for the bandages."

As every soldier in the regiment carried one in his hat, half a dozen of these were at once produced.

"Is it bleeding much?" he asked.

"Not much, Colonel."

"That is fortunate. Now find a smooth round stone, lay it on the inside of the leg just below where you have cut the trousers, now put a bandage round and round as tightly as you can do it. That is right. Now take the ramrod of one of my pistols, put it through the bandage, and then twist it. You need not be afraid of hurting me; my leg is quite numbed at present. That is right. Put another bandage on, so as to hold the ramrod in its place; now fetch a flannel shirt from my valise, fold it up so as to make a pad that will go over the wound, and bandage it there firmly. Give me another drink, for I feel faint."

When all was done, he said: "Put my valise under my head and throw my cloak over me. Thank you, I shall do very well now. Go forward and join the regiment."

"I am done for this time," he thought to himself when the men left him. "Still, I may pull through. There are many who have had a leg shot off and recovered, and there is no reason why I should not do so. There has not been any great loss of blood. I suppose that something has been smashed up so that it cannot bleed. Ah, here comes the doctor!"

The doctor was one of several medical students who had enlisted in the regiment, fighting and drilling with the rest, but, when occasion offered, acting as surgeons.

"I have just heard the news, Colonel. The regiment is heartbroken, but in their fury they went at the French facing them and scattered them like sheep. Canovas, who told me, said that you were not bleeding much, and that he and the others had bandaged you up according to your instructions. Let me see. It could not have been better," he said. He felt Terence's pulse. "Wonderfully good, considering what a smash you have had. Your vitality must be marvellous, and unless your wound breaks out bleeding badly, I have every hope that you will get over it. Robas and Salinas will be here in a minute with a stretcher for you, and we will get you to some quiet spot out of the line of fire."

Almost immediately four men came up with the stretcher, and by the surgeon's orders carried Terence to a quiet spot, sheltered by a spur of the hill from the fire.

"There is nothing more you can do for me now, Doctor?"

"Nothing. It would be madness to take the bandages off at present."

"Then please go back to the others. There must be numbers there who want your aid far more than I do. You can stay with me, Leon; but first go back to where my horse is lying, and bring here the saddle and the two blankets strapped behind it. I don't feel any pain to speak of, but it seems to me bitterly cold."

The man presently returned with the saddle and blankets. Two others accompanied him. Both had been hit too seriously to continue with the regiment. Their wounds had been already bandaged.

"We thought that we should like to be near you, Colonel, if you do not mind."

"Not at all. First, do each of you take a sip at my flask. Leon, I wish you would find a few sticks and try to make a fire. It would be cheerful, although it might not give much warmth."

A shell had struck Terence's horse.

It was dark now. It was five o'clock when the 3rd division threw itself across Maucune's line of march and the battle had begun. It was dark long before it ended, but during the three hours it lasted the French had lost a marshal, seven generals, and 12,500 men and officers, killed, wounded, or prisoners; while on the British side a field-marshal, four generals, and nearly 6000 officers and soldiers were killed or wounded. Indeed, the battle itself was concentrated into an hour's hard fighting, and a French officer, describing it, said that 40,000 men were defeated in forty minutes.

Presently the din of battle died out, and as soon as it did so, Herrara and Ryan both hurried to the side of Terence.

"My dear Terence," Ryan said, dropping on his knees beside him, "this is terrible. When I heard the news I was almost beside myself. As to the men, terrible as their loss is, they talk of no one but you."

"I think I shall pull through all right, Ryan; at any rate, the doctor says he thinks I shall, and I think so myself. I am heartily glad that you and Herrara have gone through it all right. What are our losses?"

"I don't know yet; we have not had time to count, but not far from half our number. Macwitty is killed, Bull desperately wounded; fully half the company officers are killed."

"That is terrible indeed, Ryan. Poor fellows! Poor fellows! Well, I should say, Herrara, that if you get no orders to join in the pursuit, you had best get all the wounded collected and brought here, and let the regiment light fires and bivouac. There is no chance of getting medical assistance outside the regiment to-night. Of course, all the British surgeons will have their hands full with their own men. Still, I only suggest this, for of course you are now in command."

The wounded had all fallen within a comparatively short distance, and many were able to walk in; the rest were carried, each in a blanket, with four men at the corners. Under Ryan's directions the unwounded scattered over the hillside and soon brought back a large supply of bushes and faggots. A number of fires were lighted, and the four surviving medical students and one older surgeon at once began the work of attending the wounded, taking the more serious cases first, leaving the less important ones to be bandaged by their comrades. Many wounded men from other regiments, attracted by the light of the fires, came up, and these, too, received what aid the Portuguese could give them.

The next morning Terence was carried down at daybreak on a stretcher to Salamanca, where the town was in a state of the wildest excitement over the victory. As they entered the gates an officer asked the bearers:

"Who is it?"

"Colonel O'Connor of the Minho regiment."

The officer knew Terence personally.

"I am sorry, indeed, to see you here, O'Connor. Not very serious, I hope?"

"A leg cut clean off above the knee with the fragment of a shell, Percival, but I fancy that I am going to get over it."

"Carry him to the convent of St. Bernard," the officer said to the Portuguese captain who was in command of the party, which consisted of 400 men carrying 100 wounded. "All officers are to be taken there, the others to the San Martin convent."

"I will look in and see you as soon as I can, O'Connor, and hope to find you going on well."

But few wounded officers had as yet been brought in, and as soon as Terence was carried into a ward two of the staff surgeons examined his wound.

"You are doing wonderfully well, Colonel," the senior officer said. "You must have received good surgical attention immediately on being wounded. Judging by your pulse, you can have lost but little blood."

"It hardly bled at all, Doctor, and I had it bandaged up by two of my own men. I have seen a good many serious wounds in the course of the last four years, and know pretty well what ought to be done."

"It has been uncommonly well done, anyhow. I think we had better not disturb the bandages for a few days. If no bleeding sets in by that time clots of blood will have formed, and you will be comparatively safe. Your pulse is very quiet. Your men must have carried you down very carefully."

"If I had been a basket of eggs they could not have taken more care of me. I was scarcely conscious of any movement."

"Well, you have youth and good health and good spirits in your favour. If all our patients took things as cheerfully as you do, there would not be so many of them slip through our hands."

Bull, who had been brought in immediately after Terence, was next attended to. He was unconscious. He had been struck by a round shot in the shoulder, which had not only smashed the bone, but almost carried away the upper part of the arm.

"An ugly wound," the surgeon said to his colleague. "At any rate we may as well take off the arm while he is unconscious; it will save him a second shock, and we can better bandage the wound when it is removed."

A low moan was the only sign that the wounded man had any consciousness that the operation was being performed.

"Will he get over it, Doctor?" Terence asked when the surgeon had finished.

"There is just a chance, but it is a faint one. Has he been a sober man?"

"Very. I can answer for the last four years at any rate. All the Portuguese officers were abstemious men, and I think that Bull felt that it would not do for him, commanding a battalion, to be less sober than they were."

"That increases his chance. Men who drink have everything against them when they get a severe wound; but he has lost a great deal of blood, and the shock has of course been a terrible one."

An orderly was told to administer a few spoonfuls of brandy-and-water, and the surgeon then moved on to the next bed.

Chapter XXI
Home Again

The next morning one of the surgeons brought a basketful of fruit to Terence.

"There is a young woman outside, Colonel," he said with a slight smile, "who was crying so bitterly that I was really obliged to bring this fruit up to you. She said you would know who she was, and was heartbroken that she could not be allowed to come up to nurse you. She said that she had heard from one of your men of your wound. I told her that it was quite impossible that any civilian should enter the hospital, but said that I would take her fruit up, and if she would come every day at five o'clock in the afternoon, when we went off duty for an hour, I would tell her how you were going on."

"She used to sell fruit to the prisoners here," Terence said, "and it was entirely by her aid that I effected my escape last year, and she got a muleteer, to whom she is engaged, to take me down from here to Cadiz. I bought her a present when we entered the town, and the other day told her I hoped to dance at her wedding before long. However, that engagement will not come off. My dancing days are over."

The surgeon felt his pulse.

"There is very little fever," he said. "So far you are going on marvellously, but you must not be disappointed if you get a sharp turn presently. You can hardly expect to get through a wound like this without having a touch, and perhaps a severe one, of fever."

"Is there any harm in my eating fruit?"

"I would not eat any; but you can drink some of the juice mixed with water. I hope we shall have everything comfortable by to-night; of course we are all in the rough at present. Although many of the doctors of the town have been helping us, I don't think there is one medical officer in the army who has taken off his coat since the wounded began to come in yesterday morning."

That night Terence's wound became very painful; inflammation, accompanied of course with fever, set in, and for a fortnight he was very ill. At the end of that time matters began to mend, and the wound soon assumed a healthy appearance. An operation had been performed, and the projecting bone cut off.

There were dire sufferings in Salamanca. Six thousand wounded had to be cared for, the French prisoners and their guards fed, and the army had no organisation to meet so great a strain. Numbers of lives that might have been saved by care and proper attention were lost, and the spirit of discontent and insubordination, which had its origin in the excesses committed in the sack of the fortresses, rapidly increased.

The news from the front after a time seemed more satisfactory. Clausel had been hotly pursued. Had the king with his army joined him, as he might have done, he would have been in a position to again attack the enemy with greatly superior numbers, but Joseph hesitated, and delayed until it was no longer possible. The British army crossed the mountains, and the king was obliged to retire from Madrid and evacuate the capital, which was entered by Wellington on the 25th of August. Early in September the chief surgeon said to Terence:

"There is a convoy of sick going down at the end of the week. I think that it would be best for you to go with them. In the first place, the air of this town is not favourable for recoveries. In some of the hospitals a large number of men have been carried off by the fever, which so often breaks out when the conditions are bad. In the next place, I am privately informed by the governor that he has received orders from the general to send all who are capable of bearing the journey, across the frontier as soon as possible. Another battle may be fought at any moment. The reinforcements that have come from England are nothing like sufficient to replace the gaps in the army.

"The French generals are collecting their forces, and it is certain that Wellington will not be able to withstand their combination, and if he should be compelled to retreat, it is all-important that he should

HOME AGAIN

not be hampered by the necessity of carrying off huge convoys of wounded. The difficulties of transport are already enormous, and it is therefore for many reasons desirable that all who are sufficiently convalescent to march, and all for whom transport can be provided, should start without delay."

"I should be very glad, Doctor. I have not seemed to gain strength for the last week or ten days, but I believe that if I were in the open air I should gain ground rapidly."

Nita had been allowed to come up several times to see Terence since his convalescence began, and the last time she had called had told him that Garcia had returned, being altogether dissatisfied with the feeble proceedings of the guerilla chief. She came up that afternoon soon after the doctor left, and he told her the news that he had received. The next day she told Terence that Garcia had arranged with her father for his waggon and two bullocks, and that he himself would drive it to Lisbon if necessary.

"They are fine bullocks, sir," she said, "and there is no fear of their breaking down. Last night I was talking to one of your sergeants who comes to me every day for news of you. He says that he and about forty of your men are going down with the convoy. All are able to walk. It is so difficult to get carts that only officers who cannot walk are to be taken this time."

"It is very good of Garcia and your father, Nita, but I should manage just as well as the others."

"That may be, señor, but it is better to have a friend with you who knows the country. There may be difficulty in getting provisions, and they say that there is a good deal of plundering along the roads, for troops that have lately come up have behaved so badly that the peasants declare they will have revenge, and treat them as enemies if they have the opportunity. Altogether, it is as well to have a friend with you."

Terence told the surgeon next morning what had been arranged, and said, "So we shall have room for one more, Doctor. Is Major Bull well enough to go with me? He could travel in my waggon, which is sure to be large enough for two to lie in comfortably."

"Certainly he can. He is making a slow recovery, and I should be glad to send him away, only I have no room for him. If he goes with you I can send another officer down also in the place you would have had."

Accordingly, on the Saturday morning the convoy started. Bull and Terence met for the first time since the day of the battle, as the former had been removed to another room after the operation. He was extremely weak still, and had to be carried down and placed in the waggon by the side of Terence. Garcia had been greatly affected at the latter's appearance.

"I should scarce have known you again, señor."

"I am pulled down a bit, Garcia, but by the time we get to our journey's end, you will see that I shall be a very different man. How comfortable you have made the waggon!"

"I have done what I could, señor. At the bottom are six sacks of corn, for it may be that forage will run short. Then I have filled it with hay, and there are enough rugs to lie on and to cover you well over at night; and down among the sacks is a good-sized box with some good wine, two hams of Nita's father's curing, and a stock of sausages and other things for the journey."

Nita came to say good-bye and wept unrestrainedly at the parting. She and Garcia had opened the little box and found in it fifty sovereigns, and had agreed to be married as soon as Garcia returned from his journey. As the train of thirty waggons—of which ten contained provisions for use on the road—issued from the gates, they were joined by the convalescents, four hundred in number. All able to do so carried their arms, the muskets of the remainder being placed on the provision waggons.

"Have you heard from the regiment, Bull?" Terence asked, after they had talked over their time in hospital and their comrades who had fallen.

"No, sir. There is no one I should expect to write to me."

"I had a letter from Ryan yesterday," Terence said. "He tells me that they have had no fighting since we left. They form only one battalion now, and he says the state of things in Madrid is dreadful. The people are dying of hunger, and the British officers have subscribed and started soup-kitchens, and he, with the other

HOME AGAIN

Portuguese regiments, were to march the next day with three British divisions and the cavalry to join General Clinton, who was falling back before Clausel.

"'*We all miss you horribly, Terence. Herrara does his best, but he has not the influence over the men that you had. If we have to fall back into Portugal again, which seems to me quite possible, for little more than 20,000 men are fit to carry arms, I fancy that there won't be a great many left round the colours by the spring. Upon my word, I can hardly blame them, Terence. More than half of those who originally joined have fallen, and no doubt the poor fellows think that they have done more than their share towards defending their country.*'"

By very short marches the convoy made its way to the frontier. The British convalescents remained at Guarda, the Portuguese marched for Pinhel, and the carts with the wounded officers continued their journey to Lisbon. The distance travelled had been over two hundred and fifty miles, and, including halts, they had taken five weeks to perform it. Terence gained strength greatly during the journey, and Bull had so far recovered that he was able to get out and walk sometimes by the side of the waggon. Garcia had been indefatigable in his efforts for their comfort. Every day he formed an arbour over their waggon with freshly-cut boughs brought in by the soldiers of the regiment, and this kept off the rays of the sun and the flies.

At the villages at which they stopped, most of the wounded were accommodated in the houses, but Terence and Bull preferred to sleep in the waggon, the hay being always freshly shaken out for them in the evening. The supplies they carried were most useful in eking out the rations, and Garcia proved himself an excellent cook. Altogether, the journey had been a pleasant one. On arriving at Lisbon they were taken to the principal hospital. Here the few who would be fit for service again were admitted, while the rest were ordered to be taken down at once to a hospital transport lying in the river.

At the landing-place they said good-bye to Garcia, who refused firmly any remuneration for his services or for the hire of the waggon, and then Terence was lifted into a boat, and, with several other wounded, was taken on board the transport.

The surgeon came at once to examine him. "Do you wish to be taken below, Colonel?" he asked Terence.

"Certainly not," Terence said. "I can sit up here and can enjoy myself as much as ever I could, and the air from the sea will do more for me than any tonics you can give me, Doctor."

He was placed in a comfortable deck-chair, and Bull had another beside him. There were many officers already on board, and Terence presently perceived in one who was stumping about on a wooden leg a figure he recognised. He was passing on without recognition, when Terence exclaimed:

"Why, O'Grady, is it yourself?"

"Terence O'Connor, by the powers!" O'Grady shouted. "Sure I didn't know you at first. It is meself, true enough, or what there is left of me. It is glad I am to see you, though in a poor plight. The news came to me that you had lost a leg. There was at first no one in the hospital knew where you were, and I was not able to move about meself to make inquiries; and when I found out, before I came away, they said you were very bad, and that even if I could get to you, which I could not, for I had not been fitted with a new leg then, I should not be able to see you. It is just like my luck. I was hit by one of the first shots fired, and lost all the fun of the fight."

"Where were you hit, O'Grady?"

"Right in the shin. Faith, I went down so sudden that I thought I had trod in a hole, and I was making a scramble to get up again, when young Dawson said, 'Lie still, O'Grady, they have shot the foot off ye.' And so they had, and divil a bit could I find where it had gone to. As I was about the first man hit, they carried me off the field at once and put me in a waggon, and as soon as it was full I was taken down to Salamanca. I only stopped there three weeks, and I have been here now more than two months, and my leg is all right again. But I am a lop-sided creature, though it is lucky that it is my left arm and leg that have gone. I was always a good hopper when I was a boy, so that if this wooden thing breaks, I think I should be able to get about pretty well."

"This is Major Bull, O'Grady. Don't you know him?"

"Faith, I did not know him; but now you tell me who it is, I recognise him. How are you, Major?"

"I am getting on, Captain O'Grady."

HOME AGAIN

"Major," O'Grady corrected. "I got my step at Salamanca; both our majors were killed. So I shall get a dacent pension, a major's pension, and so much for a leg and arm. That is not so bad, you know."

"Well, I have no reason to grumble," Bull said. "If I had been with my old regiment and got this hurt, a shilling a day would have been the outside. Now I shall get lieutenant's pension, and so much for my arm and shoulder."

"I have no doubt you will get another step, Bull. After the way the regiment suffered, and with poor Macwitty killed, and you and I both badly wounded, they are sure to give you your step"—and, indeed, when on their arrival they saw the *Gazette*, they found that both had been promoted.

"I suppose it is all for the best," O'Grady said. "At any rate, I shall be able to drink dacent whisky for the rest of me life, and not have to be fretting meself with Spanish spirit, though I don't say there was no virtue in it when you couldn't get anything better."

Three days later the vessel sailed for England. At Plymouth, Terence, O'Grady, and several other of the Irish officers left her, Bull promising Terence that when he was quite restored to health he would come and pay him a visit. Terence and his companion sailed the next day for Dublin. O'Grady had no relations whom he was particularly anxious to see, and therefore, at Terence's earnest invitation, he took a place with him in a coach to leave in three days, as both had to buy civilian clothes, and to report themselves at headquarters.

"What are you going to do about a leg, Terence?"

"I can do nothing at present. My stump is a great deal too tender still for me to bear anything of that sort. But I will buy a pair of crutches."

This was, indeed, the first thing done on landing, Terence finding it inconvenient in the extreme to have to be carried whenever he wanted to move, even a few yards. He had written home two or three times from the hospital, telling them how he was getting on, for he knew when his name appeared among the list of dangerously wounded, his father and cousin would be in a state of great anxiety until they received news of him; and as soon as they had taken their places in the coach, he dropped them a line, saying when they might expect him.

They had met with contrary winds on their voyage home, but the three weeks at sea had done great things for Terence, and, except for the pinned-up trousers leg, he looked almost himself again.

"Be jabers, Terence," O'Grady said, as the coach drove into Athlone, "one might think that it was only yesterday that we went away. There are the old shops, and the same people standing at their doors to see the coach standing at the gate leading into the stables. What games we had here; who would have thought that when we came back you would be my senior officer!"

When fifteen miles beyond Athlone, there was a hail, and the coach suddenly stopped. O'Grady looked out of the window.

"It's your father, Terence, and the prettiest girl I have seen since we left the ould country."

He opened the door and got out.

"Hooroo, Major! Here we are, safe and sound. We didn't expect to meet you for another eight miles."

Major O'Connor was hurrying to the door, but the girl was there before him.

"Welcome home, Terence! Welcome home!" she exclaimed, smiling through her tears as she leaned into the coach and held out both hands to him, and then drew aside to make room for his father.

"Welcome home, Terence!" the latter said as he wrung his hand. "I did not think it would have been like this, but it might have been worse."

"A great deal worse, father. Now, will you and the guard help me out. This is the most difficult business I have to do."

It was with some difficulty he was got out of the coach. As soon as he steadied himself on his crutches, Mary came up again, threw her arms round his neck, and kissed him.

"We are cousins, you know, Terence," she said, "and as your arms are occupied I have to take the initiative." She was half laughing and half crying.

The guard hurried to get the portmanteaus out of the boot. As soon as he had placed them in the road he shouted to the coachman and climbed up on to his post as the vehicle drove on, the passengers on the roof giving hearty cheers for the two disabled officers. By this time the major was heartily shaking hands with O'Grady.

"I saw in the *Gazette* that you were hit again, O'Grady."

HOME AGAIN

"Yes. I left one little memento of meself in Portugal, and it was only right that I should lave another in Spain. It has been worrying me a good deal, because I should have liked to have brought them home to be buried in the same grave with me, so as to have everything handy together. How they are ever to be collected when the time comes bothers me entirely, when I can't even point out where they are to be found."

"You have not lost your good spirits anyhow, O'Grady."

"I never shall, I hope, O'Connor; and even if I had been inclined to, Terence would have brought them back again."

As they stood chatting, a man-servant had placed the portmanteaus on the box of a pretty open carriage drawn by two horses.

"This is our state-carriage, Terence, though we don't use it very often, for when I go about by myself I ride. Mary has a pony carriage, and drives herself about. You remember Pat Cassidy, don't you?"

"Of course I do, now I look at him," Terence said. "It's your old soldier-servant;" and he shook hands with the man. "He did not come home with you, did he, father?"

"No, he was badly wounded at Talavera, and invalided home. They thought that he would not be fit for service again, and so discharged him, and he found his way here, and glad enough I was to have him."

Aided by his father and O'Grady, Terence took his place in the carriage, his father seated himself by his side, while Mary and O'Grady had the opposite seat.

"There is one advantage in losing legs," O'Grady said, "we can stow away much more comfortably in a carriage. Is this the nearest point to your place?"

"Yes. It is four miles nearer than Ballyhovey, so we thought that we might as well meet you here, and more comfortably than meeting you in the town. It was Mary's suggestion. I think she would not have liked to have kissed Terence in the public street."

"Nonsense, uncle!" Mary said indignantly. "Of course I should have kissed him anywhere. Are we not cousins, and didn't he save me from being shut up in a nunnery all my life?"

"All right, Mary, it is quite right that you should kiss him: still, I should say that it was pleasanter to do so when you had not a couple of score of loafers looking on, who would not know that he was your cousin and had saved you from a convent."

"You are looking well, father," Terence said, to turn the conversation.

"Never was better in my life, lad, except that I am obliged to be careful with my leg; but, after all, it may be that though it seemed hard to me at the time, it is as well that I left the regiment when I did. Quite half the officers have been killed since then. Vimiera accounted for some of them. Major Harrison went there, and gave me my step, Talavera made several more vacancies, and Salamanca cost us ten officers, including poor O'Driscoll. I am lucky to have come off as well as I did. It did not seem a very cheerful look-out at first, but since this young woman arrived and took possession of me, I am as happy and contented as a man can be."

"I deny altogether having taken possession of you, uncle. I let you have your way very much, and only interfere for your own good."

"You will have another patient to look after now, dear, and to fuss over."

"I will do my best," she said softly, leaning forward and putting her hand on that of Terence. "I know that it will be terribly dull for you at first, after being constantly on the move for the last five years, and always full of excitement and adventure, to have to keep quiet and do nothing."

"I shall get on very well," he said. "Just at first, of course, I shall not be able to get about very much, but I shall soon learn to use my crutches, and I hope before very long to get a leg of some sort; and I don't see why I should not be able to ride again after a bit. If I cannot do it any other way, I must take to a side-saddle. I can have a leg made specially for riding, with a crook at the knee."

Mary laughed, while the tears came in her eyes.

"Why, bless me, Mary," he went on, "the loss of a leg is nothing when you are accustomed to it. I shall be able, as I have said, to ride, drive, shoot, fish, and all sorts of things. The only thing that I shall be cut off from, as far as I can see, is dancing, but as I have never had a chance of dancing since the last ball the regiment gave at Athlone, the loss will not be a very grievous one. Look at O'Grady. There he is, much worse off than I am, as he has no one to make any particular fuss about him; he is getting on capitally, and, indeed, stumped about the deck so much coming home that the captain begged him to have a pad of leather put on to the bottom of his leg to save the decks. O'Grady is a philosopher, and I shall try to follow his example."

"Why should one bother oneself, Miss O'Connor, when bothering won't help? When the war is over I shall buy Tim Doolan, my soldier-servant, out. He is a vile, drunken villain, but I understand him, and he understands me, and he blubbered so when he carried me off the field that I had to promise him that, if a French bullet did not carry him off, I would send for him when the war was over.

"'You know you can't do without me, yer honour,' the scoundrel said.

"'I can do better without you than with you, Tim,' says I. 'Ye are always getting me into trouble with your drunken ways. Ye would have been flogged a dozen times if I hadn't screened you. Take up your musket and join your regiment. You rascal, you are smelling of drink now, and divil a drop except water is there in me flask.'

"'I did it for your own good,' says he. 'Ye know that spirits always heats your blood, and water would be the best for you when the fighting began, so I just sacrificed meself; for, says I to meself, if ye get fighting a little wild, Tim, it don't matter a bit, but the captain will have to keep cool, so it is best that you should drink up the spirits and fill the flask up with water to quench his thirst.'

"'Be off, ye black villain,' I said, 'or I will strike you.'

"'You will never be able to do without me, Captain,' says he, picking up his musket; and with that he trudged away, and, for aught I know, he never came out of the battle alive."

The others laughed.

"They were always quarreling, Mary," Terence said. "But I agree with Tim that his master will find it very hard to do without him, especially about one o'clock in the morning."

"I am ashamed of you, Terence," O'Grady said earnestly, "taking away me character, when I have come down here as your guest."

"It is too bad, O'Grady," Major O'Connor said, "but you know Terence was always conspicuous for his want of respect towards his elders."

"He was that same, O'Connor. I did me best for the boy, but there are some on whom education and example are clean thrown away."

"You are looking pale, cousin Terence," Mary said.

"Am I? My leg is hurting me a bit. Ireland is a great country, but its by-roads are not the best in the world, and the jolting shakes me up a bit."

"How stupid I was not to think of it!" she said, and, rising in her seat, told Cassidy to drive at a walk. They were now only half a mile from the house.

"You will hardly know the old place again, Terence," his father said.

"And a very good thing too, father, for a more tumble-down old shanty I was never in."

"It was the abode of our race, Terence."

"Well, then, it says mighty little for our race, father."

"Ah! But it did not fall into the state you saw it in till my father died, a year after I got my commission."

"I won't blame them, then; but, at any rate, I am glad I am coming home to a house and not a ruin. Ah, that is more like a home!" he said, as a turn of the road brought them in sight of the building. "You have done wonders, Mary. That is a house fit for any Irish gentleman to live in."

"It has been altered so that it can be added to, Terence; but, at any rate it is comfortable. As it was before, it made one feel rheumatic to look at it."

On arriving at the house, Terence refused all assistance.

"I am going to be independent as far as I can," he said, and, slipping down from the seat into the bottom of the chaise, he was able to put his foot on to the ground, and by the aid of his crutches to get out and enter the house unaided.

"That is the old parlour, I think," he said, glancing into one of the rooms.

"Yes. It is your father's snuggery now. There is scarcely any alteration there, and he can mess about as he likes with his guns and fishing-tackle and swords. This is the dining-room now."

HOME AGAIN

And she led the way along a wide passage to the new part of the house, where a bright fire was blazing in a handsome and well-furnished room. An invalid's chair had been placed by the fire, and opposite it was a large, cosy arm-chair.

"That is for your use, Major O'Grady," she said. "Now, Terence, you are to lay yourself up in that chair. I will bring a small table to your side and put your dinner there."

"I will lie down until the dinner is ready, Mary. But I am perfectly capable of sitting at the table; I did so the last week before leaving the ship."

"You shall do that to-morrow. You may say what you like, but I can see that you are very tired, and for to-day you will take it easy. I am going to be your nurse, and I can assure you that you will have to obey orders. You have been in independent command quite long enough."

"It is of no use, Terence; you must do as you are told," his father said. "The only way to get on with this young woman is to let her have her own way. I have given up opposing her long ago, and you will have to do the same."

Terence did not find it unpleasant to be nursed and looked after, and even to obey peremptory orders. A month later Mary came into the room quietly one afternoon when he was sitting and looking into the fire, as his father and O'Grady had driven to Killnally. Absorbed in his own thoughts, he did not hear her enter. Thinking that he was asleep, she paused at the door. A moment later she heard a deep sigh. She came forward at once.

"What are you sighing about, Terence? Your leg is not hurting you, is it?"

"No, dear, it has pretty well given up hurting me."

"What were you sighing about then?"

He was silent for a minute, and then said: "Well, you see, one cannot help sighing a little at the thought that one is laid up a useless man when one is scarce twenty-one."

"You have done your work, Terence. You have made a name for yourself when others are just leaving college and thinking of choosing a profession. You have done more in five years than most men achieve in all their lifetime. This is the first time I have heard you grumble. I know it is hard, but what has specially upset you to-day?"

"I suppose I am a little out of sorts," he said. "I was thinking, perhaps, how different it might have been if it hadn't been for that unlucky shell."

"You mean that you might have gone on to Burgos and fallen in the assault there, or shared in that dreadful retreat to the frontier again?"

"No. I was not thinking of Spain, nor even of the army. I was thinking of here."

"But you said over and over again, Terence, that you will be able to ride and drive and get about like other people in time."

"Yes, dear, in many respects it will be the same, but not in one respect."

Then he broke off. "I am an ungrateful brute. I have everything to make me happy—a comfortable home, a good father, and a dear little sister to nurse me."

"What did I tell you, sir," she said after a pause, "when I said good-bye to you at Coimbra? That I would rather be your cousin. You were quite hurt; and I said that you were a silly boy, and would understand better some day."

"I have understood since," he said, "and was glad that you were not my sister; but now, you see, things have altogether changed, and I must be content with sistership."

The girl looked in the fire, and then said in a low voice:

"Why, Terence?"

"You know why," he said. "I have had no one to think of but you for the last four years. Your letters were the great pleasures of my life. I thought over and over again of those last words of yours, and I had some hope that when I came back I might say to you, 'Dear Mary, I am grateful, indeed, that you are my cousin, and not my sister. A sister is a very dear relation, but there is one dearer still.' Don't be afraid, dear; I am not going to say so now. Of course that is over, and I hope that I shall come in time to be content to think of you as a sister."

HOME AGAIN

"You are very foolish, Terence," she said, almost with a laugh, "as foolish as you were at Coimbra. Do you think that I should have said what I did then if I had not meant it? Did you not save me, at the risk of your life, from what would have been worse than death? Have you not been my hero ever since? Have you not been the centre of our thoughts here, the great topic of our conversation? Have not your father and I been as proud as peacocks when we read of your rapid promotion, and the notices of your gallant conduct? And do you think that it would make any difference to me if you had come back with both your legs and arms shot off? No, dear. I am just as dissatisfied with the relationship you propose as I was three years ago, and it must be either cousin or"—and she stopped.

She was standing up beside him now.

"Or wife," he said, taking up her hand. "Is it possible you mean wife?"

Her face was a sufficient answer, and he drew her down to him.

"You silly boy!" she said, five minutes afterwards. "Of course I thought of it all along. I never made any secret of it to your father. I told him that our escape was like a fairy tale, and that it must have the same ending, 'and they married, and lived happy ever after.' He would never have let me have my way with the house had I not confided in him. He said that I could spend my money as I pleased on myself, but that not one penny should be laid out on this house, and I was obliged to tell him. I am afraid I blushed furiously as I did so; but I had to say, 'Don't you see, uncle'—of course I always called him uncle from the first, though he is only a cousin —'I have quite made up my mind that it will be my house some day, and the money may just as well be laid out on it now to make it comfortable, instead of waiting till that time comes.'"

"What did my father say?"

"Oh, he said all sorts of nonsense, just the sort of thing that you Irishmen always do say! That he hoped, perhaps, it might be so from the moment he got your letter, and that the moment he saw me he felt sure that it would be so, for it must be, if you had any eyes in your head."

When Major O'Connor came home he was greatly pleased, but he took the news as a matter of course.

"Faith," he said, "I would have disinherited the boy if he had been such a fool as not to appreciate you, Mary."

O'Grady was loud in his congratulations.

"It is just like your luck, Terence," he said. "Luck is everything. Here am I, a battered hero who has lost an arm and a foot in the service of me country, and divil a girl has thrown herself upon me neck. Here are you, a mere gossoon, fifteen years my junior in the service, mentioned a score of times in despatches, promoted over my head; and now you have won one of the prettiest creatures in Ireland, and what is a good deal more to the point, though you may not think of it at present, with a handsome fortune of her own. In faith, there is no understanding the ways of Providence."

A week afterwards the whole party went up to Dublin, as Terence and O'Grady had to go before a medical board. A fortnight later a notice appeared in the *Gazette* that Lieutenant-colonel Terence O'Connor had retired from the service on half-pay, with the rank of colonel.

The marriage did not take place for another six months, by which time Terence had thrown away his crutches and had taken to an artificial leg, so well constructed that, were it not for a certain stiffness in his walk, his loss would not have been suspected by a casual observer.

For three months previous to the event, a number of men had been employed in building a small but pretty house, some quarter of a mile from the mansion, intended for the occupation of Majors O'Connor and O'Grady.

"It will be better in every way, Terence," his father insisted, when his son and Mary remonstrated against their thus proposing to leave them. "O'Grady and I have been comrades for twenty years, and we shall feel more at home in bachelor quarters than here. I can run in three or four times a day if I like, and I expect I shall be as much here as over there; whereas if I lived here I should often be feeling myself in the way, though I know that you would never say so. It is better for young people to be together, and maybe some day the house will be none too large for you."

The house was finished by the time the wedding took place, and the two officers moved into it. The wedding was attended by all the tenants and half the country round, and it was agreed that the bride's jewels were the most magnificent that had ever been seen in that part of Ireland, though some objected that diamonds alone would have been more suitable for the occasion than the emeralds.

Terence, on his return, had heard from his father that his uncle Tim M'Manus had called very soon after the major had returned to his old home. He had been very friendly, and had been evidently mollified by Terence's name appearing in general orders, but his opinion that he would end his career by a rope had been in no way shaken. He had, however, continued to pay occasional visits, and the rapid rise of the scapegrace and his frequent mention in despatches were evidently a source of much gratification to him, and it was not long after his return that his uncle again came over.

"We will let bygones be bygones, Terence," he said, as he shook hands with him. "You have turned out a credit to your mother's name, and I am proud of you, and I hold my head high when I say Colonel Terence O'Connor, who was always playing mischief with the French, is my great-nephew, and the good M'Manus blood shines out clearly in him."

There was no one who played a more conspicuous part at the wedding than Uncle Tim. At his own request he proposed the health of the bride and bridegroom.

"I take no small credit to myself," he said, "that Colonel Terence O'Connor is the hero of this occasion. Never was there a boy whose destiny was so marked as his, and it is many a time I predicted that it was not either by flood or fire or quietly in his bed that he would die. If when the regiment was ordered abroad I had offered him a home, I firmly believe that my prediction would be verified before now, but I closed my doors to him, and the consequence was that he expended his devilment upon the French; and it is a deal better for him that it is only a leg that he has lost, which is a much less serious matter than having his neck unduly stretched. Therefore, ladies and gentlemen, I can say with pride that I have had no small share in this matter, and it is glad I am that when I go I can leave my money behind me feeling that it won't all go to the dogs before I have been twelve months in my grave."

Another old friend was present at the wedding. Bull had made a slow recovery, and had been some time before he regained his strength. When he was gazetted out of the service, he secured a step in rank, and retired as a major. In after years he made frequent visits to Terence, to whom, as he always declared, he owed it that instead of being turned adrift on a nominal pension, he was now able to live in comfort and ease.

When, four months later, Tim M'Manus was thrown out of his trap, when driving home late at night, and broke his neck, it was found that he had left the whole of his property to Terence, and as the rents of his estate amounted to L600 a year, no inconsiderable proportion of which had for many years past been accumulating, the legacy placed Terence in a leading position among the gentry of Mayo.

For very many years the house was one of the most popular in the county. It had been found necessary to make additions to it, and it had now attained the dignity of a mansion. The three officers followed with the most intense interest the bulletins and despatches from the war, and on the day when the allies entered Paris, the services of Tim Doolan, who had been invalided home a year after the return of his master, and had been discharged as unfit for further service, were called into requisition, for the first time since his return, to assist his master back to the house. O'Grady, however, explained most earnestly to Mary O'Connor the next day that it was not the whisky at all, but his wooden leg that had got out of order, and would not carry him straight.

Dick Ryan went through the war unscathed, and, after Waterloo, retired from the service with the rank of lieutenant-colonel, married, and settled at Athlone, and the closest intimacy and very frequent intercourse were maintained between him and his comrades of the Mayo Fusileers.

Terence in time quite ceased to feel the loss of his leg, and was able to join in all field sports, becoming in time master of the hounds, and one of the most popular sportsmen in the county. His wife always declared that his wound was the most fortunate thing that ever happened to him, for, had it not been for that, he would most likely have fallen in some of the last battles in the Peninsula.

"It is a good thing to have luck," she said, "and Terence had plenty of it. But it does not do to tempt fortune too far. The pitcher that goes too often to the well gets broken in the end."

The End